QUEEN OF THE SEAS
THE PIRATE QUEEN SERIES
BOOK ONE

JAMES FULLER

The afternoon sun was warm, and the air off the Atlantic coast of Catark was humid, as it was most days during this mild summer in Portugal. The smell of the sea followed inland for several miles before it dissipated within the woodlands and high-rolling hills, where those who had the means worked easier jobs on land. But if you asked a fisherman or sailor, they would all say land lovers lack the courage to face the vengeful sea gods daily. Or that they lacked the fortitude to pull lines and nets and sail across the open waters to ports far and wide, battling pirates, storms, and sea monsters alike.

In truth, it was a far simpler reason they all knew about, but none liked to think about or say it aloud. The status quo kept them where they were. If you were born to a farmer, you farmed as your father farmed, and his father farmed as your children would farm. If you were born to a fisherman, you fished. So long as you had clothes on your back and food in your belly, you had nothing to complain about—or so the preachers in church preached.

Callisto picked up another dusty rock from the roadway and packed it into her leather slingshot. It went above her head, gaining speed with each spin as she targeted an old rotting stump. With a quick snap of her wrist and the release of her index finger, the stone shot through the air, clipping the outside bark of the stump.

"'Twas a good shot," a loving voice said from behind her, "but you forgot to exhale before the release."

"No, I didn't!" Callisto proclaimed defensively, with a discouraged frown, nearly taking up her ten-year-old face. "I did everything you said! I did, I swear it, papa!"

Her father rustled her shoulder-length coal-black hair. "I am sure you think you did, wee one, but I was watching you with a careful eye. You inhaled instead of exhaled. Easy enough mistake to confuse when one is thinking too hard about the task they want to achieve."

Stomping her feet in frustration, she felt like throwing the sling to the ground and leaving it there forever. "I will never get it right!"

He burst out laughing, his sunbaked face wrinkling up in delight. "You've been practicing nay more than half a morning, and already you want to accept defeat? Already you are three times better than either of your two brothers after nearly two weeks of trying. But no, you're right, little one, you might as well give my sling back and never think of it again. A girl could never hope to master it anyways." He did his best to hide his knowing smirk.

Callisto's eyes burned with hurt at her father's words. How dare he say such a thing to her!

"I'll show you what a girl can do!" She snatched a round stone from the ground.

Soon the slingshot was whirling through the air again, but this time, Callisto steadied herself, felt the movements of her shoulder, arm, and wrist, and most importantly, the airflow throughout her lungs. She locked on her target, exhaled, and fired.

The small stone buzzed through the air and struck true, hitting the stump near dead center with a loud thud.

Callisto squealed with glee; all thoughts of forfeiting were gone. "I told you I could do it!" she boldly claimed to her father.

"I never doubted you for a second, my little sea slug."

"But you told me to give up. That a girl never could do this."

"Aye, I did just that," he knelt beside her, his sea-green eyes staring into their near-perfect counterpart, "but the real question is do you know why I did?"

He was testing her; she knew it. He always found ways to push her wit, strength, or endurance whenever they found time together, which sadly was not nearly as often as she would have liked. Life as a fisherman left little time for anything else.

"Because you wanted me to quit? Hoping I'd grow up to be more a lady, so you could marry me off to some rich man, so you no longer had to work so hard?" She knew this wasn't true, but he often joked about it.

"If only I could ever believe a lady could be made out of the likes of you. I might work twice as hard for the money to send you to a fancy school to learn!" he countered. "But you are a lost cause, my grimy little sea slug! Now, why did I say those things?"

She thought hard this time as they started walking again. What he had said had hurt her feelings and made her angry, but it was because she had been mad that she had focused harder on what she was doing. Because of that need to prove her father wrong, she believed she had been able to hit the stump the second time.

"You knew it would drive me to try harder and prove I could do it." She gasped in excitement.

"See, you aren't as simple as your two brothers claim you to be," he teased. "You can do anything, my little sea slug, anything you put that little sluggy mind to." He tousled her dirty hair again. "Don't let anyone tell you differently."

He looked up at the sky. The sun had reached its zenith and would now begin its slow descent. "Come now. We had best get moving. I mustn't be late for this meeting."

Within the hour, the pair came to a large estate on the hillside overlooking the coast. It was one of the most beautiful places Callisto had ever seen. Fig, olive, and apple trees lined the grounds in neat rows. Behind the house, grapevines cascaded up the gentle slopes until they disappeared over the tops. Dozens of workers worked methodically and with great care, knowing full well the bite of a whip was never far off as guards patrolled.

Callisto was in awe as she stepped off the dusty road and out of her wicker sandals onto the softest, greenest grass she had ever seen or felt in her life. "This place is amazing, papa!"

Her father looked concerned and anxious. "Yes, my little slug, it is very nice here. But we must not waste time. Sir Gaspar will be waiting for me."

"Oh, come now, Simao, let the girl enjoy the grass," Tito Gaspar said, walking into view from behind a large, manicured bush in the shape of a great bear as he ate a handful of fresh grapes.

Tito Gaspar was a portly man who had enjoyed his station of wealth in vast excess. His balding head was slick with greasy sweat from the mild afternoon sun. His silken robes hung over him like they would a boulder, and the buttons of his waistcoat worked hard to keep his belly from bulging too far out.

"Likely the first time in her life she has ever felt such a lush and soft thing on such tiny, calloused feet."

"Oh, it is, sir." Callisto beamed with excitement.

If the owner of this beautiful place said it was okay for her to do so, then her father would not object. Certainly, that was all he had been worried about.

"It feels so wonderful. You are so very lucky to live here, sir!"

She got down and rolled across the grass, nearly rolling straight into one of the servants tending a small rose bush.

"That I am, my dear girl," Gaspar grinned, "but luck had nothing to do with it. I worked hard to achieve all you see before you and far more than this."

Callisto returned to her feet, not even bothering to brush herself off. "What do you do?"

"Be silent, child! Do not bother Sir Gaspar. We didn't come all this way for you to waste his time with all your silly questions," her father snapped; though there was little anger in his words, there was something else.

"Not at all, Simao!" With less than friendly intent, Gaspar rested a firm, meaty paw upon his shoulder. "It is a good question indeed, young lady. One that I think we could all do with an answer." He crouched beside the young girl, his knees protesting from his great bulk. He reached into his pocket and produced a small bushel of red grapes. "Would you like some?"

Callisto's eyes widened avidly. She had only ever eaten a few grapes in her life when she and her brothers had found them half-smashed along the roadside. "I—I—would love some." She looked to her father who gave a slight nod, but his eyes seemed worried.

She took the small bunch and quickly popped one into her mouth. The taste was exquisite and made her whole body shudder as if she had just had a bucket of cold well water dumped upon her.

"Now, to answer your question. I manage people," he waved his hand around his estate, "like all the people you see here. I manage them all, they work for me, and in exchange for that work, I provide them with food and shelter. Some even make a wage in coin, depending on their skill and what they do for me."

Callisto was barely listening, she was too enthralled with the flavors and sensation assaulting her taste buds, but she nodded anyway, not wanting this man to think she wasn't listening.

"I also manage other people," he turned a scornful eye to

Simao, "like your father and many others from your little town below."

"Other fishermen?" Callisto asked, her curiosity piquing now that this nice man had mentioned her father worked for him. It was something she hadn't known before.

"Yes, several of the fishermen work for me. I buy much of the fish they bring in at a fair price to sell it to others further away inland. Now, part of my job managing people is to make sure they are doing their job and doing it to the best of their ability." He waved his hands around him at all his estate had. "None of this could be possible if I didn't, and if I didn't keep a watchful eye on those who work for me and my investments with them."

Callisto finished the grapes and nodded. She smiled at her father, who looked pale and unwell suddenly, and she wondered if the long walk in the sun had been too much for him today.

"Now, you might be too young to remember the big storm that came through here two summers ago. But in that horrible storm, your papa's boat was damaged really, really badly." Again, Gaspar glared at her father. "So badly that your poor old papa couldn't afford to fix it on his own. I am sure you understand that he can't catch fish with no boat, and no fish means no food or coin to put on the table for you and your family to survive."

Bright-eyed Callisto nodded. She remembered the storm and the fight she had heard her mother and father have a few days afterward, though she never understood why they would fight about it. It wasn't like the storm had been either of their faults.

"Your father came to see me and, being the very generous man that I am. I offered to repair his fishing boat, so he could continue to fish and provide for his family. Because children need food in their bellies and clothes on their backs." He reached into his pocket, pulled out another small bundle of grapes, and handed them to her before standing.

Simao's eyes widened as he saw a man approaching his daughter with a dagger. "Please, don't—" Gaspar silenced him with a raised hand.

"Now, it seems your papa doesn't want to pay me back the money I loaned him to repair his boat. This hurts me and makes me regret the kindness I showed him," he continued as if he was talking to Callisto, but his menacing eyes were on Simao's.

"I swear it, sir. I just need a few more months," Simao pleaded, keeping a careful eye on the man with the dagger looming just behind his daughter. "The season has started slow, but it will pick up soon. You will have your coin. I swear it by the new gods and the old!"

"Slow season, you say?" Gaspar rubbed his greasy double chin as if in thought. "Yet, Dado and Hahn have told me this season has been fruitful for them. Are you telling me those two gutter rats are better fishermen than you and your sons? Or is there something else you need to tell me?"

Simao cursed inwardly. He should have known those two would have talked against him. They were always trying to hurt him and his family in some way.

"No, sir, they have gotten lucky this year, that is all. Each year it takes time to track the new movements of the shoals. Sometimes luck is with you, and you find them quickly, sometimes not."

"Do you really think me such a fucking fool as that, Simao?" Gaspar snapped, his temper getting away from him.

Callisto snapped to attention at the man's outburst and was about to move to her father's side when a strong hand snatched a fistful of her hair and held her firmly in place.

"Papa, what is happening?" she cried, her feet barely touching the ground as the man held her painfully.

"Please don't do this, Gaspar!" Simao cried out, knowing if he moved to her, the man would cut her throat. "Stay calm, my little sea slug. It is okay. Everything will be okay, I swear it!"

"Do you think I want this? Wanted to waste part of my day with this bullshit?" Gaspar growled. "But hear me now, Simao, I will have him cut her throat and the throats of your whole family if you lie to me again! Now tell me what you've been doing with all your fish!"

Simao's shoulders sagged in defeat. He was caught, and his family's lives depended on his truth. "I have been selling part of it to another for a slightly higher price. We needed new nets and medicine from the healer. My wife has been in much pain for months, and we do not know why. But if she doesn't have the medicine, she moans and cries all night in her sleep."

"Who are you selling the fish to, Simao?"

"Radburn Lopo..."

"Out of all the people you could have sold to, my most hated rival is the one you chose?" Gaspar snapped, moving dangerously close. "Have I not been kind? Have I not been fair?" He laid a meaty fist into Simao's guts, doubling him over. "This is how you repay that kindness when I could have let your family starve and die?"

"Papa!" Callisto tried to pull away, but the man's grip was unrelenting, and instantly she felt cold steel against her throat.

"Stay still, Callisto! Do not move! I am fine!"

A kick sent him flying over to his side, gasping for air.

"Please! Leave my papa alone!"

"Your papa has been a very, very bad friend to me. He has hurt me very deeply!" Another kick sent Simao crashing into a marble bench.

8

"He didn't mean it!" Tears poured freely down her dirty face. "He is a good man!"

"I don't know how he can make me think that again! He stole from me and then had the gall to lie to my face! Do you know what happens to thieves, girl?" As the words left his fat mouth, another man handed him a hatchet.

Callisto couldn't believe what she was seeing. How could this be happening? Her father was a good, kind man; he made a mistake, that was all. Everyone made mistakes from time to time. At least, that was what her mama always told her. "Please, no, please don't hurt him! Don't hurt my papa!"

Simao stared up at the large man, his eyes pleading all that he couldn't say aloud, for his voice failed him now when he needed it most.

Gaspar sneered down at his victim. "You have two choices here today, Simao. Take your own hand, or I have my man open your daughter's throat. Choose before I grow bored and do both."

Simao swallowed the hard lump in his throat, knowing no words would change any of this now. He had sealed his fate the day he had decided to sell to Radburn Lopo. A decision at the time that had seemed harmless enough.

It had never been for long-term gains, only to get ahead so that he didn't have to borrow more money. He took the hatchet in a trembling hand, it felt impossibly heavy, and he almost dropped it. He could not meet his daughter's eyes, for his shame would not allow him. "Turn away, Callisto, do not watch this."

"No!" the fat man barked. "The girl watches so that she might learn an important lesson today about keeping one's word and the status quo and where you and her fit within it!"

"Please—don't make her—"

"You had your chance for niceties, Simao. Instead, you

chose to lie and cheat me out of what was rightfully mine!" Gaspar spat. "Now, do it, or your daughter walks the dark road today!" With a nod, the man pressed the dagger harder against her throat.

Callisto watched in horror as her father lifted the weapon. This wasn't happening; it couldn't be real. Maybe this was some sort of test, but what would he be trying to teach her in such a horrible setting? Indeed, this man who had been so kind moments ago wasn't this evil? How could such a thing be true?

The sun glinted off the polished blade, breaking her from her thoughts. She watched as if the world had slowed the scene as the hatchet came down in a smooth arc. The blade sliced through flesh, sinew, and bone. A heartbeat later, her father's wails of agony cut through the silence like the hatchet had cut through his wrist.

The man released her, and she ran to her father, slumped down on his knees, holding his left arm tightly, trying to stem the flow of blood pumping quickly from the stump.

"I am here, papa! I am here," she called to him, but his mind was distant as he stared at his severed hand upon the cobblestone. Callisto knew he would bleed out if the blood flow didn't stop. She quickly ripped strips from her dirty shirt and began wrapping the stump the way he had shown her.

"Callisto," her father mumbled in shock, "I—I am—sorry —I have failed you—your brothers—your mother—"

"No, no, papa, do not talk like that," she pleaded, not knowing what else to say.

Gaspar looked down at the young girl. "Now, remember what you saw here today. This is what happens when one forgets their place in this world. Now pick that pathetic excuse you call father up and get out of my sight before I set the hounds on you both!"

Reaching down, he picked up the severed appendage and

threw it to a massive hound by the doorstep. The dog quickly snatched it up and began chewing on it viciously.

Dusk was just about upon them before Callisto's brothers, Macario and Tad found them on the roadway still two miles from their house. Worried at their father's delay, they had hooked up the old nag to the wagon and set off in search.

They could not have come at a better time. Callisto's body ached with the strain of half dragging, half carrying their father's near limp form. He had lost so much blood that she was amazed he was still conscious or alive.

"What has happened?" Macario cried, jumping from the wagon before it could come to a complete stop. He ran to his father's aid, seeing the bloodied stump where his hand should have been. Simao's face was pale as alabaster, and thick sweat clung to his skin as his hollowed eyes starred blankly at the dusty ground.

Callisto's eyes were crusted red from the last hours of crying, her cheeks stained with dirt and grim. "He—that man —was a monster—made Father—" she couldn't force the words out, couldn't shake the vision from her mind.

"Quickly, Tad, help me get Father into the wagon. We will take him to the healer!" Macario ordered his younger brother, taking the burden from his sister. "Father? Father, can you hear me?"

"He hasn't said a word since—" she mumbled, wanting nothing more than to collapse and forget all of this. Wishing this was nothing more than a bad dream, the worst dream, but one where she could still wake up and all would be as it should be.

Tad, who usually would defy his older brother's orders at

every step, knew this was not the time for such foolishness. "By the gods, why would Gaspar do such a thing?"

Macario loaded their father into the back of the rotting wagon and covered him with an old, torn piece of canvas. "He must have discovered Father was trading part of the catch to Radburn Lopo for Mother's medicine."

"This is madness!" Tad said with bitterness. "That is no reason for an act of such nature! We will go to the Magistrate as soon as Father is in the hands of Master Cael."

"Do you think Magistrate Daan or his men will care?"

"It's their job to care. This can't be allowed to stand. This has to go against some law! He crippled Father for no good reason!" Tad countered angrily.

Macario knew nothing would be done. Father had crossed a rich man, and rich men could do as they liked with the poor common folk of the region. A few gold coins in the right hands made 'laws' pointless against their kind. But he knew better than to argue with his younger brother.

"Let us first worry about Father." He turned to Callisto. "Will you be alright to walk home? Someone needs to tell mother; she is beside herself with worry about you two."

All Callisto could do was nod and watch her brothers ride off as quickly as the old nag would go under the harsh lash she now received in haste.

It would still take her some time to get home, and she wished her brothers would have taken her with them. But their father needed help quickly, and she knew she would be an extra weight that the poor nag couldn't haul. She began the walk in the direction of their little cottage beside the sea.

Callisto's legs began shaking with exhaustion, and she was sure she would collapse if she didn't rest. She sat against a fence post in the dried grass beside one of the several homes along the road for a moment. She wasn't sure who lived here;

this part of the town was for folk far better off than her family.

With blurred vision, she stared at the quarter moon. How could that man do such a horrible thing to her father? Even if her father had sold the fish to another, he did so for a good reason. Helping their mother with her pain was a good reason for such a thing. Gaspar couldn't have needed the coin that badly. Maybe her father should have told the man the problem, and then perhaps this wouldn't have happened.

No, she quickly shook that thought from her head. A man that would do something like this would not have been so kind, even if he had pretended to be nice to her. That's all it had been, an act. He was not kind at all. He was cruel, deceitful, and a monster.

Fresh tears stung her already puffy eyes. How could she have been so stupid? How could she have fallen so quickly for the false kindness Gaspar had shown her? How had she been so blind to the looks her father had given her, silent warnings to her not to be so trusting?

"I am sorry, Father—I am a fool," she muttered to the night.

As if in answer, something soft and damp touched the back of her neck. She jumped and spun around, throwing her hands in the air, hoping to fend off the attack. But there was no attack coming as a dusty grey mare shook its head in greeting, almost as if to say sorry for scaring her.

"You silly thing." She sighed in relief and was as near to a laugh as she could muster.

She held her hand out to the horse so that it could smell it. But the animal needed no more persuasion before quickly pushing its nose under the offered palm, eager for the scratches to come.

"You heard me talking, didn't you?" she cooed, getting

behind the horse's ear. "What do you think? What should I do? I feel so helpless."

The horse pulled back and whined, stomping its front hoof into the soft ground as it shook its head.

"If only I spoke horse." She turned to continue her way home when a spark of a flame ignited within a small copse a hundred feet from the road.

"What was that?" she whispered. "Someone is in there."

Without thinking, she made her way off the road in the direction she had seen the flame. The glow was faint through the thick trees and would be easily missed from the road by anyone, but she had seen it start and knew it was there, so she navigated through the tangle of trees and thorny underbrush.

Several minutes passed, and still, she followed the pale glow further into the thicket. She looked back the way she had come and thought it strange that she had seen it from the road. From where she stood, she could see no trace of the road or anything beyond thick tree trunks and their gnarled branches.

Turning back to the flame guiding her path, it almost seemed brighter than she remembered.

You've come too far to turn back now.

Callisto paused, wondering where that voice had come from or if it had been in her head. She was certain it had been a male voice, but now she wasn't sure if she had heard anything.

Soon she pushed her way into a small clearing, and a loud gasp escaped her lips. The moon's pale light shone straight down upon the clearing, basking an ancient, weather-worn marble statue before her in an almost ghostly glow.

A single black candle's flame danced beneath the fiercely proud warrior, twice the size of an average man. The ground before him was littered with dozens of what looked like small animal bones.

The statue stood defiant as if, no matter the odds, he would win without a doubt. Firmly in his left arm was a cracked and aged shield. His right arm pointed to the sky but was empty as if the weapon he should have held was missing. The armor was like nothing Callisto had ever seen before. Even though the weather had worn most of the details away, she could tell it was impressive.

"Who are you," Callisto whispered, running her fingers along the bottom edge of the shield, "and what is this place?"

She couldn't believe that she and her brothers or the town's other children had never found this place before.

"That is the mighty Ares, the Greek god of war," a raspy voice said from behind her, "and this dear child is one of his long-forgotten shrines."

Callisto spun around so quickly that she lost her footing and fell to the hard earth. "Who are you? Leave me alone!" she cried, pushing her way back to the tree line she had entered, sure she was about to be raped or murdered for her foolishness in wandering here.

"Calm yourself, my child. I did not mean to startle you, and I certainly mean you no harm." A cloaked figure emerged from the shadows behind the statue.

The man pulled the hood back, revealing his ancient age. Wisps of matted hair clung to his sunbaked skull, and in the light, she could see one of his eyes was milky white with blindness.

Callisto almost scolded herself for her cowardliness. This old man wouldn't be able to harm her even if he wanted to. Quickly she regained her feet and brushed herself off. "Who are you, and what are you doing out here?"

"So bold for one so young. The gods do ever so favor the bold." He chuckled. "My name is Yaalon, and my homeland is far from here in one of the greatest countries on earth. Greece."

He moved over to a small wooden bench with the help of a

twisted cane and sat down with an audible grunt. "Where the gods like Ares once ruled everything the sun touched. As to what I am doing here, I am honoring a beloved god from my homeland. A god that still walks this world, even if the masses no longer believe in him and his kind." He tapped his blinded eye. "It may not be good for seeing things of this world anymore, but it has granted me a vision of what others cannot always see."

"I have heard of Greece before," Callisto replied, stepping closer to the statue. "Several of the fishermen in town have talked about going there."

"Aye, many who travel the seas would have no doubt been to Greece. It was once the strongest trading nation in all the world. Even still, it supplies the world much of what it enjoys."

"What is with all the bones around him?" she asked nervously, trying impossibly hard not to stare at Yaalon's dead milky eye.

"Unlike this new, Christian god, the gods of old required sacrifice and offerings to those who worshipped them before they would consider bestowing their favors," he explained.

"And what do you ask him for?" Callisto knew very little about any gods. Her father and mother always told her it was best to avoid talk of the gods, lest someone thought you a heretic. But needing some form of payment before asking such a mighty being for a favor made sense to her.

Yaalon's smile was crooked and rotten but showed humble kindness. "I ask for happiness, long life, protection for the family I left behind, and he one day allows me entry into the Elysian Fields when I finally walk the dark road."

"And does this god, Ares, ever answer you?"

The old man chuckled. "I am still alive and have yet to meet anyone as old as me, and I am happy enough. The rest, I have no way of knowing until it happens." He paused. "What is such a young thing like yourself doing out here so late? Surely you have a straw bed you should be in, and a mother and father likely worried sick about your whereabouts."

He looked her up and down as if for the first time. "And with the amount of dried blood and dirt upon you. I would say they would have great reason to be worried."

With a deep sigh, she told the stranger what had transpired that day and how she had come to find the shrine. She didn't know why she told him, but it felt right to do so. Felt good to tell someone who wasn't involved.

The old man whistled in genuine shock. "That is some grave tidings, little one. Far graver than anyone of your age should ever have to bear witness to. Maybe it was Ares who had me spark that candle at the perfect moment you would see it."

Callisto stared at the god's imposing figure, giving her an idea. "Do you think he would help me if I asked him?"

Yaalon shrugged his bony shoulders. "That I cannot answer. No one truly knows the will of the gods, for they are capricious and devious at the best of times. But," he held up his hands, "it could not hurt to try."

She was about to speak when she stopped, looked at the bones on the ground, and felt her insides drop suddenly. "I—I have nothing to offer him."

Smiling his crooked yellow smile again, Yaalon reached into a sack he had on his belt and pulled out a bound hare. "Here, you may use mine this night."

"But what will you offer him?" she asked, wanting to accept his offer but not wanting to steal away his gift to the god.

"Such a caring child. Do not fret about me. I have come here often enough and offer all that I can spare. Tonight, my offering to the great god of war will be helping you." He held out the hare for her to take. "I can think of no better offering I could give him."

She took the wriggling creature and stared back at the altar, almost feeling foolish now. If this kind of thing worked, more people would still do it. Her mind flashed to her father— the hatchet—the blood—her resolve fortified once more. "What is it I must do?"

Yaalon came to her aid. "Kneel before him and lower your head, he is a god, and you should feel humbled to be in his presence. Now hold out your offering as if you expect him to take it from your very hands."

He handed her a small bronze knife. "Cut the hare's throat and let the blood drip into the earth by his feet. Close your eyes, clear your mind of everything but what you want to ask him. Do not think about what you want; you must feel what you want, then ask it while placing the offering before his feet."

Callisto took the knife and held it to the hare's neck as it struggled to get free. With a quick jerk, its lifeblood began to spill out onto the earth, and within moments its frantic kicking stopped. Clearing her mind was more challenging than she expected, but soon she let out a deep breath, and the words of her soul poured out.

"I want vengeance for what Gaspar did to my papa. I want him to suffer for what he has done! I want to see his life and blood drain from his fat body! I want to kill him!"

She was startled by the words that had escaped her, and a shiver ran through her small frame. She was not a violent child, nor had she ever truly wished pain or death upon anyone. But deep down, she knew the words spoken were as accurate as any she had ever uttered.

Opening her eyes, she rose to her feet, unsure how she felt, but she did feel different. "How will I know if he answers?"

Yaalon was sitting on the bench, staring at her with much interest, his features more alive than they had been moments before. "Ares has heard your plea, child; of this, I know with certainty."

"How?"

The old man tapped his blind eye. "I watched you with my blind eye while you opened your soul for Ares to hear. I saw him lean down and accept your offering." He was in true awe. "It is something I have never witnessed before. Something I shall never forget."

Callisto almost burst with excitement before quickly feeling like a foolish child again. "You jest."

Yaalon shook his head. "I would never jest about the gods, child. Nor about something so meaningful to someone." He paused and looked back the way she had come. "It would seem Ares has seen fit to deliver you a gift for your course of vengeance."

Callisto saw the horse from before edging its way into the small clearing. "What are you doing here, girl?" She went to the animal, patting its neck. "Do you really think Ares sent the horse? Most likely, it followed me here from across the road."

"I don't claim to know the will of the gods, but from what I've seen this night, I can think of no better answer."

Looking from the horse to Yaalon, she was confused. "But why, what good does a horse that is not mine do me?"

Yaalon shrugged. "Only you can answer that." He tapped his chest. "Follow what your heart tells you. Then leap upon its back and see where it takes you. And wherever that may be, make sure you are prepared to act upon what Ares has granted for you, for not to would be an insult to his favor—and you do not want to insult a god."

Callisto looked at the statue and felt more confused than

ever. This was a stupid idea. The old gods were dead and could not help her.

"Come, girl. I will take you home before your master sees that you've gotten yourself free."

She wondered if she should go to the house and tell the owners their horse had gotten free. They would likely blame her or accuse her of trying to steal the beast. Quickly she dismissed the notion.

Wealthy people always found ways to blame those poorer than they were, just like Gaspar had done to her father! Yes, they would accuse her, maybe chop her hand off too! For a misunderstanding and a good deed! The thought burned deep within her very core, stirring a wave of anger she had only felt once before at the altar moments ago.

Her eyes locked on the horse. It looked almost like it was reading her thoughts, and again it pawed the ground and snorted its approval.

"If Ares truly did send you to me, then surely what I want is within my grasp to achieve. I can see vengeance done for my father! I can right the wrong done to him!"

Without thinking, she climbed onto the animal's back and steered it back the way she had come. The horse needed no motivation to be free of the clearing, and soon she left the town of Catark, and the altar of Ares behind her, following the trail of dried blood her father had left behind.

Yaalon watched her go and smiled. "May Ares guide you tonight, my child, so that justice will be swift."

Callisto slowed the sweat-lathered horse as she neared the large estate. With each moment along the ride, her anger had grown, and now she could barely contain herself. She wanted to scream at the top of her lungs and demand the man come out and—and—what?

Suddenly she felt her nine years of age and so very small in this great big world. What could she hope to do here? Gaspar was a grown man. A large man, with plenty of people at his beck and call, armed guards that would have no issue killing her. She was but a girl, no more than a child. Did she really think she could do anything here tonight?

The words that her father had told her often screamed at her but not in her father's voice.

"You're a girl, but that does not make you anything less than what a man can be...."

Her resolve began to return, and she climbed down from the horse, walking it over to a rocky outcrop by the road.

"You have done much for me this night." She rubbed its nose gingerly. "I pray you will still be here when I return. I shall take you home then, and no one need know what we have done."

The horse seemed to understand her and lowered its head to the sweet grass growing outside the estate, content to stay where it was for now.

Callisto moved carefully to a large shrub on the edge of the property. She needed to get her bearings; everything looked different now that it was night.

She could see several men with torches strewn throughout the grounds patrolling lazily. These men would be armed. She had seen them when she had last been here, swords, spears, and likely longbows.

The child in her screamed for her to turn around, return home, and forget this foolishness. But something more gripped her sensibilities, something more profound. She had been blessed by the War god Ares this night for her task. If a god she had never heard of until tonight would bestow his favor on her, what she would do had to be just!

She waited until the glow from the nearest torches faded, then crept along the trees, moving closer to the giant house. A house so big, it could hold nearly a third of the people in the town below with ease. Stopping, she tucked herself against the trunk of a fig tree, allowing two guards chatting idly about a whore in a local tavern to pass her by unnoticed.

With a deep breath, she sprinted the last thirty paces of open ground to the house walls. She waited for several heartbeats to hear if a call of alarm would come. When it didn't come, she knew she had made it and was safe—at least for this part, and now was all she was concerned with.

Crawling across the edge of the wall, she finally came to a large window that was slightly ajar. A small amount of light illuminated from inside. The smell of food and spices lingered from within, and Callisto guessed it had to be the kitchen. She heard nothing from inside. The cook and staff were likely long for their beds.

She climbed as quietly as possible, barely making any more sound than a mouse would. Crawling over the large counter, she slipped on the flour-covered wood and hit the floor with a groan.

Panic filled her, and she scrambled to hide beside a mountain of pots and pans. Her heart pounded as she waited, praying that she had not been heard.

Soon her eyes adjusted to the meager light, and a gasp escaped her. Cupboards and tables were bursting with food, loaves of bread, cheeses, fruits, vegetables, cured meats hanging from roof hooks, flour, sugar, and things she had never even seen before. There was enough food within this room to feed her family for nearly half a year or more!

The sight and smell of all this food made her stomach

grumble, and she realized the last thing she had eaten had been a few grapes nearly half a day ago. She grabbed some cured ham and a chuck of dried goat's cheese. Huddled underneath a table, she quickly ate.

No point doing this on an empty stomach, she thought. If she were caught, she would die with a full belly.

That was a curious thought.

Gaspar would likely kill her if she were discovered here. Yet she felt no fear right now when thinking about it. What she was doing was sanctioned by a god. How could she fail?

Looking around the kitchen, she wondered if she would have time to come back this way. She would fill one of the sacks and take it with her if she did. Her family could eat well for a week.

Full and satisfied, she moved to the far door. She had no idea where she was going or where she would find Gaspar, but she was determined not to leave until she had.

If she planned on getting justice, she would need a weapon. Her eyes landed on the small knife she had used to cut the cheese. Snatching it up, she left the kitchen, hugging the shadows the large house provided.

The house was silent as she moved down one hallway to another, checking each room and doorway she passed. With each room she searched, her bitterness for this man grew. This house was far more than any person needed or had the right to have, while others just as deserving lived in rotting shacks that did nothing to keep out the heat of summer days or the rains and wind that so often hit the coast.

The small knife was pressed in Callisto's tight fist as she slowly went up each step, spreading her weight to avoid the creaks from the lacquered wood beneath. Quickly discovering the steps were solid, little noise came from her paltry weight.

At the top of the stairs, another long hallway with several

doors along either side awaited, but a set of double doors of polished oak stood out like a beacon at the very end. She cursed herself for wasting so much time below. She should have known a man like this would place himself in the grandest of rooms at the top of the house.

Yet how was she to have known? This was the first person she had known who lived in a house with more than one level.

Making her way down the hallway, she heard footsteps from one of the rooms beside her. She cursed as she glanced around for a place to hide, but it was too late when the door opened.

The hallway filled with the bright light of a candle stick, and a middle-aged woman's chubby face appeared. She jumped back in fright at seeing the stranger standing there but was quick to compose herself as she realized it was a child.

"What are you doing here, little lass?" she whispered, checking down the hallway to ensure no one else had heard her. "This is a dangerous place for the likes of you. Come, I will take you to the kitchen and give you a little food, but stealing anything else won't go unnoticed, and the master is a cruel man he is."

"I know that fact all too well," Callisto whispered, her voice quivering with rage.

The woman noticed the small knife in the girl's hand.

"Oh, dear me." She rechecked the hallway. "Get in here, little miss, before someone is seein' you and all manner of trouble breaks out, which there will be no coming back from."

Before she could think to fight it, she was pulled into the small room, and the door was shut firmly behind her.

"What are you doing?" Callisto growled, hoping she wouldn't have to hurt this woman. She was here for Gaspar, no one else.

"I be askin' you the same question, ya wee silly little thing."

The woman looked down at the knife again. "What you thinkin' of doin' with that thing?"

"Get out of my way! Justice will happen tonight!"

It was then that realization hit the woman. "Oh, dear me, you're the girl from this afternoon, whose father—" She looked at the knife again and shook her head. "I know you feelin' like this will be justice, but it won't be. It won't change anything that's happened and will be somethin' you'll live with for the rest of your life. That is if you even get to him before he wakes up and sees you."

"If you'd get out of my way and stop wasting my time, I could!" she hissed back, her anger bubbling.

Would she have to kill this woman too? She hoped not.

"I truly am sorry about your pa, but this is no way for a young girl to throw her life away. There is so much more to live for than this."

"It's not your life to worry about!" Callisto spat, growing impatient.

Soon she would have to act, and if that meant killing this woman, then so be it! Ares had granted her favor; she wasn't about to be dissuaded by a fat housemaid.

"Now move, or else!"

With a great sigh, the woman moved from the doorway. "You won't be doing much with that little cheese sticker you have there." She struggled with some inner battle, then sighed again.

"When you enter his room, the dresser beside his wash bowl, the first drawer, has a dagger. A fine dagger, a gift he received from a nobleman of great wealth. He was wicked when he visited the estate three years ago."

Callisto opened the door, then turned to the woman again. "Why would you tell me that?"

"Your pa isn't the only person who has fallen prey to

Gaspar's cruelty." She wiped stray tears from her cheeks. "Now you do what you need to do and get gone from here as quickly as your legs will carry you, and don't let anyone see you! Else all sorts of trouble will befall your family, far worse than just the hand your pa lost."

Once in the hallway, Callisto saw only the double doors leading to her target. She could hear movement from other rooms around her and made haste, knowing she would indeed be caught if she wasted too much time. She had come too far to fail now.

Her small hands touched the polished brass knobs, and her heart and breathing quickened. It took all her power to slow them, believing anyone within the house could hear the sound of her blood pumping.

Slowly she pushed the handle until she heard the slight click of the bolt release. She held it there and waited several long heartbeats, ensuring the noise hadn't been heard from within. Satisfied that it hadn't been, she pushed slowly on the heavy door, pleased to find the hinges were not like the ones back home, which made horrible screeching sounds every time they were disturbed.

Sliding herself in, she quickly closed the door. The room was dark, only the light of the pale moon outside providing light through the three large windows along the outer walls and the glass doors to the balcony overlooking the grounds.

Waiting for her eyes to adjust, she crept towards the large bed centered on the side wall. She could see the prominent figure of Gaspar, sprawled out upon a framed canopy bed, large enough to sleep her entire family. Such refinements were ill-gotten from the backs of others for this pompous fiend. How this was allowed was beyond her reasoning.

The world was cruel and unfair, but she never expected it to be like this. Her youth and little experience made her naïve, and she promised herself then and there that if she survived this, she would change that.

The dresser the woman had spoken of was near the bed, and as quickly as she dared, ensuring her steps were true, she went to it. Her fingertips brushed against the gleaming silver handles, and she wondered how many days of fishing her family would have had to do to afford just one of them.

Her heartbeat was faster as she slid the drawer open just enough to get her small hand inside. She felt around carefully, not wanting anything within to make noise and expose her. Soon, her fingers wrapped around the blade's hilt. The sleeping man let out a loud groan and broke wind loudly before rolling onto his side.

The sudden noise and movement made Callisto jerk back in desperation in case she needed to hide. With reflexes she was unaware she had, her free hand shot out, grasped its stem, and stopped it before it could crash to the floor. In doing so, the candle holder shifted and rocked back and forth dangerously, threatening to tip over and wake her victim.

But it was too late. The noise had been enough to stir Gaspar from his undeserved slumber, and she saw him roll back over with a grunt.

"What was that?" he muttered through a yawn. "Who's there?"

Callisto scurried behind the side of the dresser, crouching down tightly. The dagger was firmly in her tiny hand. This was it. He would see her and know what she had been trying to do. Her family would be punished worse now than they already had been. All because of her foolishness! She could hear him lift from the bed and heavy footsteps on the floorboards.

Why had she come here?

Why did she think she could do this?

She was a child, not some assassin in the night.

"Stupid old woman likely dropped something again," he grumbled. "I'll lash her tomorrow for disturbing my sleep."

Callisto peered around the dresser and saw that he was completely naked and standing in front of the large chamber pot at the end of his bed. With a grunt, he began to relieve himself, and the sound of urine hitting the brass pot rang loudly throughout the room.

He doesn't know I am here!

She could escape if she stayed right here until he fell asleep again.

No!

I came here to avenge my father. I cannot leave until it is done.

But can I really go through with this?

Suddenly, the dagger in her hands felt impossibly heavy, and the weight of killing a man, even a monster such as Gaspar, gnawed at her consciousness.

The large mirror in the corner of the room caught her eye, for something unnatural was moving within. It was a powerful man, nay, she realized it was a god. Ares, the god of war, his eyes burning with anticipation as he stared at her. He pointed to Gaspar.

"Your time is now! Strike him down while he pisses. A coward like him deserves to die in his own filth for what he has done to you and your family! I have given you the perfect opportunity!" His eyes burned into hers. "Do not waste it—girl."

The words boomed in her head with raw authority, almost causing her to drop the dagger and cover her ears. She shook her head and looked again, the mirror was empty, and only Gaspar and she remained alone in the room.

It had been the same voice that she had heard in the trees where she had met Yaalon.

The god was right!

He was showing her his favor.

To fail would surely anger him.

Callisto knew naught about the gods of old, but to anger one after receiving favor couldn't be wise. What worse things could befall her with the wrath of a god?

She could do it!

She would do it!

On trembling legs, she rose from her hiding spot. The sound of urine was slowing. He was almost finished and would turn around and see her if she didn't act soon.

Fidgeting with the dagger and wondering which way she should hold it to strike, she moved forward, not wanting to give herself away before she had time to attack. The sound of urine stopped to a dribble, her heart almost with it. It was now or never! She launched forward with all the speed she could, ramming the blade deep into the rolls of the fat man's back.

Gaspar roared in sudden agony. The razor-sharp dagger tore through the flesh of his back, and he spun around. His meaty hand caught her across the side of the face, battering her to the floor. The blood-slick dagger slipped from her grip and clattered under the large bed.

"What the fuck is this?" he screamed as he looked down at her and then at the vicious wound that bled profusely.

"You wretched little bitch! I will see you and your family butchered like hogs for this!" He stepped forward and crashed to his knees, his face pale and glistening with sweat as he tried to stem the blood flow.

"Guards! Guards! Help me, you useless sods!" He realized he was in grave trouble.

Callisto knew if she didn't finish this and escape, it would all be over for her and her family. She dived for the bed and reached under for the dagger's hilt. Her fingers brushed against it when suddenly a mighty hand grabbed her ankle and pulled her back.

"I am going to wring the life from you, you fucking stupid cur!" the fat man wheezed as he tried to pull her back out.

Callisto fought for all she was worth, kicking back as she tried to claw her way back to the dagger with an outstretched hand. Her fingers brushed it again, and she could feel the man's strength waning, his pull not as powerful, and his grip weakening.

With a final kick, she was free and snatched the dagger from beneath the bed, lashing out just as Gaspar reached for her again. The blade sliced through his sausage-like fingers, and he howled, clutching his wounded hand; three fingers were missing from it now.

"Guards, help me damn you!" he gasped as he pushed himself back.

A horn sounded from outside, and Callisto knew she had only moments before armed men would burst through the door and capture her.

"I'll see your whole family skinned alive for this and make you watch before burning you alive!" Gaspar growled, though his voice seemed barely more than a whisper as he struggled to push himself further from her. The floor was slick with blood, and he didn't make it far.

"You are a monster, and tonight justice will be served!" She punched the dagger straight ahead, the blade's tip sinking through the fat of his neck.

She watched his eyes widen while she twisted the blade, opening his jugular. A warm spray of blood covered her hand and arm. Frothy blood oozed from his pain-twisted mouth. He tried to speak, but only a gurgling sound came forth. He fell back to the floor, convulsing for several seconds, and was finally still.

Callisto stood staring at the dead man triumphantly as gouts of blood stained the lush peach-colored carpet.

She had done it!

She had gotten justice for her father, and who knew how many others.

Her victory was short-lived when she heard hard-booted feet storming down the hallway just outside the door.

Sprinting for the balcony, she climbed over the side, and let herself fall without thinking, praying the ground would be soft. She landed hard but was back on her feet, running for her life as she heard the men calling out Gaspar's name above her.

"There's the killer, running for the trees! Get them!" one of the guards yelled from the balcony.

Light from torches lit up the estate grounds as armed men searched for intruders. But Callisto didn't care. If she tried to sneak out, they would surely come upon her. So, she ran as fast as her tired little legs would carry her.

"Ares, do not condemn me now!" she whispered as she came to the spot she had left the horse to find it no longer there.

"No, no, no! Horse, where are you?" she cried, fear gripping her. For she knew without the horse, escape would be impossible.

The horse moved from behind a rocky pile a moment later, and she wasted no time throwing herself onto its back and kicking its flanks hard, forcing it into a dead run down the road, the way she had come twice that day.

The night's excitement still coursed through her as she made her way across the yard to the house. Light shone through the cracks in the covered windows, telling her that her mother was up waiting for her. She couldn't wait to tell her what she had done, how she had made things right. How the debt would be gone, and they would never have to worry about that evil man again. Their lives would be better because of what she had done.

"She should have come straight home!" Macario said, worry in his words. "Something must have happened to her."

"I bet it was that bastard Gaspar," Tad interjected. "Father wasn't enough for him. He probably followed them and decided to take her!"

"We have to find her," Macario replied with more worry than she had ever heard from him.

"Find her! Find your sweet sister!" Abarrane, their mother, cried in distress. "She is out there alone, and only the gods know what is happening to her."

"I swear if that Gaspar has her, I will cut his fat fucking throat," Tad roared.

Callisto felt terrible that they were so worried about her. "I am here! I am alright," she announced as she entered the small cottage with a big grin, knowing the news she was about to tell them would make everything better.

"My sweet child!" Her mother ran to her. "What has happened to you? Where were you? Oh, my sweet heavens, she is bleeding! Get water and bandages!"

Callisto looked at all the blood now dried to her and felt a fool for not washing in the trough outside first. "No, mother, it's alright. It's not my blood."

All three of her family stopped and looked at each other before looking back, concern etched upon their faces.

"Whose blood is it?" her mother asked nervously, stepping away from her as if she had the plague.

Callisto beamed with excitement again. "I did it, Mother. I

avenged Father. That monster can't hurt us anymore. Can't hurt anyone anymore."

Macario's eyes widened as he noticed the bloodied dagger tucked away in his sister's belt. "What have you done?"

"I killed the man who hurt Father," she boasted proudly, confused by her family's weird reactions.

Her mother began to cry wildly, adding to the many tears she had already cried that night.

"No, Mother, do not cry. I killed him. He is dead now. He can't hurt anyone ever again. I did good. We are free and safe now."

"You truly killed Gaspar?" Tad asked, his eyes dancing with excitement and unease as she nodded eagerly.

"You are a stupid, stupid wretched girl!" her mother wailed. "You have brought doom upon us! How could you be so stupid?"

"No, it's alright, Mother." Callisto went to her, but she pulled away from her daughter's touch. "No one saw me; no one knows it was me. Everything will be fine. I did what was right. I had one of the old god's favor, and he helped me!"

Abarrane stood, refusing to look at her daughter a moment longer. "Macario, Tad, help your sister change and get cleaned up. I need to go look after Simao."

Finally, she turned a sharp eye on her daughter. "Tomorrow, I shall deal with this—this problem." With that, she turned away and went to the back room without glancing back.

The house was deadly silent for several long moments, and Callisto stood there in her blood-stained clothing, confused by all of this. What was happening? Why was her mother acting like this? Why didn't she understand?

"Come, we will go to the wash bin out back. No one will see you like this there," Tad said, taking the dagger from her and placing it on the counter. "You won't be needing this anymore —I hope."

"So, you really killed him?" Tad asked, stripping the blood-soaked clothes from her.

She nodded, almost beginning to feel guilty, like somehow she had done something wrong, but that couldn't be true. Gaspar had been an evil man, and now he was dead. Why didn't they see that? Wasn't good supposed to fight evil? And weren't things better when evil was defeated? Every story she had ever heard talked of such things.

How was this any different?

Macario dumped a bucket of rainwater over her head, and she nearly yelped in surprise from the sudden cold biting at her skin.

"How could you do such a thing?" he asked, handing her a bar of lye.

"I don't understand why everyone is so mad at me," she whimpered as she scrubbed the blood and grime away. "I thought everyone would be happy and proud of me. I thought for sure Mother would be relieved to know that he was gone forever."

"Proud of you?" Macario scoffed. "You killed someone. Do you not understand that?"

"He made father cut his hand off!" she shot back. "He was a monster!"

Macario shook his head. "That was between him, father, and the law. Certainly not you to take into your own hands. Not to mention how dangerous that was. You are a girl and a child. Had you been caught, they would have killed you."

"You know as well as we do the authorities would have done nothing," Tad countered. "Men like Gaspar don't get punished when men like father are concerned."

"That's not the point!" his older brother snapped, dumping another bucket of water over their sister.

"Then what is?" Tad asked with venom on his lips. "Are we to be walked upon like ants and expected to take it?"

"No, but—you know we—" Macario sighed. "If people just start taking the law into their own hands, chaos will break out. The laws are there for a reason."

"And maybe the rich bastards would finally know 'their' place," Tad growled back, handing his sister a rag. "I, for one, think what you did, Sister, is what needed to be done. I just wish you would have let me come too. I would have gladly helped gut the fat bastard."

"Tad!" Macario barked. "Do not tell her such things. You will confuse her between what is right and wrong."

"Only ones confused here tonight are Mother and you," Tad muttered. "Come, sis, time you got yourself to bed. I suspect tomorrow will not be a pleasant one for you."

Callisto followed her brother as she slipped on a fresh long shirt hanging on the clothesline. This was all so confusing.

"Don't listen to them, Callisto," Tad whispered to her as she climbed into her straw cot on the far side of the house. "Gaspar deserved what he got. You did well, even if Mother and Macario don't see it. Once Father has recovered, he will support what you did. I am sure of it."

Callisto lay there, staring up at the roof. The turmoil and excitement of the night and her family's disappointment had worn out every ounce of strength she had left.

"I couldn't have done wrong. A god granted me the means to do it. If a god helped me, it couldn't have been wrong," she told herself over and over before sleep took her.

A hand clamped down over her mouth, and Callisto's eyes shot open in a panic to see Tad standing over her.

"Shh!" he whispered. Fear was bright in his hazel eyes. "You need to get dressed quickly!"

"Why?" she asked, rubbing the sleep from her eyes. "What is going on?"

"Men are coming!" he barked. "Now get dressed. You have to leave!"

"Leave? But why?" She pulled on the clothes her brother had thrown her.

"They are coming for you!" Tad peeked out the window; dawn was still an hour away. "They know it was you."

"What?" she gasped. "Impossible, no one saw me!"

"I don't know. I was sneaking around, ensuring everything was fine, when I heard them talking to Pallos, asking them if they knew where we lived! Because some girl killed their master!"

"The old woman!" Callisto gasped. But why would she help her only to turn her in now?

"So, someone did see you?"

"She helped me—"

Tad shook his head, clearly angry with her now. "Well, now she is helping herself!"

"No, they must have—"

"We don't have time for that. If they catch you here, we will all suffer for it!" he barked at her. "But if you leave, we can claim you never returned home, and we had no idea what you did."

"Where am I to go?" she asked, suddenly very afraid and hurt by her brother's words, even though they made sense.

"I don't know, but it must be far away, Callisto. As far as you can, and it would be better if I didn't know. That way, I can't tell them if—" He handed her a small pack, refusing to finish what he had been about to say.

"I stuffed what little food I could in there, with a blanket,

36

flint, and steel, the dagger you came home with, and a few other things."

She took the heavy pack, tears welling in her eyes. "When will I be able to come back?"

"I don't know, a year—maybe two—maybe never." Tad felt sorry for her. She was so young, but what she had done had shaped this outcome, and now she would have to play it out.

The words were like knives driving into her heart. "—never—"

He was rechecking the window, and torch lights could be seen. "You have to go right now!"

"Can't I say goodbye—"

"No!" he rebuked her. "There is no time for that! I will tell them. You must go, sister. It might already be too late!"

Callisto ran to the back door and into the fading night, dawn threatening to break through soon. Tears ran freely down her cheeks as she searched for a way to run. She had never left the town of Catark before. Where was she even to go?

Just then, she heard a familiar snort and pounding of hoof on earth. By the fence was the horse that had started all of this. She didn't question it and quickly launched herself on its back.

"Take me away, Ares! Take me somewhere I will be safe!"

The horse reared up and bolted down the dirt road heading north just as several men came into view of the lane. The pounding of hooves drowned out their shout.

Callisto gasped in panic, waking suddenly from the dream. She cursed herself for falling asleep. That hadn't been part of the plan, but after all the drinks and lovemaking, the dangers of this soft, plush bed had overcome her.

With an infuriated sigh, she carefully rolled herself from

the large bed, making sure not to disturb the handsome man beside her. She caught her reflection in the full-length mirror and smirked. Her firm, womanly curves were the envy of many women and the spark of lust of many loins, male and female alike.

It had been those charming looks that made her job so much easier. Much had changed from the fateful night a lifetime ago. She couldn't believe she had dreamed of it again. It had been years since she had even thought of that night. The night that changed her life for the better as far as she was concerned, at least, better now. The first few years had been hard—very hard. Desperate and painful lessons had been learned at nearly every turn.

But she had learned and learned well.

No matter, she forced the thoughts aside.

She had a job to do, and thinking of the past was not part of it.

She slipped on her smooth black, white frilly trimmed dress, stockings, and black leather boots as quickly as she could. Once dressed, she checked on her victim.

The drug she had mixed in his wine would keep him asleep for some time. She wasn't sure how long she had slept, but it was still dark outside, so it couldn't have been that late.

At least, she hoped not.

Moving across the room to the dresser, she pulled out a pick from a hidden pocket in her outfit and deftly went to work on the small lockbox. She hoped this wasn't all for nothing. She smirked at herself as she glanced back over; not for nothing, she decided.

She had been stalking this man, this Paavo Amdre, for five days. She casually bumped into him in random places throughout the days and evenings. She could tell he had been interested in her from their first meeting. The way his eyes had lingered over her, undressing her each time their paths crossed. Married or not, the loins of men were easily seduced with bright green eyes, red lips, and suitable clothing to show off just enough flesh to stir the blood.

Skills she had learned from the best and perfected.

It hadn't been long before Paavo had begun promising her things, so long as she would give herself to him while he was in the city. He had been a decent lover, not great, but then again, the drug she had given him hadn't helped his cause. He was handsome enough, rich, and stupid. All the things she looked for in a man she wanted to rob.

The click of the lock brought her back to the task, and her eyes sparkled at the treasures inside. A hefty bag of gold and another of silver coins were quickly pocketed, along with several well-adorned rings. This was but a small portion of Paavo's wealth, and as much as she would enjoy playing a longer game to relieve him of more, there were other marks on her list, loins to seduce, and coin to be taken.

Timing was everything.

Wealthy men came and went often from the city. Some stayed for months, others mere days. She paid well for this information.

Callisto was about to slip out the door when she remembered his gold studded belt. It would fetch a reasonable price from her buyer. She was untangling the belt from his trousers on the floor when something touched her shoulder.

"What are you doing—my sweet?" Paavo mumbled, trying to focus on her; the drug lingered deeply still.

"You weren't supposed to wake up yet."

"What—what does that mean? Are you—robbing me?" He blinked several times, clearing his vision, his face increasingly concerned.

"Of course I am."

Paavo started to get up from the bed and grabbed at her. Quickly she sidestepped his groggy attempt. "You dumb bitch. I won't stand for this!"

"For what it's worth, you were very kind to me, kinder than most," she smiled sweetly, "but it's time for you to sleep some more."

"What the fuck are you talking—" A wine bottle smashed against his head, and he crashed to the floor in a heap.

Callisto stared down at him and shook her head. "A headache and damaged pride are a better outcome than some have come out of this."

She straightened her dress in the hallway and went down the stairs to the tavern below. It was past closing time, so the tavern was empty of patrons.

"So, how'd it go?" Earnest asked from behind the bar, cleaning a mug with a rag.

Callisto wondered if the mug was getting cleaner or dirtier, given the state of the rag. She smiled and accepted the cup of chilled ale he poured her regardless. A dirty mug was far from the worst thing she'd ever had to put in her mouth.

"As smooth as planned, of course. Would you expect anything different from me?"

He raised a brow at her. "Smooth, eh? I heard a crash."

She took a long swallow of the dark ale. "That's because I smoothly had to hit him with a bottle when he woke up unexpectedly."

"You were up there a lot longer than normal. I was starting to get concerned for you. Thought I might have to 'intervene.'"

"Awe, are you starting to care about my well-being, Earnest? That is a dangerous sort of affair given what we know of each other," she teased with a wink, knowing full well he cared for her, or at the very least, the profits she gave him for their arrangement.

"That bed was just too tempting tonight. I ended up dozing off." Digging around in one of her many hidden pockets, she pulled out two gold and two silver coins and one of the jeweled rings then placed them on the bar.

He scoffed at her jest, but humor shone through his eyes. "I care about my business and the dangers it could be in if you start getting sloppy."

Taking another sip of ale, she nodded. It was true. He took a significant risk helping her with her little enterprise. She reached into her pocket again and tossed another ring onto the bar.

"A small apology. I sometimes forget who else is at risk."

He slipped the coins and first ring into his pocket and slid the newly offered ring back. "It's not always about the money, Callisto." He looked uncomfortable as he fought to say something.

"Come now, Earnest, we have known one another nearly six years. You are likely the closest thing to a real friend I actually have in this god-forsaken city. If you have something to say to me, say it." She knew what it was going to be, but best for him to get it out in the open so it didn't eat at him and make him do something foolish.

"That's a sad life indeed, lass." He refilled her drink. "You have hit several big marks in the last several months. I know you only give me a small cut, and what I have gotten is a small treasure hoard. I can only imagine what you have stashed away. Maybe it's time to stop this life and give something different a go."

"You mean more honest?" She sipped the drink slower. With what she had already had that evening, she could feel her senses starting to be affected.

"Can't get nothing by you. Fine, more 'honest' if you will."

"Honest isn't my thing. I like what I do. I have a thing

against rich pricks, and removing some of their wealth from them makes me feel better about it."

"I know, I know. You've told me more than once." He sighed, poured himself a drink, and finished it in one mighty gulp. "But truth be told, it's time you moved on from here for a while."

Callisto lowered the mug slowly, regarding him carefully. "Are you breaking up with me, Earnest?"

"Aye, for a time." There was no give in his tone; he was serious. "This is a dangerous game, and you are damn good at it, lass, there ain't no denying that. But even the best players lose sooner or later. But the game you are playing, losing normally becomes fatal. For you and me."

She drummed her fingers on the bar in as much irritation as thought. This was not what she wanted to hear. She had too many plans in the works for him to back out now.

"I know this isn't what you wanted to hear, but I think it's for the best," he continued seeing the spark of anger in her eyes. "Leave the city for a year, ply your trade elsewhere, then come back once people have forgotten what you look like."

He wasn't wrong, but she wasn't ready to leave yet.

She had planned two more big marks, jobs that would see her well off for a good while. Earnest assumed she had a bulgingstash of gold and silver from all her hard work; she did not. The fact was, she had only a small stash. Right enough, it would keep her well and good for two or more years if she lowered her standard of living.

What she did came at a price. She had to pay people for good information about her targets, movements, and where-abouts. What they liked and didn't like, and who they knew and feared.

Bribes didn't come cheap, either. Specific high-ranking authority figures turned the other way because money talked.

QUEEN OF THE SEAS

Her outfits and attire cost more than she cared to think about. The parts she played had to be played correctly to work. You couldn't seduce a wealthy lord looking like a lower-class tramp.

"Are you going to say something or just stare at me with those bright green eyes, looking like you want to tear my head off?"

It was her turn to laugh. "I wouldn't tear your head off. I'd gut you and strangle you with your own entrails." She winked.

"Oh, well, good. I'll sleep easier knowing that." He was nervous as he refilled the pitcher with fresh ale.

"One more," she stated.

"What's that?"

"Just one more. Let me do one more in a few days. Then I'll lay low as you said. Take a trip somewhere and see what happens. Who knows, when I come back, maybe I'll have more interest in the 'honest' way of life," she said, but there was a plea to it. She needed him to agree. She didn't have time to set up another deal like this one and had already paid a small fortune for her intel.

It was his turn to drum his fingers on the wooden bar. "I don't like it. I really don't. But fine, you do one more. I don't even want nothing this time. My payment is you lying low after."

He turned a stern eye on her and put his hand out. "Deal?"

Smirking, Callisto shook his meaty hand. "Deal."

"Now get the fuck out of here. It's late enough as is, and I'm not as young as I used to be. Besides, pretty boy upstairs is gonna wake up mighty pissed off soon, and if you are still around, then this'll all be for naught."

Leaning over, she kissed his bearded cheek. "You're the best, Earnest. I'll catch up with you with the details in a day or two."

"Ya, ya." He waved her out with the dirty rag before bolting the door closed behind her.

Light shone through the window, bathing the small but luxurious room in its morning glory. Callisto groaned in irritation, wishing she had remembered to draw the curtains closed before crawling into bed. A handful of hours of sleep wasn't enough after last night's exploits, more so after how much she had drunk.

She had people to meet, information to gather, and items to sell off. She made it a severe habit not to have stolen possessions for more than a day or two, if possible. The coin was near impossible to track, but a family ring, or golden belt, was a good way to end up on the wrong side of the dungeon walls or with your neck in a noose.

Callisto slithered out of the soft bed, her toes digging into the thick rug. She didn't want to stand out and catch eyes this morning, so she kept her clothing choices casual. Throwing on a pair of dark grey breeches, a forest green linen shirt, dark leather boots, and a cloak, she was almost ready to leave.

Retrieving both her daggers from the desktop, the smaller one she slid into a holster in her right boot, the other strapped to her belt behind her back. She grabbed the pouch with the stolen items from under her bed and quickly hid them within a secret fold in her cloak.

She left the small apartment she rented in the southern end of Tamora. It was closer to the poorer part of the city, tucked away behind several larger buildings, making its existence known by very few.

The elderly woman who owned it. Her husband had died a few years earlier; with no income, she would have lost everything had Callisto not been lucky enough to come around. She paid twice what the old woman had asked for, ensuring the poor woman had more than the means to live out her days comfortably. But there had been a condition Callisto had set for that generosity. If anyone came looking for her, she had never been there. The old woman had agreed, and their relationship was straightforward, and interactions were almost nonexistent.

Making her way through a back door that led to a narrow alleyway, Callisto casually drifted into the morning crowd, the hood of her cloak hiding the extent of her features. She needed to get to the East end of the city where her fence would be but caution always took precedence.

She had been meticulous over the years in planning her routes, and she was more than sure no one was following her. Making several detours through the large city, slipping through vendors and shops would easily confuse anyone trying to follow her. Hard lessons had been taught the first few years on her own.

Lessons she kept to heart.

Confident she had covered her tracks, she made her way to Baron's Fish Market, a small business that was a front for more devious underground transactions. Thieves, cutthroats, and all forms of the city's scum came and went from there regularly. But it was a neutral zone to do business. Anyone starting fights or causing trouble was dealt with, never to be seen again. Baron liked things simple. Trouble was never simple and was often expensive.

Callisto pulled her hood back as she approached the warehouse. Four brutes sat out front around a small table, throwing dice. They were rough men, thugs, and killers, but with a bat of her eyes, a seductive twist of her lips, and a little cleavage, they were puppies in her hands. They glanced up and grinned.

"Morning, gentlemen. I hope all is well."

"Morning, Callisto," the man closest to the door said with as charming of a smile as he could manage with his crooked, yellow teeth. "It's been crap until now."

"Dex, if I didn't know better, I'd say you were flirting with me." She saw the slight blush the monster of a man tried to hide.

"I'd kill at least a dozen men for you, Callisto; all you have to do is ask." He grinned.

"I'd kill two dozen!" the bald man to the right, whose name she had never learned, jumped in.

"Three dozen!"

"Boys, boys!" She calmed them down with a wave of her hands. "I need no one killed today, at least not yet. But it's good to know I have options."

They all laughed proudly.

"Baron's waiting for you inside," Dex said.

"I'd best not keep him waiting."

Walking into the shop, she was assaulted by the smell of salt and fish. He was fair for as bad a man as Baron was rumored to be. As much a front as the business was, it was still a running business that turned a fair profit considering. It employed nearly three dozen workers, from fishermen to those who dried and salted the fish for sale.

"Baron, where are you?" she called out. The shop looked empty.

"In the back!" came a grunt of a reply.

Callisto slipped behind the desk and pushed open the swinging doors to where the cold room was located. Instantly her eyes landed on the man bound to a chair, his face bruised and swollen, and several deep but superficial cuts riddled parts of his gaunt form.

"Ah, Callisto, good to see you this morning. I am guessing

your evening went as planned?" the stocky, grizzly faced man known as Baron asked, his tone showing no hint of what was happening in the room to be anything out of the ordinary.

"Not as profitable as I had hoped, but well enough that it wasn't a waste of my time. Plus, he was charming enough to entertain for an evening," she replied, looking at the frightened man and wondering what stupid thing he had done to wind up here. Baron was fair, but when betrayed or crossed, he quickly reminded folk he was still dangerous. Here was not a place anyone ever wanted to find themselves.

Baron fingered through an array of knives, hooks, pinchers, and other horrendous-looking instruments. "That's a shame. I have a very interested buyer in town for a few days, willing to buy up all sorts of 'unsavory' goods at a better-than-normal price. Apparently, where he comes from, the market for such things is so high that runners have gone to other cities to get supplies for the demand."

"Well, if he is still in town in a few days, I hope to have another score by then, a larger one at that."

"Really?" Baron looked at her with growing interest, not one of lustful thoughts like most men seemed to look at her with.

Baron was one of the only men she had ever encountered, that no matter how she looked or the charm she oozed, he held no interest in her. At first, it had almost been an insult, but now she found it comforting. He and Earnest were like family.

"One so quickly after the other? Risky business, even for you."

"This one is only in town for two days and one I'd be a fool to miss out on." She shrugged. "I will take the risk. From my sources, he never misses a chance to visit the brothels while away from his wife. I will just have to intercept him before he has a chance to enjoy their pleasures when he can enjoy mine instead. Of course, my payment will be much, much higher."

Finally, Baron seemed pleased with a pair of plyers and turned back to his whimpering captive. He placed the pinchers on the man's thumbnail. "What did you bring me today?" He pulled, and the poor man wailed wildly.

With a right hook, he nearly toppled the man over. "Shut up, will you! The lady is trying to speak." With that, he pulled another nail from the man's hand, who, this time, tried not to yell, knowing his life teetered in a dangerous spot.

Callisto pulled the pouch from her cloak and dumped the contents onto a side table for Baron's inspection. It took much of her self-control to manage her expressions at the scene folding out before her. She was no meek little thing; blood and violence were something she was good and used to. But seeing someone tortured so carelessly was a gruesome sight, none-theless.

"Well, Thomas, what do you think? You are a notable thief. Should I play hardball, or should I be nice? Some good pieces here," he told her, glancing over from his bloody work. "Might keep that belt for myself. Make me look all pompous and dapper when I drink at the tavern with the boys." He put the plyers down, grabbed a pair of shears, and placed them up against the man's left ear.

The man mumbled something from behind his gag.

"Didn't your mother ever tell you not to talk with your mouth full? You just don't listen too well, do you, Thomas?" With one quick motion, he sliced the ear clean off. Thomas wailed and thrashed again, watching as his ear dropped to the dirty floor.

Baron removed the man's gag after the screaming had stopped. "I guess that one was my fault." He shrugged. "Now answer the question."

Thomas looked from Baron to Callisto and licked his lips nervously. He was terrified, knowing anything he said would get him hurt, yet to say nothing would get him hurt more.

"Well—I—I can't see too well from here, but from what I can see, those items look top-quality to the right buyers. If melted down, I'd say the jewels and gold alone would be worth at least sixteen gold, nine silver."

"That's a good eye," Baron replied, eyeing the items again. "It's a shame, Thomas, that you had to try and steal from me. You could have had a bright future." With a sudden move, he rammed the sheers through Thomas' eye. The man convulsed for several long, drawn-out seconds before finally going still.

"I'll give you twelve gold, seven silver for the lot."

Callisto knew she was being cheated but wondered if now was the time to be confrontational. "And if I tell you to go fuck yourself, will I end up tied to a chair cut to ribbons like poor Thomas?"

Baron burst out laughing. "By the gods, girl, you have a bigger set of balls than any man I have ever met. Anyone who witnessed what you did would have taken half of what I offered merely to get away from here."

Inside she sighed with relief. "I don't scare easy."

"I want that belt." Baron reached into a small pouch at his side, retrieved fourteen gold and four silver, and placed them on the table. "That's as high as I am willing to pay."

"Fine," she slid the coins into her pocket. "But next time, you open your tight purse strings a little more for what I bring you."

"So long as you bring me something of worth."

"See you in a few days, Baron."

He nodded and turned back to the two men on either side of the chair. "What are you standing around for? Clean this mess up!"

Quickly she made her way out of the shop. It had been hard to keep her composure. She had heard many stories about Baron and his cruelty to those who betrayed him, but she assumed most of them were exaggerated. She knew better now.

"Dirty business going on in there," Dex said, seeing her come down the stairs.

"Play stupid games, and you win stupid prizes," she told him calmly, though she knew her features a moment ago had betrayed her.

"Take care of yourself, Callisto. Come see us anytime," one of the others called to her as she merged onto the street.

Feeling her stomach growl, she started to head for her favorite bakery. She would need food if she were to keep at the pace she planned today.

"There she is!" someone yelled. "That's the whore who robbed me!"

Instantly, Callisto knew the voice and glimpsed Paavo Amdre and four of the city watchmen moving in behind her.

"Damn it!" she cursed, wondering if she should return to Baron's and let Dex and the others take care of this. Bloodshed wasn't what she wanted, plus Baron would likely blackball her from the shop if she brought such trouble to his doorstep, and that was something she couldn't afford right now.

So, there was only one logical opinion.

Run!

"Stop, you stupid bitch," Paavo screamed behind her. "I'll see you beaten and jailed for this!"

Callisto shoved her way through the mid-morning crowds, receiving curses and shouts from those she knocked down in her frantic wake. There was no way she planned on being caught. She checked her belt, touching the hilt of her dagger. The same blade she had used to kill her first man. She would add another to the list that had fallen to it if necessary.

Taking a side alley, she leaped over several piles of rubbish, happy she made the right choice by not wearing a dress that morning. Rounding the end of the passage, she glanced back. Only two of the five were still following.

Shit, she muttered.

They had split up, hoping to flank her somewhere.

Exiting the alley, she caught sight of the two city watchmen on the right, quickly pushing their way through the crowd, their truncheons held high. To the left, another one was coming. The yelling and commotion sparked the crowd's interest as they looked around for the cause, either to aid them or hinder the guards.

"Hey," a gruff voice called out, "hey you, lady, over here!"

Callisto turned around to see a threadbare beggar resting against a wall of a two-story building. "Little busy!" She searched for a way out.

"Up there!" he called to her, pointing to a long rope dangling from the rooftop. "Follow the arrows."

With no other options in sight, Callisto sprinted by the beggar, dropping a silver coin in his hand as she went. She leaped and grabbed the hemp rope and climbed.

Most ladies, more so ones with looks like hers, would not have been able to climb a rope to save their lives. Thankfully, that wasn't the case for Callisto. Being a fisherman's daughter, she had been climbing her whole life, even after being forced to leave that life behind. Climbing was an ability she did better than most and had been very useful in all walks of her life.

"She's up there!" one of the watchmen barked out.

"She's getting away!"

Paavo glared at her, his face a bright red as he tried to contain his escalating rage.

Safe for the moment, Callisto couldn't resist adding salt to the wound. "Paavo, my darling, I had such a wonderful time last night. I promise I won't tell anyone about your little—" She used her pinky finger to indicate his small member, and the crowd of onlookers began laughing at his expense. Callisto faked an expression of apology, "Oops."

Now his blood was boiling. "I will see you pay for this with your life! You cannot escape me!"

"And only hours ago, you told me you loved me."

"You know not who you have crossed, woman! My influence goes far and wide!"

She blew him a kiss. "Until we meet again, Paavo."

Turning back to the rooftop, she searched for an arrow and found one etched into a brick chimney. She followed it to the end of the roof. A span of five feet separated two buildings, and another arrow was seen on the other side.

"Well, a lovely stroll across the city's rooftops it is, then. Why not? I haven't had to play on rooftops in a while." She jumped, clearing the distance to the next arrow.

Weaving her way through the surprisingly junk-filled rooftop, she realized a lot more life went on up here than anyone knew. Makeshift tents and sleeping spaces littered many of the roofs she could see. A few beggars were still around, looking at her suspiciously.

A whole city above the city.

She had little time to care as she searched for another arrow and moved to follow it, hearing many more shouts from below. Had the whole of the city watch come out to find one woman? She needed to get off the rooftops and find somewhere to lay low for the day. Leaping between another two buildings, this was several feet lower. Landing hard, she dived into a roll.

The arrows were leading her toward the harbor. The salty

sea air was growing thicker with each roof she reached. Down on the streets, the sea air was hardly noticeable; too many other smells drowned it out. With nearly fifty thousand people within the city, the smell of 'humanity' outweighed the scents of nature.

The view from up here was breathtaking. Near the whole cityscape could be seen, and to the west, the Atlantic Ocean as far as the eyes could see. Ships of all shapes and sizes littered the port or just beyond. Merchants were waiting for their turn to dock to load or unload their wares. Naval vessels were waiting to dock to resupply before they took to the seas again in search of pirates and other enemies that still sailed the area.

Callisto reminded herself that she would return to the rooftops to take the view in and enjoy it when she had time again. Maybe with some company and a bottle of rum. But for now, staying ahead of her pressing trouble was more critical.

Finally, she came to another knotted rope and went down to the dark alley below. In the distance, she could still hear the yells and whistle blows as trouble moved all around her. But now, near the harbor, she could slip away in the thick busy crowds unnoticed. She would vanish in a few more minutes, and this would all be over—just another cloaked figure to blend with the masses.

"Got you, bitch!"

Callisto was slammed against a brick wall. Her eyes locked on Paavo's intense brown rage-filled gaze.

"Paavo, so good to see you again, my darling."

His hands went around her throat, and he squeezed. "You made a fool out of me! I trusted you! I could have given you things and a life no whore could have ever dreamed!"

"How sweet of you—" she managed to get out, his grip getting tighter, "but it was your cock that made a fool out of you! And I was never the whore in this. You, on the other hand."

She tried vainly to pry his grasp from her neck, but his strength would not relent. He was far stronger than she had first given him credit for. His grip tightened more, cutting off her flow of air almost completely.

"I will not be made a fool of by the likes of you, bitch! Soon you will be nothing more than another forgotten corpse in this filthy city!"

His intent was not to hold her until the watch got there. He planned on killing her here in this alleyway, where no one would find her body for days. Her vision was already beginning to blur as she gasped to draw the tiniest breath of air, but his crushing grip was near absolute.

Reaching behind her, she felt the hilt of her dagger, but being pressed against the wall made it impossible to draw. With a burst of desperation, she kicked off, pushing her attacker back half a step for only a moment before he slammed her back against the bricks.

But it had been enough.

She rammed the ten inches of steel deep into his belly.

Instantly his grip fell from her neck.

Stumbling back, he hit the wall behind him. The violence in his eyes from a moment ago was suddenly replaced with undiluted fear as his hands felt gingerly around the blade's hilt.

"You—you stabbed me—" he mumbled, looking back up at her, the hardness from a moment ago entirely superseded by his pampered nature.

Callisto grabbed the blade and pulled it clear, glad to be able to breathe again. "If you move quickly, someone might be able to save your worthless life. But I won't be so kind if you try to come after me again!"

She was about to walk away, knowing the watch would be there soon, but his words stopped her in her tracks.

"I won't stop. You will suffer for this—this—humiliation!" he coughed out weakly. "Your place in this world will be known before your miserable end!"

Cursing, she turned back to him, all humor gone now. This was not how she had pictured this playing out. And if she believed she could change his mind, she would have tried. But looking at him, she knew he meant what he was saying.

"Congratulations, idiot, you just killed yourself." The blade licked across his throat, and blood poured free.

His eyes lit up in complete and utter shock as he staggered back into the wall and slid to the mud. His hands wrapped around his neck as he tried to stem the gouts of blood pouring free.

"You—fucking—" he tried to speak as his lungs filled with blood and slowly drowned him.

"You should have just accepted the meager loss to your purse and pride, you fool," she muttered and was about to leave.

"Murderer!" a voice cried out, and she saw a small group of people staring down the alley at what had just transpired.

She ran.

To be caught as a thief was terrible enough. Adding the murder of a nobleman to such a list of crimes was indeed a death sentence.

She cursed herself.

Stabbing him in self-defense would have been bad enough, but with charm and a large enough bribe, she could have bought her way out of it. For murder, not even her charm, good looks, and all the coin she had would save her from the gallows.

The port was alive with activity, but the shouts and loud

shrieks of the watch's whistles could be heard all around her. Her eyes locked on the ships in front of her. She had nowhere else to go. All escape routes leading back into the city would be cut off before she could get to them.

Pushing through the crowd, keeping herself low, she reached the dockside unnoticed. Dock hands and sailors were busy running around the cargo ship, hauling up large nets of provisions and merchandise for whatever voyage they would soon take.

Out of places to go, she needed to slip onto a ship, but how? Too many eyes and sailors were around for her to have any hope of casually walking up the plank. She needed a better way.

There was no time to waste. She could already feel the noose closing around her as she knew the watch would draw closer.

"You there!" she called out with an air of importance to a sailor loading small crates into the net that would lift them onto the ship.

The shaggy-haired, tattooed man turned to regard her. "What the fuck do you want?" He placed another crate into the pile.

"Do not talk to me that way!" she countered boldly. "Do you know who I am?"

"Not a clue. Just another dock wench to me."

"Dock wench? Dock wench? I will have that flesh whipped from your back for such an insult!" She could hear the whistles of the watch getting closer.

The threat got the man's full attention, and he regarded her. "Then who are you?"

"My father is supplying the provisions for this ship."

"I am sure they are grateful," he grunted and went back to work.

"Well, unless you want to risk the crew's lives, I need to get on the ship!" she snapped. This fucking brute just needed to listen to her; her time was running out.

"Why?" he asked, turning around again, a look of worry on his rugged features.

Yes, finally, the hook had been taken.

"Two barrels of salted beef have turned and were meant to be thrown out but were taken this morning by mistake! I need to find them and ensure they don't leave the port. Two more barrels are on their way as we speak to replace them, plus a barrel of rum, which my father sends as an apology for the mishap."

The man scratched at his beard. "I can't be letting you on the ship, miss, but I will send someone to look for the barrels right enough."

"Don't be absurd. I know what the barrels look like. I will be able to find them faster than anyone else. It will take but a moment."

"Look, lady, I can't let you aboard the ship. I am just a dock hand," he began. "If I let you aboard without permission from the ship's captain, the dock master would have my ass."

Callisto was out of time, glancing back and seeing the watch searching closer and closer. She moved right next to the sailor pressing two pieces of gold into his palm.

"I robbed a rich man who refused to pay me for my 'services.' The watch is after me. I am as good as dead if I don't find a place to hide for a few hours." She looked up into his dark eyes. "Please."

His eyes went wide at the two gold in his palm. Likely, that was more than he would see in four months of hard labor aboard the ship.

"Fuck's sake!" he muttered. He made sure no one was

looking as he pried open one of the crates containing bundles of silk. "It'll be a tight fit but get in quick!"

No more invitation than that was needed, and she climbed in. The sound of more crates being piled on top of her hiding spot was near deafening, but she plugged her ears and tried to ignore the noise. She was hidden and safe!

The dockside would settle down in a few hours, and then she could slip off the ship and return home. She would have to lay low for a while, ruining weeks of planning. Maybe this was a sign that Earnest was right. She would figure it all out when she had time to think clearly.

The hoist began lifting the load up towards the ship. The swinging motion was incredibly unnerving, and she was sure the pitch dark wasn't helping the cause.

After what felt like forever, her crate stopped moving. Now all she had to do was wait until it was clear, and she could slip out.

A long, dull, drawn-out horn blast awoke Callisto.

Panic coursed through her every fiber. Even with her eyes open, it was still pitch black. After a few moments, she remembered the events and cursed herself for falling asleep.

Another long, low-pitched horn blast sounded.

"No, no, no!" She pushed on the crate side. "Come on! Open already!"

A sliver of light shone through the crack as she kicked again and again.

"Only two horns. That still means I have time!" She kicked relentlessly. "Open, you piece of shit!"

A third long horn blow was all the confirmation she needed. The ship had set sail already and was sailing out into open waters. It was too late to get off the ship without stealing a rowboat or a long swim, neither of which bode well for her.

The side of the crate finally gave way, and the damp, musky air of the holding bay assaulted her senses. Scrambling out of her hiding spot, she quickly ran to a portside window. Tamora, the city she had called home for the last six years, bobbed up and down in the distance.

"FUCK!" she yelled, smashing her fists into the side wall, not even thinking anyone else might be around to hear her, and to her luck, there wasn't. "Today has gone from bad, to worse, to fucking shit!" she growled, pulling her eyes away from the fading city, knowing no amount of looking at it would bring it closer.

Pressing herself against the wall, she slid to the floor. What the hell was she to do now? There was no getting back, no way off this ship that wouldn't result in a worse fate than she was facing now.

If she revealed herself to the crew and captain, they would likely throw her overboard or chain her up and turn her into the authorities for being a stowaway. Yet she highly doubted she would be able to stay hidden for the whole time they were at sea.

This was another problem; the trip could be a few days, weeks, or even months. Where it would end up was another mystery entirely. She could find herself in another country or even a different continent.

"What have you gotten yourself into now?" She laughed weakly with growing humor. "Earnest did say I should get away for a while. I guess he was right. Though I would have preferred it under my own terms with maybe a little time to pack some things."

Alas, there was nothing she could do about her current situation. Being angry and frustrated about it would not help.

At this point, she could sulk and stress or do her best to embrace it and relax, no matter how boring it would likely be.

Even if she was gone a few months, the old woman she rented from had been paid well in advance and never knew her comings and goings. Her things would be safe. What coin she did have saved was well hidden within the wallboards. She felt the coin pouch within the hidden folds of her cloak. She had enough coin to last her a while if need be. Not much she could spend it on while at sea anyway. But it might be enough to buy a sailor's silence if she were discovered.

The bulkhead was large, and the section she was in was the aft of the ship, where the more precious cargo went. Being in the back afforded her less chance of being seen, so long as she stayed behind the crates and kept her wits when others were about. They were less likely to be tossed around and damaged in rough waters.

Going back to her crate, she pushed it closer to another one and cleared out most of the silk bundles to make room for her whole body. It was going to be a long, tedious voyage. At least she would be sleeping with silk sheets, she laughed.

Callisto cut another deep line into the damp wooden plank. Eight days at sea. Eight miserably long days, hidden away with no real human contact. All she did was sleep, sneak food from the small kitchen when the cook wasn't around, and sleep some more.

The first three days, the extra sleep had felt amazing. She hadn't realized just how tired she had been. But now, sleeping had become a chore and lost its short-lived pleasure. Now when she slept, she woke up more miserable than she had been when she had fallen asleep.

On occasion, she would sneak through the stacks of cargo, getting closer to the middle of the ship, to watch and listen to the sailors in the evenings. They talked of their families, adventures at seas, storms they had been through, and pirates they had fought. Then there was the more colorful talk she was accustomed to, the whores they had fucked, money they had stolen, and drunken nights they had nearly forgotten.

She also learned that a small group of mercenaries were on board, hired blades in case of pirates. They were hard men, cutthroats, and killers. Occasionally, a few would come down and drink and talk with the sailors at night, but mostly they stayed above deck and only came below to sleep. They were the same kind of men that Baron hired to stand outside his shop.

Callisto lay on her makeshift silk bed, staring at the planks above her. She had already counted them a hundred times, counted the knots in the planks, and then counted those again a hundred times.

She was bored, restless, and tired of eating salted beef strips, smoked fish, and stale biscuits.

The Wind Spirit's cook, Eamon Gomez, seemed to be a fine cook, at least from what Callisto could smell, and the crew boasted. Sadly, Callisto seldom was able to score anything that had been cooked.

It was delicate business sneaking into Eamon's little kitchen area in the hull. Most of the time, he was in there, and when he wasn't, there was very little food left about. And so, Callisto had been forced to steal from the preserve barrels to keep fed. It was boring, but it was better than starving.

A glance at the portholes told her that several crew members would already be a few bottles into the night and sitting around swapping stories, gambling, or just getting drunk. It was the only human contact she could have, so she tried to sneak close enough each night to listen. Tonight, she hoped to get close enough to steal a bottle of something that would help her kill some time in a drunken stupor.

With practiced ease, Callisto made her way along the tightly packed maze of crates. Over the last several days, she had spent much of her free time moving dozens of them several inches, creating a tight pathway between them that she could crawl behind while remaining completely hidden.

It didn't take long before she was positioned on the far left of the hold, as close as she could get to the small group of sailors. To her surprise, two sat with their backs against the crates she was spying from, sharing a bottle of amber liquor.

These two were well known to her already. Alonso and Kadir were their names. Both were from a small coastal town in Spain that she couldn't recall. They were a simple duo, trying to see the world and earn their keep in it so they never had to return to the poor existence they had left behind.

It was something she could very much relate to.

Smiling, she settled in behind them, happy she wouldn't have to strain to hear their conversation tonight.

"Is it just me, or has the captain been in a foul mood this trip?" Alonso asked after a long pull from the rum bottle.

Kadir looked around, making sure others weren't within hearing range. "Aye, I've heard some stories as to why. Not for knowing if they be true or not, though."

"Well, come on, what is it then? What have ye heard?"

Kadir took the offered bottle and drank, wiping his lips with the back of his dirty hand. "Some of the lads were saying this was his last trip as captain of the Wind Spirit."

"What?" Alonso gasped. "That can't be true. He's been a great captain. No man in his right mind would be letting him go without good reason."

"There is a reason, see. Apparently, the owner of the ship, some rich, pompous nobleman, retired from the trade and left the ship and enterprise to his prick son." Kadir pulled out a corncob pipe and small tin of weed and began packing the bowl. "Now the thing is, the son's not as smart as the father and doesn't realize being a good captain is not easy. Rumor is, the son's got some friend who he wants to make the captain of the Wind Spirit after this trip. So, Murphy is going to lose command. They told him he could stay on as part of the regular crew. Slap in the face if you ask me."

Alonso was silent for a moment, then took a long drink. "He deserves better than that."

Kadir struck a wooden match and puffed his pipe. "Aye, he's been good to the likes of us, taking us on as he did. Nothing but a pair of dirty, greenhorns we were."

"What's to be happening to the rest of us crew then?"

Kadir shrugged and handed his friend the pipe. "Guessin' we get to stay on as crew. Or at least if it holds any real merit."

"It does," a voice said to the side of them.

Both men stiffened and looked worried for a moment.

"Captain—we were just—" Kadir began to stutter.

"At ease, men," Captain Murphy told them. "Might I join you for a round?" He pointed to the bottle they were sharing.

"Of course, Captain, of course!" Alonso handed the bottle over as Murphy pulled a stool closer and sat.

Murphy took the bottle and drank long before handing it back. "It's true. This will be my last voyage as captain of the Wind Spirit. Not sure how word got out so fast since I only just learned of it two days before we set sail," he shrugged, "but word travels fast on this tub, I guess."

Callisto could see the deep pain in the captain's eyes. The sorrow was akin to what she had seen when people spoke of loved ones they had lost. If talk in taverns held any merit, a ship was close as kin to a good captain and crew.

She nearly laughed out loud. This voyage without actual human contact and her routine were making her soft.

"What you gonna do, Captain?" Alonso asked.

Murphy shrugged. "Truth be told, I don't know. My whole life has been at sea. I ain't for any other kind of life. But I don't think I can stay with the Wind Spirit. Marcus Mangrove was a respectful and smart businessman. His son, Martin? Well, the apple fell a long way from the tree, for he is a moron if I am, to be honest."

The conversation grew quiet for a time as each man enjoyed a drink as they passed the bottle around in silent salute to uncertainty.

"I should check on a few things before my hammock calls me." Murphy stood. "I know the rumors already are making their rounds of the ship. But I'd be most grateful if you lads would keep the truth of it quiet until the trip is over. I'll address the crew before we get back. Just trying to have a normal journey one last time."

"Aye," both men said, "we can do that, Captain."

"You gentlemen have my thanks." Murphy walked through the crew, chatting to a few, and addressing others before he climbed the ladder to the deck.

"Well, if that ain't some shit," Kadir muttered.

"Might be time for us to be looking for a new ship to sail on," Alonso said. "If this son is as big of a moron as the captain be thinkin', then likely be smart not to be here when shit starts turning sour."

"You might be right, my friend," Kadir muttered. "You might very well be right."

"We should find our hammocks before we get ourselves too drunk." Alonso yawned. "Tomorrow, they want us to replace most of the ropes on the port side rigging."

"Bleh," Kadir said. "I think I will throw some die for a bit first. Feeling lucky tonight."

Grinning, Callisto's hand snaked out and snatched the half bottle of rum both men seemed to have forgotten about in their intoxicated state. Carefully, she wormed through her tunnel until she was back in her own small world of the ship.

Curling up in her pile of silks, she drank and drank some more until her world blurred, and the warm liquor took her into its warm, sleep-filled embrace.

Morning came and went, and she found herself bored and lonely once more. She'd almost wish she had a hangover, for at least the misery would be a worthy distraction.

Running a finger along the marks, she counted her nine notches in the wood. Nine days at sea. Even if they found their destination today, that would still be nine back. And that was only if they were planning on going back straight away.

She was beginning to wonder if she shouldn't try and catch the attention of one of the better-looking crewmen. Then at least, maybe she'd have some fun each day to pass some time. But she knew that was a dangerous game to try and play.

Sailors weren't known for their ability to keep secrets. More so one of that nature.

"Come on, back here," a familiar voice whispered. "No one will see us back here."

"Are you sure, Kadir?" another known voice asked nervously.

"Of course, I am sure," Kadir whispered again. "Haven't seen anyone back here the whole trip so far."

Callisto's heart skipped a beat as she realized her biggest fear was coming true. Someone was finally coming to this part of the ship. She had done well to keep her presence minimalized, so if this fated day did occur, there was a chance they would not notice that someone had been living here the whole time.

Quickly she scrambled to stuff her bedding supplies back into the crate, but they were coming too fast, and she had to abandon it and find better cover.

"I stole this whiskey from the first mate's quarters last night while he wasn't looking," Kadir said, pulling a small bottle from his vest. "Aged thirty-five years, it says."

"Thirty-five!" Alonso grabbed the bottle to read the date. "By the old gods and the new! This must have cost three whole silver!"

"Closer to four, I'd say. Comes from Ireland. You know those kilt-wearing bastards know how to make a good stiff drink! Why else would men be wearing dresses?" They both chuckled at the joke.

"Let's have ourselves likely the most expensive drink we will have in all our lives!" Alonso laughed, pulling the cork, and taking a deep swing. "Shit burns like fire!" he gasped between muffled coughs. "But tastes like gold."

"Give me that!" Kadir snatched the bottle. "Damn, that is good! Be hard going back to the swill we normally drink after tasting this."

Alonso wasn't listening; he was staring off into the corner. "What in the hell is that?"

"What is what?"

"That over there against the far wall." He pointed. "Looks like one of the crates broke open and spilled out."

"Who cares." Kadir belched. "Not our fucking problem."

Alonso was already moving towards it. "No, but something good might be inside, something worth 'hiding' for later."

Callisto cursed her luck. They would easily be able to tell someone had been sleeping there. If they told the captain or the others, the search would be on, and it wouldn't be long before she was discovered.

"What in the hell?" Alonso muttered, getting closer.

"Bloody hell, someone's been sleeping back here."

"Maybe one of the other crew, or one of them mercenaries, sneaking down here for a nap?" Kadir replied, looking around but hardly caring.

Alonso lifted several lemon peels and apple cores. "Not likely. They get to eat like kings compared to the rest of us."

The ship caught a gust of wind and shifted sharply, unbalancing Callisto, and she bumped hard into several barrels.

"Someone is here!" Kadir pulled a knife and went to investigate.

Cursing her sudden change in luck, Callisto knew it was over. It would be best to make herself known before someone got hurt and see if she could keep these two quiet. She would never be able to hide.

"No need for a blade," she called out, slowly standing up, her hands in the air. "It is just me."

"Fucking hell!" Alonso stuttered. "It's a woman!"

"Why the hell would a woman want to stow away on a shit rig like this?" Kadir asked, his knife still out as he eyed her suspiciously.

"It wasn't intentional, I can assure you," Callisto said, slowly stepping out so they could get a better look at her. She didn't look great after nine days hidden on a ship, but men stuck on a ship likely wouldn't be too picky.

"The captain ain't going to like this. Always saying woman on a ship is bad luck and all," Kadir said, his eyes taking in her figure as he put his dagger away.

Callisto walked out from behind the barrels, slowly lowering her hands. Killing these two wouldn't help her cause. Their absence would be noticed, and she wouldn't be able to hide the bodies. "I want no trouble, and I would be ever so grateful if no one else knew of this."

"We can't be keeping a secret like this from the captain!"

Alonso replied nervously.

"Wait." Kadir grabbed his friend's arm. "Maybe we can. Depends on what she is willing to offer for our silence."

Alonso screwed up his face. "You cannot be serious."

Kadir pulled him back a little. "Think about it. We may be out of a job soon and need all the coin we can muster to tie us over until we find a new ship to work on."

"Coin—" Alonso felt foolish, "of course—you meant coin."

Callisto smirked at the simpleness of these two. She had some coin for them and hoped it would be enough. If not, she bet she could convince them with something else. Something she wouldn't be too upset about having to use at this point, for her desires were already there.

Before Callisto could reply, a bell sounded from above, and the word 'pirates' was yelled.

"Sonofabitch!" Kadir spat, looking from Callisto to Alonso. "We will deal with you later. Let's get up there."

They both started for the ladder when Alonso stopped and regarded her thoughtfully. "That dagger in your boot? If any pirates make it down here, it means we lost. Use it on yourself. It'll be a better fate than what you will find with them." With that, he followed his friend to the deck of the ship.

Callisto watched them scramble up to the above deck. The sound of men readying themselves for combat was near deafening, even below deck.

"Fantastic. Pirates. That's all I bloody well needed." She gripped her dagger firmly and took cover behind the barrels filled with fresh drinking water. If anyone came down, she would be able to get the jump on them, hopefully before they had a chance to see her.

Her heart pounded loudly in her ears as the minutes passed, and nothing seemed to be happening. She could hear the crew above calling out to each other but couldn't understand what was being said. But each time she heard Captain Murphy's voice bellowing an order, she braced herself, expecting the worst to happen.

Slowly she moved to the porthole and caught sight of the pirate ship closing in at great speed as if thinking to ram the Wind Spirit. But as soon as she thought that, the Wind Spirit lurched again as the ship's prow turned towards the coming pirates, and soon Callisto could see nothing but open sea.

She could hear the cannons being loaded and knew the battle was about to start.

"BRACE YOURSELF!" Murphy screamed above.

The sound of cannons firing from a distance caused her to tense. After several moments she realized they had missed or fallen short. The ship swayed dangerously to the port side, causing much of the cargo to shift and sway, some breaking free of their holds and crashing into the side walls. She checked her surroundings, ensuring nothing was in danger of giving way near her. Dying in a fight against pirates was far preferable to being crushed by tumbling cargo.

The Wind Spirit fired its few cannons in return. Curses from above told her they had also missed their target. Orders to reload and adjust aim were given. The thunderous sound rattled her very insides and made the world seem like it had stopped in its tracks.

Each second that passed seemed like a minute. Each minute an hour as Callisto waited for the next round of cannons to fire and wondered if they would hit where she was standing.

She thought about moving but knew it was pointless. She was in just as much danger where she was as she would be anywhere down here if a cannonball tore through the ship. There was no way of knowing where one of the iron balls would strike.

Another round went off, and before she could brace herself, one struck the hull, blowing a hole clean through the stern, not far from where her bed had been. Thrown back, the wind was knocked from her. The two-foot hole was above the water line as light from outside poured in.

Before she could recover, another shot was fired, but not from the Wind Spirit. Something above was hit and came crashing down, striking the upper deck with wood-splintering force.

The ship suddenly slowed to a near stop, as if the wind had abruptly ceased to blow, and she knew the main mast must have been struck. Within moments pirates would board the ship, slashing, stabbing, and killing their way to victory, so they could plunder the wares onboard, sink the ship, and move on to their next victim.

She tried to shake the thought from her head. They could still win! The Wind Spirit's crew were well-trained and had fought pirates before. These were skilled sailors. Some had been doing this longer than she'd been alive, she reminded herself.

Callisto had heard many horrible stories of pirates in taverns from sailors or merchants. They were fierce, violent, and unforgiving typically. Sea battles were lost or won in minutes once boarding was assured. Now she would soon have a tale of her own about them if she somehow survived.

Within moments she heard shouting and orders from Captain Murphy. And soon, the sound of grappling hooks biting into the weather-worn railing of the ship echoed throughout the hull.

Dozens of bow strings hummed in union as the crew fired several volleys at the enemy. The sound of flint rifles and pistols going off was like thunder in a bad storm.

Then came the deafening battle cries.

Callisto's breathing intensified as the sound of blades clashing together suddenly filled the air. Curses and war cries erupted and were followed by the screams of the wounded and dying.

Who was winning or losing? She couldn't know, but her eyes never left the ladder in front of her.

Seconds turned to minutes, and the battle above raged on until she heard someone yell yield out of nowhere. The din of fighting died away before the sound of swords, blades, and other weapons clattered to the deck.

Someone had surrendered. Deep down, she knew it hadn't been the pirates.

Commands were barked out from the victors, and soon a shadow fell over the cargo hold. Feet appeared and began climbing down. Callisto tried to slow her breathing. She knew instantly from the clothing that this was not anyone from the Wind Spirit.

Shifting herself for a better angle, she waited and cursed under her breath. Before the first pirate had reached the bottom, another was quick to follow.

One she could have easily managed. Two would be a challenge, but she was confident, but once she saw the third set of boots coming down, she knew her chances were all but gone. They would find her, and what would happen to her would not be pretty. She considered Alonso's words before he had left and wondered if she could even do such a thing to herself.

"If you can hear me, Ares, favor me once more, and I will send you fresh souls for your army!" she whispered.

She had made a point to sacrifice to him several times a year. There had been no shrine in or near the city that she had known of, so she had commissioned a smaller statue and erected her own shrine to the old god just outside the city.

Watching the three split up, she wondered if they were

looking for people or taking stock of plunder worth taking. Either way, one at a time, if she could get the drop on them, she might stand a chance. At least until more came down looking for them. But that was a problem to worry about later.

Moving with practiced stealth, she followed the pirate, who began searching through the sailor's things, looking for something he could quickly pocket. His back was to her, and she took full advantage, moving up behind him.

"Hey," she whispered, and the pirate turned, reaching for his blade. Her dagger punched through his bottom jaw up into his brain. Warm, dark blood spilled across her hand and forearm as he jerked and crumbled to the floor without a sound.

Wasting no time, she moved on to the foredeck of the ship. She could make out the pirate as he rummaged through a crate. She lifted the pirate cutlass high, ready to strike, when she felt something press into the back of her head.

"Best be dropping that blade before I paint the hull with your brains," a pirate growled behind her.

The sword hit the floor, and she felt his hand remove the dagger from her belt. She still had the small blade in her boot; she would save it until she needed it. They would kill her, but not before they tried to have their fun with her. At least one more would die by her hands before that happened.

The pirate she had been about to kill grinned as he regarded her. "Some good treasure on this ship indeed. Hope the captain let's her live long enough so we can all have a round or two."

"Up the ladder, bitch!" the first ordered as he pushed her along.

The brightness of the day stung her eyes after nine days below deck with very little light. Bodies littered the ship, and in the short time the attack had taken place, the deck had become a collage of violence. Pools of blood soaked into the wood anywhere a brave soul had fallen. Pirates cleared the dead from the ship, leaving crimson paths that suddenly stopped as they were tossed over the side to be swallowed up by the endless sea.

The crew of the merchant's ship had taken severe losses. Out of forty-four crew members, eighteen had survived. Kadir and Alonso were wounded but alive. Her eyes lingered on those two faces. She didn't know why that made her feel good, but it did.

From the bodies she could see, the pirates had also taken losses; she counted many of their dead among the Wind Spirit's crew. The merchant's crew had fought well, just not well enough to save their skin.

Captain Murphy was down on his knees, his hands bound behind his back. Several pirate corpses littered the area around him, a testament to his prowess even at his age. Two grisly pirates flanked him on either side, their swords resting on his shoulders, a constant reminder of death if he tried anything foolish.

A large and dangerous man loomed before him. At once, Callisto knew this was the pirate captain. His long, black beard was braided with gold and ivory fetishes. He wore a jet-black captain's tricorn hat with a skull and crossbones embroidered in the front. Two polished ivory flintlock pistols tucked easily in his belt, and a jewel-encrusted sword dangled at his hip.

He commanded this group of cutthroats, and they all respected him. Out of fear or admiration? It didn't matter, he controlled them, and they would do anything he asked. But without all that, his demeanor and the sheer boldness that radiated from him was all anyone would need to know.

"You and your men fought well this day!" the pirate captain boasted, pacing in front of the kneeling man surveying the carnage still on deck. "We haven't faced a fight like that in nearly a year! You should be proud of yourself, for most, when they see Poseidon's Fury, know that death is coming. They throw down their weapons and surrender without a fight!" The pirates around him jeered. "The name Blackmane has become a legend, striking fear in men's hearts and warm piss down their legs!"

"Just kill me already. I grow tired of listening to you stroke your own flaccid cock!" Murphy spat.

Blackmane suppressed a sneer. "What is your name?"

"Captain John Murphy of the Wind Spirit," he replied, holding his head up proudly.

"Well met, Captain John Murphy of the Wind Spirit. You, your men, and your lovely ship have been conquered. So, you will listen to me stroke my cock as long as I fucking desire to!" He lashed the back of his hand across the kneeling man's face, his rings leaving jagged slash marks across the defeated man's cheek.

Blackmane stepped around him and faced the crew of prisoners. "As I have said, you all have fought well this day, proven your worth as sailors and as men of the violent seas we sail. You killed many of my crew, so many in fact that crew need replacing." He stopped, his coal-black eyes boring into them with purpose.

"True, I could sail back to one of the many ports open to pirates and find new crew, but I am also a fair and generous man when faced with opportunity. You have three options before you. You can jump from this ship and give yourself to Poseidon. You can be beaten, starved, and sold as slaves at the next port, or you can join my crew, leave behind the life you knew, and become feared pirates of the Poseidon's Fury! The choice is yours," he paused, his menacing eyes looking them over, "but I'd make the decision quickly, for time is of the essence."

Several men rose and made their way over to where the pirate captain stood, the two remaining mercenaries among them. Slowly, more hesitantly, a handful stood and made their way to stand with the pirates. Out of the eighteen survivors, eight had chosen his offer as pirates. The rest settled for whatever life awaited them as slaves, too proud, honorable, or too fearful of what the pirate life would be.

"The die has been cast!" Blackmane barked. "Now get all this plunder off this worthless pile of lumber and show our 'guests' their lavish new accommodations."

"Captain!" one of the men from below called out. "We found something special below deck!"

Blackmane turned, his greedy eyes lighting up. "What do we have here?"

"We found her down below, hiding. She killed Spitjaw! Stabbed him in the head, she did."

Blackmane grabbed Callisto by the jaw and turned her face side to side to get a better look at her. "A pretty little thing, with such fire burning in those eyes." His grin was full of malicious intent. "You picked the wrong ship to hide upon, lass."

"Oh, I already figured that out," she replied as sweetly as possible, trying to loosen her captor's grip on her arms, but neither man would relent. "Guess the chances of you being a gentleman and taking me to the nearest port so I can be on my way isn't very likely, is it?"

"You do have spirit. I like that." He laughed, showing his chipped and rotten teeth. "I might be so inclined to help you, but only if you *help* me first." He turned to the men holding her. "Bring her to my cabin and make her at home."

There was no point in fighting. Even if she got free and

managed to kill one, maybe two of them, she would be killed, or worse. The only thing she could do now was to wait and see how this would play out. If need be, she would pleasure the pirate captain. She would play the part of whore as she had had to do before, but only if she knew he would release her. If not, then she would fight to her death with what dignity she had left. Maybe then, at least, Ares would still open his arms to her in the afterlife.

Callisto was pushed towards the captain's quarters and couldn't believe how quickly men who were once honest sailors had turned pirates and fell in line alongside men who were trying to kill them only moments ago.

Though given the chance, she too would have joined them, only so she could stay alive long enough to escape later. She wondered if that was the plan for these men. Some of them, maybe, others would take up being a pirate with ease. Many of the ones that had switched sides had nothing left to go home to after the long war, and being a pirate was just as good as anything else. Sadly, that wasn't a role a captured woman would play on a ship full of violent, lustful men.

Poseidon's Fury was a large, sleek, well-maintained ship. Built for power and speed, yet still large enough to be imposing and comfortably hold a crew of seventy. Callisto guessed it had once been a British naval ship, judging by the structuring of the three sets of masts and the ten cannons lining each side. She knew very little about ships, but she knew this one was special and made it very dangerous in the hands of pirates.

Pushed within the captain's large cabin, she was in awe. It was truly beautiful within. Not something she would ever have expected to see on a ship, let alone a pirate ship. Blackmane had not struck her as a man who enjoyed fineries and beauty, yet his cabin remarkably showed otherwise.

Callisto was ushered to the port side of the room. A long

chain dangled from the roof, and another two were set into the floor.

"What the hell is this?" She started to resist.

"The captain likes his pets to be on a leash until they are broken in." The pirate who caught her down below laughed.

"Let go of me!" Now she did struggle. She did not like the looks of this and would be damned if she was to be shackled like a fucking dog.

A meaty fist to her guts was all she got for her effort, and before she could recover, her ankles and neck were clamped in chains and locked tight.

"I'd not suggest fighting the captain too long," the second pirate told her. "He likes a bit of fight in his playthings, but too much fight and you'll bring out the devil in him." With that, both men left her in the large room alone.

Callisto pulled on the chains but knew they were firmly in place and no amount of effort would dislodge them. She pulled her small dagger from her hiding spot in her boot and tried to pick the locks, but the blade tip was too big to trigger the release mechanism. Cursing, she hid the boot dagger again. She knew it would be needed at some point, more than likely to end her own miserable life.

That thought wasn't pleasant, but in the event, it had to happen, she would be in control and could make it quick.

Knowing there was nothing she could do, she took in the lush furnishings around her. Thick black and red velvet drapes covered the large back window, making it so the room could be black as night when they were drawn tight. A large, rope-suspended bed was placed against the wall opposite her. A large cherry-wood-framed canopy encompassed it; dark blue silk curtains could enshroud it. A thick, plush dark purple carpet covered the floor around the bed, making it look like something a king would sleep on.

Callisto wondered if all captains slept in such finery. From most of what she had heard, hammocks were the bedding of choice on ships. As she watched the bed, like a hammock, it swayed with the listing and tilting of the vessel, leaving the top of the bed with very little disturbance. This bed was suspended from the roof by thick hemp ropes and even anchored to the floor by more. The suspension could minimize the sway of the ship with comfort.

A large desk of polished oak with silver trim was set up in the middle of the room, close to the back window. It was riddled with papers, candles, pens, inks, maps, and other things she did not know of their use.

The artwork on the walls were erotic pieces. She knew them to be Greek and Roman in nature. She had seen several paintings of similar nature in her life and had wanted them all. Sexual displays of orgies or couples interlocked in passion and seduction. Taking what they desired from one another's bodies for lustful satisfaction. Others were scenes of battle, where a hero stood out in the wake of countless slaughtered enemies.

She would be pleased to be in such a room in almost any other circumstance, awaiting the possible pleasures. But this was not such a time. Sadly, there was nothing she could do but wait for Blackmane to come to her. She would try to seduce him, to play to his pride and lust for the female form she possessed.

It would be worth it if she could manipulate him enough that entertaining his bed for a few weeks would see her safely to shore. But she somehow doubted Blackmane would be so easily manipulated, nor did she expect him even to care. He could have her whether she fought or gave herself to him willingly; she suspected he'd almost prefer the fight.

She glanced down at her hidden blade and wondered if it would be better to end it now. But her selfish pride prevented her from doing it. She had come too far, for too long to give up hope that she could see herself out of this. Her life had been an endless journey of struggles teetering on the verge of death since that fateful day. This would be no different.

"I will make it out of this!" she told herself firmly. "I will overcome this fucking prick! I will overcome this whole fucking ship full of pricks if I have to!" She felt a fresh wave of energy course through her. "Somehow—"

The day wore on, and still, she could hear men running from one ship to another, bringing up whatever they decided was worth taking from the Wind Spirit. Now and again, she could hear Blackmane bark orders to his crew, new and old alike. Twice she heard him outside the cabin door and wondered if he would enter, but he had not.

Finally, she felt the ship lurch forward as the sails were raised to catch the eastern wind. Looking out the back window, she could tell it was nearing the evening already. Then she caught sight of the Wind Spirit, left alone as they pulled away. Then she heard someone bark a command, and flaming arrows streaked across the sky, landing on the abandoned ship. Within seconds the ship took to flames. The pirates had soaked it in oil to speed the process.

Callisto woke to the sound of the cabin door being opened. She hadn't meant to fall asleep, but clearly, the excitement, stress, and anticipation of recent events had worn her out more than she had realized. Before the cabin door closed, she was on her feet, watching her captor with a hawk gaze through the darkness, analyzing his movements. He was drunk. It was easy to see between the smell that entered the room with him and his sluggish movements and misplaced steps.

Today's victory was worthy of even the captain celebrating with his men. Or maybe he always drank with his crew; she didn't know. She knew very little of the life of pirates or life on a ship. She wished she had paid more attention to all the tavern talk.

Blackmane stumbled to his desk and used the candle he was carrying to light two lanterns hanging above. The room got much brighter. He unstrapped his sword belt and laid it along with the two flintlock pistols on his chair.

Grabbing a bottle of wine from the drawer, he pulled the cork with his teeth and drank heavily as he staggered to his bed. By the time he reached it, the empty bottle had fallen from his hand to the floor, and he hit the bed out cold.

Callisto stood there dumbfounded. Within moments his loud snores filled the room. She had been ready for anything, rape, seduction, murder, suicide, but not this. He had drunk so much that he had forgotten about her entirely.

"Guess one should take enjoyment out of small miracles," she muttered, deciding it was safe enough to get more sleep. She would need whatever strength she could muster if she were going to survive this.

Callisto woke to the sound of movement and was quick to her feet, the sounds of her chains ringing loudly in the room. The bed was empty, but soon she saw Blackmane sitting behind his desk, fully alert as if his drinking last night had been nothing.

"You are finally awake," he said, looking up from a map to regard her, "you are lucky I am in a pleasant mood this morning, or else you would have been woken with the lash. From now on, I expect you to be awake and waiting for me before I wake."

Callisto raised her brow at him. "How am I to know when you are to wake?"

His smile was full of hostility. "I suggest you learn quickly. You are a plaything to me, nothing more. You will also speak only when spoken to. Your life is mine to do with as I want. Remember that, and you might live a while. Do it well, and I might even be so gracious as to grant your earlier request."

Each word he spoke was another bitter nail into Callisto's pride, which was dangerous to wound. There would be no reasoning with this creature, no seduction, no bartering. She was far from weak and meager, nor was she forgiving.

Fine, she told herself, there will be death for both of us.

Blackmane saw the glare in her eyes, the change in posture. "You will learn to obey me, or I will give you to my men for a night before tying a cannonball to your feet and throwing you overboard!"

Callisto lowered her eyes to the floor. She could play this game and then show him where he went wrong!

"Now strip for me."

It was a command, but his tone betrayed his desire to see if she would comply. He was looking for a reason to 'train' her. To beat her and to wear her down so he could break her.

He would be in for a surprise.

Smiling as best she could, she nodded.

Seduction was an influential tool she learned to use well after she had left home. She cared not who saw her naked form; she was not ashamed of it, nor even cared to hide it. She enjoyed people looking at her, desiring her, it gave her strength, but most of all, it gave her power.

Not knowing what he fully wanted or expected from her, she selected her speed as best as possible with the chains around her. She unbuttoned her blouse slowly but quickly enough that it wasn't hesitant as she swayed and rolled her hips. She ensured her breasts stayed hidden until the last buttons had been unclasped. She let the shoulders of the blouse roll down her arms with care, building anticipation, before finally letting it drop to the floor, revealing herself to him.

Shameless, she leaned over, ensuring she was at an angle to silhouette her figure and exposed flesh, just enough to make the eyes search harder. Carefully she undid the straps to her boots, keeping the boot knife hidden but within reach. She was sure she would need it shortly.

Standing, she twisted around, blocking his view of her front. Her ass was bare for him to see in the dim light. She undid the leather belt, letting it carry the trousers down to the floor with its weight.

Glancing over her shoulder, she was annoyed that he was no longer watching her! She turned and stood fully nude, awaiting his inspection, cruel words, or arousal.

Looking up from his map, he forced a grin. "You listen well, and that body will bring me great enjoyment later." He stood and retrieved his weapon belt and topcoat. "I will have food brought to you." With that, he left the cabin, went onto the ship deck, and began bellowing fresh orders to his crew of cutthroats.

The cool salty air caressed her naked flesh before the cabin door closed, and the room was stale again. Standing alone now, she felt—deceived—betrayed—undesirable—disrespected.

"What is your fucking game!" she hissed, almost reaching for her clothes. She stopped herself from dressing, staring at the door, expecting him to return.

"I'll play, and I'll play better than you can imagine! You will regret the day you captured the Wind Spirit. You will regret even more the day you had chains put around me!"

Captain Murphy sat against the cold iron bars of one of the three holding cells within the Poseidon's Fury's back bay. Three others were imprisoned with him, and the rest of his crew occupied the other two damp cells. The mood was dourer, as each of them wondered what fate awaited them. Pirates were ruthless and just as likely to torture and kill them as they were to keep them alive and sell them as slaves.

"Twenty-three years I have sailed the seas. Twenty-three years I have fought pirates and battled storms. Hell, I've even been taken prisoner once before and ransomed back to a naval ship," Murphy said, more to himself than the others with him. "But this time feels different. This time something big is going to happen—something bad—"

"As long as that something isn't dying, I think I'd be okay with it," Kadir replied, checking the poorly stitched wound in his shoulder. He had been surprised that the pirates had even taken the time to tend to the wounded. But if they were going to be sold as slaves, the better shape they were in, the better the price, he figured.

"There are far worse fates than death, lad," Murphy told him sorrowfully.

Alonso shifted over and helped check his friend's wound. He, too, shared several deep cuts that the pirates had crudely stitched. "Ya, think of that poor woman we found before the attack. I'd not want to be her right now."

"Fucking hell." Kadir sighed. "I nearly forgot all about her, poor wench. You even told her to cut her throat before the pirates got her. I reckon she'll be wishing she listened to you now."

"Had there been time, I would have run down in the hold and done it myself just to spare her." Alonso sighed.

"You think you actually could have done that?"

"No," Alonso admitted.

"About her," Captain Murphy asked, "where the hell did she come from?"

"No idea, Captain. We were down in the hold and heard some noise," he lied, not wanting to tell the captain they were drinking the first mate's prize whiskey. "Went to look and found her bed back there, and then she popped out of nowhere. We were about to bring her to you when we heard the alarm go off."

"My da always told me bad luck having a woman on board. Likely the reason pirates took us!" the fourth man, named Aaron, spat.

"Superstitious bullshit, Aaron," Captain Murphy replied though he had said the same thing several times in jest.

"You can't really believe that, do you, Aaron?" Alonso asked.

He shrugged. "Found her on board, didn't ya, and we lost to pirates. You tell me? Seems pretty reasonable given the cages we are in now."

"I've heard it too in the taverns. Never wise to bring a woman out on the sea," Kadir piped in. "Something about the old gods don't like women in the realm of men."

"Sounds pretty stupid to me," Alonso said flatly. "I wouldn't mind a few women aboard, would give me something nice to look at when we're gone for months on end. Might even get one to warm my bed a night or two."

All four men chuckled at that, even the captain.

"Whatever happens, men," Captain Murphy called out so the others could hear. "I am proud of all of you. You are all good, brave men. You've served the Wind Spirit proudly. A captain could ask for nothing more!"

"They ain't got us beat yet, Captain!" a few called back, though there was little belief in it.

"We're still breathing. We will figure a way out of this!" another chimed in.

Murphy rested his head against the bars again. Though he had been surprised to see his first mate, Micky, trade sides so quickly. They were good men; even those who had joined the pirates had only done so to stay alive. Likely most of them would run for the hills the first time they stopped at a port.

"See me through this, and I will follow whatever plan you have," he whispered in prayer to himself and whatever gods might be listening, though he was far from religious.

Callisto rubbed at the bare skin around the shackles. The cold metal had rubbed while she paced; several places were sore and raw. But she couldn't seem to sit still. Nine days hiding upon the Wind Spirit had made her restless, and now being chained in place helped even less.

The door to the cabin creaked open again, and a middle-aged man entered. He was from the Wind Spirit's crew but had taken up with the pirates when the offer had been made. His eyes went wide as he stared at her still naked form.

"Oh, my." He dropped his eyes to the floor and half turned. "I am sorry, I didn't realize you weren't decent."

Callisto nearly laughed out loud. The first man who had come in bringing her food that morning had stared at her hungrily. Told her when the captain was finished with her, he would be first in line for a turn. She had almost expected him to try and touch her, but he had refrained. Not for any respect for her, but because Blackmane would likely skin him alive if she were touched before he had his fun.

"And I shan't be until Blackmane allows me to," she told him, "so you might as well let your eyes take in their fill, for I am sure I will be dead soon, and you'll have missed your chance."

The man looked up, but not directly at her, seeing her pile of clothing beside her. "Why not just dress? He's not even here?"

"Because I don't want to die just yet. I was told to undress, and no order was given to dress again."

He made his way over to her, keeping his eyes averted as best he could. "I am sorry about this." He placed the fish soup tray with a hunk of bread in front of her. "Nasty business being taken by pirates."

"Seems to have worked out okay for you," she replied with mild venom.

"I can see how you'd see it that way," he admitted, "joining them was about survival, not want." He shrugged. "I didn't set out to be a pirate, but now that I am one, I'll make the best of it. I lost everything in the war. The Wind Spirit is at the bottom of the sea, and so is any future pay. I am a survivor and don't wish to die if I can avoid it."

"I fear you'll make a horrible pirate if you can't even look at a naked woman."

He laughed. "I suppose you're right about that."

"What's going on out there?" she asked, deciding this man could be helpful. "Where are we going?"

"I'd tell ya if I knew, but I've only been a pirate for a day. They don't trust me, nor have they told me anything. Speaking of which, I have been here long enough. If I take too long, they'll figure something amiss is going on." He looked nervously at the door.

Before he reached the door, Callisto called to him. "What's your name?"

"Eamon Gomez."

"Thank you, Eamon."

He looked confused. "For what?"

"Not being like them. Not looking at me like a piece of meat." She could see him blush slightly.

"I may be a pirate now, but I'll not let that destroy what my ma and pa taught me about respect." With that, he left her alone.

Callisto nearly laughed out loud. "Eamon, you will be the worst pirate the sea has ever known with ideals like that." She sighed. "I hope you don't have to be a pirate for long."

Finally, evening came, and Blackmane entered the chambers much earlier than he had the night before. He had been drinking again, but this time seemed to have more control of himself.

His dark eyes turned to regard Callisto, who stood looking at him. "Why are you still naked?"

"You never told me to dress," she replied, hoping being asked a question was an invitation to speak.

"Ha!" He grinned maliciously. "I guess I didn't. You learn quickly."

"I want to live," she told him frankly.

He unbuckled his weapon belts and placed them on the desk. "How badly do you want to stay alive, little wench?"

She smiled coyly. "Bad enough to do whatever a pirate captain tells me to do."

"You surprise me." He stepped closer, his eyes taking her in as if for the first time. "The fire in your eyes when you were first brought over from that merchant ship burned with pride, with fight." He looked her up and down. "Yet here you are, bare to the world, meek and willing. What happened to the fire? The fight?"

"Fire will get you burned if you let it get out of control, and fight will get you killed when you are outmatched. I am not so stupid as to believe I hold any upper hand here. I will do as instructed if it means I will live to see another day and another after that."

"Beautiful and smart, a dangerous and fun combination," he mused as he took off his topcoat and hat. "You will please me tonight. If I am not pleased, you will die." Reaching into his pocket, he threw a key down at her feet.

"Don't bother thinking about running, a thousand miles of sea in any direction you look and a ship full of killers that'd stop you before you could even hope to get over the side."

Callisto picked up the key and carefully unlocked the chain around her neck, instantly relieved to have it off. A few more moments, and she was free from her restraints. She glanced at the desk where he had dropped his weapon belts. Instantly thoughts of running swarmed her mind, but he was right. Where would she go? She would never make it before he was on her.

Her only options were to please him and do it well.

"Come here, whore, before I grow bored with you."

She straightened herself up and went to him. He was a head taller than her, thick set, with barrel shoulders and a slight gut. His dark hair was thick and greasy, and only his beard seemed well-kept. Her hands went to his trousers, and slowly she began to undo the drawstring, keeping her eyes locked on his, trying to build his lust. The more he was built up, the quicker it would go, and the sooner it would be over.

Reaching her hand down, she teased his cock, surprised to

find it still flaccid. She saw a glint of something behind his eyes. Was he resisting to see just how good she could be, she wondered?

With her free hand, she slowly unclasped the buttons of his black silken shirt. All the while, her other hand continued to play with his manhood, teasing it, trying to get it to stir. She pushed his shirt away, revealing his broad, hairy chest, a man's chest, the kind she generally would like. She might have enjoyed it if she wasn't being forced to do this.

"You are trying my patience, whore!" he growled, his breathing getting more profound, more agitated.

His eyes burned with something dark, something she couldn't quite place. Finally, she pulled his trousers free, letting them drop to the floor. She smirked up at him and lowered herself to her knees. Then she saw the nasty, thick scar running up his thigh and into his manhood. The kind of wound that would cripple lesser men.

"Now you know my secret." His tone was hollow and dark.

Callisto looked up at him again and realized what she had seen behind his eyes, shame. "I can work wonders with my mouth."

He backed away a step. "Don't touch it!" he growled. "You've seen it. You know the truth! What kind of man am I now? One that can't even get it up! I can't rape. I can't fuck!"

"Fucking doesn't make a man."

A thick hand slapped her face hard, almost throwing her backward. "Don't fucking patronize me, bitch!"

This was it. He was going to kill her no matter what. Nothing she could say or do would bring him peace of mind and spare her. She glanced at her reflection in the polished silver wine urn on the desk. Her eyes glimpsed a familiar figure she hadn't seen in a long time. "Ares—you haven't abandoned me!"

"What the fuck did you say?"

Callisto glared back at the pirate captain, her fury rising, knowing she wasn't alone now. "You're right. A tiny useless prick attached to a fat useless prick!"

His eye burned with violence, and he grabbed a fist full of her hair and screamed, releasing her instantly. "What the fuck was that!" He pulled his hand away quickly, blood gushing from a deep wound across his palm.

"Your mistake!" Callisto reached back and pulled out her small boot knife hidden within her braids. She rammed the blade up into his groin and twisted, feeling the spray of blood upon her skin.

Blackmane stumbled backward, tripping on the trousers still around his ankles, and crashed to the floor.

Callisto wasted no time and leaped upon him, driving the small blade down into his chest. "Die, you fucking piece of shit!"

He reached up and grabbed her throat; his grip was powerful. Instantly Callisto knew she was still in trouble, and already she could feel her face turning red as she struggled to breathe.

Twisting the knife, she felt his grip lessen, but he was still choking the life from her. Quickly before she blacked out, she wrenched the blade free and slammed it down again. His grip faltered, and she sucked in a quick breath before the pressure returned.

"You'll die before I do, bitch!"

Callisto could already feel the room spinning and knew he would be correct if she didn't think of something. She pulled on the blade, the strength in her arms fading as she fought against the blackness.

Kill him!

Hearing the voice, she glanced at the full mirror in the room. Ares was glaring at her in disappointment.

Do not fail now, or all my help will be for nothing!

A surge of strength flooded throughout her limbs, and the blade plunged once, twice, three more times. Each time Blackmane's strength diminished more and more until, finally, his arms collapsed to his side.

Blackmane weakly chuckled as blood seeped from his mouth. "You've killed yourself—my men—will kill you—" Finally, he went still, blood pooling beneath him.

Staring down at the body, she slowly regained control of her breathing. This hadn't gone the way she had planned. With the captain dead, she was also dead.

"I was dead anyways. At least it won't be by a limp-cocked urchin like you!" She spat on his corpse. "I need an idea—a plan—but what!"

"Your destiny is now!"

Callisto looked around the room. She had heard the voice and words as if the speaker had been right there. "Ares?"

"You only have one chance now—seize it and rise above all others!"

Her eyes lingered on Blackmane's weapon belt, seeing the ring of keys. She grinned. "The gods favor the bold!"

With her head downcast, Callisto left the captain's chambers, messily dressed in her clothing. Using blood from Blackmane, she made it look like her lip and nose were bleeding.

Only a skeleton crew manned the deck at such a late hour. The rest were either drinking or sleeping down below in their hammocks. If she was lucky this night, most of them would be drunk and passed out by now.

"Hey, what the fuck are you doing out here?" someone called from the top deck.

Fearfully she turned to face the one-eyed pirate. She held up the silver urn she had found on the desk. "The—the captain —wants more wine."

"Then you fucking best get to it, bitch," the man snarled dismissively, "the captain doesn't like to be kept waiting!"

"Where—where is the—wine?" she asked helplessly, noting that this man would die by her hand at some point.

"Where the fuck do you think it is?" he growled. "Below deck, aft of the ship! Don't think of hiding, either. If you aren't back soon, I will come looking for you. And you won't like that!" The look he gave her was devilish. "But I will."

Lowering her head again, she continued to the first of two entry points down into the ship's hold. Slowly she descended the ladder. She could hear several voices near the front of the hold, but in the rear, it seemed mostly quiet, and she was thankful for that.

Once below, her fragile demeanor faded instantly, and she scanned her surroundings. Three pirates sat around a small table gambling off to the ship's starboard side. By the several jugs of ale around them, they were well into the night, and plenty distracted.

Several hammocks lined the port side, half occupied with snoring men. Laughter roared out from the front of the hold, and she quickly ducked down and began her way to the aft of the ship.

As she neared the back, she passed by most of the stolen cargo and more from other ships they must have plundered, along with the cask of wine she had claimed to be after. Soon she saw a large, thick door, it was slightly ajar, and she could just make out voices. Slowly she crept closer until she could peer through the crack.

"Drink up, you fucking pieces of shit!" a pirate drunkenly

grumbled as he pissed over three poor captives in a cell. "Come on, you said you were thirsty!"

While the pirate was distracted, Callisto moved into the room, staying out of view as she came behind him.

The men in the other cell noticed her, and she quickly brought her finger to her lips to silence them. She was thankful they understood and averted their eyes.

"Come on, you fucking cowards, drink!" he roared as he shook the last of his piss on them. "Or maybe it is that you're hungry? Got something from the other end to stop your bellies from grumbling."

Callisto stepped in behind the drunk, and before he had a chance to notice her, she kicked out his knees and ran her dagger across his throat. He tried to grab at her but too quickly his lungs filled with blood, and he collapsed in his final death throes.

"Well, you were the last person I thought we'd ever see!" Kadir gasped in surprise.

"How in the seven hells did you get down here?" someone from another cell asked.

"Most of them are either drunk or passed out." Callisto wasted no time and quickly put the ring of keys to work, opening the three cells.

"Be it far from me to look a gift horse in the mouth and question a rescue, but what now?" Captain Murphy asked, this turn of events throwing him off guard. It was great to be free, but for how long?

"What do you think we do?" she snapped, eyeing all the men before her. "We take the bloody ship!"

Some of the men looked hopeful; others looked from one to another with uncertainly and dread. "There are only ten of us! Against a whole ship of them!" Alonso whispered.

"And eight of your crew walks among them," she reminded them, "it is unlikely they will be so keen to fight against their former comrades. Most of the pirates are either drunk or asleep. If we do this quickly and without hesitation, we should be able to take the ship within minutes, with very little of a real fight!"

Her words were gaining ground among them, but they were looking to their captain now for a real plan.

She looked the middle-aged man up and down. He was a solid man, and his eyes showed he was intelligent and calculated. "It's either that or I killed Blackmane and freed you for nothing. If that's the case, you might as well get back in those cells, and I'll take this fucking ship by myself."

"You killed Blackmane?" Several whispers erupted from the group.

"Truly?" Murphy asked her, picking up the dead pirate's sword. "Blackmane is dead?"

"You think he let me stroll along the ship because of his good nature?" She pulled Blackmane's silver flintlock pistols from behind her back as proof.

Murphy nodded. "More than enough proof for me." He turned to what was left of his crew. "Alright, we will only get one chance at this. We were dead men moments ago, but now there is a trickle of light where we might yet still be alive come morning. Let's go kill some pirates!"

"We need weapons," Kadir said, not wishing to kill the momentum of his speech.

Before Murphy could reply, Callisto cut in. "You'll have them, slowly, as we kill pirates. There are several sleeping just beyond this hold, reeking of rum. They should be easily taken. After we take the hold, you'll have enough weapons to deal with those on the deck."

Captain Murphy nodded, amazement clear on his face. "She's right. It's the only way we stand a chance."

"What about the defectors?" someone asked.

Again, before the captain could reply, Callisto answered. "I've already talked to one of yours. Eamon. He and most of the others only joined to stay alive and plan on running the first chance they get. My guess is once they know you are free and fighting, they will join in on our side."

"Eamon is a good man," Captain Murphy replied. "I have known him twelve years. If what you say is true, then we might have more help in this than we thought." He looked at the two pistols and dagger she had. "It would help if you gave those up to my men. If we are successful, I will send someone to get you when it is safe."

Callisto set a dark gaze on him. "If you think I am going to sit here like a scared woman while 'men' do all the fighting when all our lives lay in the balance of this, then you are sorely mistaken."

Before he could reply, she tucked the pistols back into her belt and crept from the room, dagger in hand, not waiting for his retort.

Kadir came up beside Murphy. "Damn, sir! That is one dangerous woman right there."

Murphy grinned. "Best we not let our savior down then."

Quickly they followed behind her, the men more than willing to let her take the lead into dangers unknown.

At first, Callisto wasn't sure if they would follow, but soon she heard the shuffling of feet behind her and sighed with relief. She needed them; there was no way to do this alone. Moving along the side of the hull, she used the stolen cargo to hide as she skulked towards the hammocks full of sleeping pirates. Nine days hidden aboard the Wind Spirit had given her plenty of practice in sneaking around a ship unnoticed. She used those skills now as if her life depended on it, for indeed it did.

Captain Murphy and Kadir moved up alongside her; they were the only two with weapons.

"If we strike the three at once, we can move on to the other two while the men arm themselves. From there, we can move to starboard and take out the seven sleeping there," Murphy whispered, pointing to the three sleeping pirates.

She nodded and was ready to move when he grabbed her arm.

"Are you sure you want to do this?" he whispered. There was no condescension in his tone, merely concern.

"I have killed before, twice already this night. I can kill again and again and again if I need to." She shrugged him off and moved into place.

Murphy watched her go for a second. What had this woman endured in life that had made her so hard and ready to fight and likely die? He shook the thought from his head as he motioned for the others to take their places. If they lived through this, he would be sure to ask her.

The pirate before her was older. Scars crisscrossed his face, arms, and bare chest. He had survived much in his life, but a woman, he would not. Glancing at the others, she threw her hand over his mouth and pressed the blade deep into his soft neck, slicing through his jugular as if it were nothing more than fish flesh. His eyes shot open and filled with panic, but already his lungs were filling with blood, and his limbs were weak. After several small jerks he was still, succumbed to death's grasp.

The men moved forward, relieving the dead of their weapons. Swords and daggers were handed out, and one pistol was given to Murphy.

"Now we have them!" one of the men said eagerly.

They moved on to the starboard side, where seven more pirates slept. The sound of the men gambling only a few dozen feet away was trying to their nerves as they slipped past the opening to the other side unnoticed.

Callisto stepped up to her victim and noticed at once it was Eamon. She steadied her blade as the others went to their grizzly task. Once the others were dead, she clamped her hand over the man's mouth. His eyes came alive with fear and only calmed slightly at the sight of her with a blade hovering about his face.

"We are taking the ship. You are either with us or against us," she whispered to him, removing her hand, her blade at the ready for any sign he might betray them.

Eamon glanced over and saw his crewmates grim-faced and bloodied. "By all the gods, new and old, I am with you!"

"Good, I have a job for you," she told him.

"Anything," he replied, getting down from his hammock as quietly as he could.

"What is going on?" Captain Murphy asked, beginning to feel annoyed that this woman was making decisions when all their lives were at stake. But he refrained from voicing his resentment. There would be time for that later if they survived.

"Those three men over there all have rifles." She pointed to where the pirates sat gambling. "There is no way we will be able to clear that ground and take them out without them getting off a shot or alerting others."

Murphy could see her point and felt stupid for not seeing the problem himself. *Damn this woman! Who is she, and why is this so easy for her?*

"What are you thinking?"

"We use bait."

Eamon was already beginning not to like the sounds of this, but he kept a brave face on. "What would you have of me?"

"Bring them to us." She grinned.

Eamon stepped nervously into the swinging lamplight the three pirates were using to gamble by. They regarded him with disdainful glares, not having yet accepted him as one of their own.

"What the fuck do you want?" a burly man missing an ear snarled at him.

"To be fucking sleeping," he replied, doing his best to sound undaunted by the man, "but Telmar told me to come to get you three. He heard the prisoners plotting something about escaping and wants us to help him give them a thrashing for good measure."

"Why the fuck did he send you and not come himself?" one of them asked.

Eamon felt sweat beading on his neck and shrugged. "I asked him the same thing, and he told me if I didn't want to have my throat cut open while I slept, I'd fucking do as I was told."

The three pirates laughed and stood from the table. "Well, we can take a break from our game and break some skulls."

Eamon led them through the hull towards the aft of the ship. Once they had cleared the open space and were among the cargo, the ambush struck. It was timed flawlessly. All three pirates lay dead within a handful of heartbeats, likely unaware they were even dead.

Captain Murphy nodded proudly to Callisto. "I hate to admit it so openly, but we'd not have gotten this far without you. You, my lady, are a dangerous sort, and because of you, we might just manage this."

"I am not a lady," she countered boldly, "and this is far

from over. Several more still sleep in the bow, and then at least a dozen on deck."

Murphy passed one of the blunderbusses to one of his men. "Ah, but now we are fully armed and have the advantage of surprise still with us."

"Captain!" one of his men called quietly.

"What is it, Jonas?"

"We took care of the other sleeping pirates. Calvin and Byron were there; they are with us again, sir. But the bow of the ship, sir, is locked. Byron said that's where a score or more privileged pirates sleep. He wasn't sure how many of them were in there but said, near a third of the crew, he reckons."

"That is good news indeed. Where are the others?"

"They said they were up top."

Murphy rubbed his short-bearded chin. "Meaning we might have an easier time taking the deck than we had hoped."

"What about the other pirates?" Jonas asked nervously.

"Block off the doorway with crates and barrels," Callisto told him. "They will be locked in there. Once we take the ship, we can deal with them at our leisure without risking spoiling our advantage."

Jonas looked from Callisto to Murphy. "Sir?"

Captain Murphy regarded her calmly, but his irritation was growing. She was right, and that would be the best course of action, but he was unused to having orders given that weren't his. More so, he was beginning to feel inferior to her quick mind for strategy in this.

"Stop wasting time, damn it!" Callisto hissed. "Just do it!"

Jonas needed no more motivation and gathered three others to see the job done.

"You overstep yourself," Murphy told her firmly. This wasn't the time for this, and he knew it, but he had to know his men would listen to his orders when given, not hers.

Callisto caught the irritation in his eyes and held it with her own. "Why, because I am a woman? Might I remind you, you'd all still be being pissed and shit on by pirates if it wasn't for me."

"Your gender is not what I meant. I am the captain here, and my men take orders from me, not you. I'll not deny your usefulness, it has been most remarkable, and I am grateful, as are my men, but they are MY men."

Callisto rolled her eyes. "Strangest thank you I've ever heard in my life."

Alonso rushed up to them. "They are locked in, sir, and the men are ready to swarm the deck at your command."

Callisto stepped back and waved her arm. "By all means, 'captain,' command your men. Maybe you'd like me to hide, so I don't get hurt."

Murphy fought back a snarl at the woman's impudence, yet he also had to fight a slight grin. "Let's get this over with, shall we? Do not kill them if we don't have to. We will try and force a surrender!"

The northern breeze held a crispness, making the early summer night tranquil. Light waves lapped at the ship's sides as it sailed calmly northwest in no hurry. They were nearly fully loaded with stolen cargo and would sail back to their home port and sell off the goods for a favorable profit.

A handful of pirates played dice upon a barrel near the ship's bow, and several others walked the length, watching the sea and sky for any sign of ships or storms.

Reeves was at the helm, lazily steering the ship. He had been Blackmane's quartermaster for nearly five years since the previous one had been killed in a battle. The same battle that had won them Poseidon's Fury and began the legend of Black-mane and his dreadful pirate crew.

Reeves had assumed the promotion would come with many perks, and it did, at times. But he had hoped never having to do night duty again would have been one of them. But Blackmane and his first mate, One Eye, had the day life, and he was stuck steering the ship all bloody night, nearly every fucking night. Not to mention everything else they wanted him to do. Now they had eight recruits he needed to train up. It was almost too much for him.

The title often gave him perks in taverns or with the whores. The pay was good, or at least better when they docked. But the amount of actual work it was made it almost not worth it, and he wondered if he should tell Blackmane he wanted to go back to just being part of the crew.

Quickly he dismissed the idea. The captain was just as likely to kill him as he was to grant it to him. No, that was wishful thinking. He was more than likely just to kill him.

Movement caught his attention as the deck's two hatches swung open and armed men clambered out. "So much for a quiet night." He chuckled, having no intention of moving from the helm. He suspected life was about to change, good or bad. He was always one for an opportunity.

Within moments the deck was full of armed captives from below.

"Surrender and keep your lives this day!" Captain Murphy yelled out. "Fight, and no mercy will be shown!"

Four pirates from the ship's bow drew their sabres and charged. A round from the rifles took three down in a spray of blood. The fourth had his guts spilled across the deck by a vicious sword blow.

The remaining pirates looked from one to another and then to Blackmane's cabin, expecting to see their battle captain rush to their aid. Unsure whether help would be coming or not as the seconds ticked by and no other pirates emerged from below deck.

Callisto knew a fight was going to happen, these men needed to see the truth, and if she was going to control the situation, she needed to be the one to control it. She opened the cabin door disappearing within; the sound of a blade on flesh could be heard, and men from both sides stared on in confusion, tensions high.

Blood splattered, Callisto exited the cabin, and several gasps came from all around her. She stood before them, proud and determined, her gaze hard and unrelenting, lifting her arm, showing them the head of Blackmane.

"Your captain is dead. I killed him with the blessing of Ares, the old god of war, before freeing these men and killing most of your crew below." She tossed the head in front of the line of pirates, still armed and ready to fight.

"The ship is mine. Now lower your weapons." Her gaze lingered on them, seeing their confusion, anger, and uncertainty. She needed to make a stand. "You all have two options, and you will make them right fucking now. Follow me as your new captain blessed by the old gods or get the fuck off my ship and start swimming!"

Several murmurs and curses arose from pirates and the newly freed merchant crew. This was a shock, and none of them had expected it.

Captain Murphy stared at her, his mouth hanging open. Surely, she hadn't just claimed ownership of Poseidon's Fury by the power of the old gods? Clearly, he had heard her wrong. And yet, he knew he hadn't. She had seen the moment for what it was—when power would be handed over, one way or another.

All this time, he expected it would be him to take control

since he was already a captain, and here this strange, unexpected woman took the reins, just like she had this entire night. He couldn't help but grin and wondered if she could pull it off. If she could, it would be one of the greatest moments he had ever witnessed. She would likely die one of the worst deaths he could fathom if she couldn't.

Callisto waited several long moments, her vibrant green gaze passing over every man, gauging and judging them. She was surprised to see several pirates and the Wind Spirit's crew nodding as if accepting it, Kadir and Alonso among them.

"Well?" she called out, her tone leaving nothing to debate.

"I'll not sail under some fucking wench!" a pirate growled, holding his sword threateningly.

Callisto walked towards the man who stood half a head taller than her. Fear gripped her with every step. But her eyes were cold and merciless, which caused the man to step back, unsure of what was happening. She stopped just out of his blade's reach. "Then get the fuck off my ship!" she ordered, pulling the flintlock pistol from her belt and firing it into his chest.

The shot took him square in the chest and threw him over the ship's rail, where the sea swallowed him. A crimson stain lingered in the water before it dissipated into nothingness.

Callisto turned back to the men on board. "Anyone else?"

"Sure as shit, we'd all have died here soon enough if not for you. As weird as it is to have a woman command a ship, I'll follow you, "Alonso said, stepping towards her, "I owe you my life—Captain."

Kadir threw up his arms. "Well, if he is gonna follow you, I guess so will I. His mother wouldn't take too kindly to me if I left him alone, Captain."

Murphy shook his head as he looked at the night sky to whatever god might have heard him, and after what she had claimed, it was hard to think the old gods weren't listening. "You have a cruel sense of humor," he muttered, stepping forward. "I guess I, too, am your man—Captain."

This drew several gasps from his crew, but soon they followed suit, some more willingly than others.

"I'll not fucking ask again!" she barked, staring threateningly at the pirates, who still seemed unhappy about this insane turn of events.

A shot fired behind her; she ducked and swung around. The other pistol in her hand was ready. Callisto saw the big man at the helm slip his gun away. A giant, one-eyed pirate fell face first by her feet, a dagger in hand. She knew him as the man who had first talked to her when she had left Blackmane's cabin. The ship's former first mate.

"I, for one, am with you, Captain." He glared over the remaining pirates still holding firm. "Come on, you fucking cunts! Blackmane is dead and was a vile prick anyways! How much worse could it get?"

A bald pirate stepped forward, his sword lowered, his eyes hard. "What gives you the right to take this ship from us?"

"I killed your shrivel-pricked captain. I freed your slaves from under you and overtook the ship with more swords and certainly more brains. That is what gives me the right!" she spat but held up a hand. "But I am not taking the ship from you. This ship can still be your home. All that has changed is who is in charge."

"And what do you know about being a pirate?" he asked in disdain.

She smirked dangerously at him. "I know how to kill, and I know how to take a ship from under the noses of a whole crew of some of the world's most feared pirates. I know enough."

"Aye, that you did, I'll give you that. I'll follow you—for now," the pirate said, his eyes full of intrigue.

The flintlock pistol snapped up and pointed straight at the pirate's face. "Know this and know it well. You'll die if I sense even a moment of treachery from you."

"That's a good start, Captain," he replied. "Name's Barraka."

"What about the fucking rest of you shit stains?" Callisto called out, trying to keep her demeanor hard.

Murmurs rippled out, but weapons were lowered and sheathed.

"I can't fucking hear you!"

"Aye, Captain!" the crowd of milling pirates called out, some more enthusiastic than others.

"Good, now clean up this mess on my ship!" she ordered firmly. "Kadir, Alonso!"

Both men snapped to attention. "Yes, Captain?"

"Go below and bring up a barrel of ale and a casket of rum. After tonight, we could all use a drink!"

The men laughed at the jest, and the tension seemed to ease just a bit as they slowly began clearing their former comrades' bodies.

Callisto looked up at the giant of a man at the helm. "What is your name?"

"Reeves."

"You have my thanks. You saved my life. I won't forget it."

"Anytime, Captain," he replied with a boyish grin. "Where to, now?"

"Where were we heading?" she asked, having no real idea what to do at this point.

"We were heading to Kelters Bay to unload and sell our stolen goods. But I don't much figure we can go there now," the big man said.

"Why not?" she asked.

"Kelters Bay is run by a madman named Sharktooth, who

happens to be Blackmane's older brother. Wouldn't do us well to sail up in his brother's ship after you killed him and all."

Callisto nodded. "I see your point. Where can we go to sell our cargo and get resupplied?"

Reeves laughed. "Only one place I can think of where you'll have a chance at being taken seriously as the new captain—Captain. No disrespect, of course."

Callisto rolled her eyes. "Only a little taken. Where is this place?"

"Six days due west, five if the winds favor us."

That would give her time, the time she needed to learn enough about being a real captain to fake it, and time to know who on this ship was really with her and who wasn't. "What is this place called?"

"Glacia's Palace. But it's not a real palace," he paused, "well, I guess there is actually a palace on it. It's a small island, ruled by someone you'll either love or hate."

"Get us there!" she ordered and went to the cabin as Blackmane's corpse was dragged out. "Murphy, a word and close the door."

Callisto entered her new quarters and began to shake uncontrollably once the door closed. She grabbed the front of the desk to steady herself, fearing her legs would betray her. Truly her whole body felt like it would simply quit on her right that moment.

Murphy came to her side. "Are you alright?"

Quickly her nerves settled, her body was hers again, and she burst out laughing in near hysteria. "Alright? Ha! I've never been better! I just took over a bloody pirate ship!"

"Yes, you did," Murphy replied, his tone not overly thrilled with this prospect.

"How the fuck did I do that?" She gasped.

"I'm still asking that myself."

She turned to him and bore into his mist-grey eyes. "Why did you follow me?"

Murphy sighed. "I prayed for a way out of that cage and told the gods I would follow whatever direction they threw my way." He chuckled. "Then you slit a pirate's throat in front of me."

He grew serious. "You know most of those men can't be trusted? Likely most of them will try and rape and murder you the first chance they get."

"Men like that have been trying to rape and kill me nearly my whole life. None have succeeded so far." She poured two goblets of red wine on the desk and handed one to him.

He took the offered cup. "Then let's make sure it stays that way. I will have my most trusted men keep watch on the pirates."

"You have my thanks." She downed the wine in a single gulp and poured herself another.

"Speaking of pirates, what shall we do with the ones in the hold below?" Murphy asked.

"Leave them there. We will deal with them later once we make it through tonight." She paused, looking at him with concern. "I will need a first mate. You want the job?"

"Been years since I was a first mate. Kind of a demotion from captain," he rubbed his unshaven chin, "but it is a big promotion from the slave I was only minutes ago. I am sure I can handle it. At least until we get somewhere safer."

"We both know this was your last trip as a captain."

"How did you...." He shook his head and laughed. "Even the stowaway knows the talk of the ship."

"Heard it from your own mouth, actually."

"How did you—I only told Kadir and Alonso the other night."

Callisto smirked. "And I was right behind you, hidden by

the crates." She paused. "I will need something else from you, something we must do in secret. I was hoping you could teach me to become a proper captain. I know little of ships. If I am to rule over this crew of cutthroats and killers, I will need to know what the fuck I am talking about and when to talk about it."

Murphy rubbed his weather-worn face. "I think I can manage that. It wouldn't hurt for you to learn how to use a sword and to fight."

"Done," she told him. "Thank you."

"I cannot promise I or the others will stay with you once we dock. We aren't pirates. We are sailors, not ruthless killers."

"I know, but I need you to be my crew for now."

"Aye, for now, we can do that." He nodded. "So, what is your plan now that you've taken over one of the most feared pirate ships the seas have ever known? Do you actually plan to remain here once we dock?"

She stood tall and took the captain's hat from the desk, placing it on her head. "I'm going to become the most feared pirate the seas have ever seen."

The sound of hard-soled leather boots clicked with a slight echo throughout the long naval adorn hallways. If one of experience had been listening, they would have been surprised at how awkward and forced the footfall timing truly was for someone with such a strict, composed stature.

But today was different. Today, the world had gotten a hundred times better for Captain Stephan Belfield, and his world was already well into what he had always dreamed of.

At eighteen, he had enlisted in the navy. Having spent a good portion of his life on or around ships, helping his father, who had been a naval dockmaster in London. This low birthright would have seen him nowhere in life. But his father had been well-respected for how well he kept the docks in order, day after day, year after year.

With a word from his father's lips to Jacob Knight, a man, his father, had watched grow from a greenhorn to Commodore in a decade and a half and had become a good acquaintance over the years. Within days Stephan had been placed under his command and on the flagship Paradise.

It had been an honor far outreaching what his low status should have afforded him. One he never allowed to be taken for granted. He had worked his hands to bloody blisters day after day, month after month, doing whatever was needed, even long after his shifts had ended.

Within two years, he had learned every inch of the Paradise and survived six battles with pirates. Quickly he had risen in the eyes of the veterans on the ship, and word of mouth had spread his name to many superior officers.

Four years into his naval service, he had found himself the first mate of the Sea Lion. One of the four sister ships to the Paradise. The Sea Lion was the lead battleship. It was fortified with ninety men, all veterans. Two rows of a dozen cannon's a side, longbows, and rifles for each man had made The Sea Lion the perfect lead ship for battle. It made up for what it lacked in grace and speed in raw ferocity.

Two years later, Captain Mark Sapmore of The Sea Lion had taken ill and passed away. They had been at sea and two weeks from any known port. As was right, Stephan had taken command. In those weeks, they had battled two storms that had nearly seen them sink and a fierce battle against a well-known pirate ship. But he had seen them through, kept the ship afloat, and captured a pirate vessel they towed back with them.

It was then he was given the rank of Captain of The Sea

Lion by Commodore Jacob Knight. His low birth was forgotten by anyone who had once brought it up among the officers.

It had been the proudest moment in his life and one he had wished to share with his father, but before he had made it back to London, his father's heart had given out. Now twelve years later, at thirty years of age, he had gotten the final piece in his dreams.

His hand touched the polished silver door handles. He could hear voices beyond and knew they were awaiting his arrival. He was running late. The thought usually would have irked him greatly, but today it was a faint annoyance in the back of his mind.

Stephan took a deep breath and held it for a second to calm his excitement. Boyish excitement had no place beyond these doors, and Stephan was well known for his firm beliefs in protocol. These were stoic men, military men.

"Let's not keep them waiting any longer, shall we?" With a final nod to himself, he entered the large conference room. "My apologies, gentlemen, for my tardiness—" he began.

"I should have you whipped publicly for making us wait, Captain Belfield!" a rough old voice grumbled from the far side of the command table piled with maps and documents.

A tingle of fear ran up Belfield's back. "Again, I—"

The speaker, General Marcus Carpton, stepped out. "That is, of course, unless you name the child after me." He winked.

Stephan felt the fear wash away and was surprised to see everyone in the room smiling at him.

"Congratulations are in order, it would seem." Commodore Jacob Knight clapped him on the back, almost like a father would to a son, and in truth, the man was as close to a father figure as he had now.

"Thank you, sirs. You are all too kind." His excitement slipped out only a little.

QUEEN OF THE SEAS

"What is it, a boy or a girl?" Lieutenant General Ralph Wineton asked eagerly, puffing on a thick cigar.

"It was a boy, sir," he replied, trying to keep his composure.

Marcus chuckled. "Look at this man. His wife just bore him his first son, and he is standing here all stiff as a tree, trying to keep decorum even still. At ease, man, at ease! Rejoice a little; you are a father now. The business will come later, first, a moment of pride, a drink, and a cigar."

"Thank you, sirs. It is a great feeling." Stephan was at a loss. He had never seen these men this way. Jacob, he had known for most of his life and had seen him casual and open, but the other two had only ever been formal in his presence.

"What did you name the boy?" Knight asked.

"After my father, sir."

"Ah, yes, a good name Johnathon, and a good man he was. Not a day goes by that I don't miss that man and how he ran the port. Gone through three replacements, not one of them can even come close to your father." The General nodded.

"You do me and his memory a great honor, General."

Ralph Wineton handed him a glass of strong brandy and a cigar. "Come, Stephan. Let us toast to your good fortune and your son's health!"

Everyone raised their glasses, drank, and made idle chat for several long moments.

"Not to rush the joyous event, Captain Belfield, but we called you here because there is business to attend to," General Carpton said, placing his cigar and glass down.

"You may have heard the rumors by now that there has been a vast increase in pirate activity. Sadly, it isn't a rumor. There have been many more attacks on merchant ships, and even four of our military ships have fallen prey. Two rest at the bottom of the sea with their crews. One made it back with minor damages, and another made it back, but the damages might cost more to repair than the cost of building a new ship."

"Bloody pirates!" Wineton cursed. "They are growing bolder each year! And it seems for everyone we sink, two more set sail! We are stretched too thin as it is after the war! We need another hundred ships to protect our seas from this scourge!"

Commodore Knight stared out the large bay windows at the city and the sea beyond. "Ever since Blackmane captured Poseidon's Fury, that act alone has stirred the hornet's nest. Pirates have grown braver, knowing our prized ship was taken." He sighed and turned around. "The war was hard on everyone, the common people most of all. Lands were destroyed, fathers, sons, and brothers were killed, and families were left with nothing. Now pirate ships overflow with plunder and riches, and honest men flock to that life hoping to share that wealth with their suffering families."

"Truly honorable men wouldn't stoop so low as to join ranks with pirates!" Wineton folded his arms.

"And where does a man's honor lie most?" Knight asked. "Country or family?"

"Country, of course!" the lieutenant replied without hesitation.

General Marcus cut in. "Awe, yes, to men like us, where our country and government have given us much, seen us through, paid us well, and our families have never suffered a day for it. I would strongly agree, Lieutenant. But country and government have far from kept these people safe. Their lives were pawns and casualties in a war that never concerned them. In this, we failed them, and many of them know it and hate us for it. If your country cannot protect you, you must protect yourself." He took another sip of his brandy. "This is why so many men are turning to the life of piracy."

"The state of the regions is disastrous. We don't notice it much here in London, for the war did little lasting damage here," Stephan added, "but farmlands were ravished. Whole towns and villages were burnt to the ground, leaving people broken, confused, and with nothing. Some won't recover for years to come. We need to give them something to hold onto, a purpose. Something to make them take pride in their country again, to believe in their government once more."

General Carpton and Commodore Knight exchanged glances.

"And what do you propose?" Carpton asked.

"Well, General, we need more ships, but those ships need crews to man them. We need to rally the people back to wanting to fight for their country and home. We must show them that they still have a place in this world and can make a difference for the better. I suggest we send out envoys and spread the word that the navy is looking for eager and willing men to join us. We petition the Governors and even King William the third to invest in more ships. By the time they are built, we will have men trained to sail them."

"Hmm," General Marcus replied, rubbing his chin. "Interesting proposal. But how would you feed them? Pay them?"

Stephan smiled inwardly to himself as he had expected the question. "Many surrounding towns' and cities' populations were greatly reduced during the nine years of war. Many homes and businesses remain empty. We offer contracts of service. Men pledge ten years or more. They receive a house for their families. Others with experience can take over abandoned farms, and with a small grant from the government for tools, seeds, and equipment, they can get them growing again. We can rebuild much of what was lost and fill our ranks again. Starting will be a large sum, but once farmers and businesses run again, taxes will level things out within a decade. More so if we can end the pirate problem quickly."

Again, the General and Commodore exchanged glances, but there was a brief nod this time.

"You are a bright young man, Stephan Belfield, and your wisdom follows along much with our own but with added insight," the general said. "We shall push for your ideas to come to fruition. But in the meantime, we need you out there." He pointed to the seas. "Doing what you do best. Hunting pirates!"

Stephan stood to attention and saluted. "Yes, General." He turned to Commodore Knight. "When shall we sail, sir? I can have the Sea Lion ready to sail by this evening if you wish, but I would request until morning to give the men a final night with their families."

Jacob Knight picked up his hat from the table. "You will do no such thing, for you are no longer captain of the Sea Lion."

"Sir?" Stephan felt his stomach lurch. What had he done wrong?

"You are no longer a captain." Knight held out the Commodore hat. "You are now Commodore Stephan Belfield of the naval ship Paradise in service to William the Third, the King of England."

Stephan felt his knees go weak. For a moment, he thought they would buckle beneath him. His mouth was suddenly dry, and he felt himself wobble. "I—I—"

"I hope you are trying to say you accept," General Marcus grunted. "Many good men were reviewed for such a position, but Commodore Knight here swears that there is no finer than you. I have studied and watched you grow into the finest of men and an even finer captain. Men like you are rare, Stephan, and regardless of birth or status, some men need to be given rare opportunities for the betterment of the world."

Finally, Stephan found himself. "I am honored, sirs! Truly honored."

"A new son and a bloody promotion!" Lieutenant Wineton clapped him on the back. "Doubt any day from now till the end will ever give such rewards!"

"What about you, Commodore Knight?"

Knight smiled. "I will soon be commodore no more, but a general like Marcus. Ah, I shall miss the sailing, but my bones are too old for months at sea. My arms too slow to be parrying pirate blades with confidence."

He sighed. "It is a younger man's world as it should be. Besides, there is no other man I would leave my ship in the hands of than you, Stephan. Take care of her for me, and don't let a pirate sink it."

Stephan saluted with more pride than he had ever done before. "As if she were my own daughter, sir!"

"Now get on out of here," Knight told him. "You have a baby boy who needs to feel his father's strong arms. And a wife to tell about a promotion! Hold them closely, Stephan. In two days, I want you ready to sail."

"Yes, sir!"

The events of the evening had run long into the night. Callisto was sure morning was only a few hours away. But she had been too alert to sleep, her position too new. She had needed to be seen on the deck with the men she hoped would soon respect her enough to call her Captain in earnest.

The wound of the night's events was too fresh and too bizarre for them to simply accept and continue. No, this was different. A woman captain? A woman pirate captain, no less. It was unheard of and would not be easy to shift.

Once the bodies had been removed and sent over the side, the blood stains were swabbed and scraped clean. She had personally opened the rum and ale cask Kadir and Alonso had retrieved. She had filled mug after mug with liquor and passed them around, trying to gauge who was with her, who still needed convincing, and who would never accept her.

It was a daunting realization that most did not or would not support her. Even many from the Wind Spirit lacked support, and she was sure they were only following orders because of their loyalty to Murphy.

These were hard men, and worst off, they were harder pirates. The upset they had suffered at the hands of a captured woman was a deep wound for many, she could tell. If it wasn't for the eighteen members of the Wind Spirit having all the rifles and pistols now, she was sure there would be mutiny, and her reign would have been over before it could begin.

The survival of everyone on the ship dangled in a precarious balance. The survivors on the Wind Spirit outnumbered the pirates only by three, but sooner or later, the pirates locked below would have to be freed, and then the odds would be more than two to one.

Even with the rifles and pistols in the hands of the Wind Spirit's crew Callisto was unsure if that would be enough to hold back an attack if the pirates decided to fight.

Callisto paced her newly won quarters like a caged tiger. A thousand thoughts and questions assaulted her in an endless cycle. The truth was, she had no answers to these questions, at least not yet. And no matter how many times she asked and tried to decipher them, there were no answers to be had at this time.

It would be a dangerous waiting game.

Finally, she retired to the plush hanging bed, doubting she would sleep but hoping for even a few meager hours to help her reset for the following morning chaos she was sure would be waiting for her.

But sleep did find her...

The sky was crystal clear and vibrant blue. The world opened up before her in every direction she looked. It was breathtaking, a sight she doubted any mortal had ever seen before. It was as if she was standing at the top of the world. She knew at once this was no ordinary dream.

"In a manner of speaking, that is correct," a deep, powerful voice said behind her.

Callisto's heart began to beat faster. She knew that voice, and it was the same now as it had been every single time she had heard it, from the first time that night so long ago as a child. The god of war —Ares—

"What is this place?" she asked, too afraid to turn around to look at him.

"Mt. Olympus," the god replied, "the home and birthplace of the true gods of this world."

"It is beautiful," Callisto whispered, feeling him close.

"Maybe one day I will show it to you in person," Ares said close to her ear.

Callisto's heart was beating faster. She did not know what to do or what to say. She had only caught glimpses of the deity through her life in reflections. Never had he visited her in her dreams.

"Would you like to look upon a god?" he asked, his voice smooth and intense.

"I would."

"Then turn and face me, Callisto, my chosen child." It was almost a command.

It took her a moment to gather her wits. This was a moment she had dreamed about often in those first few years, but never had she imagined it would come true. Slowly she turned, her eyes downcast, not knowing if she should look him in the eyes.

Her gaze landed on his sandaled feet and polished bronze greaves. Her breath caught in her throat. He was really here with her, standing before her. Was it just a dream, or was it something truly more than that?

"This is a dream world, yes," he told her as if reading her thoughts, "but I am here within it. Look me in the eyes and know that I speak the truth."

She lifted her gaze past the black leather pteruges to his hardened body and molded black leather cuirass studded with silver fetishes. Finally, she reached his face.

Instantly she was pulled to his dark, golden-brown eyes that radiate power, control, and violence. He had a chiseled jaw, sharp nose, and shoulder-length jet-black hair that connected to a cropped beard. He was everything she pictured him to be and more. The statues and artwork she had seen of him could never begin to do him true justice.

"You honor me with your presence." she finally managed to say, feeling like a child.

Ares's expression was cocky and assured. "I do indeed, as I have rewarded you much since that fateful night you heard my name for the first time. I will still reward you if you prove your worth to me."

"I am but your humble servant." She lowered her head in a slight bow and felt his hand upon her chin, lifting her head back to meet his mighty gaze.

"I have many faithful servants," he told her. "That is not what I want from you, Callisto."

His touch was captivating, sending a shiver through her whole body. "What—what is it you want from me then?"

"I want you to become an embodiment of my power on earth. I can grant you much power, riches, strength, fear in the hearts of *your enemies, vengeance on those who cross you," he explained, his hand still upon her chin. "I can make you the most feared pirate the world has ever known." He smirked. "Do you want that?"*

"Yes!" she nearly cried out. "More than anything!"

"Good."

"What must I do?" She was nearly begging.

He grinned at her eagerness. "I will have tasks for you, and you will spread my name across the world once more. Mortals will know the old gods are far from forgotten, and they will learn to love and fear us once more!"

"Yes, yes!" Callisto nodded. "I will spread your name far and wide."

"Good," he caressed her cheek and stepped back, "but before you can do any of that, you must first wake up and fight."

Callisto did not understand and was about to ask when his hand flashed out and struck her face so hard her world began to spin as she stumbled back and fell from the cliff face...

Callisto's eyes shot open just in time to see a dark figure standing above her, ready to plunge a dagger down. With reflexes defying her half-asleep form, she rolled to the side as the blade slammed into the mattress.

Snatching the flintlock pistol under her pillow, she rolled off the side of the bed. Her killer was already scrambling up after her. The gun fired, taking her opponent in the chest, and throwing him back before he could reach her. But before she had time to think, thick arms wrapped around her from behind.

"You stupid bitch!" a beer-soaked voice hissed. "Thought you could just take over our ship, and we would do nothing!"

Callisto struggled to free herself from the pirate's grip, but he was strong, angry, and fully intent on killing her. She looked to the cabin door. Where the hell was Murphy or the others who had promised to stand guard? Had they betrayed her too? She noticed the cabin door had a chair wedged against it and could faintly hear the calls and pounding from outside.

"I'm going to gut you like a fucking fish!" the pirate growled as he fought to control her.

It was a small relief to know those she trusted hadn't betrayed her, not that it did her any good since she was likely about to die.

No!

The god of war had put his faith in her, and she would not die here and now!

Slamming her head back, she felt the crunch of a nose breaking, and the pirate's grip loosened. She stomped down on his foot and pulled free, throwing herself into a roll across the bed and grabbing her dagger from the nightstand.

"You're gonna pay extra for that." He started around the bed, drawing a knife from his belt.

"So afraid of me you have to attack me in the middle of the night while I sleep!" Callisto berated him. "Fucking coward!"

He just grinned a rotten-toothed grin. "Pirates don't become great by fighting fairly. You'd know that if you were a pirate!"

"You're right. I thank you for the reminder." She had nowhere to go, and he was almost around the bed. She snatched a bottle of rum from the nightstand and threw it on the floor in front of him. It shattered, spilling its contents all around him.

"You missed." He laughed.

"Did I?" Callisto asked, lifting the burning candle from the nightstand, it took a moment, but the pirate's eyes lit up with sudden fear at what she was suggesting.

"You wouldn't dare—" he stammered, "you'd burn the whole ship!"

Her smile boarded on mad. "If I am to die, I might as well take everyone else with me!"

"You're bluffing!"

"Try me!"

Without a second thought, the pirate lunged forward, and Callisto threw the candle at him.

Instantly he released his knife, grabbing for the flying candle, catching it in both hands moments before it hit the rum-soaked planks.

"Ha!" he cried out in triumph.

Callisto wasted no time and was already before him, her dagger punching up into his lungs. She stared into his shock-filled eyes as blood spilled down across his chest.

"I think you are on to something about not fighting fair." She blew out the candle before it fell from his grip as he crumpled to the floor.

Callisto kicked the chair from the door and opened it to see an armed Murphy, Reeves, Kadir, and Alonso.

"Captain, are you alright?" Murphy asked, seeing her blood-drenched arms and peering into the cabin to see the two bloodied corpses.

"Yes," she growled, "no thanks to any of you and whoever was meant to guard my door tonight!"

Kadir dropped his gaze. "I only went to the rails to take a piss. I wasn't gone more than a moment," he insisted.

"Long enough for these two curs to sneak in," Murphy barked at him. "You'll be flogged for this."

Callisto stared hard at Kadir, searching his eyes for betrayal, malice, or any other sign that might be there that he was against her. But it was not there. All she saw was a man afraid and ashamed.

"There's been enough bloodshed and pain this night." She looked back into the cabin and at the growing crowd on the ship deck. "Besides, this might prove to be worth more in the end."

"What do you mean?" Murphy asked.

"Drag those bodies out and let the men see them before you throw them over the rail," Callisto ordered Reeves and Kadir.

"Listen up, you fucking maggots!" Callisto screamed out at the crew. She glared at the men before her, as cold and threatening as she could.

"These two fucking cowards snuck into my cabin and tried to kill me in my sleep. Yet here I stand," she looked over and nodded, and the two dead pirates were discarded over the side, "and there they go."

"I took this ship. It is mine by right of fucking conquest! It will remain mine, and the ship's tow rope will drag the next son of a cowson who tries to kill me until they drown or until I catch a big fish! Now get back to work!" She spat at their feet, turned, and returned to her cabin.

Callisto parried the thrust wide, barely having enough time to turn aside the knife angled for her midsection before another downward slash came her way. Sidestepping, she lunged for her opponent's unprotected side, but cold steel defeated her. She knew she didn't have time to bring her blade up to protect her exposed front. She jumped back and hit the ship rail. Out of room to run, she held up her hands and yielded.

"Enough," she gasped, sweat stinging her eyes, "I yield again, damn it."

Murphy sheathed his cutlass. "You are getting better."

Callisto splashed water from a rain barrel on her face before taking a long drink. "Don't lie to me; I was awful. I never even came close to scoring a hit."

"How could you have?" Murphy replied honestly. "I have been wielding a sword most my life. You have been doing so for four days."

She kicked the rain barrel. "I can't spend the next twenty years learning to fight in hopes of holding my own against someone! I will be long dead before then. There have already been three attempts on my life in nearly as many days! I need to get better, faster."

The morning after the first attempt in her cabin, three others had tried to confront her and throw her overboard. She would have been if it had not been for Murphy, Reeves, Kadir, and Alonso.

She had kept her word, and all three men had been dragged behind the ship for nearly a full day before being cut free. Whether they had still been alive or not, no one knew.

After that, she hoped things would calm down, and the crew would finally accept her, or at the very least stop trying to murder her. But still, she knew the tension and hate were simmering just beneath the surface for many of the men.

On the third day, a pirate was caught trying to release the others still in the hold. He had been dragged to the top deck kicking and screaming. She glanced up at the corpse of Blackmane still hanging from the beam. It was gruesome and smelled, but Reeves had told her to make a show of strength.

A dangling body was a good reminder.

"You certainly do," Murphy agreed, "and you will. Your form has improved greatly. You are starting to understand the movements between sword, dagger, and body and how to make them one. The strength in your shoulders and arms has increased as you no longer drop your blade when struck. In short, you are doing well, but it will still take time."

He watched her put on her belt again and pointed to the two ivory pistols. "In the meantime, keep those primed and within reach at all times."

"When do you plan on releasing the pirates in the hold?" Reeves asked from the helm. "Been a long time, those boys are going to be hungry and pissed right off, and I can't say I'd blame them."

"And hopefully weak and not in the mood for a fight," Callisto replied with all seriousness.

Reeves shrugged. "They are pirates, Captain. They are always ready to fight. There are a few decent men in there. But I know them all, some better than others. Men of reason," he paused and shrugged, "as reasonable as pirates come, that is."

"How much longer until we reach Glacia's Palace?"

Reeves pointed to a tiny dark speck in the distance. "Few hours if the wind holds."

"Good." Callisto went to the upper deck rail and looked down on her crew, a mixture of merchant sailors and pirates. The tension was still evident, but things aboard were running smoothly.

"Alonso, Kadir! Gather six men from the Wind Spirit, arm them with rifles, and release the pirates in the hold. Bring them up top! It is time I had a word with them."

"Yes, Captain!"

"You think this is wise?" Murphy asked, checking his blunderbuss and pistol.

"Not likely." Callisto shrugged. "But I cannot leave them in there forever. I want that space for my crew, who are committed to me. Get those who can be trusted ready for action and those who cannot be trusted unarmed and separated from the others. I don't want any surprises we can't handle."

Murphy nodded and set off to his task.

Callisto looked out to the sea and watched the small island getting closer. It was still nothing but a black smudge on the horizon, but every minute it slowly grew.

What awaited her there, she wondered?

The last few days had been so demanding. Between the attempts on her life, the sword practice, learning about charts and maps, parts of the ship, how to sail, and everything else that happened on the ship, she was physically and mentally exhausted.

Several times she had almost broken down and made Murphy captain. But deep down, she couldn't. She had been chosen for this by Ares! By the god of war himself! This was her destiny, and she had to see it through. She wanted to see it through more than anything.

She was destined to be on this ship. Everything that had happened on that fateful night so long ago had led her to this moment. To this fate. She could feel it. As much as she wanted to deny it, as much as she feared it, she knew it was true.

It was only a matter of how long she could manage to stay alive that was the problem.

Commotion on the deck informed her the pirates were being brought up. She steadied herself but stayed focused on the small island.

"Play this right, or many people will die soon," she whispered to herself. "You might very well be one of them."

Calmly, she turned around, standing straight and firm, her face stern and demanding as she walked towards the stairs, looking down at the row of twenty-four pirates. A few looked angry, others confused, bitter, thirsty, and hungry, and all looked too weak to want to start trouble.

This was good; this was what she had hoped for.

"I should have left you mangy curs down there and just cleaned up the mess once you were dead! Doesn't look to be a set of balls among the lot of you!" she bellowed down to them, only going halfway down the stairs.

Too close would be dangerous. She needed a better read on things before she pressed her luck. Yet she also could not allow herself to appear weak. These men were like sharks, a moment of weakness was like the smell of blood, and they would tear her apart.

"Know this, and know it well, Blackmane is dead! Cut his filthy head off myself," she pointed to the mast where the rotting corpse had been hung, "and now I, Callisto SinClair, am captain of the Poseidon's Fury."

Several grumbles could be heard from the line of men, even a few from beyond them from men she had hoped she had already persuaded. It would take time to convince these bastards she was a worthy captain. Yet time was an enemy. She needed a crew now, one that she didn't have to fear being stabbed in the back by every time she went near them. She needed their respect and their trust.

"Fuck it," she whispered to herself, clearing the stairs, and walking down in front of the line of prisoners. Their eyes were hard, hate-filled, and worried.

"Let me make this plain for you inbred pricks to understand! I need a fucking crew of pirates! A crew that I can trust to do as they are told, one whose respect I can depend upon!"

"Respect is earned, wench!" a tall, scarred-up man said from the line. "Why would we respect you? Why would we follow a fucking woman? What will you do? Offer us our lives if we follow you. And if we refuse," he looked up to the dangling corpse, "offer us death?"

Callisto looked the pirate up and down. He wasn't overly

large, but what was there was lean and powerful. He was a fighter and, by the sharpness in his eyes, a thinker. The others almost seemed to move closer to him, so he was a man who was liked or respected among his peers.

"He died because he tried to kill me like a coward. If you are going to try and kill me, have the decency to challenge me to my face! I am just a 'woman' after all. I offer you two choices." She ran her gaze over everyone, prisoners and crew alike. "Sail with me to plunder, riches and adventures, or," she pointed to the growing island, "we part ways at Glacia's Palace. Those who wish to leave will be given their pay and then are to get the fuck off my ship! Those who wish to stay will be given the same when we dock, to enjoy whatever delights they wish until we set sail! Those who are here, I expect to be here ready to swear their loyalty to me as their captain! Those who are not, to Hades with you!"

Walking to the center of the deck, she drew her cutlass. "Any one of you that has a problem with this and wants me dead, this is the only chance I'm giving you. Challenge me here and now, or forever hold your fucking peace!"

Murphy felt his gut clench. She wasn't ready for this, not even close. She was decent with a blade, but the men on this ship were killers. Maybe a handful she could best in single combat if she were lucky. The rest would cut her to ribbons.

He made sure his own sword was ready. He would protect her if he had to, though he doubted it would make a difference.

The pirate stepped forward, grabbing a blade from one of the pirates who had already accepted her. He squared himself with her, his eyes burning with interest. "And if I cut you down here and now, then what?"

"What is your name?" she asked.

"Weaver."

"Then, Weaver, I guess you get to be captain. But I ask but one small request."

The pirate laughed. "And what would that be?"

"If I do lose, you honor my terms. The merchant men who want to leave get their coin, and no harm comes to them."

Weaver stood there shocked for several moments before slamming the blade into the deck and turning to the rest of the crew. "Did you fucking hear that?"

Pirates and sailors alike looked at one another, confused, before looking back to Weaver.

"Did you hear what she just requested!"

"Aye!" several shouted, still not sure what he was getting at.

He pulled the blade from the wood and pointed it at her. "What captain have you ever heard say such a thing for any of their crew knowing death was near? What captain have you ever known to give pay even if they know you aren't to be coming back?"

He ran the sword lightly across his arm, smearing it in blood. "On my blood, I will follow you, Captain Callisto SinClair, until the gods see fit to take me to the world beyond this one! My blade and my life are yours!"

He turned a glare onto the others. "What say you, you fucking pricks? Will you follow Poseidon's Fury's new captain, or will you be trying your luck at Glacia's Palace?"

Several looks and murmurs were thrown around before four more prisoner pirates stepped forward, took the blade from Weaver, and made the same oath. Several other pirates came forth and made the same pledge.

Callisto stood there, watching this unfolding before her, a feeling of pride and wonder flooding her. It was happening. It was truly happening. The weight of fear melted from her.

"Captain!" Reeves called down to her.

"Yes, Reeves?" she called up to him. "What is there to report."

"Few more hours, Captain, and we will sail into the harbor."

"First mate Murphy."

"Yes, Captain?"

"Take Weaver and another and bring a chest from my locked storage. Pay the men and add an extra gold for everyone who swore a blood oath!"

Murphy grinned inwardly. "Aye, aye, Captain!"

"And Murphy."

"Captain?"

"Get them some food and water before they fall over dead."

The last of the vibrant red liquid poured into the crystal goblet. The owner lifted it gingerly, inhaling the sweet, exotic aroma. It was a shame. This was the very last of the Massandra Sherry on the island. The last she was likely to see in a long time.

"A shame," she muttered. "Now I will have to go back to that other swill." She laughed.

In truth, the other 'swill' was just as expensive and highly sought after, but since she had discovered this rare vintage, she had wanted nothing else for a long time. She wondered if those traders would ever find their way back here.

It had been nearly four years since they had stumbled upon her island after being stuck in a storm. She had agreed to let them dock to make their repairs. In exchange, they gave her a third of their wine shipment.

After tasting it, she had told them to bring her more, and she would pay handsomely for it. But they had been honest men, and this was far from what could be considered an 'honest' place. But it was her place, her kingdom, her world. She was the queen of every inch of this island and every soul upon it.

"Your highness," a soft voice said.

Glacia pulled her attention from the amber liquid to the slender blonde servant. "Yes, Macy?"

"The Poseidon's Fury has been spotted pulling into port," the girl replied, averting her eyes to the ground.

"Blackmane," Glacia muttered. "I thought I told you not to come here again."

She swirled the wine several times before downing it in a single swallow. "Macy, tell Gavin to round up the men and meet me at the docks. Let him know there is likely to be a fight that needs to end quickly."

"As you wish, your highness." Macy's head bobbed up and down.

"And, Macy." Glacia walked over to the servant girl.

"Yes, your highness?"

Slowly she lifted the girl's face until their eyes met. "Am I so hideous that you do not wish to look upon me?"

Fear brushed the girl's eyes. "No, your highness! You are very beautiful! The most beautiful woman I have ever known!"

"Then why do you avert your eyes whenever you see me? Am I such a monster?"

"I—I—I do not know, your highness." The girl's cheeks flushed brightly.

Glacia stroked the girl's cheek, lifting her chin back up. "I asked you when you came here to never lie to me. Why would you do so now?"

"I'm sorry, your highness—It's just—It's jus—" she stuttered, her eyes fearful and excited, "the way you look at me—it makes me feel—"

"Good?" Glacia finished for her, her finger running under the girl's soft pink lips. "Alive? Desired?"

Swallowing nervously, Macy nodded.

"Never be ashamed of that feeling, Macy. Never fear it, and never run from it." She kissed the girl gingerly on the cheek. "For if you do, you may miss out on a world of possibility."

"Ye—yes—your highness."

"Good, now go tell Gavin. Then I want you and the other acolytes to go to your rooms and await my summons." Glacia watched the girl leave. "For things might get bloody this afternoon, and I'll not have any of you hurt."

Lines were thrown down to hesitant dock hands as the Poseidon's Fury pulled into the large docking yard in the large, natural cove. The water was more than deep enough, saving a great deal of time loading and unloading supplies. Glacia's Palace was one of the only docking yards outside of large cities where a ship of Poseidon's Fury's size could pull up straight to the island's long wharves.

The wharf was alive with activity. Half a dozen smaller ships were busy loading or unloading their goods, be it whether they were their original wares or stolen was easy to tell by the crews that worked them. Four of the ships were smaller pirate vessels, crewed by hard-looking men, killers, and cutthroats all. Reeves had informed Callisto that Glacia's Palace was a haven for all who docked there. Any fighting on the island or within three miles of sea was swiftly dealt with and the combatants would be seen as an enemy forevermore.

"Captain!" Reeves called, standing beside her on the deck as the lines were tied. "There is something else you should know."

"What is it?" Callisto looked at the large man. He easily had a foot on her and likely a hundred pounds.

Reeves scratched his shaven chin. "Well, last time Blackmane and we were here, there was a bit of a 'disagreement,' and we were told never to return on the punishment of death. Due to Blackmane killing another ship captain and all."

"And you didn't think it important to tell me this before we sailed into hostile territory?"

"Well, since you ain't Blackmane, and the Poseidon has a new captain, I'd suspect that problem wouldn't matter anymore, and we'd be welcome again." He glanced up at the armed men rushing down to the dock. "Though with the welcome crew arriving, I suppose it would help if they knew that information sooner rather than later."

Callisto watched nearly forty men and women making their way down from the hillside towards them, blunderbuss, pistols, and swords in hand. All around them, dock hands and crews were quickly withdrawing safely from the ship.

"Lovely," she mused.

It was known to her that anyone who used the port had to pay tribute, a sum of ten gold and ten silver, and on top of that, something special from the ship's cargo as a 'gift.'

"Reeves, find Murphy, double the tribute, and bring me Blackmane's head in a sack."

Reeves nodded. "Aye, Captain, that might just be the direction to smooth this all over."

"And Reeves," she called to him before he had gone more than a few paces, "from now on, be sure to tell me everything before the problem arises."

"Yes, Captain, sorry 'bout that."

"No backing out of this now," she told herself, checking her sword and pistols. "Let's see how this plays out." She walked down the boarding plank towards the island's growing army.

"Blackmane, I told you never to set foot on my island again!" a commanding voice called out, moving through the crowd.

Glacia stopped in her tracks as she neared the front. "Who are you? Where is Blackmane?"

Callisto bowed slightly. This woman was beautiful, her fiery red hair catching the breeze. "My name is Callisto SinClair. I am the captain of the Poseidon's Fury."

"Impossible!" Shock was clear across her face.

"Look out below!" someone yelled from above, and a sack hit the planks between them.

"What the hell is that?" Glacia asked, eyebrow raised, her troops eager for a fight.

"A gift and the answer to your other question," Callisto emptied its contents, "and proof of the possible."

Blackmane's rotting head rolled across the dock.

Several gasps worked through the crowd, and weapons were lowered.

Glacia stepped forward and examined the head before kicking it off the dock into the water. "So Blackmane is finally dead. Who killed him?"

Once more, Callisto bowed. "Is it truly so hard to believe it was me?"

Vibrant blue eyes scanned her from top to bottom. "Frankly, yes. Not to insult you, of course, but I have known Blackmane for a long time. He was not an easy man to kill."

She stepped around Callisto, taking in every aspect of her. "But he is dead, and you now stand before me," glancing up, she saw the Poseidon's crew looking down, "and since no one else is stepping forwards to claim credit, I guess I am left wonderfully surprised."

"Captain," Murphy called over as he carried a small chest down to the dock, "I have what you asked for."

He set it down between the two women.

"And what is this now?" Glacia asked.

"My crew told me that to dock here, there was a customary tribute to be paid, and I am far from one to displease a kind hostess." Callisto kicked open the top, showing the gold and silver coins.

Glacia's brow rose again. "That is far more than what is required."

"I like to make a good first impression."

A smirk crossed Glacia's full ruby lips. "An impression you have made."

She nodded, and one of her men picked up the chest and walked off. "I suspect you have wares you'd like to sell and supplies you'd like to buy?"

"Among other things, yes."

"Good." Glacia turned and started to walk off, her hands held behind her back. "You and three of your crew may dine with me tonight. I will have someone come and get you. Until then, my man, Hogarth, will show you and your crew their accommodations."

"You have our thanks, your highness," Callisto called to her as their hostess vanished among her people.

"That went better than expected," Murphy said once the armed men had begun to disperse, and regular activities began on the docks again.

"Yes, it did," Callisto smiled. "Find out what you can about this Glacia. I want to know all that I can before dinner."

"I'll see what I can do." Murphy nodded.

"And Murphy,"

He stopped and regarded her.

"How many men do you think will be gone by morning?"

"I'd imagine close to half, maybe a few less."

"Will we still be able to sail?"

He sighed. "That all depends on which ones leave. But either way, we will need more hands. As it stands right now, we have enough, but another three or four bodies would be helpful. If we lose half of what we have now, we'll be in trouble if we plan on sailing for more than a few days."

"I was afraid of that."

The door closed as Callisto, Murphy, Reeves, and Weaver took their seats in the ornate carriage. The carriage was pulled by four of the biggest and most beautiful black and white horses any of them had ever seen and was built from polished cherry wood and trimmed with enough silver and gold to feed a village for months. It was more than large enough for all four of them to be comfortable, even with Reeves and Weaver's larger size. The seats were crushed velvet, stuffed with goose down, and Callisto was sure she had never felt anything so remarkable on her ass.

"Never expected to be riding in style like a king." Weaver grinned, running a hand across his bald scalp, looking out the side window. "A man could almost get used to something like this."

"Except you'd have to stay on land to use it," Reeves put in sourly. "It's nice and all, but I'll take the crashing salty waves of the sea any day."

Weaver shrugged. "If I could live like a king, I think I could do without the sea for months on end. Not that I would not miss it, but I think I'd be too busy drinking and fucking myself into an early grave."

"What did you find out about our hostess?" Callisto asked, doing her best to seem unfazed by the luxurious ride and the chatter of her two seemingly most trusted pirate companions.

"Her full name is Glacia Von-Silverblade. She founded this island nearly twenty years ago. Rumors of how she came to be the island leader vary. Some claim she was shipwrecked here, and the crew and her slowly built it into what it is. Others claim she is a runaway from a wealthy family, that she stole her family's wealth, hired a small army and ship crew, sailed here, and set up shop. Another rumor—"

Callisto held up her hand to stop him. "I don't want hearsay. I want facts, truths, the known."

"Right," Murphy cleared his throat. "She is said to be fair but very dangerous. She has over four hundred men and women on the island under her payroll, most ex-military, mercenaries, or pirates. When her rules are broken, she has been known to go to the extreme to make examples, and public executions seem to be a favorite, though assassinations have been known to happen. The methods range from simple hangings, beheadings, to the more drastic, blood eagles, skinning, or burning alive."

"Aye." Weaver nodded. "Seen a few of those myself when I was here before, grisly business, not something you forget nor something you want to find yourself on the wrong end of either."

"Fear is a useful tool for keeping those who might step out of line in line. Couldn't hope to rule an island such as this when pirates and cutthroats are your main clientele without a show of force from time to time." Callisto nodded. "Anything else?"

"She is very ostentatious and likes to make a grand show for those around. Hence our elaborate ride, I would suspect. Also, she is very carnal in every sense of the word. It is said she is a follower of Aphrodite," Murphy finished with an uncomfortable cough. "It would be my advice that we play this carefully. She might be just as likely to kill us all as she is actually to feed us."

"Sounds like my kind of woman." Callisto grinned, very intrigued by the part of the Greek Goddess of beauty and love. That might play as common ground for her and this woman.

"By the old gods and the new!" Reeves whispered in awe, looking out the window as they pulled through a set of large iron gates into an impressive animated garden.

Strange and beautiful trees, plants, and flowers grew in an array of vibrant shades and colors. Lush bushes and trees were trimmed and sculpted flawlessly in a mosaic of exquisiteness. Pathways throughout the garden varied with colored sands or small rocks, bringing a unique and colorful feature to the already impressive sight.

"There are trees and plants here I've only ever seen half a world away, and others I have never seen," Murphy whispered, trying to take it all in. "I have been to some of the richest merchants' mansions and never seen such a garden. The cost to make this possible would have been worth a king's ransom or more."

"It would appear Glacia is truly a queen of her island," Callisto replied, finally giving in to the awe of what was around her. She, too, had seen some impressive estates and gardens in her lifetime, but this was something else entirely.

The carriage pulled up to an equally extraordinary manor, nearly a castle in its own right. A half-dozen marble pillars lined the front, as thick as a barrel and nearly twenty paces between which held up a vast sundeck above.

The well-dressed driver, who appeared to be no more than eighteen, opened the door for them, and a lithe brunette in nothing more than a thin toga and sandals awaited them as they climbed out.

The woman bowed gracefully. "The mistress is waiting for

you in the back garden if you'll follow me." Without waiting to see if they would follow, she made her way up the marble steps to the vast, bronze-studded oak doors, large enough that eight men could walk abreast.

Callisto followed, with her three companions behind her, gawping and gasping at all they saw. She would have joined them, but she needed to keep her head, keep from being distracted by all this wealth and splendor before her.

It was a manipulation tool to throw people off, intimidate, shock, and blind weaker minds to the truths that awaited. She had no doubt it worked, and often, for it was working on her as well, as fear and envy grew with each step. But she would keep her calm. She would not allow this to distract her from her course. She had a god-granted destiny to fulfill, and she would be damned if she weren't going to succeed.

She closed her mind to the wonders they passed, ignoring the sculpting, paintings, and other beautiful works of art that littered the walls and nearly every corner. Shut herself off to the brilliant-colored water pools fed by naked statues of elves, angels, and other mythical beings. She stopped her eyes from wandering to the several beautiful half-naked male and female servants who were busying themselves with various tasks. She truly hoped there would be time to enjoy the sights later.

"What manner of business does she do to be able to afford all this?" Murphy muttered. "Trading with pirates and merchants can't bring this much wealth."

Weaver grinned. "Whatever it is, I wouldn't mind getting in on some of the action."

Finally, after what seemed like forever, they reached the back, where stained glass doors were wide open, leading them out into the back garden. Instantly the smell of cooking meat, roasting vegetables, and spices overtook their senses, setting their stomachs to growling. None had gone without food, but after weeks upon a ship with only so many options that the ship's cook could concoct. The smell of real cooked food was overwhelming.

The back of the mansion was even more impressive than the front as they stepped out onto a large, forest-green marble veranda. Several guests mingled around tables arranged with fruits and sweetmeats, or kegs of ale, bottles of wine, and large glass bowls mixed with liquored fruit drinks. Others focused on chess games, cards, dice, or mud wrestling happening off to the sides of the building.

Several beautiful, nearly nude male and female servants mingled between guests, ensuring they had all they needed and, of course, to be pleasing to the eyes. It was all nearly too much to comprehend, like something from an erotic fairytale.

Beyond the veranda was open lush grass where a handful of guests lazed about, talking and drinking, enjoying the soft sweet smells around them and the grass between their toes.

Further back was a huge natural stone pool fed by a small cascading waterfall above a small cliff face. A handful of guests and servants swam naked within the pool, laughing, diving, flirting, and sexual exploration for all to witness.

"Your guests have arrived, your highness," the servant girl said with a curtsey.

Glacia turned from the two men she was talking with to her new guests. "Thank you, Gabriella." She caressed the girl's cheek. "Be a peach and tell Luca that they have arrived and to start bringing out the food. I am sure they are hungry."

The servant seemed to shudder pleasantly from her touch, her cheeks reddening a little. "Yes, your highness."

"Please, come, sit and enjoy." Glacia gestured to the large open table, already set with much food and drink. "I am sure the last few weeks have been very trying for you. I know all too well how long ship voyages make you yearn for the comforts only land can provide. I do my best to provide all that I can for my guests."

Dipping her head, Callisto took a seat closest to their hostess. "You are most kind and generous."

"I can be," Glacia smiled, but behind it was a world of intrigue and danger, "for friends and good acquaintances."

"I wonder what I will be categorized after tonight," Callisto asked, casually lifting a glass of red wine.

Glacia drank deeply of her wine. "I, too, wonder that very same question." Her smirk was dangerous. "Only time will tell, I suppose."

"I don't mean to cut in here in your subtle female pissing contest, Captain," Weaver cut in, not caring at all as he looked to their host, "but is that pool for anyone to swim in—and are the girls in there—available for enjoyment?"

"It would be a waste if others couldn't enjoy them as much as I enjoy them myself," Glacia replied, refilling her wine, "and I mean that about both your questions."

Weaver's excitement was almost uncontainable as he looked to Callisto. "Captain, with your permission, I would enjoy a swim before the food arrives."

"I, too, think a swim would refresh me nicely!" Reeves quickly jumped in, as eager as a youth.

"It would be rude not to indulge in our host's gracious liberties." Callisto nodded to them and watched them down their wine in single gulps before stripping down and diving into the clear waters. "Not going to join them?"

"Not today, Captain," Murphy replied, pulling his eyes away. "It would be foolish to leave you fully unguarded in an uncertain place." He glanced at Glacia. "No disrespect intended."

"None was taken," she replied. "Many feel that way, but I assure you, on my island, as long as my laws are followed, no harm comes to anyone. This is a safe haven for all those who I allow on it. Your dear captain here is as safe as she ever could be, and from the sounds of it. Safer than she has been in a while."

"Be that as it may, if it's all the same, I'd rather not stray too far," he replied, not backing down.

He was not sure what good he would be if something did happen. It had been requested their weapons stay within the carriage, and he had never been much of a fist fighter.

Glacia turned her attention back to the pool. "Whether the softest of poets to the hardest of pirates, boys will be boys when the pleasures of life are offered so freely," Glacia commented, watching the two pirates swim over to a group of naked women who were acolytes of hers.

"Interesting way to say 'influence' them." Picking up a handful of grapes, Callisto popped them into her mouth, enjoying the sweet juicy flavor. Still, to this day, grapes were her favorite treat.

"It is good to see I was correct about you with my first impression, and you aren't just some stupid wench who got lucky in killing a legend and taking command of one of the most dangerous ships this side of the world."

"I try not to disappoint, but I'd be lying if I said luck didn't play a small role in what transpired on the Poseidon, among other things."

Glacia let out a good laugh. "Oh, believe me, darling, I have no doubt a lot of what transpired was luck." She leaned closer. "But that intrigues me more than calculated ploys do. What were you before you found yourself a prisoner at sea?"

"What makes you think I was a prisoner?" Callisto questioned, though she instantly felt stupid for it. She was trying to have a battle of coyness and wits with a woman far more equipped than she was at this point.

The island's queen smirked. "You wouldn't have been on a pirate ship as anything else, dear girl."

"Before I found myself reluctantly on the Wind Spirit as a stowaway and sadly later a prisoner on the Poseidon, I was a professional thief—of sorts."

Her eyes raised in interest. "I would not have pegged you as a thief, for you don't have the look of one. Too clean, too put together, and certainly too beautiful for the shadows of the streets. Pray tell what it was you stole and how?"

"I seduced rich men with a sweet smile, sensual curves, and the whispers of what pleasures closed doors could bring. Some took hours, some took days, and a few even took weeks, but all fell for my charms sooner or later. Once alone, a little milk of the poppy into their wine, a little tussle in the sheets to get the blood flowing quicker." She poured herself another glass of wine. "Then I would take anything of value from them and slip out. It was a decent life."

"Clever girl." Glacia had a new sparkle in her eyes. "We women need to use what we have to carve our paths through the ranks of men if we wish to get above their booted feet." She folded her arms. "But there is something we should discuss before we get too formal with one another."

Callisto tipped her glass to her. "By all means, I wish to discuss much with you."

"Then I will make this plain, for beating around the bush has never been my strong point. I wish to purchase the Poseidon's Fury from you."

"You want to what?" Murphy nearly spat out his wine.

Glacia held up her hand. "Let us face it, Callisto SinClair, you are no pirate; neither of you are. Piracy is a hard, deadly game that I do not believe either of you has in you when it comes down to the brass of it."

"Now it is true you could indeed take it back to London,

and I am sure you would be well received to return it to the British Navy; they might even pay you a sizeable finder's fee, but I will give you a better price without a doubt. I will also set you up on one of my own ships to take you anywhere you wish to go and start your new life with enough gold, silver, and gems you will never want again. So you know that I am serious about my offer." With a wave of her hand, several prominent men carried three heaping chests full of wealth.

There were chests of gold and riches within her cabin upon the Poseidon's Fury, to be sure, but not like this. Callisto couldn't contain her composure at the sight of such wealth, and she gasped in delight. Her eyes danced with possibilities as her mind flirted with all she could do. She could be as rich as lords and kings with a simple answer.

The life she could live.

A glint of sunlight hit something in the garden pulling her attention away from the gold-laden chests. Before she realized it, she was up and moving toward it. Something deep within her called to her to investigate.

"Captain?" Murphy asked, standing and making to follow, but an up-raised hand from Glacia stopped him.

"Likely just needs a minute to digest," the hostess told him, taking a sip of her wine as she watched the other woman move behind the bushes to a remote and quiet area in the vast garden.

A sly smile crossed her red lips. "Interesting."

The pull to wherever she was headed was strong, almost forceful, as her feet moved with purpose through the perfectly manicured bushes and trees. Her breath caught in her throat as she stopped in front of the god of war in the flesh.

"Ares?" Callisto whispered, stepping closer, only to realize it was a life-sized statue and not really the god in the flesh.

Callisto marveled at the sheer reality of the stonework,

running her hand over the smooth flawlessness of its chest and shoulder, slowly walking a complete circle around it. It was not him, but she could feel his power there, pulsing from the stone figure like the intense heat from a flame.

She looked back the way she had come. How had she seen it from the table when she could not even see the table itself from here? No, he had called her here for some reason. Like he had called to her half a lifetime ago when she was a child.

She thought of the gold and the life it could buy her if she accepted Glacia's offer to sell the Poseidon's Fury.

"Ouch!" Callisto pulled her hand from the statue as if it had burned her. She inspected her hand, but no such marks marred her fingers. Curious, she touched the marble again. It was cool upon her skin.

"I am going to sell the ship," she said aloud and instantly snapped her hand back. The stone instantly felt like it was on fire. This time the experience left her hand with a raw soreness.

"So, you are there—" she whispered, admiring the statue closer.

"Who are you talking to?" Glacia asked from behind her.

Callisto turned to the woman. "Mostly myself, or at least, so I had thought."

Glacia smirked and strolled closer, admiring the statue herself with folded arms. "How did you know this was here?"

"I caught a glance of it from the table," Callisto lied and knew Glacia would know this. But she didn't know if she should tell this woman her secret, at least not yet.

"Hmm," Glacia mused, her eyes looking her guest up and down. "Come, let us get back to the party, least your friend gets the wrong impression of things and thinks your life is in danger."

They walked silently back to the elegant table, now laden with food fit for kings and queens.

"Is everything alright?" Murphy asked nervously.

"Yes," Callisto assured him and sat once more.

"My offer?" Glacia reminded her, waving her hand to the small fortune before them.

"It is a most generous one that anyone but a fool would refuse," Callisto's smile radiated confidence far beyond her understanding, "but I am that fool."

"Interesting. I didn't take you for one," Glacia replied, almost hurt by the refusal. "Care to tell me why?"

"Simple, I don't want to return to my 'normal' life. Fate led me onto the Wind Spirit, and fate led me into the clutches of pirates. It also made me a pirate captain of one of the most feared ships the seas have ever known. It would be rude of me to throw all that away for a few handfuls of gold and silver." She looked out across the sea in the distance. "When there are mountains of it out there just waiting for me to take!"

"Are you sure about this?" Glacia asked. "This is the final time I shall offer to buy this burden from you."

"Maybe you should think about this a moment longer," Murphy told her, his eyes large and round as he took in the chest of gold. "It might be a better path for you—for all of us."

"Everything in life worth doing starts off as a burden." Her eyes went from Murphy to Glacia. "I am prepared to do what I must and to Hades with anyone who believes differently!"

Her attention landed on Murphy. "My offer stands with you as well. If you don't have it in you to become a pirate, don't be back on my ship come morning. I will harbor no ill will."

"Captain, that isn't what I necessarily meant—" he stuttered, but an upheld hand stopped him.

"Deep down, you and I know it was," Callisto corrected him. "Leave us. Enjoy the sights, food, and drink. Think long and hard about where you wish to end up on the morrow. If I do not see you come morning, I wish you well in whatever ventures you choose."

Murphy looked about to say something and then stopped, stood, and wandered away from the table, his head hung low.

"I hope for your sake that he is back on your ship come morning," Glacia told her, watching the middle-aged man wander away like a dog that had just been kicked. "There is an honor in him that if he gives it to you fully, you'll never need to worry about his betrayal."

"I hope you are right, but I need no more half-hearted crew members if he is not."

"How well do you trust your 'new' crew?" the island's queen asked.

Sighing, Callisto put down her wine. "Sadly, not enough. I believe some of them are with me, others likely only until the right moment arrives, and a better portion will likely try to kill me before the week is over, and those are only those that will return to the ship tomorrow. Either way, there is a chance I won't have a large enough crew to sail off your island come the morrow anyways."

"Do you trust me?" Glacia asked, all coyness and games gone from her voice and features.

"A bold question for someone with your power whom I'm only just met. I want to, more than you could ever know." Callisto searched the woman's sea-blue eyes; they were stunning, and she found no hint of treachery.

"That is fair, and in your position, I would feel the same. Let me earn it then," Glacia stood. "Follow me. There is something you must see."

Callisto followed the strange and radiant woman, feeling slightly out of place and nervous. Her fingers felt for where her sword and pistols should have been. She almost laughed. If this woman wanted them dead, they would be dead, and two pistols and a poorly wielded sword would not change that. The weight of the boot knife reminded her that if things did turn poorly, she would do her best to take this marvelous woman with her to the other side.

"Why do you have a statue of Ares, the Greek God of War, in your garden?"

Glacia slowed her steps. "It is a strange wonder that you even knew who it was," she smirked, "but then again, I suspect you are full of strange wonders. In short, I have many statues and shrines of gods and goddesses of new and old across my island."

"You are a believer then?" Callisto asked, walking side by side with her host. "Of the old gods, that is."

"Only a fool wouldn't believe once they had been blessed by one of them, as I feel you know all too well." Glacia stopped outside a stairway that led down into an underground bunker. "Might be why I do this small favor for you now, even though it goes against my rules. Might your beauty have made my head spin, or maybe I just want to see another woman rule part of this world that I cannot."

She led the way down the stairs. "A mystery for us both to unravel as time goes on."

The thick wooden door opened, and the smell of torch smoke and fear spilled out as the two women left the world above and entered the subterranean layer. Smoke from the torches stung their eyes as they went down to where voices could be heard in a room beyond.

"Nothing happens on my island that I don't know about or hear about," Glacia explained, no hint of ego in her words, only a matter of fact.

"Normally, I don't interfere with things of this nature, but as I said above, something about you made me think I should

—even before this evening." She pushed up the iron door revealing five of Callisto's crew.

"What is the meaning of this?" Callisto asked, eyeing the five men, two of whom she had thought were on her side since the beginning, another who had sworn a blood oath with Weaver.

"Captain!" one of the men called desperately. "Help us!"

"These men were plotting with several other pirate captains seeking shelter in my bay. Plotting to kill you and overtake Poseidon's Fury. They all had different ideas and plans involving you dead and someone else sailing away in your new ship."

"Explain yourselves!" Callisto growled at the men chained to the wall before her.

"What's there to explain, bitch!" the pirate on the far right spat. "We'll not take orders from a fucking whore, nor will we be the laughingstock of the seas with a female captain! One that doesn't even know a thing about ships or the sea!"

Callisto glared bitterly at them. "And do you all feel this way?"

"The only way you survive this, bitch, is to relinquish the ship and stay put on this little island with your new friend for a while," the man in the middle barked, and all the heads nodded.

"Thank you for bringing this to my attention." Callisto's jaw was firm as she struggled with the reality of just how big a problem this was still going to be. "What happens to them now?"

Glacia spread her arms wide. "They are your crew, I'll leave that up to you."

"One of your rules is no one is allowed to kill on your island, is it not?"

"It is. But what happens aboard your ship to your crew in my harbor is none of my concern."

"Have them brought in chains to my ship come morning."

"As you wish," the island's queen replied, "let us get away from the trash and enjoy the evening to come."

"There's more of us!" one of them yelled as the two women walked away. "You didn't catch us all!"

The door to the underground cell closed, and Callisto took a deep breath, trying to clear her senses.

"My spies are on it. If others are found, they will also be brought to you in chains," Glacia assured her with a soft hand on her shoulder.

"Am I a fool to think I can do this?"

Glacia stepped closer, running her hand along the younger woman's jawline. "Most likely, yes, but nothing ventured, nothing gained."

"I need a fucking crew I can trust," Callisto told her, enjoying the softness of her hand. "If I am constantly worried about a knife in my back, I will never be able to become a true pirate captain."

Glacia looked her up and down. "I may be able to help you with that or, at the very least, point you in the right direction. But first, if you are going to captain one of the most feared ships this side of the world, you had best start looking the part."

"Hard to find fitted clothing for a woman on a ship full of men." Callisto looked at the clothes that barely fit her. All of them were sized for a man larger than herself that she had altered slightly to fit her. It wasn't until then that she realized she must have genuinely looked a fool.

Another smirk rolled across Glacia's full cherry lips. "Well, we aren't on a ship full of men right now. We are on an island ruled by a woman who has fashionable taste. I believe I have what you will need to look the part, come."

The gulls cried out their song to the morning sun, which was climbing from the ocean depths. Or, as she had learned years before, it was Helios, the sun god racing his flaming chariot across the sky, chasing his sister Selene, the goddess of the moon, from the sky.

The view from the third-floor balcony was breathtaking as Callisto stretched her smooth, naked body, welcoming the cool caress of the morning sea air upon her skin. This was a view and a marvelous place she could get used to.

She glanced over her shoulder to the two naked, still sleeping figures occupying her bed. A strong young man and woman who had eagerly been awaiting her arrival the previous night. Gifts from the hostess to ensure any sexual desire was taken care of.

A shiver of delight coursed through her at the flood of memories. A gift that had not gone to waste and one that she wished she could enjoy again this morning before she had to go back to reality. Alas, reality was knocking, and she knew the chariot that would take her back to her ship already awaited.

Looking over at the small pile of clothing on the floor, she grinned. The clothes that Glacia had found for her had fit perfectly, giving her a new look and air of authority. She quickly dressed but could not help but admire her new look in the mirror.

Callisto ran her fingers over the soft crushed velvet of the black blouse. It was low cut, showing off a seductive amount of cleavage, and trimmed with sky-blue silk. The long sleeves were trimmed with white silk and silver thread. At first,

Callisto had been unsure about the top, but Glacia had told her she was a beautiful woman and flaunting that only added to her position of power. Now that she was seeing it again this morning, she had to agree.

A dark, leather, armored corset clasped around her midsection, protecting her vitals without hindering her movements. It would turn all but the most powerful dagger thrusts.

Soft black leather breeches fit her snugly but provided her with easy and agile movement without hindrance. Leather boots capped with blood ruby studs fulfilled her new look. A dark grey leather belt lazily rested across her enticing hips, holstering her two ivory pistols, dagger, and another gift, a cutlass made for a woman.

She was transformed, hardly recognized herself, and now looked every inch the part of a true pirate captain.

"This is the first day of the rest of my life."

"You look stunning," a soft voice said from the bedside, "like a pirate queen."

Callisto stepped over to the blonde woman, only a handful of years younger than herself. Her name was Katrina, and she, too, was breathtaking. Callisto cupped her chin and lifted it to her lips, kissing her gently. "Thank you for that."

The girl smiled. "For last night? A pleasure I would gladly do again and again for you."

Callisto had to force back her growing arousal. "Thank you for that too." She stopped at the doorway.

"I hope we meet again." She left the room and made her way to the awaiting carriage.

The docks were full of life already. Sailors, merchants, pirates, and dockhands worked side by side in their shared goals of loading or unloading their ships for trade and profits. There was a simplicity to it here. Everyone knew they were safe from threats, safe to conduct business and rest, and so men acted as such. It was almost amusing to think that here they would drink, gamble and converse together as comrades, and later today, they might find each other on the open sea and try to kill one another.

Now she was part of that world.

The carriage pulled up to the large dock that moored her ship. The stolen cargo that had once occupied its hold was now removed—traded for provisions, mild ship repairs, and a decent size chest of silver.

"There you are!" Murphy said, worry evident in his tone. "I did not see you again the whole evening and thought something unruly might have happened."

"Your worry is touching, Murphy. But as you can see, I am fine."

Reeves whistled long and low, a goofy grin splitting across his face as he tried not to stare too hard at the display in front of him. "I would say more than fine, Captain. You have the look of someone in control and command."

"Yes, much has changed since last night. Today is a day for revolution and new beginnings."

"You'll be happy to know your prisoners are already on board," Murphy told her as they began their walk towards the ship. "Glacia thought it prudent to bring them before things got busy."

"I suspect she was right in that. Too many eyes on such a thing might look like she was breaking her own rules, which would only hurt her image." She took a long, deep breath of the fresh sea air. "How many did we lose?"

Murphy sighed. "More than I'd like to think about. Twenty-three haven't returned."

"I see." She bit her bottom lip. "Where does that put us?"

"Thirty-six have remained with you. We could sail for a few weeks if we had to, but it wouldn't be long before the men were worn out and exhausted. And think nothing of trying to pick a fight with another ship."

"I have a plan, but I need more men, fighters preferably, even if it's just temporarily for a week, maybe a day more," Callisto muttered bitterly. She wasn't surprised; few had stayed with her, but she had hoped for more.

"I might be able to help you with that, Captain," Reeves said, climbing up onto a stack of crates to overlook the dockyard. "Listen up, you bunch of fucking ugly cunts!" he called out over the morning drum of noises, drawing the attention of nearly two hundred individuals.

"The Poseidon's Fury needs a few fighting hands for a week. Equal take for anyone who joins! Once the job is done, we will drop your smelly arse back here with a pocket full of loot! We only need a score of bodies, and we be leaving with the tide, so hurry your arses if you have got a mind for it. If not, sod off under your mother's knee-stained skirt!"

"We could use more than a score," Callisto told him.

"True," Reeves admitted. "But if we have too many of these cunts aboard, they might think of causing some trouble, and we won't have the numbers to stop them. Better to have a few less but keep the upper hand."

Murphy nodded. "What he says is true."

"Besides, the fewer of them that make it back with us, the less you have to pay out." The tall pirate winked.

"Alright, I am not entirely sure what treasures will be on the ship we are after," Callisto admitted.

Reeves' laughter boomed out. "Captain, there is always treasure to be had. Hell, worst off, we take a ship, keep it as our treasure, and drag it back here." He waved his hand around. "Be at least a score or more of these thieving bastards that would buy another ship for the right price."

Already a handful of sailors, mercenaries, or pirates lined

up beside the ship. They all were hard-looking killers and cutthroats—just the type of men she needed.

"Reeves," she regarded him, "see to picking the worthiest of the bunch. Murphy, get the rest of the ship loaded and let us get ready to sail. We have a limited window to catch our prey, and if we miss it, then I don't know what we will do."

"If you don't mind me asking, who are we after, Captain?" Murphy asked.

Callisto stepped onto the boarding plank. "We are going to go get us some new crew members. One's that I know we will be able to trust." Her face turned grim. "But first, I must deal with those I cannot."

Her crew was working here and there. All regarded her with new eyes as she passed. Everyone single one she passed nodded and called her by her new title, and their tones were more earnest than before.

She could see in their eyes the new attire was making an impression. But she was confident the men still aboard with her were as trustworthy as she could expect. They had all opportunity to leave or try and betray her, and they had chosen to stay. She found Weaver barking orders at someone and went to him. Hopefully, after this, the men here would be hers without a doubt.

"Weaver," she called to him.

The big, lean man turned around with his crooked smile. "Captain, good to see you this morning." He took her new look in approvingly. "And looking mighty fine indeed. A new look fit for the power you now hold."

"Figured if I expected others to accept me, I had best look the part."

"A wise choice."

"Grab a few men and bring up our honored 'guests.'" Her tone was stern.

"As you wish, Captain."

Callisto gripped the deck and breathed the fresh sea air, steadying her nerves. She needed this to work, needed to be in complete control, focused, and unrelenting. She was a pirate captain now and needed to embrace that role entirely. She could not half-ass this endeavor. Much like her life beforehand, she would need to be calculated and in control.

The five prisoners were hauled up on deck in chains and gagged just as the hired fighters were brought aboard. A strange mixture of emotion and anticipation flooded the ship as the prisoners lined up along the railing facing the port for those below to see.

"You can do this," she whispered to herself.

Taking one more deep breath, she stood confident. Now was her time. This was her ship, her crew, and it was time she made damn sure everyone fucking knew it.

Turning, she pulled one of her pistols and fired it in the air, immediately drawing every eye from the port below to her. "Good, now that I have your attention!" she bellowed out to all those who could hear her—those who could not were moving closer.

"I am sure you've all heard by now that the Poseidon's Fury is under new management! I am sure you've heard a woman now claims to be its captain." She let her stern gaze linger on the growing crowd below. "That is true, for you are now looking at her! I am Callisto SinClair, Pirate Captain of the Poseidon's Fury."

She pointed down at the five prisoners lining the railing. "These men were once crew members to the former and now very much dead captain. Like everyone here, I gave them a choice. They decided that trying to kill me was a better choice, and they chose wrong!" she growled, letting her words hang in the air.

Without another word, she drew her sword, plunged it into each man's chest, and kicked them over the rails into the water below. Gasps and murmurs filled the air around her, both aboard her ship and on the dock.

"Let's this be a warning and a lesson," she called out, her tone dark and ruthless. "I will not be trifled with! And to any who think to harm me, my crew, or my ship, you'll have to swim through an ocean of blood to do it!"

Her crew's sudden cheer rang out, and those on the docks seemed transfixed by her display. She could see many talking or whispering. Glacia had been right, and this would be discussed for a while now. This act would spread, and respect would be given because of it. Though, in truth, she doubted that would stop half the other pirate captains from trying to kill her once she was at sea, she would deal with that once it came. Right now, she had a goal to achieve.

Callisto turned to the new dozen hired hands and eyed them coolly. "Welcome aboard my ship. Do as you're told and fight when the time comes, and you will be rewarded well when this is done."

She let her stern gaze hold theirs for a long moment. "If you do not listen or I even hear a murmur of betrayal, I will slit your bellies open and strangle you with your own entrails! After, I will pluck out your eyes and burn your ears shut so you will wander the underworld blind and deaf for eternity, never to know peace!" She slid her cutlass back into its sheath. "Do I make myself clear?"

Every one of the men shouted out. "Aye!"

Many of their expressions changed, some with mild respect, others with a slight fear creeping across their features.

"Good! Now get to work!" She turned her attention to Reeves. "Reeves set course for the southeast with all haste!"

"Aye, aye, Captain!" He climbed the steps to the wheel.

The northern wind favored them, speeding the ship at an impressive pace of nearly five knots. If they raised the other sail, they could achieve closer to six, but the other ships could not keep up. As much as Stephan would have enjoyed seeing just how fast he could get the Paradise, they had a job to do.

The Paradise easily cut through the small waves, spraying a fine salty mist that helped keep the ship deck cooler against the rising heat of the early summer sun.

A mile off portside was the Sea Lion, off the starboard side was the Sea Glory, and making up the stern was The Highlander. All four ships sailed in perfect formation. They were all veteran crews with only a handful of greenhorns totaled among them. They had been under the command of one of the finest naval leaders and had seen nearly a hundred sea battles between them. A finer naval party there was not.

Commodore Stephan Belfield took a deep breath of the morning air while standing on the main deck. It was refreshing and invigorating, quickly clearing his mind to the task of the day before him. He was a commodore. He still could not believe it.

He smiled at the memory of when he had told his wife, Mary, how her eyes had lit up with excitement, knowing they finally had everything they had dreamed for. The start of a new family and a regal and proud profession that paid handsomely.

With the elevation of their family name, no longer would the surname Belfield be considered lower class. Now it would ring proudly off tongues and be remembered for greatness. His father would have been proud of him. This he knew for sure.

Mary had only been crestfallen for a moment when he told her he had to sail in three days and would likely be gone a handful of months. He knew she had just hoped he would have had more time to spend with his new family. But she had quickly wiped away the tears, knowing she was a sailor's wife, and this was nothing new. Nearly half of their eight years together had been spent apart.

He had left her in good care. She would want for nothing now. Her mother and sister were minutes away, and he hired the help of a maid to see to anything that needed doing around the house while he was away.

Stephan smiled again. Yes, his wife was in good hands, and so was their son, and he was out there doing what he loved: sailing the sea and hunting down pirates. His life had been blessed, of that, he had no doubt. God was smiling down on him for his service in ridding the world of the vileness that preyed on the weak and innocent.

His hand went to the silver cross around his neck, a gift from his wife when they married. He carried it with him wherever he went. It gave him hope and reminded him of home.

They had been at sea for nearly a fortnight and had already chased down one small pirate ship. There had been no boarding; the ship had been old, aged poorly due to lack of maintenance, and of no value. The pirates had been flying unknown colors. They had sunk the vessel in a single sweep of the cannons of all four ships.

Stephan had refused to risk a single life in his command on such an unimportant catch. His first mate James Featherstone had questioned such actions, claiming the ship might have treasures on board. Gold doubloons, silver, gems, silk, and many other things pirates plundered from the innocent merchant ships.

Naval laws stated a crew was entitled to twenty percent value of plunder recovered from pirates. It added much incentive to hunt them down. But as Stephan had noted, the ship had been sailing away from known ports and sat high within the water. It had been fresh on the waters, looking, hunting, and empty of anything of value.

The crew seemed more than willing to put the cannons to target practice. Out of the eighteen cannons to fire, only three missed their target. But that was enough to sink the rotting ship and the miscreants aboard it.

"Commodore!" Tomas Hill called down from the crow's nest.

"Report?" Belfield called back.

"Wreckage off to starboard side!"

"How far?"

Tomas looked through his eyeglass again. "Two nautical miles."

Stephan nodded. "Carpenter!"

"Yes, Commodore!" a tall, wiry man with a growing bald spot called up from below.

"Signal the other ships, perimeter sweep, starboard one nautical mile from the wreckage. We are checking for survivors and any indication of what ship it might have been."

"Aye, aye, sir." Carpenter moved off to his station next to the communication pole to relay the order to the other ships through a colored flag system.

A skilled Relay Messenger earned a more than fair wage aboard a naval ship. When the ships were further apart, he used a mixture of ingredients to yield colored smoke to signal orders over longer distances. It was a skill set that took years to master.

"You think this is leftovers from the pirates we sunk the other day?" Jacob Wheeler, the Paradise's helmsman, asked as he moved the ship closer.

"I highly doubt it," Belfield replied, leaning over the deck railing as they began to pass by debris.

"They traveled in this direction and wouldn't have been around this area yet. Plus, they weren't loaded with anything. By the looks of it, this was a fair size merchant ship. It would have been well stocked with goods."

Jacob shrugged. "Could it have been the ship was attacked but was on a return journey home empty? Pirates were angry and sunk it?"

Already Stephan was shaking his head. "No, if it had been empty, the pirates would have taken the survivors as slaves and towed the ship back to a port to sell to the highest bidder or use for themselves, given their own ship's state."

"Means there's another pirate out here," James Featherstone reasoned eagerly.

He was twenty-five years old; his family was noble, wealthy, powerful, and high-ranking in London society. His father and grandfather had both been generals in the army. But James had always dreamed of sailing the sea.

James remembered the exact moment his mind had been made up. He had been eleven, and his family had ridden out on horses across his family's vast estate which edged the coastline. That is where he had witnessed a spectacle he would never forget.

A pirate ship and a lone navy ship locked in battle only a mile from the shoreline. He could still hear the deafening roar as banks of cannons fired, ripping through both ships and sending a spray of smoke and debris high in the air. The volleys of arrows that cut through the air, the loud booms of flintlock pistols or blunderbuss rifles. The battle cries and the screams as men met their deaths.

It had been a glorious battle to witness.

Finally, after an impossible time for two ships to engage one another without a winner, the naval ship launched grappling hooks, locking the pirate ship close and boarded. From there, it was only a matter of minutes before the pirates were executed and thrown overboard, and their ship torched and left at the bottom of the sea.

From that moment, James knew he wanted to do that. He wanted to sail and hunt pirates. To be in the middle of such action where life dangled in the balance, and if you aren't the best, you are a corpse.

It had taken more than a few years to convince his father that the navy was where he wanted to go. It was a family tradition to become soldiers and lead men in battle.

He had promised his father he would lead ships into battle against their country's enemies and pirates alike. He would rise through the ranks quickly with their family's powerful influence, captain a ship of his own, and one day rank Commodore. With a fleet of ships following his command.

With the right words in the right ears and donations made to the right purses, James quickly rose through the ranks, years faster than any others could have dreamed of.

James had no illusion that his new ranking as the first mate of the Paradise hadn't been bought and paid for. But he also knew he had worked endlessly to ensure he did know what he was doing. He listened and learned quickly and followed orders to the letter. He hoped that after this adventure, he would rise rank again and hopefully captain one of the ships in the Paradise's fleet or even another fleet.

He looked over at Commodore Belfield. He was a man of common birthright who had toiled and proven himself relentlessly through the years to achieve the impossible rank he now held. At first, James had been envious, jealous, and even angered by it. But serving under the man now, he felt honored, inspired even. Stephan Belfield was a leader, sharp of wit, smart to action, and calm of mind. A perfect mentor and one, if he pleased well enough, would see him in a captain's hat in short order.

"This isn't a new wreckage," Jack O'Bryan, a weathered crew member, said, poking at the rubble with a long pole, "at least not in the last week, maybe longer."

Belfield moved down to the lower deck to look over. "What makes you say that?"

"Debris is too far spread for one thing." Jack pointed to the colored flags being raised from the other ships, indicating they were still finding debris far and wide.

"For another, look at how waterlogged everything is." He pointed to several larger pieces floating near them. "They don't ride high in the water, but low and bloated, meaning they have been soaking for many days. Few more, and they will sink to the bottom of the sea."

Stephan listened intently to everything the man said, always eager to learn something new. "Good eye. I believe you are correct in your assessment. Further proof is the burned timbers and lack of that lingering odor of burnt wood in the air."

"Any idea of what ship it might have been?" James Featherstone asked, his eyes scanning the horizon, praying to see a pirate ship in the distance. But if what they said was true, the pirates would be long gone.

"Doubt we will ever know," Commodore Belfield replied, turning and climbing the steps back to the main deck. "That is unless we find the pirates that did this and ask them nicely." He chuckled.

"Where to, Commodore?" Jacob asked, his hand resting keenly upon the wheel, the crew waiting for new orders before they set to task repositioning the sails and rigging.

Stephan Belfield closed his eyes, taking a deep, controlled

breath. In truth, he had no idea which direction the pirates who had done this might have gone. They could be anywhere by now if it had been a fortnight ago. But one thing he had that he always trusted was his instinct, and thus far, it had seldom led him astray. It was like some innate gift he had been born with, a gift from God he'd like to think. A gift he had been granted for this very purpose.

"Commodore?" Jacob asked again, eager to be away from here.

"Set a heading due west," Stephan replied, finally opening his eyes.

"Permission to speak freely, Commodore?" Jacob Wheeler asked before barking orders to the waiting men.

"Granted."

"A fortnight west is rumored to be a pirate-friendly island called Glacia's Palace," the helmsman informed. "The likes of us might not be too welcome around those waters."

"I have heard rumors of such a place," Belfield replied, still staring west.

"Aye, not a place the like of us should be sailing near if you ask me," the helmsman said.

"If it is a haven for any ship, then we shouldn't have an issue sailing to the island unharmed." Belfield looked over at his helmsman firmly.

"It's not the sailing to the island where the problems will occur, Commodore." The helmsman shivered while looking nervous. "It's the leaving the island alive that I fear will be the problem."

"Your concerns are noted." Stephan nodded. "Now set the course."

"Due west, at your command," Roberts replied, his tone wary and fearful. "You heard the Commodore! Due west, you slackers!"

"A pirate island, you say?" James asked, standing next to Stephan. "How exciting. Do you think the rumors are true?"

"Yes, I do," Stephan replied with a glance at the younger man.

Here was a man who was the exact opposite. Where he was of low birth and had worked bitterly hard to achieve what he had now, James Featherstone had not. Born within a wealthy, high-ranking family, the man had easily achieved what would have taken others thrice as long with nothing more than placing money in the right hands.

Even now, his new position as a lieutenant on the Paradise had been paid for. Not that James wasn't a capable sailor and had so far shown he would likely do well as a lieutenant, but he had not earned the position, leaving a bitter taste in Stephan's mouth.

When news of the transfer had come to him the day before they had set sail, Stephan had wanted to protest. But he knew better than to make waves in his new position of power. He would judge James Featherstone fairly on his skills upon this ship and not on his birthright and give his report when they returned from there. This sort of thing happened and often in the world of high-ranking families.

James bit the bottom of his lip in excitement. "Do you think we will have to fight our way in or out?"

"I am hoping neither will be the case."

"What are you hoping to find there?"

"With any luck, we will find Blackmane and the Poseidon's Fury. They hunt these waters often enough."

"It is a big sea to get that lucky," James reminded him.

Stephan tried to roll his eyes away from the young man's view. "Indeed."

"Then why are we headed in that direction? Why take such a risk when the likelihood of finding that target is so slim?"

"Because if nothing else, it will be good to remind them we are out here hunting, just as they are," Stephan stated, simple as that. "Now, gather a few men and ensure the cargo holds are well strapped down. I smell something in the weather."

James looked as if he was about to protest but quickly shut his mouth and nodded. "Yes. Commodore."

Stephan stared straight ahead, a slightly unnerved feeling tingling in his gut. It was an unusual sensation and almost made him second-guess himself. Should they be sailing so close to such a place? Would this put him and his men in unnecessary danger? The idea was absurd and almost made him laugh out loud. Every moment at sea could be dangerous, from storms to sickness, to pirates, and even the will of God.

Something had told him to sail in this direction, and he would not start second-guessing himself now.

Callisto parried a thrust aimed at her heart and nimbly sidestepped the ensuing dagger poised for her midsection. With a quick twist of her wrist, she launched her own attack, slashing the new cutlass at her attacker, forcing him to jump back as the tip just missed the boiled leather chest guard. She kept the pursuit with a backhand slash and a dagger lunge, slowly gaining back the ground she had lost only moments ago.

Her confidence grew bolder as she swept away another quick attack and responded with another combination of her own. She could win this. Movement from the corner of her eye alerted her to a new threat from the helm. She spun away to block a hastily downward chop from Reeves' longer blade.

"What the fuck!" Callisto growled under the weight of his

attack as he continued to bear down on her with his superior strength.

"Time to die," he grinned at her, "Captain."

Before she had time to think, she felt cold steel on her neck from her first opponent.

"Once more, you find yourself dead, Captain," Murphy said from behind her, removing his blade and sheathing it.

Callisto stepped back, slamming her blade home at her hip. "Only because Reeves thought it would be a good time to interrupt."

"Yes, he did," Murphy reached for the water jugs waiting by the helm on a small table, pouring two tin cups full, "but he did what I asked him to do earlier."

"Why? I was finally doing well."

"A fight is seldom ever one-on-one on a ship or land, for that matter. A fatal blow can strike at any time from any direction. You may be a better swordsman against the enemy in front of you, but that does not mean another blade will not come for you before you can finish them. You must be alert to everything around you and ready to react."

"Lovely, so I need to have eyes in the back of my head now." She grabbed the offered cup and drank.

"In a manner of speaking, yes." Murphy shrugged.

"How does one manage to stay alive in a battle, then? I was barely holding my own against you, and now there is another I must contend with suddenly," she asked, trying to keep the bitterness from her tone.

"Luck does play a role at times," Murphy admitted. "But given your lack of battle experience, there was another course of action you could have taken which could have given you a fighting chance."

"And what was that?"

"Retreat."

She scoffed.

Murphy spread his arms wide. "Truly. Had you retreated when you saw Reeves' attack coming, it would have put more distance between us, giving you more time to evaluate the new situation you were faced against."

"I still would have had two enemies to fight, and now both would be coming at me at once," Callisto countered.

Murphy placed his cup down. He held up his hand to stop her from a retort she was about to launch at him. "But it would have gotten you out of the immediate danger of death, even if only for a few more seconds."

"In a fight, a few more seconds can mean the difference between seeing tomorrow or not. Anything can happen. Another crew member could have seen your plight and come to aid you. The ship could shift suddenly, causing your enemies to become off balance giving you a perfect opportunity to even the odds. A stray arrow, bullet, or a hundred other things could happen in those few seconds to turn the fight back in your favor. Yes, these things may appear slim, but slim odds are better than the death you would have just faced."

Reeves turned back to them. "Or giving yourself the space, you might have found your enemies do not fight well together and hinder each other more than help."

"Fine, you're right." She wandered over to the rail and stared out at sea.

"Do not feel defeated," Murphy said, standing beside her. "You are doing far better than I expected you ever would. You have a natural balance and reflexes that would have taken others years to hone."

He pointed at the new blade at her side. "Having a sword more to your size has proven where much of the trouble was coming from. I suspect another few months, and you will be able to hold your own against half the men aboard this ship."

"Stop trying to humor me," Callisto growled, still bitter about the test. "Flattery is for the bedroom, not swordplay."

They were right, and she knew it. She knew she should have retreated the moment she saw the attack. But she had felt powerful, what she imagined a real pirate captain felt when in a fight.

She had felt immortal.

"I am being honest," he replied, almost as if the comment had hurt him. "I would never give someone falsehoods about such a thing as their readiness for battle."

"I know." Callisto sighed again, releasing her bitterness. "I need to be better; I need to be faster, stronger, fiercer, and awed by all that see me!"

"Captain, I can assure you, you are awed by most of this crew already in your new attire." Reeves winked back at her from his post.

"Gods, man!" Murphy grumbled. "Some bloody respect. She is our captain, for Christ's sake!"

"At ease, Murphy." Callisto laughed. "He is right. My looks will either be helpful or a hindrance. I have long grown used to that. But I need more training, and by others. If I just practice with you, I won't learn how others fight, styles, and movements."

"It wouldn't hurt for some variety in your practice," Murphy agreed.

"We can see to that," Reeves agreed. "Start with those we trust fully, then work your way through the crew. See where you stand among them. Show them you mean business and mean to lead them as fiercely as they require a captain too."

"Ship ho! Two points off the starboard side!" Rusty Juan, a small, wiry man with unmatched eyesight, called down from the crow's nest. "Two masts—flying the Spanish flag. One bank of oars—twelve a side!"

Murphy whispered something to Callisto, and she strolled up to the rail of the main deck and called out., "How close?"

Rusty Juan looked through his eyeglass again briefly. "Three miles, a stone throws more maybe, North by northeast."

"That's our target, gentlemen!" Callisto called. "You ready for a fight?"

The crew showed their eagerness with a deafening battle cheer and raised their swords to the sky.

"Reeves, set a course to rake her starboard side," Callisto commanded, feeling the excitement building in her once more. "Hoist the black flag!"

"Shall I have the cannons readied, Captain?" Murphy asked.

"No. I want to take the ship in as close to one piece as possible. The information I was given said they didn't have cannons aboard, just fighting men and slaves. We will make a pass and litter them with fire arrows to cripple their sails and rake across their oars, leaving them dead in the water for us to plunder!" Callisto called out.

It had already been planned with the help of Reeves and Murphy, but she needed the crew to believe it was from her. Most of the crew realized she knew very little about sailing a ship and even less about being a pirate. But she had to win them over, make them forget she wasn't raised at sea as they had been.

"AND HEAR ME NOW!" Callisto barked out over the noise of the crew. "The slaves aboard that ship are our prize! Do not kill them! If they surrender, we will honor it! Do I make myself clear?"

"AYE, CAPTAIN!"

"Good. Weaver, go below and retrieve a dozen bows. I want the best four sharpshooters up the masts with a dozen arrows.

The others will only need four apiece. Someone light that goddamn brazier already," she barked out. "We can't shoot fire arrows if we ain't got any fire, you fucking halfwits!"

"Well done," Reeves said from behind her. "You certainly are picking up the language quickly."

"I have good teachers."

"You sure you want me to stay aboard?" he asked.

"I'm told you are the best helmsmen on this ship. I wouldn't want anyone else for my first battle."

Reeves grinned. "Ya, but I'm the one that told you that."

"Are you telling me you lied?"

"Might be that I overembellished a bit." He shrugged. "You know, pirate and all."

Callisto laughed. "Well, until you prove your embellishment wrong, you're staying where you are."

"If we can take this ship as easily as you hope, it'll increase your chances of winning these pricks over," he replied.

"That's not the only way to win them over," Callisto smirked, taking the stairs down to the main deck to her cabin.

Once inside, a cold sweat dampened her body almost instantly. Excitement and fear raged a dangerous battle within her—each warring with the good counsel she had been given the day before.

Murphy and Reeves had counseled that she stay aboard the ship until the fighting was over. That way, she would remain out of danger from the enemy and possibly her own crew, who might still think of putting an end to her. The crew would not hold it against her, at least not yet. Neither thought she was ready for battle.

It was good advice, and she was sure they were correct, and she had accepted the idea, not wanting to end up dead in her first real fight. But Weaver had come to her that night in secret. He knew many of the men well. It had been his advice that she should lead the attack over. If the crew saw her standing in the front lines and one of the first over the rails, it would gain her much respect in their eyes.

He had assured her he would fight beside her with two others he trusted. They would keep her safe at all costs. He had given his word—the word of a pirate no less, but she believed him—needed to believe him.

At first, she had wanted to say no, but what he had said had been truth. If these men were ever to respect her, she had to prove she was just as willing to bleed and die as she expected them to be.

Covertly, she had agreed with Weaver, told him she would be there, but not to tell the others. They still expected her to remain safely aboard the Poseidon's Fury when the boarding happened. She could not wait by and let others risk their lives if she would not do likewise.

Her stunt on the docks of Glacia's Palace had granted her only a mere portion of the reverence she truly needed over these fucking brutes. She needed them to adore and love her, but most of all, she needed them to fear what she was willing to do.

Pouring herself a mug of red wine, she leaned against her large cabin room desk and drank deeply to steady her growing unease. Face down men who had spent decades battling at sea, killing, raping, murdering their way through life. Within an hour, she would be testing all Murphy had taught her so far and more.

Fear gripped her relentlessly, and her breathing started to become erratic. What had she gotten herself into? Who did she think she was? Why did she ever think she could do this? Why hadn't she just accepted Glacia's offer to sell this damned ship for a fortune!

"Destiny."

Callisto looked up and into the large mirror across from her. A dark, powerful, shadowy figure illuminated within. She knew who it was—who it always was.

"Destiny—" she whispered back.

"*Have I chosen wrong?*" the god of war asked bitterly. "*Are you as worthless as all the others?*"

"No!" She pushed herself from the desk, standing proudly.

"*Prove it to me! Prove that I have not made a mistake leading you to the path of greatness! Prove to me you can be everything I have offered you! Everything I have given you!*" the voice boomed angrily. "*The world is yours for the taking. All you must do is stop being a fucking coward and take it!*"

"I am no fucking coward!" she screamed, throwing the mug across the room. Hearing that word was worse than a blow to the face.

The figure started to dissipate from the mirror. "*Then prove it with blood or your life!*"

Rage and shame flooded through her. How could she be so pathetic, so weak! She was fucking chosen by a god! And here she was, cowering in her cabin, fighting her fear of what she needed to do. How could she ever expect to be a pirate captain if she were afraid of what captains needed to do?

She steeled her gaze in the mirror. "You want blood? I'll give you fucking blood!"

Callisto grabbed the red wine from her desk and drank deeply from the bottle. It was no longer nerves she was trying to calm. No, now she was fueling a violent tidal wave threatening to overwhelm her.

If she were to embrace what the god of war had given her, she had to embrace it fully, which meant risking her life in battle. Ares has mocked her and yet spoken the bitter truth.

Today she would earn her place as captain of this ship or die in the trying. Either way, she would earn these pricks' respect! Straightening herself up, she stood tall, glaring at the reflection in the mirror before her.

Callisto checked her pistols, ensuring they were primed and within easy reach, and straightened her tricorn hat, ensuring the skull and crossbones were visible.

She gripped the door handle to her cabin, her hand deathly calm as she walked out onto the main deck and to the men of *her* crew.

"Report!" she called out as her eyes adjusted to the brightness of the afternoon sun.

"The winds favor us today, Captain. We are coming up on her starboard side!" Reeves called down to her. "Won't be long now until we can see the whites of their eyes!"

She straightened defiantly. So be it, then. The god of war wanted her to fight. Then she would fucking fight! It wouldn't be long now until the air was filled with the roars of battle and the screams of dying men. Her own would be among them.

"Good," she replied, looking to the men checking swords, axes, knives, and other weapons they would take over the rails with them.

"Who are we?" she cried out to the gathering men. They looked at her oddly, unsure of how to answer.

"I said who the fuck are we?"

"Pirates!" several called out.

"We are fucking pirates!" Callisto confirmed, adding strength to her words as she walked among them. "But we are so much more than pirates! We are warriors! We are killers! We are the things nightmares are made of! We take what we want and give nothing back!"

Every man on deck was gathering around.

"This sea," she pointed out into the great blue surrounding them, "this sea is OURS!"

The crew roared their eager excitement.

"And they are trespassing!" Callisto pointed to the slave ship they were closing in on.

The ship sprang alive with new energy as pirates readied themselves for battle, eager to spill blood.

"That was a hell of a speech," Murphy said, coming up behind her as he checked that his gear was in order. "We should get you up top where you'll be safe."

Callisto had dreaded this part but knew it would come. "That isn't where I am needed this day."

She drew her cutlass as Weaver, Alonso, and two others she had not learned their names yet strolled up beside her, as Weaver had called it, a protective guard to see her through this alive.

Murphy looked as if he were about to protest but stopped, knowing it would not make a difference and knowing they did not have the time to argue anyway; they were seconds away from clashing with the other ship.

"Fight well, Captain, and I better see you when this is done."

Callisto thanked him with her eyes and stalked off to the rail, pushing her way through until she was front and center. The men around her were whispering and muttering their confusion at seeing her standing beside them, armed for the fight. But quickly, those whispers became grunts and nods of approval.

"The fiery lass that took a pirate ship will fight with us?" a gruesomely scarred man said beside her.

"I fight with my crew," Callisto replied coolly as she stared ahead, remembering the man's name was Slimy Fife.

"As it should be—Captain." Slimy Fife nodded.

The distance between ships lessened, heartbeat after heartbeat. Two-hundred yards—a hundred and fifty—a hundred—

"Enemy arrows comin' in!" Rusty Juan called down from the crow's nest.

The Poseidon's crew ducked below the rail, but most of the arrows fell short of their mark, and only a few hit the bottom side of the ship.

Another two volleys came, and only half a dozen arrows found the deck. One man was killed, another with a shoulder wound that he hardly noticed.

"OUR TURN!" Callisto yelled.

The command was given, arrows were lit, bow strings were pulled taut—eighty yards—sixty—a dozen burning arrows streaked across the gap between ships, then another volley followed. Several missed their mark and disappeared in the sea's rolling waves, others riddled the deck or found raised shields, but a handful found their target, and that was enough. The arrows were never about killing men. Within seconds the slave ship slowed, losing its wind as its sails burned up.

"Doesn't look like too many fighting men on deck." Weaver rolled his shoulders and flexed his fingers around the haft of his twin axes. "Should be an easy fight. And no matter how hard they try to row, they'll never escape us now."

Callisto grimaced. She certainly hoped so.

Weaver gripped her shoulder. "I'll keep you alive, Captain, just don't stray too far from my side."

Poseidon's Fury cut past the windless ship. Several more arrows cut across the water, and a few screams could be heard. The Poseidon's Fury swung around sharply to take its prize on its starboard side.

The minutes passed like hours as Callisto's heart pounded painfully in her chest. The anticipation of the fight made her dizzy, turning her stomach into knots, but she held firm, kept her face stern, and her eyes on the enemy ship. She could feel the eyes of her crew on her. They were judging her, scanning her for weakness, for fault. Waiting to see her turn and flee so they could know they had judged her correctly.

She refused to give it to them.

"Grappling hooks at the ready!" she screamed out as they once again cut the distance. She could see the men on the other ship standing at the ready, with swords and axes gripped tightly, determination set across their faces. This was life or death.

It was almost time.

"Fight like the devils you are!" Callisto raised her blade high.

Barbed hooks soared across the gap and clattered across the deck. The hemp ropes were pulled fast and hard to set them into the enemy ship. Some fell away, not finding a hold, others were quickly thrown overboard by the Spanish crew. But most bit into solid wood and held as the ships were slowly brought together. But those that held were in danger of being cut.

"Sharpshooters!" Callisto cried at the top of her lungs.

Instantly the four men she had assigned to the main staff let loose. Iron-tipped arrows cut down any brave enough to try and cut the lines. As good as they were, a handful of lines were still severed, but it was too late. The ships were joined.

All the sounds around her faded like she was in a bubble as the ships closed together. Callisto could see the grim-faced slavers and mercenaries aboard the Phantom Chaser cursing and jeering wildly. Very few of them looked eager for this fight.

Glacia had explained to her that the ship was under crewed and most of their provisions had spoiled on their long journey. They were hungry, tired, and weak, and their morale was defeated. They had hoped to sell slaves at Glacia's Palace so they could provision themselves again, but she had refused them.

Callisto had asked her why *"I do not support that vile trade. I would rather see them starve to death at sea,"* had been the reply.

Several of the crew had abandoned the Phantom Chaser to find places among other ships on the island. It was how she had gathered the information.

It was ripe for the plucking.

"You ready for this, Captain?" Weaver yelled to her over the jeers of both crews.

"I was born ready!" Callisto called back as the gap was near closed.

"Rifles!" she cried out, and nine men from the Wind Spirit stepped through the pirates and fired into the waiting enemy without mercy. Several went down in a spray of blood. At this distance, it would have been impossible to miss.

"With me!" Callisto bellowed, leaping over the rail, one of her polished ivory pistols firing into the man's face directly in front of her, sending him flying back into his comrades.

She landed where her first victim had been a heartbeat before. Instantly, she found herself fighting for her life, parrying a thrust for her throat. She tried to counter with an attack of her own, but already another blade slashed down at her from her side. She swept the attack wide with surprising reflexes and kicked up, catching the man in the groin. His guard fell, and her blade plunged into his chest.

Before she could pull her blade free, another enemy was upon her with a battle roar, swinging his axe for her head, but before his blade could strike her, an arrow took him in the neck, and he pitched back.

Another man fell over the side as Weaver cleaved his skull with his hatchet. He grinned at her like a foolish boy. "Fun, isn't it?"

Callisto wasted no time and pushed forward, stabbing and slashing wildly at any she did not recognize. Men fell from her blade or were distracted long enough to fall from another as she forced her way forward. Weaver and his hand-picked group fought on either side of her keeping the enemy from flanking her.

Soon she was clear of the fighting and was thankful for the moment to catch her breath. But from the corner of her eyes, she saw trouble as the captain of the ship and a handful of others were hauling the slaves onto the deck.

"Defend the ship and win your freedom!" the captain screamed in terror, seeing his men being cut down quickly.

Already a dozen slaves were on deck, looking around confused, scared, but eager for the promise of freedom. She needed to act, and now! Glacia had told her the ship held nearly fifty slaves. If they all joined in the battle, her crew would be overtaken.

Scooping up a fallen blade, she sprinted towards the Phantom Chaser's captain, leaving the fighting behind her, but not before hamstringing an enemy who was engaged with Slimy Fife. The battle would be theirs if she could quell the slaves from joining before it was too late.

"Stop her! Stop them! Your freedom, I swear it!" he wailed.

Callisto did not want to kill any of them if it could be avoided. It would be hard to win them over as a new crew if she started butchering them. But there were too many of them coming at her. There would be no way to avoid bloodshed, and even then, they would overwhelm her.

She slammed a sword into the deck and pulled her silver flintlock pistol. "STOP!" She fired into the air.

The slaves slowed their advance, confused. Even the fighting behind her slowed to a stop as they looked back at what was happening.

Callisto stepped back from the blade. "Surrender now, and

our hands will spill no more blood!" she called out for all to hear.

"Don't listen to her, you fools!" the captain cried out. "They will kill us all and enslave you again!"

A large burly, dark-skinned man snatched up the blade as he ran forward and swung an overhead chop for Callisto. It was clumsy and ill-planned but held a raw power behind it. She parried it, though she was sure her wrist had almost broken in doing so. She kicked out, hitting her attacker's knee, causing him to buckle to the deck. Her blade rested on his neck.

"I am a pirate, not a slaver." She scanned the crowd. "What is your name?"

He stared up at her with hard, determined, dark eyes. "Afia."

She lowered her blade from his neck. "As of this moment, you are free."

"She lies!" the Phantom's captain screamed. "They are pirates! They lie, steal, cheat, and kill! She is deceiving you all!"

Callisto pushed past the emancipated, filth-stained men to stand before the captain. "I am all those things and more, but I'm not the one who had these men chained to a ship as cargo." She pressed her cutlass to his chest.

"Mercy!" he begged, dropping to his knees. "You swore no more bloodshed if we surrendered!"

Callisto lowered her sword again. "Aye, I did." She turned to the weary men before her. "This man and his crew enslaved you like cattle to be sold to whoever would buy you! I'll not deny you your right to revenge."

"What? You can't do this to—" His voice was cut short as blows and kicks rained down on him from the former slaves of his ship.

Only fifteen crew remained alive from the Phantom Chaser.

Her crew had them unarmed and corralled near the main mast. "Afia, are any of these men worth the air they breathe?"

The dark man stood beside her, blade back in his hand. "No," he sneered. "They are all vile Spanish dogs."

Callisto nodded. "That is a shame. Some of them look like they would have been capable crew. Put them in chains, cage them and search the ship for anything of worth. Let's drag this tub back to the island!" she ordered.

"Wait!" the dark man called to her, and she turned to regard him. "What happens to us?"

"I'm glad you asked. The choices you make from now on are yours. This ship is ours, and we will take you back to Glacia's Palace, and from there, you are free to do as you please. But I do have an offer you may be interested in."

Afia raised a thick brow.

"I did not come by this ship by chance. I came here solely to free the slaves aboard this ship."

"But why?" he asked.

"To offer you a new life."

"There it is, Commodore," John Baker, the Paradise's helmsman, said when Glacia's Palace was finally in view without the need for the spyglass. "Likely the most dangerous island for us to sail near in all the seas."

"A beautiful island, set in the middle of nowhere," Stephan replied. "Hard to believe it is so dangerous for honest men like us."

"Aye, a beautiful place, full of wonder that draws you in while the vipers and jackals slip in behind ya to slit your throat," John muttered.

"Lieutenant Featherstone, how many ships do you see?"

Stephan asked.

"Fourteen," James replied, shifting the spyglass. "There might be a few more that I cannot. But I see the colors of Stoutleg and his two ships, One Ear's colors on three ships, and Blood Eye flying three ships. The rest fly colors that are unknown to our records. The Poseidon's Fury is nowhere to be seen."

"Three high-profile pirates." Stephan began pacing as he calculated the risks. "Capturing and defeating those three alone would send a clear message across the waves far and wide. Even if we were only to capture one of those captains and a handful of the crew for trial."

"You cannot think to try to attack them while they reside on the island," John said, worry in his tone.

"I would love nothing more," Stephan admitted. "We could not hope to defeat them all if they mustered up a defense against us. Nor do I know enough about the island's defenses and its ruler to know what they are capable of."

Stephan grabbed the railing of the Paradise and stared hard across the waters towards the island. "I would not gamble such a risk as of yet. They will see us out here. They will know we are here, waiting."

"But won't that give them time to devise a plan to attack?" James asked.

"When have you ever seen rival pirates ever work together?" Stephan asked honestly. "They may make a plan to come out in force, but the moment they see one or two ships crippled, they will flee like the cowards they truly are, leaving the others to their watery graves."

"No honor among thieves," John spat.

"Two ships are coming off the port side!" Tomas, the lookout, called down.

James Featherstone shifted his spyglass. "By god!"

"What is it, lieutenant?"

"You are going to want to see this with your own eyes." James handed him the glass.

"The Poseidon's Fury—"

John Baker quickly moved to the helm. "Shall we intercept her, Commodore?"

"Yes, a full flanking maneuver," Stephan ordered. "We board her and take her intact!"

"What in the nine hells does that mean?" James Featherstone muttered, pointing back towards the island where a thick red smoke curled up into the sky.

"Smoke signals," Stephan replied. "They know we are here and are trying to warn any others who might be going to the island, no doubt."

"Sir," John asked, "are we still to intercept?"

"Yes."

Colored flags soon went up the main mast in communication with the Sea Lion, The Highlander, and the Sea Glory. They would all know their roles in the coming conflict as they had hunted as a pack for nearly two decades.

Soon the Paradise's sails were hoisted, and the ship lurched back into motion towards the two oncoming ships, one that was once the British Navy's prize ship.

"Commodore," Lieutenant Featherstone called out as he kept a watchful eye on the island.

"Report?" Stephan asked.

James pulled his eye from the spyglass. "All sorts of movement happening on the island now."

"What does it look like?"

"Heavily armed soldiers are marching from the town towards several ships," James explained. "Ships that fly the colors of the island."

"Steady the course, Mr. Baker," Stephan commanded the

helmsman. "Blackmane will be in chains before this is over, and the Poseidon's Fury will be back in British hands. Lieutenant Featherstone, keep an eye on the island."

"Glacia's Palace is in sight, Captain," Reeves called down from the wheel.

Callisto looked back at her captured prize and grinned.

It had gone better than she had expected. They had lost nine crew members in the fight, seven of the mercenaries and two of her own. Four had been badly wounded, though they would recover.

The journey back had been eventful for her. She saw admiration in their looks and less contempt in many of them now. When they spoke to her, there was a level of respect in their tone. And not a single attempt on her life had been made since the fight, though she still slept with a guard at her door, her pistols ready and one eye open.

"What in the hell is going on at the island?" Murphy muttered, taking up his spyglass as a red smoke lingered in the sky from the island's center.

Weaver dropped his rope and moved over to get a better look. "Warning signal." He took the glass from Murphy. "The island has unwelcome visitors, it would seem."

"What is the problem?" Callisto said, seeing the smoke.

"Shit," Weaver spat as his gaze settled on the four British ships making their way toward them. "It's the Paradise and her naval fleet of pirate hunters."

"Is the island under attack?"

"They are bold but not stupid, Captain," Weaver replied, handing the glass back to Murphy. "The island is safe, but we have a big fucking problem sailing our way."

"Can we get to the island without a fight?" Callisto asked.

"Not likely," Weaver told her honestly, with more than a bit of concern.

"Can we fight our way through?" She looked at Weaver and Murphy.

"Only if you wish to meet your maker today," Weaver said.

"The Paradise and her fleet are the best fighting fleet the sea has ever known," Murphy explained. "We would last only a few moments against them in open battle."

Callisto gripped the railing until her knuckles were white. "What of those on the island? It looks as if ships are being made ready to sail out and meet them. Will they join us in a fight?"

"Only if those British bastards sail within the range of the island, Captain," Reeves said. "What happens out of that range is none of Glacia's concern. She won't allow the battle to be joined unless her borders are crossed."

"Her ships, yes, but what of the other pirates? Do you believe they would sail beyond the safeguard to help us?" Callisto was near begging.

Reeves shrugged. "They are pirates. Unless they expected a sizable reward for their efforts, they'd not risk their ships and crew more so—" he paused as he considered his words, "more so for the likes us."

"Fucking pirates." Callisto spat at the irony of it.

Even faced with a common enemy, they would not put themselves at risk for the betterment of one of their own. Callisto felt the weight of that statement, 'their own.' She was not one of them in their eyes, at least not yet, and likely never since they may very well be killed shortly.

"What are the chances we can punch through and make it to the safety of the island's border?" She chewed her bottom lip.

"They are already moving to intercept us," Murphy replied. "If they mean to sink us, we will be done for before we can hope to defend ourselves. If they mean to take us afloat, they will cripple us, and the fight will be on, but each of those ships has nearly eighty fighting men, all veterans. We may bloody their noses, but ultimately, we will be defeated."

"Are you telling me surrender is the only option?"

"We are pirates, Captain. Even if we surrender, we will still hang," Weaver explained. "To turn and flee is the only way we may live to see another day."

We are pirates...

Those words struck a chord with her as she remembered not long ago when the two men came into her room to kill her the first night she'd had the Poseidon's Fury.

"We are pirates!" Callisto roared to all those on deck. "And pirates do not fight fair!"

She turned to her crew, many of them looking to her for guidance, others looking at her with scorn for what they would believe was their end because they sailed under her.

"Prepare for a fight, arm yourself, and load the cannons. I want them ready if we need them."

"Captain?" Murphy and Reeves asked together.

"You cannot be serious," Murphy said. "You are sentencing us all to death."

"This is madness!" one of the hired crew called out. "You'll kill us all."

Several others grumbled their agreement.

"Fucking woman trying to play at being a pirate!" another growled, turning to face the others. "The only way we survive this is to turn tail and flee and hope the gods and wind are with us."

"If there was ever a time for you to have faith in me, now is that time," Callisto said with a fire in her eyes.

The hired man ignored her and was gaining momentum with the others.

"Throw the bitch overboard, and let's get the fuck out of here," he commanded and turned back just as the barrel of Callisto's pistol pressed under his chin.

"This is my fucking ship."

The gun went off, spraying the man's brains across those near him as his lifeless body hit the deck.

"Get this corpse off the deck, go below, and bring up the prisoners," she bellowed at those around.

"By god, there is no way!" James Featherstone gasped.

Stephan turned his attention back to his first mate. "Lieutenant?"

James pulled his eye from the spyglass to look at Stephan. "They are preparing for a fight, Commodore."

"What are you thinking, Blackmane?" Stephan asked out loud as he tried to calculate what the dangerous pirate might try and do.

"I—I don't see Blackmane, sir, but there is a—" Featherstone paused. "There's a woman—"

"A woman? A prisoner?" Stephan took the glass and focused it. "What game is this?"

"I don't know, Commodore, but she seemed to be leading them."

"What sick game are you playing, Blackmane?" Stephan muttered and could only imagine what cruelty that poor woman had gone through on a ship full of pirates.

"Commodore," one of the artillerymen asked, "do we ready the cannons?"

Stephan licked his lips as his mind raced through a dozen

scenarios. He didn't want to sink the Poseidon's Fury if he didn't have to. To win the ship back would be a significant boost to the navy and a severe wound to the pirates' confidence within the region. But he also would not put his men at serious risk just for a pile of lumber and ropes.

"Commodore?" the man asked again nervously as the two pirate ships drew closer and those around the island began sailing out.

"Make them ready," Stephan ordered. "We will wound her if we have to, but we still have to get her home." The man dipped his head, relaying the order to those waiting by the massive iron weapons.

"Light the braziers and ready the arrows," Stephan commanded. "We will cripple her sails and catch her dead in the water. Sinking her is a last resort!"

Colored flags went up the flagpole, relaying the orders to the other three ships in the fleet as they moved into better countermeasure positions.

"They have prisoners on deck." James lowered the glass and turned to Stephan, his face at a loss for words. "They—they are using them as human shields, I think, sir."

Stephan felt his face flush at the thought.

Such a move was unheard of, even among pirates. He had been prepared for a brutal fight if need be. He had even made peace with sinking the prized ship if it came to that. But this? This was something he had not considered. This was a cowardly act, and he had never been forced to make a decision in all the years such as this one.

"Commodore," an officer called to him as oil-soaked arrows hovered above flames. "Sir, they are in range. What are your orders?"

Stephan's throat was dry.

He knew they could cripple the enemy's sails, but if the

enemy planned on using innocent lives as shields, boarding would be impossible without losing those lives. He had sworn an oath before his betters and God to protect the innocent. That oath now had him against a wall.

"Commodore?"

"Stand down," Stephan whispered.

"Sir?" both James and the officer asked together.

"Stand down!" Stephan bellowed, finally finding his voice.

"Truly?" James asked, confused. "We have them ripe for the picking. A few prisoners may die, but we will stop the pirates and win back our ship."

"Alert the other ships to stand down!" Stephan said more forcefully, doubt pulling at him. "We do not engage! Let them —" The words once more caught in his throat. "Let them pass."

The flags man quickly sent up the colors, ensuring the other ships knew the new orders as the crew on the Paradise lowered their weapons in confusion as the Poseidon's Fury sailed by them.

Stephan ran to the railing and stared across the hundred feet to the enemy ship, his eyes locking on the imposing woman staring back at him, a look of cold victory clear upon her face as she passed.

"Who are you?" Stephan whispered. "And how did you come to be leading that ship?"

The Poseidon's Fury's crew cheered in triumph as they entered the protective ring of the island's guard. The crew couldn't believe what had happened. Their bold captain's suicidal plan had worked, and not a single shot had been fired, blade crossed, or drop of blood spilled.

"By the old gods and the new." Weaver breathed a sigh of relief. "It fucking worked! How did you know that they wouldn't fire on us?"

Callisto's fears finally subsided. It had been a vast gamble, and she had barely expected to work. But it had worked! And now she could feel something different aboard her ship. Something that had never truly been there before. Her crew was proud, and she could feel it in the air, see it as they went to work bringing the ship into the bay to dock. Their voices were full of wonder and awe.

"A lucky guess that our enemy has a higher code of morals than we do."

"Just wait until they find out they spared the lives of a handful of slavers when they are just as hunted as we are." Reeves burst out laughing, clapping Callisto on the back. "I knew you would be a fun one to follow."

The Poseidon's Fury sailed into the harbor and was greeted by cheers of admiration. For among those, none would have attempted something so suicidally daring in the face of those four ships.

"Captain, Callisto SinClair." An older man beckoned her as Callisto stepped off her ship. A man she had seen with Glacia when she had been here last. "A daring and fine display of prowess. A fitting play for your growing reputation as a pirate and Captain of the famed Poseidon."

Callisto dipped her head. "And you would be?"

"My apologies. I am Gavin Santiago. Glacia's captain of the guard."

"Should you not be out there," she pointed to the ships protecting the bay, "chasing off the filth that has formed around the island?"

"Nay, my place is on land, first and foremost. Others far more capable than I protect us from the water."

"What can I do for you, Gavin Santiago?"

"Lady Glacia would like to see you at once." He gestured to the two horses waiting for them.

Callisto mounted the awaiting horse and followed Gavin up the road to the hilltop palace, with several armed guards following them as escorts.

"I thought the island was a safe place?" Callisto asked, riding up beside Gavin.

"As safe as it can be, but it only stays that way because we keep a show of force. Pirates being the unsavory sort that they are, often need reminding." He glanced back to the naval ships just beyond the border. "And that is a good as reason as any to ensure we are showing that force now."

"Am I really so unsavory?"

Gavin chuckled. "I have no idea what exactly you are or what you are capable of. But from what I just witnessed, you might just find yourself in the history books soon enough."

"The world will know my name before I am done with it," Callisto stated matter-of-factly.

"I would bet against any man who doubted you. But know such fame as you are hoping to gather does not often end well for your kind."

"Fisherman, merchant, whore, soldier, pirate, at the end of all our roads, dead is dead," Callisto said coldly.

Gavin nodded, conceding the point.

"So, what does Glacia want?"

"I cannot say. I was merely told to retrieve you for an audience."

"Why the horses and not the carriage this time? Does Glacia not wish to impress me with her riches anymore?" Callisto asked jokingly.

Gavin smiled at her. "It would seem a foolish thing to hide you after what you just accomplished. Let the people see and admire you. Let them talk of the female captain of the dreaded Poseidon's Fury who made a mockery of the most feared naval fleet this world over."

It was Callisto's turn to concede the point. One she was happy to do, for now, she did notice the looks the few folks that passed by were giving her.

"I am not sure you fully understand what you have done."

"Care to enlighten me?"

"I could," Gavin admitted, "but I think it will be more rewarding when you realize it on your own."

Soon they were dismounting in front of the palace's front doors, and Gavin walked Callisto into the main room and up several flights of stairs until they reached the top of the palace.

"The lady awaits you." Gavin bowed and stood aside.

Callisto stepped through the pearl string doorway out onto the large open rooftop, just as grandly decorated as the rest of the palace was. There she spotted the lady of the island overlooking the bay, where her ships and a handful of others waited to see what the four naval ships would do.

"You wanted to see me."

"I am glad you joined me," Glacia said, still overlooking the bay.

"When the lady of the island sends her captain of the guard to collect you, I don't feel like there was much choice."

"You're not entirely wrong in that reasoning." Glacia turned with two goblets of red wine in hand, offering her one. "I see you were very successful in your venture, bringing in the slave ship. I hope it wasn't too much trouble and bore the fruits we had hoped for?"

Callisto accepted the glass and drank, washing the taste of the sea from her mouth. "It was, in more ways than one, I am hoping."

"Congratulations are in order then. I suspect you wish to

sell your second ship. I know someone in the market and could help broker a fair price."

"I have made other arrangements for it."

"Oh?"

"Near half the prisoners aboard the Phantom Chaser have agreed to sail under me, at least for a time."

"You know you could have demanded of them as many as you wanted. You are a pirate after all. Their choices were limited," Glacia explained with intrigue. "More so when faced with death at the end of a pirate's cutlass or an endless swim."

"I would have been no better than their merciless captors at that point. I do not wish to have a crew of slaves or men who resent me. I likely still have enough of those already. The choice was theirs. I gave them all their freedom."

Glacia laughed lightly. "You are the strangest pirate I have ever known—certainly, the most pleasing to the eyes. But you may also be the smartest. Go on, tell me more."

"I have made a deal with the others in exchange for the Phantom Chaser."

"You have given them the ship?" Glacia was surprised. "A ship like that would have fetched you a chest of gold. Something you will need if you wish to continue your new enterprise. The pirate's life is not a cheap one."

"Several of my crew made that same argument. But I took my share of wealth from the ship. The rest is theirs to begin their new venture as pirates. Under the condition that twenty percent of their take is given to me for the first three years."

"You have been studying up on your role." Glacia applauded.

"I have been told you can help arrange such a thing. When they return, you will hold in trust my coin?"

"I have been known to make such arrangements for a small fee. I could do such a thing for you."

They both looked out at the bay, where tensions were growing higher, and a fight threatened to break out at any moment.

"How do you plan on dealing with these unwanted visitors?" Callisto asked.

"I have not figured that out yet. I had thought they would have sailed away by now, knowing they could not hope to win if they started fighting for my island. Yet, they remain."

"If you need me to help, my ship and crew will help fight them."

"That may be needed, but as an absolute last resort. I don't intentionally plan to start a war with the British navy."

Callisto shrugged. "You have more than enough ships to deal with them."

"Yes, I do. But once word spreads that it was done, by next year, I'll have fifty naval ships surrounding my island, and that would be the end of all I have built, and I will not risk that for anyone," she stated flatly.

"You would surrender who was here to save yourself?"

"Yes." Again, Glacia's tone left nothing to doubt. "Survival often comes with a cost to those around us."

"Would that not hurt what you have built?" Callisto asked honestly. "If those you have come to rely on for trade and information. If they believed they were no longer safe here for fear of being turned over to the enemy at the first show of force?"

"They are pirates. They will do what is most profitable to them, and I am the most profitable port they will find for five hundred miles. They may hate me, but most already do. But they will not let that stop them from sailing here to sell their stolen wares and resupply empty stores."

"Can you be so sure?"

"You have not been a pirate long enough to understand the

whims of an empty coin pouch or the biting pains of an empty stomach at sea." She paused. "I do pray it never comes to that, though."

Callisto finished her drink and set the glass down. "I thank you for the wine. I will return to my ship and crew if that is all."

"You do not wish to stay the evening?" Glacia asked, almost hurt. "I already had your room ready for you, with a certain two lovers eager for your return to the sheets."

The thought of such an evening did pull at her and almost won out. "I should return to my ship. My crew needs to see me there, to know that I am with them."

"They will be out whoring and drinking their wages away by now." Glacia laughed. "But I am not finished with you if you would indulge me a little more of your time."

"I am at your mercy."

"Come now, Callisto SinClair, do not treat me as such. With respect, yes, but as a better, nay. We are women of intelligence and power both with our will and from the divine."

Callisto's brows lifted at that last part. "The divine?"

"Let me be as bold now as you were out there. I know you are favored by the old gods, or at least one. Poseidon? Zeus? Hades? Athena? I cannot say for certainty, but I know it to be true, and I know you know it to be true. I knew it before you even sailed Blackmane's ship to my bay. Though in truth, I did not know it would be you who was delivered to my doorstep or by what means. But the old gods do enjoy a show among their playthings. And yes, we are their playthings. Never forget that small fact."

"Are you saying you speak to the old gods?"

Glacia waved her hands around them. "I would love to take full credit for all I have, but it was not achieved solely by my own will. I have had—help as I know you have."

"Aphrodite?" Callisto asked eagerly.

Glacia nodded. "We are sisters of the divine, blessed by powers greater than the world has known since the time of Hercules, Hector, Achilles, and all the other mortals who have paved their way into history forever."

Callisto chuckled. "Are you saying no person has been able to achieve greatness without the aid of the gods?"

"I am sure there has been a handful, but who is to say for sure? I only speak of which I know, and what I know is I am here ruling an island of cutthroats, pirates, and thieves in which any other time one such as myself would be no more than a tavern wench or worse." She motioned around them once more. "Yet everything before us, I was able to take! To create and to mold to my design all because I sparked the interest of the old gods."

"Ares," Callisto told her. "When I was ten."

"Truly? The god of war? I would have wagered Poseidon." Glacia sat back against the railing. "I am surprised at that, yet it does make sense. His strength and passion do have the means to spark the loyalty of men to follow."

"Is the only reason you have helped me because of this?" Callisto asked. "Because of the gods?"

Glacia smiled. "I help those who can help me."

"What is my debt to you then?"

"I guess we shall see," came her reply.

"But do not think of our relationship as purely transactional." She ran a hand across Callisto's cheek. "No, never that, not with what we both know. We are so much more than that. We are sisters in the cause of bringing back the power of the gods that time has nearly forgotten."

"The two of us against the world of men?" Callisto joked.

"Yes, the two of us against the world of men." Glacia brushed her lips against hers. "Think of all we can achieve."

Callisto smirked. This one was dangerous but exciting, and

exciting was always worth exploring.

"So, tell me. How could you build such a palace here in such a short time?" Callisto asked. "I would think something of this splendor would have taken decades to build, let alone ship such vast materials to. It would have cost a king's ransom and more."

Glacia placed her empty glass down and took Callisto's hand. "Let me show you one of my little secrets."

Moving through the palace and down deeper into the vault of the place. Torches led the way down the hallway, which opened up into a vast room near the size of the palace's main floor above.

"What is this place?" Callisto whispered in awe, for even though they were underground, the place shone with brilliance as if somehow the very sun from outside had found its way within. As she looked around, she noticed the large mirrors placed at angles that directed a sunbeam from above down into the temple, bringing the very sun beneath the ground.

"This is an old Greek temple to the goddess Aphrodite, the goddess of beauty, love, and desire."

"It is breathtaking."

"Truly it is," Glacia agreed. "All this was here centuries before I was even born. But, like many of the great temples of the old gods, it was abandoned and forgotten over time. That is until I found it and helped restore it to even greater glory." She smiled proudly. "Now, it is my home, and this island my small kingdom."

"How long have you been here?"

"Nearly two decades now."

"You must have been no more than a girl when you found this place. How did you manage to do all this at such a young age?" Callisto asked in awe.

Glacia smirked. "I was not much younger than you are now when I came across this place."

Callisto stared at her in doubt. "There is no way you are that old."

"Older than I appear."

"How is that possible? You look little older than I?"

"The gods work in mysterious ways."

Callisto ran her hand across the large marble statue of the goddess Aphrodite. A statue very much like the one she had come across of Ares a lifetime ago.

"How were you able to do all this?" Callisto asked.

"You are not the only one with seductive powers," Glacia remarked.

Callisto nearly laughed. "Your abilities clearly outmatch my own."

"Not always the case, I am sure." Glacia sat beneath an impressive statue, her eyes staring off at nothing. "I was a nobody once—a servant for a rich family, but she—" her hand grazed over the feet of the statue, "she changed that for me.

"The family I served traveled by sea for business and pleasure. On one such trip, we were caught in a storm. It blew us around for many days before we were finally free of its grasp. But we were lost, and the ship was damaged heavily. For days we drifted at the mercy of the sea, the crew repairing what they could in hopes that we would once more find the wind again that would carry us home.

"At night, something strange began to happen to me when I slept. I felt her calling to me in my dreams, the goddess Aphrodite, though I had no idea who she was at the time. But I felt her there, reaching out to me, beckoning me to her.

"On the fourth night I felt her, she whispered to me. Told me how close I was to her temple island and powers and rewards I could never imagine, but if I didn't do something quickly, we would sail right past." Glacia paused and sipped her wine.

"I woke in the dead of night, climbed to the top deck, and tried to convince the helmsman he needed to change course. Being a woman and a servant, he ignored me and told me to fuck off." Her eyes went dark. "But Aphrodite's call was too strong, her promises too sweet—the helmsman was the first man I ever killed."

Silence filled the room for several long moments.

"With the ship free to roam, the goddess guided it in the night. In the morning, we were in sight of the island. There was much chaos over who killed the helmsman, but no one suspected me."

Glacia smiled widely. "I still remember when my feet first touched the island's sands. The feelings that overcame me are the same ones I feel still every day I awake here. I felt at home, truly home. As if my entire life had led me to that very moment.

"That night, the goddess came to me again, stronger than before. For the first time, I could see her in all her glory. She told me of this temple and the vast treasures within. She told me what she wanted me to do while leading me here to this spot we sit now in the dead of night. She promised me I would no longer be a servant to anyone but her. That I would rule this island in her name and have the power of a queen over men and women.

"The next morning, I left the temple, dressed in gowns fit for a goddess. I remember little of that morning, except the captain and crew of the ship fell to their knees upon seeing me, promising me anything I desired of them." A wicked smile crossed her face. "I made them kill the family I once served."

"We filled the ship's hull with much treasure and returned home. The men were paid well to keep silent on where the island was so we could return. And return, we did, but with a fleet of ships carrying what I needed to begin to rebuild. It took over a decade to prepare this place and a decade more to perfect it.

"An impressive tale," Callisto admitted. "But how did you find yourself in league with pirates? Why didn't they simply overrun you and take everything for themselves?"

Glacia smirked. "That will be a tale for another time. A girl can't give up all her secrets in one evening. Now tell me about you and how you ended up here. You told me part of it, but now we better understand each other. I would hear it from the beginning."

Callisto told her of that day a lifetime ago when she had gone up the hillside to visit Gaspar with her father.

"I don't like this one bit," John Baker grumbled, not for the first time, as several others pulled back on the oars.

"I noted it the first time you mentioned it," Commodore Stephan Belfield replied distantly, staring straight ahead.

Glacia's Palace, a small island with only one bay large enough to land ships. The rest was guarded by jagged reefs and sheer cliff walls where the ruins of ship masts could be seen sticking up through the crashing waves. Ships who had either hit the reef or been foolish enough to attempt an attack and met their doom.

The Sea Lion had circled the island twice during the night and once that morning, looking for a weakness. A place to land where they would not have to fight through an army of enemy ships. There had been none to be seen. The only safe way onto the island was here, which was now heavily guarded.

No one on the four ships had slept that night. High alert

had been a priority for fear of an attack coming in the dark. Pirates and their ilk were always waiting to slit the throats of sleeping men. But no move had come against them. They merely had dropped anchor and waited menacingly, their cannons angled straight ahead.

As experienced and battle-ready as Stephan's fleet was, it would be no match for the powers before them. It was true. He expected they could have sunk a half dozen ships with little trouble, then they would have to flee, and if they were pursued, they would likely be picked off one at a time by the sheer volume of enemies. Not in a pitched battle, that was.

There was the realization that several other ships had been seen just beyond the horizon, clearly aware trouble was brewing around the island due to the red smoke drifting into the sky steadily. If they started a fight, they would be fighting on all fronts in short order.

No, they could not win this in a straight fight. They had almost decided to pull anchor and sail away, hoping to catch any pirates beyond the view of the island. That was before they had seen the rowboat flying the white flag of truce that morning.

The islanders had brought a message from the self-appointed queen. An open invitation to come ashore and speak, under the safety and protection of the lady herself, regarding this situation they found themselves in.

How daft did they think he was to take himself and a select group of men away from his ships into enemy territory to be murdered? At first, Stephan had almost outright refused such a foolish notion. But he had bitten his tongue at the fast refusal, seeing once more the Poseidon's Fury in the bay just beyond his grasp.

He had asked where Blackmane was, and the reply was dead. A new captain, a female captain, now commanded the prized naval ship. And that had given Stephan much to think about. There could still be a way to take back the ship without bloodshed.

It was a risk, and even now, as they rowed towards the island past enemy ships whose crew glared down at them, wanting nothing more than to open fire, no move was forthcoming.

"Is the chance of recovering the ship truly worth this risk?" James Featherstone asked, fear clear on his face.

"We go for more reasons than just that, lieutenant," Stephan replied.

"Sir?"

"Information," Stephan explained. "If we can retrieve Poseidon's Fury, that will be wonderful. If not, we will return with much-needed knowledge about this island and those who reside upon it."

"I don't think we will learn much, sir," James admitted. "We will be watched closely and are hated by every soul here. No one will tell us anything."

"Not everything needs to be told. An attentive man can gather much. What can you see? What do you hear? What are their movements like, are they organized, weapons, or defensive? A dozen or more things can be learned by simply observing your surroundings."

He turned to the twelve men he had been allowed to bring to the island as an escort. "I expect you all to be sharp and absorb all that you can. Anything we can learn may help us in the future."

"Do you plan to report this to the generals back in London?" John asked. "In thoughts of taking the island in a war?"

"I will report all that we discover. What transpires after will be up to the generals to decide."

Soon the boat slid up to the dock only a stone's throw from where the Poseidon's Fury was being resupplied. A score of armed men was waiting for them.

"Greetings, Commodore. My name is Gavin Santiago, captain of the guard in this lovely slice of heaven. I am to escort you to her Lady Glacia for your discussion."

"Not the warmest of welcomes," James grunted as he looked over the line of armed men glaring their way.

"Be thankful you are welcome at all," Gavin replied with a mocking smile. "Before we go any further, know this: only you, Commodore, and two others may accompany you to the lady. The rest of your men will remain within the dockside tavern just over there." He pointed to a nearby spot.

"The owner is under strict orders to serve your men free of charge so long as they do not cause any disturbance. Furthermore, your men will be allowed to keep their weapons for their own feeling of safety. But know that the punishment is death for anyone who breaks the peace on this island. Several of my men will remain with them for their protection to help dissuade any altercations there could be with those you have made enemies with."

"You forget yourself. We are British navy officers," James spat. "You have no jurisdiction to set such a punishment over us."

"Your titles mean nothing once you step foot on this island, boy," Gavin replied, his tone cold and dangerous. "You would do well to remember that, lest you say something that won't be overlooked, and I set your ass back into your boat whimpering like the child you appear to be."

James Featherstone bristled at that but was wise enough to hold his tongue, even though all around knew it was killing him to do so.

"You will keep the peace, gentlemen," Stephan ordered.

"We are guests, and we will honor that as naval officials of King William the Third."

"Commodore." Gavin motioned to the wagon that awaited. "If you would be so kind, her highness is very busy, and already we have wasted enough time." His eyes lingered on James as he spoke.

"Featherstone, Baker, with me," Stephan ordered, though he wondered if bringing James was wise given his reckless conduct. It would be something he would remember to talk to the man about.

The wagon bounced around and was an uncomfortable ride for the three sailors. Stephan suspected their driver was intentionally trying to hit every rut he could find along the way. It also was not lost on them that several carriages had come down from the direction they were heading. Fancy carriages that looked more like they belonged in the streets of London than an island full of vile cutthroats. They were not welcome guests and would not be treated as such.

Deep in his thoughts, Stephan tried to sort out the possible mind games that were indeed being played at this very moment. Anyone who could achieve all of this and keep hundreds of the fiercest and most vile pirates in check was dangerous. But more so, he was preparing himself for the mind games that were soon to come.

He had dealt with pirates and these abhorrent types most of his life, and he knew their minds and the treachery behind their every word. But he also knew he was in the midst of the hornet's nest and had to play this carefully if he expected to leave the island alive with his men. He held no false hope that this woman would remain faithful to her word if she so decided it was not in their best interests.

Once more, Stephan questioned his course. He might very

well have signed all their death warrants with this brash exploit.

His contemplations were broken as they turned a bend and caught sight of the structure that gave the island its name, Glacia's Palace. All three sailors gasped at the sight, never having seen such a thing anywhere but in the richest cities they had visited. In truth, even many of those did not compare to the sheer elegance of this place.

"How in the nine hells did this happen?" John asked in wonder.

"Off of the stolen goods of honest men," James spat. "Fucking pirates." He turned to Stephan. "How many men died so that this monstrosity could be built? How many ships ladened with goods were pilfered so that this bastard island could thrive like only a truly civilized country might? This is an insult to all we hold true, Commodore."

Stephan had barely heard his words, for he was truly in awe of this spectacle. Never in his entire imagination could he have thought it possible for an island of pirates and thieves to achieve such a thing. How many more such islands of killers were prospering like this? This only proved they were desperately losing the war.

They pulled up to the magnificent front doors, where a row of armed men awaited on either side, ensuring there was only one path to take, and that was where they were to be herded.

Stephan kept his head high, his posture perfect, and wished his two comrades were doing the same, but both were drawn in and forgot themselves. This was the time to show the strength and prestige of their station, not to gawk in bewilderment like common fools.

They were led through the marvelous structure, hardly believing each room or hallway they entered was as impressive as the one they exited. Soon they found themselves on a vast marble veranda. Tables of sweet goods, exotic fruits, cheeses, and smoked meats had been prepared, filling the air with the smell of food that would set anyone's stomach to grumbling in anticipation.

"I present to you, her highness, Lady Glacia, ruler of the soil your feet now have the privilege of touching," Gavin announced proudly.

Glacia turned to face her three guests, smirking at the twinkle in two of their eyes at her low V dress that cut down to her navel, exposing hints of the wonders of her body. She smiled. Men were so easily distracted, except the commodore, who fought it well.

"Welcome to my island, gentlemen," she greeted them sweetly.

Stephan stepped forward. "I am Commodore Stephan—" his words were cut short.

"I know very well who you and your fleet are, Belfield," she cut in like a blade through flesh, the sweetness of her tone gone. "I would like to know why you and your ships are here, hindering my clients and business, and becoming an eyesore from my balcony?"

Stephan's eyes darkened. "If you know who we are, then you should know what we might be doing here, *my lady*." He put venom within the words.

"What I know is you are very far from home, in seas full of dangers that have humbled stronger men." She matched his venom with her own, and the guards around the area shifted their weapons to exaggerate the point.

Stephan was suddenly reminded of the immediate dangers they were in. "You do know your clients are mostly pirates? Wanted men by the crown? All who aid, harbor, and assist such criminals are thereby deemed traitors to the crown."

Glacia laughed cruelly at him. "The only crown here that

matters is mine, lest you forget you are on MY island, far from your country, jurisdiction, and that fat little king of yours."

"My jurisdiction is the open sea," Stephan replied boldly, "making my reach far."

"If you are thinking of attacking my island or those residing upon it, pirates or not, you believe yourself stronger than you truly are, Commodore. There will be no victory here for you. But I will do you the honor if you wish to meet your Christian god in a hail of cannon fire and blades."

"The British Navy does not take well to such threats, my lady."

"Nor do I, Commodore, and it is I who you need to worry about at this moment. Neither your king nor God will protect you from the consequences of your words or actions here. There is only I." She strolled up to mere inches away, holding back her smile as she could see him tense. "I ask again, Commodore, what is it you want?"

For one of the very few times in Stephan's danger-filled life, he felt a cold sweat beading around the nap of his neck. He was at the line. If he crossed it now, he and his men would be killed long before they could even hope to draw their weapons in defense.

"I do not wish any such altercation with you, your island, or even those mooring here at this given time," he replied calmly. "I am here for the Poseidon's Fury."

"That is a bold claim to make."

"It is a ship of the British navy and is the property of the king."

"Was," Glacia reminded him. "It has not been for many years if my memory serves me."

"Yes, well, be that as it may. It is a prized naval ship we have been commissioned to return or destroy."

"That might be difficult, given it already has a captain and crew that I assume are quite fond of it," Glacia smirked.

"I am sure they are, but I am also aware that Blackmane is dead. I wish to speak to that new captain to see if terms can be reached for its surrender."

"Callisto SinClair is the captain now. Truly she is a wonder to behold, both in beauty and in her capability of such a crew."

"So, it is true then?" James Featherstone cut in. "A woman captains Blackmane's ship?"

"Stolen ship," Stephan quickly corrected.

Glacia once again laughed with genuine mirth. "It is very true, gentlemen. She killed Blackmane with her own hands, even brought me his head in a bag. You might still be able to find it beneath the waters of the dock if the crabs haven't picked it clean by now."

"By god," James muttered, with more than a bit of admiration, for Blackmane had been known as one of the most dangerous pirates to roam the seas.

"What is more impressive is how she managed to get past four of the most dangerous pirate hunters on the seas without needing to fire a single shot from her cannons." Glacia knew those words would sting. They were meant to.

"Aye, using slaves as human fucking shields like a cowardly woman," John Baker grumbled.

"Correction, slavers of the ship she has just conquered. Men that you hunt just the same as pirates, no doubt."

Stephan felt his stomach lurch. He had thought they were innocent men, merchants, or traders—but slavers! He had been made a fool indeed.

"All the same. I would like to speak with this Callisto SinClair," he said, trying to keep his shame from his eyes and voice.

"You will likely find her down at the docks, aboard her

ship. I will have my men escort you." Glacia smiled sweetly. "I have no quarrelwith you speaking to her about surrendering the ship, and if she so chooses to, luck will have truly favored you this day."

Stephan dipped his head. "You have my thanks."

They turned to leave.

"Commodore," Glacia called, and they turned back to regard her. "We need not have a problem so long as you don't make one."

Callisto stepped out of her cabin into the late morning sun and warm sea breeze sweeping from the north. She had spent a good part of the night talking with Glacia. What they had talked about and what had been shown to her had opened her eyes to a larger truth about the world she had found herself in. She had learned much and shared much of herself.

More gods were at play, moving others around like pieces on a board game. Helping those they favored accomplish things ordinary people could not even dream of.

When she had been forced from her home as a young girl, she had learned to read and discovered several stories about the old gods and those they had favored. She had always dreamed that she was one of them without truly understanding that she was. But now she saw that with perfect clarity. Ares blessed her, and his power and strength were with her.

Callisto smiled. One day, stories would be written about her in the same light as those of old.

"Morning, Captain," Murphy said, climbing down some rigging to join her. "You look in a fine mood."

"I am," she admitted. "Today is the first day of the rest of my life."

Murphy scratched his head. "A bit of an odd saying, but I am glad you are in high spirits. Most of the crew didn't return last night, likely sleeping off the effect of a long night of drinking."

"They deserve it."

"Provisions have been arranged for this afternoon. We will be fully stocked and ready to set sail on the morrow if that is your wish. If we can get out, that is." He glanced at the warships still just outside of the bay.

"If we must stay a few days, so be it," Callisto said. "I am sure the men will find no fault in that."

"Aye, I am sure you are correct, but there is—" He paused and scratched his head again.

"What is it?" Callisto asked. "What is the problem?"

"Well, coin, to be frank." He spoke. "We are running low. The coffers are thinning with what you paid the men when we first arrived, the mercenaries, recruits, repairs, and provisions. We could have used the coin selling the Phantom Chaser."

"I know," Callisto admitted. "But I am looking long-term. They will provide us with extra coin when we return from their own ventures at sea."

Murphy didn't look convinced. "That is, if they honor it, they are becoming pirates. They are not known to be the most honorable bunch. Nor do they have much experience being pirates. Who is to say they don't get defeated their first time trying to take a ship?"

"I have faith in my decision," Callisto assured him, though, in truth, she was beginning to see her error. "Plus, I needed that show of faith so the others would join our crew. I now have a crew I can mostly trust, or so I am hoping."

"Aye, there is reason in that to be sure." He agreed. "From

what I've heard, most are talking highly of you right now, especially after our daring escape."

"How much coin do we have?"

Murphy flipped open his ledger. "Enough for wages and to have the ship stocked partly again, so long as no major repairs will need to be done. In short, when we leave here, we will have to leave here to hunt. And pray we find a worthy find."

"What do we have here?" Callisto muttered, stepping away from Murphy to the front of the ship. A wagon flanked by a score of guards was making its way down from the palace.

"Rumor has it the commodore of the Paradise and some of his men came ashore this morning to broker some sort of peace with the island."

The wagon rolled right down to the dock, right in front of the Poseidon's Fury, the escort fanning wide to keep those who might prove foolish from attempting harm on the three naval men's lives.

Gavin dismounted and walked to the wooden dock towards the ship, seeing Callisto and Murphy staring down. "A good morning to you, Captain SinClair."

She nodded to him.

"I hate to disrupt you, but it would seem the Commodore here would like a word if you would grant it," he called up, "though the choice is purely yours if you wish to accept."

"This is an interesting turn of events," Callisto mused, staring down at the Commodore and his dozen men who had been ushered over from one of the island's many taverns.

"A trap?" Murphy asked.

"A foolish place to try something like that." She gestured to the hundreds of men and women gathering closer to see what was transpiring.

"He is a dangerous man," Murphy told her. "One does not raise to such a station without knowing his craft well."

"I have dealt with men like that my whole life." Callisto grinned. "Let's go see what the good commodore wants of me."

Stephan Belfield and his men waited at the edge of the wharf, watching the new captain of the Poseidon's Fury make her way to them. She was undeniably beautiful, exceeding even the stature of beauty London had come to know among the noble women. She would have fit in at any royal table, and no one would have questioned her right to be there. Nay, they would have felt less in her presence. And in all Stephan's life, he had never seen such a creature as this.

"My lady SinClair, thank you for choosing to meet with me," Stephan began.

"If this meeting is to go any further, you will address me correctly, Commodore," Callisto said with authority. "It is, Captain SinClair."

Stephan held her gaze, finding the notion ridiculous, but he held those thoughts back, though he knew his eyes spoke volumes. "Captain SinClair."

"I am a busy woman," she said with emphasis on 'woman.' "What do you want? Maybe you are here to apologies for almost attacking my ship and crew while we tried to make berth? Or maybe how that didn't go as you had planned? Because if you are going to apologize, you must get down on your knees to do it."

All around them, laughter and jeers sprung up.

Stephan did his best to suppress a sneer. "I ask that we discuss this matter privately, maybe upon your ship."

"Anything you wish to say to me, you can say in front of my fellow brethren of the sea." Callisto boasted, though she wondered if that had been wise to do. She still doubted many of them would consider her as such.

"As you wish—Captain. I hear you have defeated Blackmane and are now Captain of the Poseidon's Fury. A ship you may well know belongs to the British Navy and is the property of King William the Third. A ship we would have back sailing under our colors. I am at liberty to offer you fair compensation for the return of our ship."

"My ship," Callisto corrected him.

Stephan cleared his throat. "A sum of which will set you and your crew well on their way to honest and moral lives."

She burst out laughing. "That would have to be a mighty sum, Commodore. I am not so sure your king has that deep of pockets."

Again, those in the crowd of men and women laughed at the commodore's expense.

"I am also at liberty to pardon the crew of the Poseidon's Fury of all crimes of piracy. Giving them all a clean slate to start their lives anew without fear of prosecution."

"Is that all, Commodore?"

Stephan was surprised by the question. "What do you mean?"

Callisto threw up her arms in dramatic dismay. "Merely the offer of coin and a pardon for crimes committed. Do you think that is enticing enough to leave behind all of this? I already had a better offer and turned it down."

"My la—Captain, you must realize this in no life for a woman. The fact that you survived Blackmane and this long among these degenerates is truly a shock. But to continue this path will see you dead or in chains."

Callisto's eyes flared with anger. "You would do well to watch the words coming out of that mouth of yours, Commodore." Several of her crew were already moving through the crowd to gather behind her. "These degenerates, as you call them, are my crew, and I'll be damned if I stand by and let the likes of you call them down!"

Cheers erupted all around them, and for a moment, it seemed a riot would happen as hands quickly moved to blades.

"You are making a mistake!" Stephan pressed, stepping forward. "You don't understand what you are getting yourself into, woman!"

Callisto's hand lashed out, striking him across the face and forcing him back a step. "Listen well, navy pig. You are greatly mistaken if you think to goad me into submission for a moment because I am a woman."

Stephan sucked in a deep breath. "This is your last chance, Captain SinClair. Once this conversation is over, the next talking we do will be out there on the open sea under cannon fire and steel."

"And this is the only warning I shall give you, Commodore, so hear me loud and clear," she hissed back. "If you do not get back on your ship and sail far the fuck away, I will take everything you hold dear from you before I end your life." With that, Callisto turned on her heels and walked back to her ship to the cheers of everyone around.

"Well played, Captain." Reeves grinned, climbing aboard the ship, several others in tow, all looking worse off for the night of debauchery.

Callisto said nothing as she watched the commodore and his men climb back into their rowboat. Something stirred inside of her as Stephan Belfield stared back at her, and she knew this would not be the last time she dealt with this man.

Glacia stood staring out at the bay from atop her palace, watching two more heavily damaged ships limp their way into the safety of the harbor. Smoke from a rain of flaming arrows still wafting from their sails and decks, the rigging was tangled and ruined, and timber dangled awkwardly from the destruction of cannon fire.

These were not the first ships to return to the island in such a condition. Nearly a dozen vessels had come in the last six days looking much like this or worse. Some were barely afloat and needed weeks, if not months, of repairs before they could set sail again.

All of them returned with similar stories. The Paradise and its fleet of pirate hunters were out there, just beyond the horizon, attacking any ship making its way to the island that did not surrender. For every ship that made it past, it was rumored two did not.

Glacia felt her anger rising more each day. Yes, business was good. Her crews were profiting from repairing the damaged ships, trading supplies, and housing crews in the many taverns and inns where all men did was drink, gamble, and whore.

But she knew it could not last forever.

Fewer ships would attempt to reach her island if this continued for much longer. Fewer still would be afloat to do so, and trade would plummet, leaving the island bare of the supplies required to run such a profitable business.

This siege needed to end.

She mustered up the eight ships she had at her command and set them patrolling the perimeter of the islands. They were to intercept and help any ship that got close enough to make it to safety, and if they came into range of enemy ships, to engage only if victory could be assured.

But the commodore would not gamble in getting close to the island. They stayed far from pitch battle with her ships but close enough that their presence was known, watching, waiting. Knowing sooner or later, they could and would cripple the island.

Glacia knew sooner or later, the commodore and his fleet would have to leave their waters and resupply. The closest place they could do that would take them a month or more. But the damage to the island and her clientele would be significant long before then.

The offer of a sizable reward would be given to any ships that would join together to chase these invaders away. A sizable amount that would vastly lessen her treasury had still been turned down. No one, it seemed, was willing to take such a risk, and many had found their moments to sail free of the island in hopes of escaping. If they made it, she didn't know.

"Fucking pirates," she cursed.

Something needed to happen, and soon.

"Aphrodite, I could use your guidance, speak to me," she pleaded.

Stephan Belfield stood on the aft deck, watching the smoke rise while the last echoes of cannon fire disappeared as the Sea Lion and the Highlander finished off their latest catch. This would mark the ninth ship they had laid to the bottom of the sea in the last week, with nearly twice that they had wounded but had ultimately gotten away.

They had been sent out to send a message to pirates and vagabonds alike. A message Stephan was taking complete seriousness in sending. By the time they were finished here, pirates would lessen their ventures from their hiding spots, only coming forth when they desperately needed to. And Stephan and his hunters would be waiting for them.

Generally, if they could take a ship without putting it to the bottom of the sea, they would have. But with what they were doing here, their holds would have been full of prisoners by the end of the third day. And feeding and guarding such unruly guests would have taken more time, men, and supplies than he was willing to waste.

Let them perish in the waters they had chosen to sin upon.

Stephan knew his pride was deeply involved in this now. He knew it and would not deny it. He had been scorned deeply upon that island by two women, no less, in front of several of his men. Such things could not go unanswered.

He had fought too long and hard to get to where he was. He sacrificed too much blood, sweat, and tears year after year to make himself the man he was today. He would not let the pompousness of two women shame him or his position. Nor would he let them forget just who they had crossed.

To stop this from happening, equal opportunity had been given to both, more than equal in his mind. He had given Callisto SinClair a better offer than he would have given anyone else simply because she had been a woman, and she had mocked him. Nay, she had threatened him as if she could begin to claim she was somehow his better.

This massacre fell upon their shoulders.

"Another bad day to be a pirate." James Featherstone, lieutenant of the Paradise, rose proudly, standing beside the Commodore.

His eyes burned with the thrill of all of this. This was the reason he had wanted to be in the navy. These were the battles he had dreamed of all his life. For what they had done already, his name would be forever remembered in the history books for his part in it.

"We have wounded them deeply," Stephan confirmed. "But it will not last much longer. We run short of arrows, iron balls, and black powder. Not to mention water and food will have to be rationed if we stay much longer."

James scoffed at that. "We have more than enough to sink

a dozen more of these miscreants. Then we can leave, resupply, and return tenfold to finish what we started!"

Stephan grinned slightly at that, for that was his plan if his superiors would agree. But his eyes kept lingering back to the island, where the prize he wanted more than anything at that moment remained.

The Poseidon's Fury.

Returning with the famed naval ship in their possession would be a triumph that would set this war in their favor. He would make the Poseidon's Fury his lead ship, raising him in the eyes of any who doubted him still. It would also strike fear in the hearts of any pirate who spotted her.

"We will play out this dance a little longer," Stephan confirmed to his lieutenant. "Leave a lasting mark that hopefully sends them far and wide, never to return."

"We should begin taking prisoners, a few captains, and high-ranking pirates. It would do well to return with something the crown can use as a spectacle for the people. Hanging a score of pirates has always brought the commoners closer. Plus, it will deter them from thinking about joining the ranks of pirates."

The Commodore nodded, for indeed, it was true. The hanging of pirates was always a sure way to discourage more from joining them. "Relay it to the other ships. A score of prisoners, no more than that."

Callisto gripped the worn brass-handled door, willing herself to push it open and join those inside, many of whom were her crew. A crew that it would appear had indeed begun to accept her for her bold exploits that had seen them this far.

It was not that which held her in place.

She had drunk many nights with her crew aboard their ship and had even been, for the most part, at ease. But there was more than just her crew within this place. There were men from a dozen ships within the establishment. Men she didn't know or trust. Frustrated captains who might very well break the island's peace to lay her low in hopes of bringing her head to Commodore Stephan Belfield for safe passage away from here.

Callisto gripped the handle harder. "Fortune favors the bold," she growled, knowing to hide upon her ship was not helping her cause among those she wanted to be equal with, nay, better than.

Pushing the door open, she entered the dimly lit tavern. Her senses were assaulted with the smell of pipe tobacco, cheap ale, and cheaper sex. A smell that took her back through the years of her past life. A life that much like now had hung in a web of danger and chaos.

All eyes turned to regard her, and silence took the place for the briefest moments before cheers erupted and mugs of ale were held high in her direction. Before she had taken a dozen steps, a barmaid had a drink in each of her hands.

"I hope you have a thirst this night." The barmaid laughed. "Already, a score of drinks has been ordered for you."

This had not been the welcome she had expected. She lifted each mug in the air for all to see, put one after the other to her lips, and drank them back as quickly as she could. As the last bit of foam hit her lips, the tavern broke out into cheering her name.

"Captain!" Alonso called out, motioning her to a group of tables where a score of her crew sat drinking, eating, and gambling.

"I knew I'd find you worthless lot here," Callisto bellowed back with a grin.

Several of them laughed with her and held up their tankards in salute.

"Not much else to do at the moment," Weaver grumbled, staring into his nearly empty mug.

"Aye, there's sad truth in that," Callisto agreed.

"Not going to lie, Captain, we are going a little stir-crazy being stuck here like this," Weaver explained. "It is one thing to be here for a break of our own free will, aye, that is good times. But to know we are stuck here and cannot leave is leaving me with a bitter taste. Only so much drinking and whoring a man can do before his coin runs out and tempers flare."

"We should try and break out," Jonesy cut in from one of the other tables. "Like a few of the others have."

"Bleh," Byron grunted, "we don't even know if any of them made it free. For all we know, they could be sitting on the bottom of the sea."

"Worth the risk, I'd say," Jonesy replied bitterly. "Gonna become a land lover if we stay here much longer."

"The Paradise and her fleet can't remain out there forever," Callisto said, sipping a new drink handed to her. She would drink but would also ensure her wits remained about her. "Sooner or later, they will run themselves dry of ammo and need to find a port."

"Bleh, that could take another week or more," Jonesy argued. "Things around here are sure to be getting violent before then. Already half a dozen have broken the peace and struck blades. This place is wound up tight and sure to snap. It won't matter how many guards Glacia has to stop it."

That gave Callisto pause, for it was true. The tenseness in the island's air had changed, and with crews of pirates, many hated rivals were forced to parley day after day. It was only a matter of time before those strings that held it together frayed and snapped.

"You have talked to Glacia. What is her plan?" Weaver asked, and many ears turned her way. "By now, she must have an idea of what to do. This is her island, after all."

Callisto had talked to the island queen several times, and this had been a conversation that had come up often. One she knew Glacia had had with several of the captains. The issuewas that no captains would commit their ships to the fight, fearing the worst for themselves or betrayal from their rivals. If they were to engage, they feared the others would sail past, leaving them to their doomed fate.

"Plans are being made. A solution will be found," Callisto told them, knowing it was only partially a lie.

"Bleh, not soon enough," came several replies.

"Let us not worry about tomorrow when tonight is still in front of us!" Callisto called out, lifting her drink.

Callisto woke on a strange hilltop overlooking a narrow valley and knew she was once more in the magical world of Ares. He had finally come to her call after days of praying for him to give her guidance.

An army gathered on either side. The army on the Northern side was vast, easily outnumbering those of the South ten to one. Yet the smaller army seemed not bothered from here, almost eager for the fight.

That surprised Callisto, for she could see no way they could defeat the large enemy that would soon march upon them.

"Seems foolish of them, doesn't it?" the husky voice of Ares said as he appeared beside her.

"They cannot hope to win against such a force in a pitched

battle as this. It would be better for them to run and pick their time to strike," Callisto confirmed.

"What makes you think this was not their mindset?" the god of war asked.

Callisto waved her hand out at the scene before them as if that should be obvious. "They are outnumbered and will crumble before such an army. No matter how strong of arm and skilled fighters, they will tire by the sheer volume of enemies before the enemy runs out of fighting men to send against them."

"That is what they hope the enemy believes as well."

"What strategy could they possibly have that would see them the victors?"

"Wait and see my pet."

Horns blew from the North, and the great army began its march forward, slowly and organized as they had trained their whole lives to do. Yet the defenders of the South remained still, unbothered, and unmoved.

Once the army of the North reached halfway across the valley, the men charged, smelling an easy victory of their lessers.

Suddenly a horn blew from the South, and the men moved with practiced ease, pulling back camouflaged netting, revealing scores of strange wooden contraptions beneath.

The war machines looked like a vast ladle pulled back and resting upon a wide square frame. Torches were touched to pitch-covered boulders cradled within the large buckets and quickly took flame.

Callisto gasped in awe as massive fiery stones were hurtled through the sky to descend upon the ranks of the charging enemy. The boulders collided with men and horses alike, repeatedly crushing scores of soldiers like bugs beneath a boot heel.

Soon the enemy ranks broke in utter confusion and terror. Some men ran for the enemy, hoping to close the distance and escape the bombardment while others thought to retreat, getting in the way of those trying to reach the front.

All the while, death rained down upon them.

Within moments nearly half the larger army was dead or too wounded to fight, and soon the battle became a rout as the army from the South formed ranks and charged, cutting through the once large enemy like a sickle through wheat.

"A well-prepared battlefield can easily defeat a larger enemy," Ares explained.

"I do not see how this will help me now," Callisto admitted. "Battling on land is nowhere the same as at sea. Nor do I have an army to command. I do not know what this will do to help me."

"This is all the help you shall receive from me regarding this. Do not disappoint me."

With that, the god of war faded into nothingness.

Callisto cursed as she stood there, upon the ridge line, watching the battle play out repeatedly, trying to discover what the god of war was trying to show her.

"I know what needs to be done!" Callisto's eyes shot open, and she jumped from her bed. The effects of the night of heavy drinking nearly toppled her over for her efforts.

The dawn was still hours away, but this could not wait.

She ran to the horse pen and roused one of the sleeping beasts, not even concerning herself with a bridle and saddle. As soon as she was mounted, she fled from the dock towards the palace. Yelling and curses came from behind her as the stable man noted her stealing one of his beasts.

Callisto raced up the empty roadside as fast as she dared in the dark, not wanting to injure her borrowed mount.

Slowing the horse as it neared the palace entrance, four

riflemen were already coming towards her, weapons at the ready.

"What do you want at this hour?" one called out.

"I need to speak with Glacia," Callisto replied, climbing down from the horse's back.

"Then you best come back when she is awake."

"Just rouse her and tell her I am here!" snapped Callisto, having no time for this bullshit. "I need to speak with her."

"Look here, Captain," the man started to say.

"No, you look." Callisto stepped right up against the barrel of his rifle, not an ounce of fear on her face. "I know how to break the siege. Now go and wake Glacia."

The man looked back to the others, and they all shared a look before one nodded and took off inside.

"Come on then," the guard grumbled in defeat.

Callisto paced feverishly in the waiting room she had been escorted to. A thousand thoughts of how this would work played through her mind. A thousand different battles, a thousand different endings, and a thousand different scenarios.

"If anyone else thought to wake me at this hour, I would have them publicly executed," Glacia muttered, even at being disturbed in the middle of the night.

"I know how to break the siege!" Callisto said with fire in her voice.

Glacia had been told as much but seeing the passion in this woman's eyes and the power in her voice, she knew something big was about to happen.

"Do not keep me in suspense."

"I will need a dozen of you finest craftsmen, three black-smiths, as much lamp oil as you can spare, and flour, lots of flour!"

Glacia eyed the woman up and down with a smirk,

wondering just what she was planning. "You will have it if it means an end to that bastard besieging my fucking island."

"Are you certain about this, Captain?" Reeves asked, watching the anchor lines to the dock slip away as the ship started to drift into the bay. The call was given, and the sails were raised.

"It will work," Callisto said, trying to hide the doubt in her voice.

It had to work.

It had taken nearly three full days of hard work to ready her plan, but it was finally complete and ready to be used.

A small catapult was mounted at the bow of the Poseidon's Fury and two of Glacia's guard ships. It sat upon a greased iron swivel so that it could be easily aimed to port, front, or starboard. But the large baskets would not hurl large stones like those she had witnessed in her dream, but a score of clay jugs filled with flammable oil.

They had tested the new weapons in the dark of night to ensure they worked and to have an idea of the distance they would fire. After a few dozen test fires with false ammunition, they were confident they could hit their target if they could get close enough.

It was that part that was worrisome, they would have to be within range of cannon fire, but worse was that until the payload was launched, they were at risk of their ship going up in flames if the jugs were damaged.

Callisto was prepared to take that risk. She suspected they were the big prize. The ship that Commodore Belfield wanted to bring back at all costs. And so, she doubted and prayed they would not open fire with their cannons.

Each of the three ships was loaded with a single round,

using all the island's oil it had to spare. They would only get one shot with the catapults. After that, it would be fight or flight if they missed.

Much risk rested on this plan, risk that Callisto had forced upon her ship and crew, even against many who voiced their disapproval, calling it suicide. She had given them a simple choice, sail with her in this attack or to get the fuck off her ship and never return. Only two had left.

The plan was a simple one.

The Poseidon's Fury would lead the attack, as Callisto knew the commodore would focus his fleet's full attention upon her. Once she had their attention, Glacia's two guard ships would sail out to support and take their shots in hopes of crippling two other ships in the Paradise's fleet. From there, it would be a free-for-all with those who were left to flee or fight.

Once the ship was set to sail, and they had caught the western breeze, Callisto hailed her men around the top deck, knowing they needed encouragement.

"I know many of you doubt this course of action, thinking I am a fool, whereas many of you applaud it. But we are not alone in this, nor have we been alone since I became your captain!" It was time to tell them. However, there had already been whispers.

"Many of you heard me cry out in our battle with the slavers to Ares, the god of war of olden times. He is my patron. I pray to him. I fight for him. I sacrifice to him! He lends me his strength, his wisdom, and courage!" she told them proudly and was surprised to see many nodding as they believed in the old gods, as many seamen still did.

"He is with us today!" she called out. "He demands the blood of our enemies!"

The men cheered, even those who likely did not believe her

claims, cheered, for the energy engulfed them, and they needed that before they entered this possibly fatal fight.

"You know the plan, and you know your roles. Now let's sink these fucking bastards and show them who we truly are!"

The day had finally arrived when the Paradise and its fleet of hunters had to set sail from the island to find a safe port to resupply. Their vast arsenal of weapons and ammunition was all but depleted, leaving them dangerously exposed for the trip home if they were to find enemies in front of them.

Commodore Stephan Belfield didn't worry about that, for any pirate or enemy alike would turn and flee before the four warships, not knowing a chance for victory might have been there.

He bit into an apple. It was soft and bruised in several places. Another day or two, and it would have been too rotten to eat. That was another problem. Their food was dwindling, and half rations would need to be put in place before they would see a safe port.

Today they would sail away from this place, this haven for pirates, thieves, and debauchery. But they would return as soon as they could, he vowed. He had to return home with news of all that had transpired, with a score of prisoners and a dozen tales of battle.

This had been a good journey. No, they hadn't been able to bring back the Poseidon's Fury, but they had eliminated a dozen pirate ships and their crews, wounding and crippling a score of others.

The sea would be a little safer for at least a short while.

Stephan tossed the apple core over the railing and turned to address his crew. Their months at sea had ended, but his voice caught in his throat before a single word could be uttered. It was time to tell them they were going home.

Snatching the spyglass from his pocket, he focused on the ship leaving the island, and his pulse raced with anticipation.

The Poseidon's Fury had finally come out!

"To arms!" Stephan cried out when he finally found his voice.

"Commodore?" John Baker asked, suddenly roused from daydreaming at the helm as all those on the ship began preparing for a fight.

"She is finally trying to break out." Stephan pointed.

"With all due respect, Commodore. I am not sure we will have the firepower to take her," John said. "The Poseidon's Fury is near equal to our own."

"I know the number of every iron ball and arrow on each ship," Stephan snapped back with more venom than he should have. "We have more than enough to sink her if it comes to that. But I do not want to sink her. We will capture her. Flank her on both sides, and board her from port and starboard. We outnumber their crew five to one with our combined strength!"

James Featherstone climbed the stairs to stand by Stephan at the stern. "It looks like the little bitch is coming to play after all. We should take her back in chains to be hung with the rest. See how smart-mouthed she is when she spends a month in her own filth."

"If we can take her alive, we will. Any who surrender will be taken prisoner. The crown will be especially interested in them," Stephan agreed. "But the real prize is getting our ship back. That, my lieutenant, will be the cherry on our cake after all this."

James's eyes lit up. "If we take her Commodore, might I ask a favor?"

"And that would be?"

"Might I take command of her for the trip home?"

Stephan raised a brow. "Why would you want to? It will be filled with the stench of pirates."

James looked out at the tiny figure of the Poseidon's Fury moving closer and shrugged. "Call it morbid curiosity."

"If we can take her in one piece, I'll grant it."

The Poseidon's Fury's crew watched as the naval fleet began their communications and repositioning, hoping to flank them on both sides for an easy board and capture. But they wouldn't be able to form up before the first engagement with the Sea Lion happened. But they expected the Poseidon to try and flee, not fight. That would be their downfall.

As much as Callisto wanted the Paradise and Stephan Belfield, the Sea Lion was the true threat. Slower moving it was, but it had nearly twice the crew and twice the cannons as the other three ships. If she could cripple it or sink it with her payload, half the battle around the island would already be won.

The tricky part of this plan was trying to stay ahead of the Sea Lion's cannons. If they were caught under a hail of fire, this would be over before they could begin.

It was a risk, a great risk.

The next part of the trick was to keep their surprise hidden until they were in range, much like the smaller army in her dream had done. They needed to catch them by surprise and make them believe that the Poseidon's crew were going straight for a boarding attempt and not open fire.

"We are coming to the point of no return, Captain," Reeves

said, gripping the wheel tightly, anticipating what would come next.

"Keep us small and in front of them," Callisto called to him. "Don't let us get caught along their starboard side! We don't need them to open fire on us!"

"Murphy!" Callisto called down to him. "Get the boarding party ready and make it look real!"

"You heard the captain, you sea dogs! Make it look good, or you've killed us all!"

"Weaver!" the captain bellowed.

"Yes, Captain?" the tall man called back and waited with five others for their particular task.

Callisto locked eyes with him. "Make ready."

Weaver nodded nervously. He and the others had been tasked with their plan's opening scene. If they didn't play it right, they would be dead or in chains by the morning's end. Neither was a favorable prospect, and all had doubts about whether it would even work.

The Poseidon's Fury was closing fast with the Sea Lion as the two ships raced towards one another. But Kadir kept his eye to the spyglass, watching the enemy's every move, waiting for that final moment when the Sea Lion would turn sharp to starboard to cut them off or to open fire.

"Rusty Juan?" Callisto called to her man in the crow's nest.

He licked his lips nervously. "Not yet, Captain!"

Callisto gripped the railing as she watched the ship speed closer. So close now she could see their mouths moving as they called out to each other. The order would be given any moment now, and the enemy ship would turn sharp to cut them off, forcing them to turn to port into the three oncoming enemy ships or steer starboard and risk the cannons and boarding.

"Juan?" Callisto called again, her nerves beginning to unravel as each second seemed a lifetime.

"Hold!"

It had to be perfect.

"Hold!"

Silence settled on the Poseidon's Fury as every crewman held their breath, knowing this was it. The moment this whole crazy plan truly began and ended, either in victory or in death.

"NOW!" Rusty Juan screamed.

Reeves spun the wheel as fast to starboard as he could where a dozen men pulled and cranked ropes, adjusting them to keep the sails full. They could not slow down, and they had to keep that hair's breadth ahead of the enemy.

The Sea Lion also turned hard to starboard, but moments behind them and the bigger, heavier warship could not hope to turn as gracefully nor as prepared.

"Weaver, now!" Callisto cried out as she saw the Sea Lion's cannon hatches pop open.

Even though the Poseidon's Fury cannons were not aimed at the enemy but somewhat ahead of them, torches went to wicks. They weren't trying to hit the Sea Lion. The cannons weren't even loaded with iron. The long guns on the starboard fired in a vast spray of flour, creating a blinding screen against their enemy. Stealing their sight and, hopefully, their aim.

"Hard to port!" Callisto screamed, knowing each second wasted was a second closer to failure. "Alonso, get ready!"

Once more, Reeves threw his weight into the wheel, pulling with all his considerable strength as the crew went fast to work, shifting the sails once more the other way to help him.

The Poseidon's Fury lurched to port, cutting abruptly in front of the path of the blinded Sea Lion. So sudden was the maneuver, even knowing it was coming, two crewmen lost their foot, slammed into the railing, and held on for dear life.

The enemy, though blinded, took their shot, thinking the pirates were just beyond the distraction. Cannons erupted through the white haze between them, except the Poseidon's Fury was no longer there, and its port side directly faced the Sea Lion's bow.

"Now!" Callisto cried out through the cannon fire as she caught sight of the first of the Sea Lion's crew to realize the ruse that had just been played.

Alonso cut the rope holding back the catapult's arm.

Time seemed to slow as the thick wooden arm snapped up, and a score of clay jugs soared between the two ships, scattering down the Sea Lion nearly from bow to stern. The jugs shattered and sprayed oil in every direction, soaking men, timber, rope, and sails alike.

A dozen arrows were put to flame.

"Fire!" Callisto grinned viciously, seeing the sudden understanding of what had just transpired on their enemy's faces as flaming arrows soared towards them.

Instantly, flames sprung to life, consuming timber, rigging, and flesh without remorse. The screams of men burning to death filled the air in a deranged macabre song.

But not everything went as planned as the Sea Lion's ram slammed the Poseidon's stern. Timbers along the hull cracked, and a man was thrown over the side of the Poseidon to the unforgiving waves below.

The collision only slowed the Poseidon's Fury a little as they sailed away from the screams of the dying and men throwing themselves overboard, hoping to escape the inferno that had become their ship.

Callisto stared back at the destruction and knew the Sea Lion was doomed. Her plan had worked. It would sink to the bottom of the sea along with most of its crew.

Glacia's two guard ships had already covered half the distance from the island, ready to join in the fight. A dozen pirate ships were not far behind. Whether to join in the fight or to take the moment to break free was unknown.

"Captain," Reeves asked, looking back as the burning ship and the three other naval ships finally came around the fading flour screen, "should we turn back and assist?"

"No, we have done our part in this deed. Let the others finish the fight," she ordered. "Steady our course southwest. Let's go hunting!"

"Faster!" Commodore Belfield screamed, seeing the Sea Lion about to engage with the famed pirate ship. They needed to get there to ensure they could take the ship intact. To cut off any hope of retreat they might have. This was their chance to capture the ship, and it was not a chance he planned on letting get away.

Stephan wasn't worried about the Sea Lion. He had been aboard it for many years and knew it could handle anything this woman captain could throw at it. The Sea Lion was the strongest and most capable in battle of all four ships in his fleet.

The sound of cannons was heard, and out of nowhere, a white cloud of smoke appeared, blocking Stephan and the other ship's view of the fight before them.

"What the hell?" Stephan muttered.

"Where did all that smoke come from?" James asked as the two ships disappeared before their eyes.

Stephan grabbed the spyglass. "It's not smoke."

"Then what is it?"

Commodore Belfield felt a tightness growing in his chest. Something was wrong. "I don't know, a trick of some kind."

Within moments flames leaped into the air above the

strange white dust cloud, mixing it with thick, curling black smoke.

"By God!" James Featherstone gasped. "What did the Sea Lion do? How did they get a fire going like that?"

"No!" Stephan cried out, losing his composure and feeling his heart sinking, along with his prize. "We want her afloat. You damned fools!"

"Commodore, look!" A crewman pointed to the southwest.

Stephan turned to see the Poseidon's Fury sailing clear of the cloud, not on fire or in any distress. "What? How? But that means...."

"The Sea Lion!" James bellowed in realization that their warship was going up in flames.

"Mr. Baker, bring us up to starboard!" the commodore ordered as he watched several of the Sea Lion's crew jump from the burning ship into the water, trying to escape the certain death that had become their ship.

"Commodore, look!" the helmsman shouted, pointing to several ships making their way from the island towards them. "If we stop, they'll be on us in short order. We don't have the firepower to stop that many ships! If we stay, we will join the Sea Lion at the bottom of the sea, no doubt."

"We cannot leave them! Now set us to the starboard side! Ready ropes to haul them up!" Stephan turned to James. "Get the Highlander and Sea Glory to intercept and open fire! Hold them back as long as possible!"

What was happening?

How was this possible?

Out of a thousand scenarios he had played in his mind, nothing like this had even occurred to him.

Stephan felt as if his entire world had just taken a mighty blow. He had studied under the best and brightest minds in naval history. He had known life at sea fighting pirates was dangerous, and that his life could end at any time in battle. But never before had he believed he could not prevail so long as he remained calm, and his men followed the commands he gave them. But this was becoming a situation he could not control. This was a situation that was very quickly unraveling everything he had believed.

They were weakened with their limited weaponry, and now the strongest ship of their fleet was burning dead in the water, with a dozen ships threatening to engage them in combat.

The Paradise slowed, tossing a dozen lines into the water, trying to rescue their drowning comrades. There were scores of them scrambling to grab hold of a lifeline. Well, there were already dozens of bodies facedown and unmoving, some still smoldering from the flames that had taken them.

Screams suddenly tore through the distance, and those aboard the Paradise stopped to witness greedy flames engulf the starboard side of the Highlander as if it had been dried grass. But even from here, everyone on the Paradise knew there would be no saving it. The Highlander had been as quickly defeated as the Sea Lion.

"What weapon could they possibly possess to do such a thing?" James Featherstone gasped.

A cold sweat hit Stephan as he watched in horror while another ship under his command went up in flames. The sound of cannons shattering through planking and the screams of the dying were all he could hear. Its crew was forsaken to the deadly waters or the arrows or blades of pirates.

"Sir! Sir!" Lieutenant Featherstone grabbed Stephan's arm.

Stephan snapped back to attention. "What is it?"

James stared at him as if it should be obvious. "We need to retreat. Now!"

"We cannot leave our men behind," Stephan argued, though there was little conviction in his tone.

"All is lost, Commodore. We retreat now, or we join the others in death, and all we have learned is for nothing."

Stephan licked his lips, fighting every ounce of his pride, telling him to find a way to win. If he had just a little longer to think, he would figure out a way to turn this battle around. To win! But even he knew they had lost and were moments away from the grim fate the others would face.

"Fuck it!" James growled, pushing by Stephan. "RETREAT! Make haste!"

The Paradise's crew jumped into action, not caring where the order came from, only that it had finally come. Death was in the air, and they had already witnessed two of their ships and crews engulfed in flames, and the Sea Glory was surely to join them.

Stephan nodded his approval to his lieutenant but could not find his voice as he stared ahead at the utter ruin he had brought upon them. This defeat was his, and their deaths were because of his pride.

The Poseidon's Fury cut through the three-foot waves with ease as the dawn of a new day slowly lifted from the watery horizon in the east. They were still traveling southwest towards a known trade route between Puerto Rico and Ireland.

They hoped to catch a heavily ladened ship full of rum, spices, and tobacco heading to Ireland or a ship full of silks, wool, teas, and foodstuffs heading to Puerto Rico. Either one would be an excellent start to refilling their depleted coffers.

They had sailed more than two hundred miles from Glacia's Island and the battle they had helped start and hopefully helped finish, knowing at least two British ships had met their end.

Callisto knew that such a thing would weigh heavily on Commodore Belfield, knowing he had led all those men to their deaths. If luck had it, the others would have given chase and put The Paradise beneath the waves. But deep down, she knew that wasn't the case. Deep down, she knew he was still alive, and they would one day meet again.

The Poseidon's Fury had not escaped unscathed. The collision with the Sea Lion had left an eight-foot hole in the back of the hull. Thankfully they had the supplies to make minor repairs to such a hole. They wouldn't sink, but they would take on some water that would need to be bailed out often. When next they found a port, they would need to have a shipwright repair it properly.

Callisto filled her lungs with the salty air, and even though it had only been three months since she fled from Tamora, she felt more at home here and now upon this ship than anywhere else. She knew in her heart this was where she was meant to be. Everything that had happened from that fateful day to now had been for this.

"Captain, what are you doing at the helm?" Reeves asked, climbing from below deck to relieve Three-Fingered Pete, the night helmsman. "Where is Three Fingers?"

"Likely drunk and passed out in his hammock, I would hope," she replied. "I relieved him a few hours ago. I was awake, and this is something, as captain, I should know how to do. What real captain can't steer their ship?"

"None, as far as I know. But steering the ship is easy. It's just this big wheel going side to side. The real impressive part is knowing how to read the compass, astrolabe, maps, and charts."

"Three Fingers told me to keep the sun behind my left shoulder, and we'd be fine."

"Aye, close enough."

"But you're right. I know very little of these things, and I should. You will teach me."

"I think Murphy would be better suited as a teacher for that kind of thing," Reeves admitted. "I have never taught anyone much of anything."

Callisto grimaced. "I would prefer you to do it. After our battle, Murphy has been—distracted."

"A few of the Wind Spirit's crew seem to be struggling to digest what we did."

"We won and only lost one of our own. The plan worked as well as we could have expected it, given what we were up against."

"You are made of different stuff, Captain, but the Wind Spirit were merchants, not pirates. Sure, they know how to fight and defend themselves. But they watched honest men burn to death or be swallowed by the sea." He shrugged. "That can twist a man in his core. Make him question himself."

"You are so much more than you appear, Reeves." Callisto's brow lifted. "You look like a pirate and act like a pirate. But when you talk with me, I could swear you were far more than that."

"I wasn't always a pirate. There was a life before all this."

"What were you before you found yourself in this life?"

"You wouldn't believe me even if I told you."

"Try me."

Reeves glanced around to ensure no one was listening. "My father was a small but respected sculptor in Spain, and my mother was a handmaiden for a noblewoman. When I was born, my mother had been allowed to bring me to work. The noblewoman she waited on also had two young children a little older than me. I was raised mostly within those walls for the first twelve years of my life. Learning as the noble children did, to read and write, proper etiquette, and more."

"A start to life many could never dream of."

"Aye, it would have seemed just that to an outside view. And was something my mother and father told me often to be grateful for," Reeves said with a hint of bitterness.

"Clearly, it didn't remain so?"

"I was never seen as an equal, not among the nobles of the house, not among the staff, and certainly not among the two I grew up beside. I was always the 'dog' as I was often referred to. They looked down on me, treated me like their personal slave, and that was the truth of it. The lady of the house allowed my mother to bring me into their home for just that reason. To allow her children to lord it over someone. To give them practice."

"The noble class can be cruel indeed. I have had my fair share of run-ins with many," Callisto agreed. "What happened?"

"There are only so many times you can kick a dog before it bites back." Reeves' eyes darkened. "My mother was little more than a slave for these people. To do as she was told, regardless of what it was, even if it was for the sexual urges of two boys hardly older than her own son."

He took a deep breath. "I killed them all one night. I slit the lord and lady's throats while they slept, nailed their bastard children to a wall, and skinned them alive. I stole everything I could carry before setting the house on fire."

"I thought I had done good and had freed us from that torment. My mother and father shunned me. They took what I had stolen for themselves and turned me in to the authorities."

He was silent for a long time, and Callisto believed that

was all he would tell and was about to say something when he finally continued.

"Because I was so young, I was spared the rope and instead sold to a Spanish merchant as a rower." He held up his scarred hands. "I spent four years rowing that fat bastard's ship around before pirates finally attacked us. When we were boarded, a few of us got free and attacked, killing the fat merchant and several of his guard before the pirates took over the ship." The darkness faded a little from his eyes, and he finally grinned. "I think you know the choice I made after that."

"That is quite the tale," Callisto replied. "One that resonates with much of my own. I suspect many of those on the ship have tales of similar woes."

"Nay, Captain. The rest of these cunts were born gutter rats and will die rats," Reeves joked. "What is your true story? What were you before we found you as a stowaway and before you killed one of the fiercest pirates on the seas?"

"Another day, perhaps," Callisto said, not wanting to relive that memory.

Reeves turned his attention to the bow of the ship. "Where did you get the idea for that?"

"Not sure you'd believe me if I told you."

"The god you spoke of?" Reeves asked. "I don't know much about the old gods or the new. I know of Poseidon only because some of this lot still make sacrifices for him before we leave port. But I never truly gave them much thought."

"Poseidon is Ares's uncle."

"You truly believe this god talks to you?"

"We are still alive, aren't we?"

"By that logic, someone could make that claim every time something bad happened, and they survived."

"Do you think I am lying?"

Reeves looked her up and down but ended up shaking his head. "If you are, you believe it."

"Do you believe we will have any issues with the recruits?" she asked him.

Reeves chewed his lip. "Hard to say."

Callisto cocked a brow. "How is it hard to say when you are the quartermaster? Is it not your job to know these things?"

"About that." He scratched his head. "I'm not a very good quartermaster. Blackmane made me take the position when the man before me was killed. It came with a pay increase, and well, one didn't think to say no to Blackmane and hope to —prosper."

Callisto nodded, catching on to what he was hinting at. "Who would you give the position to?"

"Old Half Beard likely would do the job better than most. He's been sailing since he was still at his mother's tit. Been a pirate longer than most of the crew has been alive and crossed more blades than most of us put together too. Though slowing down, the old dog is still as sharp as a whip and has a few tricks to teach. Heck, truth be told, I order him to do half my job already."

"Do you think there are others who may feel the same as you in their jobs and duties?" she asked him.

Reeves shrugged. "Most of these bastards are just here for the coin and fighting. Hard but simple men that just need someone to point a coin in front of their noses." He paused and added. "But keep an eye on Murphy. A pirate ship is no place for weakness. A first mate can't be weak in the face of necessity. The men won't stand for it and won't respect him for long. And pirates who don't respect those in charge of them—well—go missing or are found dead."

"He'll come around," Callisto said with confidence. "He

was a sailor and captain for a long time. He will harden himself to what happened."

"I hope you're right."

The next four days were uneventful, which seemed to be preferred by most of the crew. They sailed the open waters southwest, the crow's nest always occupied, searching the horizon for sails and opportunity. But each day ended as it began, with horizons clear of prospects.

The crew spent their days cleaning the ship and trading stories among each other as they began to blend as one crew. The original crew of the Poseidon's Fury showed those of the Wind Spirit and the new recruits from the Phantom Chaser how things aboard a pirate vessel were done in their crude manner.

All three small groups seemed to merge as well as one could have hoped well the ship's new quartermaster, Half Beard, beat them into shape, often literally. Each man found their best-suited role with the stern help of the ship's new quartermaster, and soon the running of the ship fell into place as if the crew had sailed together for years.

Half Beard took to his new position with earnestness, and no one aboard the ship would have guessed he had been anything but quartermaster his whole life. Battle tactics and maneuvers were drilled over and over again until each man aboard could easily fall into their place. Ensuring they could be counted on to fulfill their role in any coming fight when the time came. And once they were perfect, he drilled them again, harder, faster until all they wanted to do was throw themselves overboard.

More than once, fist fights broke out, and each time Half Beard gave out twice as many licks as he received and put the men back in line. And once a man from the Phantom Chaser pulled a knife, thinking of silencing the old brute once and for all. A skilled throw from Weaver had a hatchet buried in the man's back before he got close. Callisto had finished the job by using the same blade the man had tried to use to kill Half Beard to cut his throat and throw him overboard. After that, everyone fell in line, and the ship's daily duties ran smoothly.

Callisto spent her mornings learning maps, charts, and how to sail the ship she now commanded. She often spent time with the crew while they worked, learning to tie different knots, adjusting ropes, sails, and even how to load the cannons. What all working parts were, what they did, how they did it, and why they were important.

Her afternoons were spent crossing blades with one crew member or another with Reeves and Weaver hands on hilts close by. But no attempts had been made on her life. The Wind Spirit crew was hers now; she knew none of them would move against her. Those from the slave ship seemed more than willing to accept her as captain after she had given them their freedom. Even those of Blackmane's old crew, though only a score remained aboard the ship, had fallen in line after recent events. Though doubt still nagged her when she found herself alone with too many of them.

Many still glanced at her with a hint of contempt, not liking the mere fact that a woman held authority over them. But they kept themselves in check, and none had said or done anything to warrant action.

If this were indeed her destiny and the path Ares wanted her to walk, she would walk it, and sooner or later, she would have her crew bound to her. In truth, she wondered if this was just how it was for a captain. Did they ever really trust their crews? Were they ever safe from a dagger in the back or mutiny?

Callisto parried a final attack, off-balancing Kadir, who

stumbled forward. She turned and slapped the flat of her blade across his rump as he tried righting himself.

"Fuck," Kadir muttered, knowing he was defeated. "I thought I had you again."

"You almost did." Callisto slipped her sword into its scabbard, smiling that she had finally defeated him.

Out of the score of the crew she had practiced against, only a handful had she been able to defeat. Several had been stalemates, and others had proven their years of experience over her with little remorse. But she was improving and hoped she would soon be able to stand against most of the crew.

"You have come a long way from the random stowaway we found below deck." Kadir laughed, wiping the sweat from his eyes.

"And you have fallen into a pirate's life rather well for an honest man," Callisto countered.

Kadir's smirk left, and he merely shrugged. "My father always used to tell me you have to sail at best you can with the waves that find you, not against them."

"Wise words."

"He was a prick most of the time." Kadir laughed. "But he had his pearls of wisdom."

"How is Murphy doing?"

"Captain?"

"I have seen you and Alonso sitting with him at times, talking. I have seen very little of him, and he seems to be avoiding me."

"Honestly, Captain, he doesn't say much. Me and Alonso do most of the talking. Normally of our times together on the Wind Spirit. But he hasn't been right in the head since we set the Sea Lion ablaze," Kadir replied, clearly having his own dark thoughts about the battle. "It was a dirty business for those of us not used to such affairs."

"Do you regret it?"

"I have a lot of regrets in my life, Captain," he admitted, "but staying alive isn't one of them. Though I'd be a bold liar if I didn't tell you I have had to harden a part of me because of it."

Callisto respected that honesty and couldn't argue it, for she had felt a slight change in her soul that day. "Go and get Murphy up here. I need to talk to him. I will be in my cabin."

Callisto poured herself a glass of watered wine. She was drinking more than usual, a habit of the job, she suspected—a job she was taking to with a practiced ease to all who were watching.

In truth, she spent her nights questioning everything she had done since the beginning. From the moment she had killed Blackmane and freed Murphy and the Wind Spirit crew. It had all just come to her as if it had been rehearsed. But the truth was, even knowing Ares was with her, she felt doubt in all of this.

She smiled down at the drink in her hands. "At least I have you to help me sleep and silence the thoughts in my head."

A knock at the door pulled her from those thoughts.

"Enter."

Murphy stepped into the cabin. He looked a wreck, with dark circles around her eyes and his face unshaven for a week. "You wished to see me, Captain?"

"I have barely seen the whites of your eyes since we set sail," Callisto replied, regarding the once imposing figure, who now looked longer in his years than he was. "The men need you. I need you. Old Half Beard is our new quartermaster, yet he has also fulfilled most of your duties as first mate. It is not a good look for either of us."

Murphy shrugged as if it hardly mattered. "You seem to be getting along well enough."

His tone was one of defeat, and Callisto felt a true worry for him. "Talk to me."

"What is it you need of me, Captain?"

Callisto threw her glass at the wall beside Murphy as she stormed towards him in frustration.

"I need my fucking first mate to be of sound mind!" she screamed an inch from his face. "I need the one person on this ship I fucking trust the most, helping me sail this tub and its unruly crew! Yet you have been hiding below deck like a dog that has been kicked."

"I—I—" Murphy sighed. "I just can't."

"Can't what?" Callisto pressed. "Sail? Navigate? Teach? Watch over the crew? Have my back? Fight? Kill? What is it that Murphy cannot do any fucking longer?"

Murphy opened his mouth to speak, yet no words would come.

"You have killed before. Men have fallen to your blade. What was done needed to be done. We did not ask for it. Hell, we even tried to wait it out. But we dealt with it as it needed to be dealt with, as pirates deal with things."

"I am not a pirate," he told her mournfully.

"You are now, as am I and everyone else on this ship."

"I tried—for you."

She grabbed him by his dirty shirt and shook him bitterly. "I need you to try harder."

"I can't," he whispered.

"No," Callisto growled, shaking him harder. "I will not accept that bullshit! You can, and you fucking will!"

"Ship ho! South to southeast, port side!" Rusty Juan called from the crow's nest.

Callisto sneered at Murphy and shoved him back. "Get below deck and grab your fucking gear. We have work to do, and I need you by my side for this. We can't let this one get away. We need plunder."

Out on the deck, her crew was fast to work, eagerness in their movements like a pack of wolves finally sighting a meal after days of their stomachs growling in bitterness.

"What do we have?" she called up to Juan.

"Two masts, moving slowly northeast. Not sitting too low in the water, but low enough. I suspect they have something on there for cargo," came the call back. "Flying a French flag, only four cannons aside."

"You hear that, men!" Callisto shouted. "Fine plunder to be found on French ships! Fine food, silks, and spices for Mr. Pewter to make this crap we have been eating bearable! Oh, and do not doubt a chest or two full of gold and silver for our coffers!"

If the men truly needed more encouragement, that was more than enough as they readied themselves for the coming fight with a new fire.

"Ready the cannons Half Beard," she commanded. "But let us not risk sinking her before we take what we need from them!"

She turned her attention to the helm and knew Reeves didn't want to be there. He wanted a fight, not to be stuck at the wheel once more. "Get Three Finger Pete at the helm! Reeves, Murphy, you are with me!"

Reeves grinned like a boy. "Aye, aye, Captain!"

Murphy merely complied as he strapped on his sword belt, something he had not worn since their escape from the island.

The French ship tried to outrun them, but with only two masts and the wind not in their favor, the Poseidon's Fury had them within three hours. The race was over, and the fight was about to begin.

The French ship cut hard to port and opened fire.

"Down!" Callisto screamed.

Iron balls thundered into the bow of the Poseidon's hull, punching two holes through the timber while two more skipped across the deck, blasting through the railing harmlessly.

"Ram them!" Callisto screamed.

Counting the minutes, she knew it would take a well-organized crew to reload the long guns. But the French crew knew they had no chance and quickly abandoned the cannons, drew blades, and lifted their rifles.

Bullets clipped into the railing and deck as they got off a single volley before the Poseidon's Fury ram crashed into their flank and spun them to the port side of the Poseidon. With the skill of expert seamen, the pirates' sails slackened, losing the strength of the wind as they ground hull against hull against the smaller vessel.

Grappling hooks bit into the wood, locking the two ships side by side. A handful of the French crew chopped at the ropes trying to separate the two ships before the pirates could board. Those not chopping fired their rifles up at the pirates, wounding one too eager for the fight to keep back from the railing.

The French crew timed their shots well, keeping the pirates fearful of jumping the rail to board as the thick ropes were cut one after the other. The lock would be lost at this rate, and the chase would begin anew.

Frustrated, Callisto stepped forward and fired her pistol, clipping an enemy gunman in the shoulder. "Now!" she screamed, and two bullets bit into the wood right beside her.

A dozen pirates stepped forward and fired at the first thing they saw, wasting no time aiming and risking being shot in return. Four enemies went down, and others stumbled back and took cover against the sudden hail of bullets and arrows.

"Board!" Callisto screamed, and her men fearlessly leaped into the waiting enemy below.

By the time Callisto's feet had touched the deck, nearly a dozen enemies were dead, and the French crew were already throwing down their weapons in utter defeat, knowing it was over.

"We surrender!" the French captain bellowed, dropping to his knees. "Do not kill us!"

"Wise decision." Callisto kicked the kneeling man onto his back. "What are you carrying?"

"Mostly spices, wool, silk, and two dozen crates of wine," the chubby captain whimpered. "Please, it is not much, and to take it will ruin all I have worked for."

"You need to worry about today," she sneered, "not tomorrow."

Callisto turned to her crew. "Secure the prisoners and empty the ship but leave enough food—" her words caught in her throat, her ears suddenly ringing as something tore into her side.

"Captain!" Reeves screamed, his blade slashing down behind her.

She glanced back to see the captain's severed hand and pistol clatter to the deck, and Reeves lay the man low with a mighty punch.

"You sonofabitch." She lifted her hand from her side to see dark blood.

"Alonso!" Kadir screamed, rushing to his friend's aid.

Confused at what was happening, Callisto turned to see Alonso, who had been only a few feet behind her, drop to his knees. His hand holding his guts, a dark red patch began to grow across his tanned vest.

"I—I'm—sorry—Captain—I was—too slow—" he muttered before falling back into Kadir's arms.

Callisto felt her rage building as she turned back to the defeated captain, who was starting to come back around. "You fucking idiot!" she spat.

"I would have let you live! I would have let your crew live!" She pulled one of her silver flintlock pistols and pushed it into the blubbering man's mouth. "You killed yourself and your crew this day!" She pulled the trigger, painting the deck with the man's brains.

The ship was silent as death as men from both crews waited for what came next.

"Captain, you're going to bleed out." Reeves was at her side helping steady her. "We need to get you to the ship." Already strong arms were bent down from the Poseidon to retrieve her.

Callisto was lifted onto her ship, and there, a dozen feet away, stood Murphy, his eyes downcast. "Where were you?" she screamed weakly. "You were supposed to be watching my side!" She staggered towards him but found little strength in her feet, and once more, Reeves was there.

"Captain, what are your orders?" Weaver asked. He had heard her declaration, as had everyone else.

"Plunder everything from the ship." She didn't take her eyes off Murphy. "Then set it ablaze and make him watch tied to the main mast. The death of these men is on your hands. And know this, if Alonso dies," her eyes burned violence, "so do you, Murphy, so do you."

"You heard the captain!" Weaver called out. "Get to fucking work!"

Before her cabin door closed, the screams and begging of dying men from the French ship could already be heard.

The bottle trembled in his hand as he tried to fill his glass for the countless time that day. He wanted to blame it on the ship's swaying but knew that was a lie; he was deeply under the influence of the potent rum. An influence he had been under for a week now.

Stephan had never been a heavy drinker. He had limited nearly all base pleasures that other men over-indulged in. He prided himself over others for his ability to drink only a little in celebrations. But the clear liquor was all he felt was keeping him together at this point.

It was undoubtedly the only thing that allowed him to sleep without having to hear the screams of his men as they had burned or were dragged beneath the lapping waves of the merciless sea around that wretched woman's island.

The thought of that despicable place and what had transpired put the glass to his lips again, and he drank, letting the potent liquid burn down to his very soul—trying to burn away the memories of failure—of death that rested upon his shoulders.

Images of the Sea Lion and The Highlander up in flames from the devious employment of deck-mounted catapults filled with oil jugs flashed before his eyes. He wanted to scream —or maybe he was screaming and didn't realize it anymore as his throat had long ago gone raw.

They had had to retreat from the battle before it had even begun. Everything had happened so fast, so precise, so perfectly executed by the enemies it had seemed unreal.

He had ordered rope thrown to Sea Lion's crew to try and rescue those who had jumped into the waters to avoid the deadly fires that consumed it. Only nine had made it aboard, nine out of ninety-six souls. Scores had remained in the waters, trying desperately to swim to the Paradise, seeing a chance at survival.

A chance he had had to deny them.

Stephan finished his drink in a single swallow.

The only way any of them would survive the calculated attack had been to flee, so the order had been given. An order that had refused to leave his lips, and so his Lieutenant, James Featherstone, had ordered it, as Stephan had watched his men flounder in the waters, desperately crying for help, knowing their lives were forfeit.

The Paradise had abandoned the Sea Lion to its fate, and so too had the Sea Glory seeing The Highlander engulfed in flames. The Sea Glory had fired her cannons at the oncoming ships, buying itself time to escape. But the Sea Glory had taken much damage in those first few moments, wounds that had slowly filled her hull with seawater—slowing her down while a handful of pirate dogs nipped at her heels.

The Paradise had circled, firing off two volleys of her long guns, hoping to force the pursuing pirates back into a retreat. But the baying hounds had tasted blood and wanted their meal.

The Paradise had abandoned the Sea Glory to the hounds, knowing the only way to avenge all they had lost was to escape and make it home. Only back in London could they muster a new force, tenfold in size and strength, and avenge the hundreds of good, proud men they had lost. Their deaths could not be in vain at the hands of this scourge.

Stephan filled his drink again, spilling more upon his desk and papers than went into his glass.

Images of the Sea Glory being circled by the four pirate ships that had chased them for three days flashed in his mind, and fresh tears cut a path down his unshaven cheeks. On that day, after that command, he had felt the last of his resolve crack inside.

They were still nearly a fortnight from London. A fortnight

before, he would have to give his report—explain how his pride had gotten hundreds of Britain's finest sailors and loyal soldiers killed. How he had lost three of King William's strongest naval vessels in a fight they should have avoided altogether if he had given the order to leave days before.

They would court-martial him. Strip him of his rank, take his house, and put him back where his peasant blood demanded him to be. Beneath the heels of better men...

...or...

...they would lock him away in chains, in a cell beneath the cold ground like so many pirates he had put there before.

No, he decided.

He would ask for the rope.

Beg for it if he must.

Better to hang and end it all with the last shred of dignity he could hope to collect. Maybe then his wife and son wouldn't have to hang their heads low in shame at every look from another.

Stephan glanced at the pistol on his desk.

He could end it now.

Save them all the trouble of any of this.

His fingers grazed the polished oak handle, lingering on the smooth cold iron of the barrel trigger.

"You best not be thinking of doing something foolish," James Featherstone said as he closed the cabin door behind him.

Instantly, Stephan pulled his hand back, shame filling him. "What do you want?" he slurred.

James knocked the empty rum bottle to the floor. "I want you to get your fucking head together, get out there, and show the men you haven't broken down like a whimpering child."

Stephan sat back in his chair and glared at his lieutenant.

"You dare to speak to your commodore in such a manner? I could have you locked in chains for such a thing."

James nearly laughed in his face. "I wouldn't dream of talking to the commodore of the Paradise in such a way." He leaned forward on the desk, his face mere inches from Stephan's. "But the drunk in front of me is not that man, so I will talk to this drunkard before me however I see fit."

"There are all dead because of me." Fresh tears brimmed his eyes. "All of them."

"Nonsense," James snapped. "They are dead because pirates overwhelmed us while we did what the crown asked us to do. It is a hazard of the job. Most times, we win. Sometimes, we do not."

"I should have commanded us to leave days before when we knew our supplies were low. I should have known they would try and break out when we were weakened."

James rolled his eyes. "So, you are a seer now? You know the future? If so, then yes, you should have known and, therefore, sailed us far, far away long before it happened."

Stephan glared at the man for his sarcastic comment.

"You are just a man, Stephan, as I am just a man. We cannot know everything about everything. You were just about to sail us home after doing our job liberating the sea of several pirate threats. What happened was tragic, but your fault? Nay. The fault rests on the pirates. None of this would have happened if they were not out here."

For a moment, Stephan felt a little of the guilt lift. "The crown and others will not see it as such when I give my report."

"They will if I am standing beside you and tell them as such. You are a hero among these men, well-loved among all who know you, and I am rich and come from a family of prestige and honor," James reminded him. "Our word will erase any doubt from their minds."

Stephan sighed. "But it will not erase it from my own."

James looked down at him with disgust. "How did you ever rise above your birth? I admired you once upon a time, even wished to be like you." Now he shook his head. "How could I be so blind as to the weak man before me."

"How dare you!" Stephan clambered to his feet, nearly falling back as his impairment almost swooned him.

"How dare I?" James laughed. "How dare I?" He pointed to the door. "You have men out there who need you! Who has just been through the hardest blow to their pride and world. They lost far more than you out there, yet you sit here hiding in the dark, trying to purge your shame, only proving to any who doubted you that they were correct to do so. How dare I? No, Stephan, how fucking dare you!"

The Commodore fell back into his chair in defeat. The words came as a fiercer blow than any physical attack could have.

"I am giving you three options." He pushed the pistol closer. "Take the coward's way out or be on the deck in the morning, ready to command this ship and these men." He paused. "Or I will take full command and have you in irons for failing your duty to the crown."

Stephan watched the lieutenant leave his cabin and was assaulted by every word the man had thrown at him. He grabbed the gun, put it to his temple, and screamed.

Lieutenant James Featherstone stood at the bow of the Paradise, looking back at the crew as they slowly gathered on the main deck after being called to attention. The dawn was among them, and so was the time for him to make his decision and inform the men that Commodore Stephan Belfield would no longer hold command and would be locked in irons for the remainder of the trip home.

It was not an easy decision, though he would be lying to himself if he wasn't excited by it. He would step into the role, and hopefully, upon their return, he would find himself higher in his ranking for it. Or at least closer to achieving a captain's title. Maybe they would hand him over the Paradise.

He had given Stephan a choice when in truth, due to the man's fall into despair, he hadn't needed to. But he had feared taking control of the ship against him. Mutiny upon a naval ship was an ugly beast and often spelled disaster for all involved. But he knew he was righteous in this course, and the men would support him.

They were defeated, haggard, and full of bitterness and despair. They needed a firm leader now more than ever before. He would become that leader and lead them home and gain their respect.

Steadying himself, he took a deep breath, about to address them when the door to the commodore's cabin opened. His voice caught in his throat as the impressive figure of Stephan Belfield stepped out. He was cleanly shaven and dressed now as fine as James had ever seen him.

Stephan climbed the steps to the upper deck and looked down upon the crowd of sailors. His hawk gaze swept over all of them and came to rest on James, where he gave the slightest nod. The man had made him see the error of his anguish. Had forced the uncomfortable truth into the open and forced him to decide.

A decision had been made.

"I must issue a grand apology to each and every one of you," Stephan said loud enough for all to hear. "My absence the last several days is inexcusable. I failed you when my presence was needed the most. For that, I pray you can one day forgive me."

He paused, letting his words reach them, gauging their looks and movements. Had he lost them already, or could he win them back to his side?

"The defeat we suffered wounded me greater than any physical blow could have. I felt like a failure and mourned deeply for our lost comrades, as I am sure you all are. We lost friends, family, and men we have known for months, years, and even decades, men we have lived and fought beside."

"I feared my leadership and pride had seen us fail and fall into ruin. But nay," he took a deep breath, "it wasn't anything we did that saw such a horrific event come to pass. For we are righteous in our cause, but even the righteous succumb to defeats. But only in remaining defeated are the righteous truly beaten!"

Several cheers came forth.

"We do honest work for God and the crown of King William the Third! It is these scum of the sea, these pirates and murderers, that have chosen the side of evil! To pray upon the weak and wreak havoc on the goodly folk of the world. We are all that stand in their way. We have had our noses bloodied, but we few survived. We few will live another day and seek justice for what these demons have done!"

More cheers now filled the ship.

"The pirates have chosen to side with the devil, and so to hell, we will send them!" he cried out. "Bring up the prisoners!"

James felt his lungs burning and realized he had been so caught up in the speech that he had been holding his breath. How was it possible, he wondered. How was it this man, who only hours before had been in such emotional ruin that he was contemplating taking his own life, was now standing before them as if it had never happened? Proud and majestic, like a true leader of men.

Within minutes five shackled pirates were brought to the deck, battered, bruised, and bloodied but full of hate and fire as they had been since the moment they were taken.

Stephan steeled himself for what was to come as he marched down to stand before them.

"You are here charged with the high crime of piracy and treason to the crown and King William the Third," Stephan shouted. "How do you plead?"

"Fuck you, naval pig dog," one spat.

"Your sentence is death and will be carried out here and now, for I refuse to suffer your existence any longer," Stephan hissed, pulling his dagger and ramming it into the man's chest.

The pirate struggled for a moment before death stole his strength, and he fell to the deck, his last breath escaping him in a sputter of blood.

In kind, Stephan stood before each man and bloodied his dagger until all five laid dead at his feet.

All around, the ship broke out into bitter cheers for justice.

Stephan turned back to them, his suit now splattered with their enemies' blood. "Get this filth off our ship, and let's go home."

Callisto woke in a cold sweat and tried to roll over, but her left side screamed in protest, and she almost retched from the effort. Flashes of being shot aboard the French merchant's ship came back to her, and so did the sight of Alonso holding his guts from that same bullet.

"Be at ease, Captain," a soft voice said from the dim lamp light of the room.

"What has happened?"

"You were shot."

"I know that much already." She winced as she carefully repositioned herself. "How long have I been out?"

"Almost two days," Toothless Jack said, pulling up a stool.

He was the closest thing to a surgeon the ship had, and next to Angus Pewter was one of the only two that were seldom expected to fight in a battle.

"You will live to be sure. The bullet glanced off your ribs, breaking two of them in the process. You'll be in pain for a few weeks but will heal fully so long as you take it easy."

"Alonso, does he still live?"

"He does, at least for now," Jack admitted. "Though he did not fare as well as you. I was able to remove the bullet from his guts and sew him up, but there was damage inside. I have seen men survive such wounds before, but many more die from them." He shrugged. "It will be up to the gods to decide now."

Callisto gripped the man's boney arm. "You do whatever you can to keep him on this side of the living. Do you hear me?"

"Of course I will, Captain," he replied nervously. "But you must accept the likelihood of him—"

"Do not let him die!" she demanded, her grip hardening.

"Captain, I am merely—"

"You deny the gods on this one. They do not get to take him, not yet." Her tone left no room for debate.

"Yes, Captain, of course."

Callisto relaxed then, though she knew it would not be Jack's fault if Alonso died. The thought of whose fault it was soured her mood deeply.

"What of Murphy?" She winced as she sat up further, and Jack handed her a glass of water.

"He remains tied to the mast, as were your orders."

"Help me out of this bed. I must get up and see to something."

"Captain, I must insist you remain in bed for a few more days," he argued. "The wound is still fresh and has barely had time to close. Moving too much will tear it open again. Anything you need done—"

"Fucking hell, Jack, I said help me up!" Callisto growled.

"I don't know why I even bother." Jack sighed, offering his hand. "No one from this damn ship ever listens to me anyway."

Slowly Callisto was lifted from the bed and realized for the first time she was naked from the waist up, and it was only Jack's wandering eyes had clued her in.

"Surely you have had your fill of this sight while you worked on me." She rolled her eyes. "Now, get me a shirt."

"Yes, Captain, sorry." He dipped his head and fetched her a fresh shirt from the armoire. With his help, she dressed, leaving her vest behind but ensuring her weapons belt was around her waist.

Jack opened the door, and she stepped out onto the ship's deck, where her crew stopped what they were doing to look back at her, surprised that she was already on her feet.

"Captain," Reeves said, by her side in an instant.

Callisto held up her hand to stop him before he could say what she knew he was about to. "I will rest when I am dead, and I am a long way from dead."

"Aye." Reeves nodded at her bitter resolve, though he could tell by the strain on her face each step was taking its toll.

Callisto locked eyes with Murphy, who quickly downcast his own. His arms were bound above him as he dangled, his feet barely touching the deck. The joints of his wrists, elbows, and shoulders were red and purple and swollen angrily after being suspended on his feet for days.

"Because of your incompetence, I, your captain, was shot, and a valued crew member lays on what may end up being his deathbed!" she shouted, loud enough for everyone on deck to hear. "Explain yourself!"

Murphy slowly lifted his gaze to try and meet hers, yet he could not find the strength to do so. "I failed you, Captain. I am sorry."

"Sorry?" Callisto slapped him across the face. "Sorry? That is all you have for me? For the crew whose lives you fucking endangered?"

"I—I am not a pirate—," Murphy whispered. "I don't think I have it—in me to live life like this. I tried to tell you in your cabin before the—attack."

"I gave you the same choice as everyone else back on that island!" she shouted, feeling suddenly betrayed. "I told you when we were at Glacia's not to be back on this ship if you didn't have the heart for it!"

"I thought I could, thought it was fate—but now...."

"You are weak, Murphy!"

"I am..."

She slapped him again. "You are a fucking coward!"

He let his head dangle there in defeat.

Callisto turned to Reeves. "What is the punishment for such actions?"

"The lash, Captain," Reeves replied.

"How many?"

Reeves swallowed hard. "Ten."

"Bring me the whip."

"Captain, you are injured. I will administer the punishment."

"The whip!"

Reeves returned moments later with a bullwhip and reluctantly handed it to her.

Callisto gripped it tightly in her hand and could almost feel the weapon's violence and hunger.

"Hold him," she ordered. Her voice was cold and distant.

Two crewmen came over, turned the first mate around, and stripped his shirt from his back, baring his flesh as they held him against the mast and slipped a piece of leather between his teeth.

"You are hereby removed from your duties as the first mate of the Poseidon's Fury and, at this moment, no longer a member of my crew." She cocked the whip back. "I take no pleasure in this, but you've left me no choice in the matter."

The whip cracked out, and Murphy's scream was muffled only by the leather he bit down on. The effort made Callisto dizzy as she felt fresh blood oozing from her wound.

The leather piece slipped from his mouth by the third, and his screams of agony were no longer stifled. Some turned away, not wanting to see anymore or remembering the punishment themselves. Others watched every moment with disdainful satisfaction knowing Murphy deserved every violent moment for his failure.

Again and again, the whip tasted his back, crisscrossing bloody lines down his flesh. His screams were rendered to mere whimpers now as he no longer had the strength to cry out.

The whip returned, and Reeves' strong hand held her arm in place. She turned a bitter eye towards him at being stopped and was about to scold him.

"It is done, Captain." He told her with a grim nod. "That was ten."

She let him take the whip from her and felt herself almost fall to her knees; her fresh shirt was already stained with blood from her wound that had torn back open.

"Clean him up but leave him chained to the mast," she

ordered. "He is to remain there and receive half rations until Alonso either steps onto the deck or dies. If Alonso dies, Murphy with join him over the side attached to a cannonball."

Callisto stumbled back into her cabin, where Toothless Jack waited with his arms crossed and shaking his head at the fresh blood that dripped from her.

"I don't want to hear it," she warned him.

"Of course not," he muttered in reply, grabbing his bag of supplies and helping her back to the bed.

For the next four days, Callisto had remained as much in bed as she could, taking Toothless Jack's advice and resting her wound to avoid tearing it open again.

She had gone on deck earlier that morning at calls they had sighted another ship. Their hold was far from filled, and more would be needed to make this trip a fruitful success.

Callisto held no notion that she would be joining in the fight. To make such an attempt would be suicide, but she needed her presence seen. To have the men know that she was with them even when wounded.

But the winds had not favored them, and after nearly a whole day of chasing, their target had slipped beyond the horizon with no hope of them catching up. They had given up the pursuit, knowing there would be others.

Now on day five, her wound had closed enough that simple movements were of no risk to it any longer. Her muscles were sore and tight, and she needed to move about the ship to speed up the healing process, though nearly every step upon the rocking ship felt like a punch to her mending ribs.

Callisto had one destination in mind as she left her cabin that morning and saw Murphy, his leg chained to the mast like a dog. His skin was red and blistering from the days in the sun with no reprieve. His back was scabbed and bruised but slowly healing. She felt terrible and nearly had him released but quickly hardened herself to such a thought when she remembered her destination.

Carefully she climbed below deck, nearly falling down the damp stairs twice, and only saved herself from such embarrassment by the ropes dangling from above.

"Captain," several of the crew said, seeing her joining them below deck as they slept, drank, gambled, or killed time before their shifts began.

"At ease," she replied as she passed to where Toothless Jack sat next to a ghostly pale figure.

"How does he fare?" she asked, not realizing the man had been dozing off.

"Oh, Captain!" he gasped in worry. "Sorry, I didn't know you were coming down. I was just catching a small rest."

She rested a hand upon his shoulder. "Even you need sleep. How is he?"

"I thought for sure we'd have lost him a handful of times," he said honestly. "But his fever seemed to have finally broken, and he has come around for a few minutes here and there the last few hours."

"He will live?"

"He is not out of trouble yet, but if he can stay awake long enough to eat and drink, I believe he will. His wound has closed, and I have done everything in my power to stop infection. But he is weak, and it will take him a fortnight or more to recover his strength enough to be back on deck to do any real work."

Callisto nodded. "Can he be moved?"

"Moved?" Jack asked. "Whatever would you move him for —Captain?"

"Yes, moved," Callisto confirmed. "To a more comfortable spot, where he may heal and rest better."

"With all due respect, Captain. The middle of the hull is the best place for him. There is less movement of the ship here to jar him around. I don't think there is a better place aside from—" he paused, "aside from your cabin."

"Aye, that was what I was thinking," she confirmed. "Gather a few men, oversee the move, and set him up in my cabin."

"Captain?"

"Make it happen." She squeezed his shoulder again before she left.

Callisto made her way above deck again, saw Reeves and Weaver standing at the helm, and joined them.

"You are looking far better, Captain. More color in the cheeks, less blood on your clothes," Weaver said as she reached them.

"Good, but I still feel like I was shot." She shared in the laugh. "And the blood made me look like I belonged, even if it was my own."

"A hazard of the job at times." He pulled open his vest to show three such wounds that riddled his torso. He pointed to one below his shoulder. "Half the bullet is still in this one. Hurts like a bastard when it gets cold."

Callisto decided to cut to the chase. "The ship has a job opening. Will you take it if I give it to you?"

Weaver's grin faded as quickly as it had come. "First mate?"

"The ship requires someone who will not," she turned a sharp eye to Murphy below, "forget themselves."

"Captain, I—"

She stopped him short. "Do not take the position if you do not want it, Weaver. But I trust you. You know the crew, and

264

you know the ship inside and out. You have stood by me since I released you from the hold those months ago when you could have cut me down. Yet you didn't. Why was that?"

He rubbed his bald head. "I thought about it, aye, almost did too. But you're too pretty a thing to kill."

Callisto rolled her eyes at the statement. "You let me live and command a pirate ship because of my looks?"

"Nay, I didn't cut you down because of your looks. I followed you because I saw something in your eyes, Captain. There is a power there, a destiny that I can't even begin to explain." He shrugged. "And I wanted to be a part of it."

Callisto burst out laughing. "That was a far better answer."

"You have yet to disappoint either. So, I'm thinking I made a good decision."

"Then make another good decision and be the ship's first mate." She was serious again.

After a long moment, Weaver nodded. "Aye, why the hell not."

Reeves threw up his hands. "What about me? Not even going to ask me? I even saved your life that day."

"Pfft, you didn't want to be quartermaster because it was too much work for you," Callisto reminded him. "First mate is far more work with the likes of me as a captain."

"Aye, that's fair," Reeves replied. "I'd make a horrible first mate anyways on account I owe half these thieving bastards coin."

They all watched as Alonso was brought up from below and carried into her cabin. Murphy's eyes went wide with excitement initially, but that was quickly doused by shame.

"What's this now?" Weaver asked.

"I'll not have him die," Callisto said. "He was the very first to join me. To believe in me."

"You are something else, Captain," Reeves said. "Might be

that I get hurt next fight so that I can join you in your bed." He winked.

Once more, Callisto rolled her eyes. Men would be men.

"What are we to do with Murphy?" Weaver asked.

Callisto stared down at the defeated man, and again her heart hurt, and she felt a pang of regret. She could not blame him. He spent his whole life an honest man only to be thrust into a pirate's life because of her. But she had given him a choice, and he had made it only to falter now and almost get her and Alonso killed.

"What would you have me do?" she found herself asking for she indeed was at a loss.

"Will Alonso live?"

She nodded. "It seems most likely, though not ensured just yet."

"Then leave him where he is," Weaver stated coldly. "It is good for the men to know they are expected to perform their duties. And that you are firm but fair in your punishments. The fact that he still draws breath when Blackmane would have cut his heart out is a testament to your fairness."

"I am not Blackmane. I can be cold, but I am not heartless."

"A rare trait for one in your position. A weakness some might have seen at the start, but I suspect you are gaining more respect because of this."

"Good."

"But if Alonso lives, what then will become of Murphy?" Weaver cleared his throat. "You know as well as I do that he cannot remain with us. The crew will never accept him back."

"When we return to Glacia's Palace, we will leave him there. He can find his own way to whatever life he wishes to live on his own."

"Aye, that will work," Weaver said.

"I don't suspect he will be there long," Callisto admitted.

266

"He knows his way around a ship. Someone will pick him up in short order."

"That is only if he gets aboard one before rumors of his cowardice spread," Reeves said.

Callisto shrugged. "That'll be his problem, not ours."

"Maybe Glacia will offer him a position on the island. Might be something more to what he is used to," Weaver added.

Deep down, Callisto liked that option. For at least then, she would know the man was safe.

"Not liking the looks of those clouds." Reeves pointed, seeing a darkening on the horizon.

"A storm, to be sure," Weaver agreed.

Callisto pulled out her spyglass and took a closer look. "Can we stay ahead of it?"

Reeves shrugged as if it didn't matter. "We can or we can't. But we will sure try. Best we prepare for it, batten down the hatches, and get everything secure. If we get pulled in, it will be a hell of a ride."

Callisto stared at the darkening clouds and felt a chill run up her spine and knew they wouldn't be able to escape this storm. She felt a strange fear grip her. Dying in a fight or by betrayal she had made her peace with. Dying in a storm had not been something she had thought about. And now that she was thinking about it wasn't a thought she liked.

Within hours the black rolling clouds had overtaken the early evening sky. Flashes of lightning lit up the seas while the thunder vibrated the very timbers of the ship.

The wind increased, whipping at their sails, speeding the ship along and keeping them on the outskirts of the building storm. It kept the crew's hopes up that they would be able to stay ahead of it until it died down if they could only hold a little longer.

But that was a wish that was short-lived.

Within an hour, the rains had caught up with them, pelting the ship and its crew relentlessly, making everything aboard the ship slick and visibility low. Barely could they see a hundred yards in any direction. Only when lightning flashed could anyone get their bearings and see what troubles were rolling their way as they were assaulted with powerful wave after wave.

Standing at the helm next to Reeves, Callisto kept looking back, trying to gauge just how far they had slipped into the mouth of the storm. The waves around them were growing, crashing against the hull, and drenching everything on the deck.

Several of the crew were working nonstop, bailing water from below, from the cracks in the hull, and now from the water that flowed down the hatches below deck. It would be a full-time commitment from anyone not on the top deck until the storm subsided.

"Will we make it?" Callisto yelled to Reeves, whose muscles bulged against the strain of controlling the wheel against the force of such fierce wind and waves.

"This is nothing," he called back with a nervous grin, but his eyes betrayed his worry as he kept glancing back at the storm that gave chase. He was already tiring, his hands raw and blistered from battling the rudder.

But he would hold.

He had to.

Several crew members were needed on deck to adjust the sails for their fight against the relentless winds and endless waves. The rest were in the hull, bailing the endless water that would be their death if they didn't keep up. Those on deck tied themselves to ropes anchored to the ship in anticipation of what was to come, and many had begun to whisper prayers to Poseidon or other gods that might hear their pleas.

"You should go to your cabin, Captain. This is no place for you to be if things worsen," Reeves told her, and his expression informed her things would be getting much worse before this was over.

"I'll not abandon the top deck while members of my crew are on it," she called back, though deep down she wanted nothing more than to hide and wait for this to be over.

"It won't matter soon," Reeves yelled over the storm's fury. "If it gets much worse, we will have to cut the sails and suffer the mercy of what comes."

Within another hour, the waves reached up in the darkness twenty feet and more, battering the ship as it battled over them. The rigging and masts groaned in protest as they endured the ferocious winds. All knew it was only a matter of time before they would give out, leaving them to ride out the storm with no control.

"You cannot escape me...."

Callisto looked to Reeves. "What did you say?"

Reeves could barely hear her. "What?"

"Did you hear that?"

"Hear what?"

"Run all you want, but I am everywhere...."

Before Callisto could say anything, a mighty wave crashed into the side of the ship, causing it to list to port, throwing her to the deck where she skidded into the railing. She cried out and knew she was going over when a strong hand grabbed her moments before she went over the side.

Weaver was there, hauling her to her feet. "Captain," he screamed, "we can no longer fight the storm. We must drop the sails before the wind tears the rigging to shreds."

"Do it!" she screamed, but she needn't have, for it was already too late. They had waited too long.

A loud groan rent the air as a large crack ran up the length of the front mast before the thick wood snapped halfway and pitched over the side, breaking and tangling sails and rigging as it went. The Poseidon's Fury lurched to the starboard as the weight of the ruined mast and sails caught the waves and began dragging the ship to the side, threatening to capsize it.

The crew scrambled to untether the remaining sails before another mast broke and ruined them. But as the ship was dragged further to starboard, they couldn't keep their footing. All thought of anything else fled their minds as holding on desperately to anything they could became all that mattered as the end loomed moments away.

"We must cut free or be dragged to our deaths!" Weaver bellowed as he half fell down the stairs to the lower deck, trying to get to the tangle of ropes still holding onto the broken mast over the side.

"You think you can sail my seas without my permission? Think I would overlook you forever, SinClair?"

Callisto felt her blood run cold. "Who are you? What do you want from me?"

"What is owed to me!"

Rising before the Poseidon's Fury was a wall of water, a wave, sure enough, that would utterly destroy the ship and anyone aboard it in its wake. But time seemed to stop as Callisto scrambled down the stairs to the main deck. She could see the sheer terror in her crew as they braced for the mighty wave that would end them.

Still, she forced herself forward to the ship's bow, determined to be at the forefront of that destruction. Feeling the call of whatever was out there, demanding she go there and face it.

The ship shifted violently as Weaver and three others

finally freed themselves from the broken mast, and two men were thrown over the side. Their ropes snapped by the sheer force of the violent movement. Yet Callisto managed to keep herself aboard as she slammed once more into the railing but held on through the agony of her broken ribs and fresh blood streaming down her leg.

She caught sight of Reeves trying desperately to make his way to her, abandoning the wheel to the whims of the unforgivable sea. Others who saw her reached for her, calling her to them so that they could tie her to something.

She ignored them, knowing her place was at the front of the ship as the massive wave loomed above, ready to crash down upon them and snuff out their meager existence.

"Come to me, or I will take everything!"

The closer she got to her destination, the less the wind and rain howled against the tattered sails. The harder she fought to make her way forward, the fewer waves pounded ruthlessly against the ship. As she fought the storm and its bitter rage, her determination seemed to filter into the very timbers of the ship, defending it against the might of the sea.

Finally clawing her way to the ship's bow, she forced herself onto unsteady legs. Her broken ribs screamed at her in agony, but she ignored the pain even as it threatened to take her breath away. Fighting relentlessly, Callisto pulled herself up to face the giant wall of water that would doom them.

"I am here, damn it!" she screamed. "What would you have of me, oh great and mighty Poseidon? Tell me what it is you demand!"

Lightning filled the sky, stealing the night from them as the colossal wave parted, leaving only the titan figure of the sea god, Poseidon, before all to see. A hundred feet tall, he stood even with the lower half of his body still beneath the turmoil of the sea. He gripped a vicious trident in his right hand, and his grey and weed-strewn hair and beard whipped around in the wind.

"You have finally come, mortal." His voice was like thunder and drowned out the rest of the world.

The ship hung in the balance as the storm whipped in a frenzy around them, but those aboard were granted a small reprieve as they gaped in awe at what they were witnessing. Something out of tales bards sang about in taverns about exaggerated events none truly believed.

"By the gods," Reeves mumbled as he stood beside Weaver and several other crewmen, who were all wide-eyed in horror and wonder.

"Poseidon..." Weaver whispered.

"I am here before you," Callisto called to the mighty god of the sea. "I beg you to spare my ship and its crew!"

"What right do you have to ask of me anything, mortal? When you have scorned me all this time."

"I am a patron of Ares," Callisto reasoned as if that should make a difference.

The sea god's bellowing laughter caused many aboard the ship to cover their ears, fearing they would go deaf from the sheer power of his voice.

"And what meager power does my wretched nephew hold over my domain?"

"None, your greatness."

"You stole a ship from a patron of mine. One who offered me much, and yet you have offered me nothing! Tell me why I shouldn't drag you and your crew to the ocean's depths, where I will make your souls my slaves for eternity?"

Callisto swallowed the growing lump in her throat. "I did not realize I was scorning you, oh great one. Had I realized, I would have corrected it. What must I do to make this right?"

"What will you sacrifice?"

"Gold! Silver!" she cried back instantly.

"I can have all of that here and now!"

"What do you want, oh father of storms?"

"A soul."

"Whose?"

The god of the sea grinned maliciously.

"Chose one of your crew, throw them into my depths, and I shall spare you this time! One soul to save them all, and you may reign as Queen of the Seas."

Callisto glanced back at her crew. All of them had climbed on deck now, wondering what was happening. They stared in amazement at the scene folding out before them. But all of them had also heard the god's declaration, and all began to look around, wondering who would be sacrificed to save the rest.

"Captain!" Weaver called out, and when she looked at him, he looked down at Murphy, who was still clinging to the mast, his eyes as wide as the rest.

Murphy had failed her.

He had failed them all and almost had gotten her and Alonso killed. His life had already been forfeited, and her good graces were the only reason he was still alive. The crew hated him and would never accept him back, even if he had wished it.

No one would miss him.

No one would blame her for sacrificing him to save them all.

It was a fair trade.

"Chose now, mortal, for I got bored!"

It was an easy decision, plain before her, yet she could not do it. Could not throw the poor man to his death. Even now, he meant something to her.

"I have chosen!" she cried back to the god.

"Who?"

Callisto looked back at her crew and smiled before throwing herself from the ship's bow into the cold depths of the sea.

"No!" several men cried out, but she was gone.

Lightning and thunder violently exploded all around them, deafening and blinding everyone aboard the ship as the spell was broken and the winds, rain, and waves crashed into the ship anew.

Reeves tried to stand but was hit by someone and thrown back by the fresh assault. Grabbling on, he held on to them, not knowing who it was or what was about to happen now that the storm had them once more.

They were all at the mercy of Poseidon now.

The heat of the late morning sun beat down on the battered deck and those who lay twisted and tangled upon it. The storm had finally ceased and released the Poseidon's Fury from its grasp, leaving them floating in the mild currents that remained behind.

Reeves groaned, lifting his head, and shielding his eyes from the sudden brightness that assaulted him. He had survived and felt the shifting of the timbers beneath him. So too had the ship. At least enough that it was still above water.

He tried to move, but a weight rested across him, and he remembered the person he had caught when the waves had struck.

"We are alive," he grunted. "Now get the fuck off me."

A soft moan escaped the figure.

He glanced down to see a tangle of long matted black hair. "Captain?" he gasped, moving the wet hair from her face.

"Holy shit, it is you!" He held the back of his hand near her mouth and felt her breath.

She was alive.

"Captain." He shook her gently. "Captain, we're alive."

Callisto slowly began to stir.

"What—what happened?" she croaked, her voice rough and dry.

"We're alive—" Reeves replied. "I think we are anyways. So that's a pretty good start. But more importantly, you—how did you survive? I watched you go over the rails into the sea."

Callisto pushed herself off Reeves and stared at the destruction around her. The Poseidon's Fury was afloat, but it had suffered greatly in its survival. "I guess I wasn't up to Poseidon's tastes."

"I would say you were more than up to his tastes, seeing as how he let us live."

The crew was beginning to come around as if a spell had finally been broken, and they were returned to the grim world they knew. Many of the crew were wounded, with cuts, bruises, and broken bones, and many would need attention.

She got to her feet and had to grab the shattered railing to keep herself from collapsing. "We survived," she coughed. "Gather everyone. I would know who we lost and who all is wounded."

"Captain," Slimy Fife stepped forward, many others behind him, his already gruesome features magnified by the fresh cuts and blood dried to his face.

"You saved us from the might of Poseidon himself. I saw you crawl to the ship's bow to defy him, to save us! Even when he demanded a sacrifice, you refused to give him any of us, even though," he glanced at the still form of Murphy, who had not yet stirred and very well might be dead, "there was another option to be had. For us, you gave yourself to Poseidon, the father of storms."

Those who had survived gathered around her on the deck, muttering and talking to each other, but their eyes did not stray from her as if they were seeing her for the first time.

"You saved us," Jonesy said. "I saw it."

"I saw it too," another called out and several more chimed in before all of the deck was alive.

"I apologize, Captain, for being stupid enough to doubt you," Barraka said. "You are the Queen of the Seas, by the father of storms' own words! Let it be known now and forever!"

Every man on the deck dropped to their knees one after the other and began chanting those words.

"Queen of the Seas! Queen of the Seas!"

Callisto had to hold back the tears that threatened to escape her as her chest filled with pride. She had done it. Finally, she had won them over fully. They were her crew, without a doubt.

"Captain, we have work to do." Weaver was the first to pick himself up off his knees. He looked around at the state of the ship and knew, with the list to port and how low in the water they sat, that they were taking on water and likely quickly.

"Aye," she agreed, being pulled back to the reality of their situation. "Alright, you sea slugs!" she barked. "We are alive, but we are not safe. Find any crew that might be trapped and injured. Toothless Jack, gather your bag and tend the wounded. The rest of you get me a report on what supplies we still have and a damage report of every inch of this ship."

"Aye, Captain!" came the hearty reply as men picked themselves up and quickly got to work.

"All it took was offering yourself to a god to save their

worthless lives," Reeves said, hardly believing any of it, though he had witnessed it with his own eyes.

"What do we need to do?" Callisto asked Weaver, who was still taking in the mess.

"Captain, I—" he shrugged, "I don't really know at this point. The ship will stay afloat, but it will take us days to sort out the rigging and sails to see if we can even get something up to catch a draft to limp us along to find a port."

"I don't even know where we are," Reeves admitted. "That storm blew us all over the place. Tonight, if the sky is clear, I might be able to get us an idea, but it'll be a crap shoot if we are even remotely near any known ports."

Callisto had barely heard a word of what they had said as she felt herself become dizzy and collapse. Only the quick reflexes of Reeves catching her stopped her from hitting the deck.

Callisto woke as an arm draped over her, and she was suddenly aware that she was not alone in her bed. Panicked, she reached for the pistol she kept on her nightstand, but it wasn't there. Soon her memory cleared, and she remembered who she was sharing her bed with and, more importantly, why.

"Where—where am I?" a suddenly perplexed Alonso mumbled, his voice weak from over a week of fighting a fever and deadly gut wound.

"Be still, Alonso," Callisto said. "You are safe."

"What?" His eyes shot open. "Captain—I—what—why am I your bed?" His face flushed. "Did I—did we—what in the nine hells!"

"At ease," Callisto told him, looking down at his hand, which was still around her waist.

He pulled it back quickly and winced as the sudden movement jarred him, causing him great pain. "Captain, I'm sorry. I don't know what happened. Why am I in here?"

"No need to apologize," she told him. "You are here because we were both wounded in our last fight, and you almost died. I thought it only right to allow you to get better rested here where you would be safer and more comfortable. Though it seems you are well on the mend and shouldn't need my bed any longer."

His hand went to his stomach, where he felt the thickness of the bandages. "You were shot—I was shot. I don't remember anything else."

Callisto pulled herself from the bed, wincing as her side sent a wave of agony through her. Battling the storm on deck had set her healing ribs back. "It has been an interesting adventure since."

"How long?"

"Ten days."

"What the hell happened? I thought we won?" He looked around the cabin, seeing that the desk was overturned, and nearly everything was scattered across the floor, mixed with broken timbers and glass.

Callisto laughed. "We did, and I guess we survived the larger one that followed, but barely. We were caught in a violent storm," she explained. "But do not worry. The others will tell you all about it in due time. For now, rest. I will send Jack in to check on you."

She paused at the door and looked back at him. "Alonso, I am grateful you survived, for I would not have enjoyed what would have happened if you didn't." She left the confused man and stepped back onto the deck.

Her crew was fast at work, repairing what parts of the ship they could. A dozen men dangled from the two masts that had not been destroyed. Most of the rigging had been untangled, and tears in the canvas sails were being sewn with haste.

"Captain, how do you fair?" Slimy Fife asked with genuine concern as he came from below with a coil of rope.

"Better. My swim with Poseidon took more out of me than I expected."

That drew a grin from the man and several chuckles from those nearby.

"Another half day, and we will have what we can of the sails repaired," he informed her. "We won't be able to go fast, but we won't be dead in the water."

"Good."

"We have other problems on our hands," Weaver said, coming up behind her.

"How many did we lose?" was the first thing she asked.

"Three must have fallen overboard, for we found no trace. Two others we found below, crushed by cargo. Five are wounded with broken bones that will keep them held up for weeks. So long as infection doesn't set in, they will recover."

That was better news than she feared it would be after what they had endured. "I suspected worse, to be honest."

"It gets worse," he admitted. "Much of our food and water were destroyed. Food we have a fortnight's worth if we ration, a bit longer if we cut tightly. But fresh water, a week, maybe a day or two longer if we cut rations deeply now," he explained with more than a little worry as he glanced around the endless sea around them.

"Once we know where we have landed, we will make for the first port we can," Callisto confirmed the dire news, "as quickly as we can."

Callisto turned her attention to Murphy. Alonso would survive. She was sure now, and so too, it seemed, would

Murphy. She was truly glad about that. She had not enjoyed the idea of having to kill the man.

"Kadir."

"Yes, Captain?" The young man made his way over.

"Alonso will live. He woke and is doing much better," she informed him, to a great relief to him.

"Praise the old gods and the new."

"Unlock Murphy. His punishment is at an end."

"What are we to do with him now, Captain?"

What to do with him indeed, Callisto mused. The crew would never accept him as one of them, but she couldn't have him not pulling his weight while aboard, or he would surely end up dead.

"Take him below, have Toothless Jack check him over, feed him and give him a day to rebuild his strength. Tomorrow he will work hard doing whatever the crew demands of him. If he doesn't, throw him overboard."

Murphy glanced up at her. His eyes were sunken in with dark circles around them. His skin was dark and burned like leather, but he was alive, even if he would have wished it otherwise.

"Do you understand that?" Callisto growled at him.

Murphy nodded slowly.

She stepped forward and kicked him. "I asked you, did you understand that?"

"Yes, Captain."

Callisto leaned down to face him. "I am not your captain anymore, Murphy. Nay, you lost that privilege when you betrayed the crew and me. You are still alive by my good graces, only because of the part you played in me staying alive those first weeks."

Murphy chuckled weakly. "A slave then. Thought you didn't believe in that?"

The words stung her, but he wasn't wrong, and she hated him for it. "A worker, one of lower value than the rest of the crew. And only until we get to a port where you will be on your way, never to show yourself to me again. Kadir, get him out of my fucking sight."

Callisto paced her freshly organized cabin as she tried to calculate possibilities to improve their situation. It had taken two more full days to get the sails and rigging repaired enough that they could finally catch the wind and begin moving of their own accord.

Where the Sea Lion had collided with them had been torn open again in the storm, and they were taking on water, causing the ship to move sluggishly. All supplies had been shifted to the starboard side in the hull, causing them to list to that side. But the damage was further from the waterline, and even though they still were taking on water from a dozen other more minor cracks, it was less worrisome now. But still, four men had to remain there, bailing buckets of water from the hull back into the sea through the large hole in the side.

Reeves had discovered their general whereabouts the evening before when the night sky had cleared, and that had come as a bitter reality. They had been blown far from any known trade routes and were still a fortnight from any port that was known to them. Worst, those ports were not pirate-friendly by all accounts.

Their only hope for survival was to find a ship to board. But with one of the masts destroyed and the other two barely working, the chance of catching one would be nearly impossible. If they came across another ship, they would have to play possum, hoping the ship would not realize them for pirates and come to aid them.

After surviving the storm and the quick pace of work needed to get the ship sailing again, they were all exhausted.

They had enough water for six more days if they remained at one-third rations, but the men were weak. At this rate, even if they were to overtake a ship somehow, they would be too weak to win in a fight.

They had lost half their cannons to the sea, and half the ones that had survived would not fire until they were fully repaired. But even without that, only a few small barrels of gunpowder had survived. Slimy Fife guessed maybe a dozen shots could be fired before that, too, was depleted.

"You let us survive your wrath so that you could leave us to die in the open sea?" Callisto muttered bitterly to herself.

It would not surprise her if that were precisely what Poseidon had decided to do. And not for the first time did she wonder if she had made the wrong choice. Maybe she should have given Murphy to the god of the seas.

She sighed.

It was pointless to think about now. What was done was done.

She grabbed a small mirror, the only mirror to have survived undamaged. "Talk to me, Ares!" she pleaded. "I need you. I need your guidance now, more than likely ever before. What can I do? How can I save everything I have won? Everything you have helped me achieve?"

She stared long and hard at the mirror as the minutes slipped by, but no answer was forthcoming. No divine help had come. Even her dreams were void of the god who often came to her when she needed him. Had he abandoned her, she wondered? Was it because she had thrown herself to Poseidon to save herself and the crew?

"What else should I have done?" she yelled in frustration. "Would you have preferred me to have just died? All of this would have been for nothing. All of it! And where were you in that time when I needed you against the might of another god? Your uncle, no less?"

She reached for a bottle of rum but stopped herself short of drinking it. That would not help her in the end. It would only dehydrate her further than she already was, making things worse in these final days.

A knock on her door pulled her from her brooding thoughts. "Enter."

Weaver stepped in and closed the door behind him. He looked haggard, and his once olive-firm skin was gaunt and sagging from his large frame.

"Tell me you have good news?" She already knew from the look on his face this conversation would be anything but.

"I wish it were so."

"Out with it."

"With rations low, the men are getting bitter and harder to manage. Already a dozen fights have broken out and needed to be stopped."

"I know this; unless it rains, I can do nothing about it."

"The men know this. That is not what they grow bitter about, Captain." He cleared his throat. "It is Murphy."

"Murphy? What had he done now?"

"Nothing, in truth. He is doing what he has been told to do and does it without complaint. But he is no longer part of the crew. In truth, he is nothing more than an extra mouth to feed and, worse, to give precious water. Water that we have little of."

"They expect him to survive without water?"

"No," Weaver admitted, "but they also don't care if he survives. The majority of what can be done to the ship is done. His labor is no longer seen as—necessary."

Callisto felt her heart grow heavy. "All they see him as is an extra ration they will not receive."

"Aye, it will only worsen in the coming days. I fear soon they will move against him, as they might start doing against each other. Lessening the mouths on board to prolong themselves."

"What would you have me do?" she asked plainly.

Weaver rubbed a calloused hand across his bald head. "I like it no more than you. I respect Murphy, he was and still is a decent man, and I do not fault him for not being able to embrace this life. He is not like us. It is not in his blood and mind. To cut him off will satisfy the men for at least a short time longer before things begin to get dangerous for all of us."

"Taking what little water we have allowed is a death sentence. Will he survive two days? Maybe three? It would be kinder to kill him and be done with it," she muttered.

"I will see it done if you wish it."

"No, I do not wish it!" she growled. "He receives no more water and no more food. When he dies, he dies. The men are not to touch him, and he works no longer."

Weaver dipped his head and left.

"Fuck!" Callisto screamed.

These were the decisions she didn't want to have to make. These were the ones that balanced life and death with mere words uttered from her lips in situations where the moral lines were grey. This was the part of being the leader—the captain so hard.

Murphy pulled himself onto the deck with weak and shaking limbs. His strength was nearing its end, and so was he; he knew it and had accepted it. This would be the second day since his ration had been cut, and those rations had been meager. It would be his last day on this earth, he had decided.

He would no longer suffer and would die with what pride he could still muster.

He held no ill intent against the rest of the crew, for their water would be gone in another day. They would join him in whatever afterlife awaited any of them soon enough. That brought him little pleasure, though, for he had grown fond of many of them, even if they all hated him now. This was the worst fate for a sailor to succumb to. One not even deserving of pirates.

The deck was nearly empty this early in the morning. Most of the crew groaned and tried to get what restless sleep they might find below as they fought against thirst and hunger pains that chewed at their insides. Those few on night watch were too weary to notice his presence or simply didn't care anymore.

Murphy pulled himself to the broken railing, where a gap had yet to be repaired. He was thankful for that, for he was unsure he would be able to haul himself to his feet.

This would make it easier.

Staring at the coming dawn, he closed his eyes and thought of his wife. A woman he had spent nearly twenty incredible years with before she was taken from him by pneumonia three years before. He didn't care which god received him so long as they would allow him to see his wife again.

They had never had children, for she had been barren, or he had been impotent. They never knew which was the guilty party, for it hadn't mattered to them. Instead of resentment or blame, they had accepted that that wouldn't be a part of their lives and simply enjoyed each other.

"I am coming, Lynda," he whispered, opening his eyes to throw himself to the rolling sea.

At that moment, when his eyes opened, he saw something dark on the horizon. And before he pitched over the side, he paused, rubbing at his dry, weary eyes, and felt his heart nearly stop in his chest.

"Land..." he mumbled, for his tongue was swollen, his throat dry, and barely any sound escaped.

"Land!" he tried again and found a little more strength.

Pulling away from the railing, he spotted a crewman and flailed his arms catching the pirate's attention.

"What, old man," the man grumbled, his voice with little more strength than Murphy's. "You want me to throw you overboard? I'm not sure I have the strength for that, even though you deserve it."

"Land," Murphy muttered again and pointed to the skyline.

"What did you say?" The man made his way over. "What do you want, fool? What are you even doing up here?"

Murphy could no longer speak and just pointed with a trembling finger.

Following Murphy's finger, the man's eyes went wide.

"Land!" he found what voice he had.

"Land!" he cried out louder, finding the attention of the others on deck.

"Land!" came the cry from several voices.

Soon the whole ship was alive, men scrambling onto the deck with the promise of land and the hope of survival glimmering in their faces.

Callisto was pulled from her uncomfortable sleep by Reeves barging into the cabin full of excitement.

"What has happened?" She shot from her bed, thinking an attack or storm would be bearing down upon them at any moment.

"Land!" he cried. "Fucking land in sight, Captain!"

Hardly slowing to dress appropriately, Callisto burst from the cabin to join the others on the deck of the Poseidon's Fury to witness their salvation ahead. Several small islands dotted the horizon before them, surrounding a larger island at the core. Lush green trees and flora could be seen through the spyglass, meaning there would be fresh water aplenty. For indeed, there was land.

"Get us to those islands!" She needn't have said anything, for the ship was already sailing towards them. Yet she had to make it official for herself even if no one else cared.

The crew grew eager with every mile they put closer to the islands. Knowing they would soon have their fill of water and food, or at least, they desperately hoped. A restored sense of life filled them now.

"What is sticking up from the water's edge around the island?" Reeves wondered as they drew closer. So close now that they could smell the sweetness of foliage on the salty breeze and hear the cry of sea birds that called the islands home.

Callisto pulled out her spyglass and took a closer look. "They look like—masts from ships run aground."

"Guess we aren't the first to find the place," Kadir said.

"I wonder if others inhabit it," Reeves put in, knowing that often such hidden islands were home to indigenous tribes.

Weaver put down his spyglass. "I see no reason to believe so. No smoke and the beaches look clear of anything aside from ship wreckage."

"That is a lot of sunken ships," Alonso said as he tried to count the masts that could be seen, his tone problematic, and he had to steady himself on Kadir's shoulder.

"Likely ships caught in storms trying to find shelter smashed against the reefs," Weaver replied. "We will take her in nice and easy and take the longboats ashore. We need not risk any more damages to the ship."

"Gather what weapons we have, and make sure the men are armed when we go ashore," Callisto ordered. "I'll not be caught by any surprises if anyone calls this place home, be it by choice or by mistake. Some of these lost ships might still have men trapped on the island. They may be friendly, or they may be desperate."

"If there is, might be that we get ourselves some new crew," Reeves replied, hopeful, for they could use several more hands if they hoped to take another ship before finding their way back to Glacia's Palace.

"Aye, and with all the wreckage, we should be able to salvage enough to do most of the repairs," Half Beard said with new hope.

"First things first. We make sure we are alone, find water and food, and let the men have their fill if we can," Callisto said, not taking her eyes off the islands. "From there, we will figure out a plan for the ship."

Within a few hours, they had dropped anchor as close to the center and largest island as they dared. Four longboats were lowered into the water and rowed to the sandy beach awaiting them. They would go back and collect the others before they ventured too far inland. She wanted most of her force with their feet on the ground to search for water quicker.

Callisto was in the first boat and made sure she was the first to touch dry land. She was the captain and would lead them into whatever dangers lurked there. Or hopefully, whatever deliverance they might be able to find.

She ordered four men to stay behind on the Poseidon's Fury in case others on the island might think to capture and sail away with their ship. Murphy had been among those four, and she prayed he would still be alive when she returned. Three were left behind to watch over their longboats and to see what they could find among the wreckage in the sand.

"Weapons at the ready, and fan out twenty paces," she

ordered as they made for the tree line. "Call out if you see anything of note."

Slowly the weary men made their way into the shade of the trees, gripping blades, pistols, or rifles tightly. Feeling relief from the beating sun instantly and, with it, the smell of fresh water somewhere on this island.

It did not take them long to discover signs that others had indeed been here. Within minutes, calls came down the line of discarded possessions, human bones, clothes, long-dried blood, and footprints. Though on inspection, none could confidently say how old they might be.

On it went. Each minute felt like an hour as the crew moved slowly through the thick growth of the forest, anxious for the call that someone found water. Nothing else mattered to any of them right now. No amount of gold or silver would matter if they all died of thirst.

It was slow moving through the island's thick vegetation, and Callisto was weak. Soon cutting a path with her blade became nearly impossible, the weight of her sword becoming hopelessly heavy.

"WATER!"

The call finally came.

The line broke apart instantly as men raced to where the calls were coming from, each man eager to wet their tongue in whatever water or mud puddle that might have been found. As they broke through the screen of trees and growth, they came upon a large spring nearly fifty feet wide and a score deep spilling forth from the rocks in a small clearing.

There was no control over the men now, and even if Callisto wanted to, she wouldn't have. Men dropped their things and pushed their heads deep into the cool water. They were gorging themselves until their bellies were plump, only to try and force more down. Many stripped dirty clothing and dived in, wanting to feel the coolness of the water on their sunbaked skin.

Callisto tried to contain herself and show some restraint, but she couldn't, not with this. Soon she too was waist-deep in the cool waters, cupping water into her mouth as if it was the greatest thing she had ever tasted. And in truth, at that moment, it was.

"Captain, look there." Javier nudged her, pointing to the trees surrounding them that were teaming with bananas, mangos, and a small furry fruit known as kiwi.

Captain Callisto SinClair felt true relief flood over her. With plenty of water, food, and hopefully enough wreckage from the ships surrounding the island, they could resupply and rebuild the Poseidon's Fury to get them back to a safe port.

They would survive this ordeal.

Though their coffers were low, she would find a way to fill those. But one problem at a time. They would live, and that was enough for now.

"Drink your fill, lads," Callisto called out, climbing from the spring, feeling more alive than she had in a week. "Fill your water pouches, grab an arm full of fruit and head back to the beach so our comrades may fill their bellies next and take some to those still upon the Poseidon."

Reeves splashed more water upon his face. "This is truly a godsend, but something about this place gives me the chills. The air has an eeriness, but I cannot place it."

"When we return to the beach, gather five others, and explore a little more. I would know that we are truly alone."

"Aye, Captain. I'll see to it."

Callisto grabbed his arm. "Do not get yourself killed out there, Reeves." She squeezed. "Be sure to return to me."

Reeves grinned boyishly. "Aye, Captain, I think I can manage that."

The mood on the beach was boundless liberation, as empty casks were quickly filled with water and brought out from the spring to be enjoyed in abundance. Baskets heaped with fruit were shared all around as the crew indulged for the first time in nearly a fortnight until their stomachs were bloated and hurt. No rations were to be had any longer, at least not until they were back on the ship and sailing away.

Reeves returned a few hours later with no signs that anyone was still alive on the island. However, they had seen more proof that there had been survivors of the many wrecks. Bones, clothing, trinkets, and makeshift shelters they had come across. But nothing that had been fresher than several months.

But almost as importantly, Reeves had brought back meat, having found a pack of wild pigs. They took down two fat beasts and dragged them back to the beach to roast.

Callisto leaned back against a large rock, a half bottle of rum in hand. They had brought a score of bottles ashore to enjoy, though all had been instructed not to overindulge. She needed them to be functional in the morning, for there was much to be done before they could plan to set sail once more.

"A fortnight, maybe a few days more, by mine and Half Beard's account," Weaver said, plopping himself beside her, his chin dripping with fresh mango juices.

"That long?"

He shrugged. "Likely. We will see if we can salvage a mast from one of the other ships to suit our needs. If not," he pointed to the trees, "we will have to fashion a new one. It won't be pretty, but it should get us on our way faster than we can now. The ship took much damage in that cursed storm. It'll take time to patch everything. Best take our time doing so, to do it right. That way, if caught in another storm, we might survive without having you throw yourself overboard. Or if fates are kind, we might still fill our hold with plunder before we return."

"What of the cannons?" She sipped her rum.

"Aye, those will be a problem. But there might be a few we can use from the other ships. Hoping to find some iron balls and powder that isn't ruined." Again, he shrugged. "Won't know until we start exploring. Might even be some of these ships have some treasure on them. We could certainly use some of that."

Callisto couldn't disagree with that notion.

"We will stay as long as we must. It will give the men time to recover and build their strength before finding what more fate has in store for us out there." Her eyes went to the sea.

"With the Queen of the Seas leading us, how could we not win no matter what the old gods or new throw our way." He laughed, taking a long swig of the bottle she passed him.

"I'm not sure I would go that far yet." She chuckled.

"You heard Poseidon. I heard him, and they all heard him. Like it or not, my dear Captain," he grinned, "you are the Queen of the Seas now and forever more."

She took the bottle back and drank. "Guess I better not disappoint."

"I don't think you could even if you tried to."

Callisto woke on the beach beside her burnt-out fire to the sound of arguing. "What the hell is going on?" she muttered, sluggishly getting to her feet, the effects of her drinking slowing her.

"Captain, Jonesy went off to have himself a shit see but hasn't returned," Javier, one of the men who had joined the crew from the Phantom Chaser, stated, his eyes wild with distress. "Been damn near an hour since anyone saw him last."

"Has anyone gone looking for him?" she questioned.

"Aye, Captain. Me and a few others just got back, searched all the way to the spring we did. Thinking he might have gone to get a drink or have a swim. Ain't found nothing of him, nowhere," Javier huffed, clearly concerned, as the two seemed to be good friends on the ship.

"Calm yourself, Javier. I am sure he is out there. Likely partly hungover and stumbling around a little lost. Or maybe he caught sight of one of those wild pigs and gave chase in hopes of bringing us all back some ham for breakfast."

That brought a few laughs and grunts of likelihood from those around.

"I don't think so, Captain," Javier persisted. "I think there's something out there, something that got him. Some of us felt eyes upon us last night. And others swore they heard strange noises out there."

Callisto finally nodded. "We searched the area yesterday and found nothing to make us concerned about any threat on the island. I am sure he is just lost. It isn't that large of an island. He will find his way back in short order."

She could tell several men weren't convinced and seemed bothered by something. This was the last thing they needed. "Javier, get three others and go search for him more thoroughly. Be back by midday if you can't find him."

"And if we can't find him, Captain?"

"Then I will stop work on the ship, and we will all go looking for our lost man."

"Thank you, Captain," Javier said, and he picked three men and went off into the trees.

"And if you see any pigs, shoot them and bring them back!"

Callisto called with a laugh, betting they find Jonesy face down in his vomit.

"He speaks true, you know." Kadir came up to her when all the others were gone.

"About?"

"Feeling something out there last night. Me and Alonso were sharing a bottle and heard some strange noises and calls coming from the trees."

"Animals, nothing more," Callisto reasoned.

"Maybe, but nothing of the likes I have heard before, and with this many men on shore, not too many animals foolish enough to get that close." He looked back at the crew. "A few of us felt it. As if something was watching us."

"Take heart, Kadir. If something were out there watching us, it wouldn't think to be foolish enough to attack a beach full of pirates," Callisto said, making light of the conversation, for there was no reason to believe it otherwise. "We are easily the most dangerous things on this island."

Kadir nodded half-heartedly. "Aye, you are right there, Captain. Sorry for wasting your time. I just thought you should know."

Javier and the others returned just before midday without Jonesy and with news none had wanted to hear. They had found the man's tracks and followed them to a sinkhole a quarter mile away. His hat floated on top of it.

The rest of the day, the crew worked hard on repairs. Pulling what they could use from the scrap littering the beach and other ships they could access from the water. They had discovered three cannons aboard an upturned ship down the beach that was still functional. It would be a slow process of several days to unload them from the other ship into the long-boats to take back to the Poseidon's Fury, but it could be done.

The undamaged canvas was recovered from several ships,

and new sails were being constructed for the mast they had lost. But they had found no masts that would serve their needs. They would need to go into the trees and find a suitable tree with a straight enough trunk to make do.

That night was a somber event. Though the men were still in good spirits, the fate of their comrade weighed heavy on all of them. Too many had been lost of late, so they shared drinks and roasted wild pig in Jonesy's honor.

The next morning trouble started anew. As Callisto was discussing the day's plans with Weaver and Half Beard, Reeves and Three-Fingered Jack rushed over.

"You two best come look at this," Reeves prompted.

Several of the crew had gathered around their water barrels. Four of the ten barrels had been cracked along the bottom. Clear markings could be seen around the gaping holes, proving they were tampered with by a blade of some sort.

"That's not all I found either," Reeves pointed to the coils of rope they had piled nearby along with the canvas. Most of them were cut to pieces and ruined beyond repair.

"Who did this?" Weaver growled at the men around him. "What purpose would this serve? Did you all enjoy nearly dying at sea?"

"It was none of us," some of the men said, and everyone else around quickly agreed.

"Who else could it be?" he yelled. "One of you had to have done it. There is no one else on this bloody island!"

Callisto stepped forward. "Whoever did this, step forward now. On my word, five lashings are all you will receive, but if we are forced to root you out, it'll be death and not a quick one." Her voice left nothing to debate.

No one stepped forward, and they all shifted their gazes from one to another with accusations of guilt.

"Who was on watch last night?" Callisto demanded, her

eyes burning with the promise of violence now.

"Javier and Marcus," Half Beard, the ship's quartermaster, said.

"And where are they?" she asked, not seeing either within the crowd and near all the men were present.

The men looked around in confusion, none having seen either of the two since the evening before.

"Find them damn it!" Callisto snapped.

"Something strange is going on," Weaver said as the men began searching the beach for their missing crew.

As much as Callisto wanted to argue the point, she couldn't, for she was beginning to believe they weren't alone on this island after all. There was an eerie energy in the air this morning. If she could feel it, she knew so could everyone else.

Callisto, Weaver, and Reeves joined in the search near the tree line, searching for anything that would make them believe either of their missing crew might have foolishly gone inland alone. Something that would indicate foul play of some kind from her men, or something else.

"Found some tracks," Reeves called out as he inspected the scuffs in the sand that continued inland.

The trio followed the tracks for a hundred meters when the first true sign that they were on the right path was discovered.

"It's Marcus's shirt," Reeves said, picking up the discarded garment.

"His shoes are over here," Weaver called after exploring further.

"Did he decide to run through the woods naked?" Callisto muttered, barely believing any of this.

They continued forward, hoping they would soon find their half-naked man passed out in a drunken stupor. But soon, they found his belt and slacks hastily removed and thrown to the side.

"There's blood here," Reeves called, dipping fingers into the dark liquid. It was cold but hadn't clotted or dried.

Callisto moved past where more blood could be seen, and deep marks were in the soil as if something had been dragged. She followed them, Weaver and Reeves forming behind her, their blades drawn as more blood and a clear sign of a struggle could easily be seen.

"There." Callisto pointed to a small opening in the ground. "He was dragged into that hole."

They stopped in front of the sloping hole in the ground, a burrow of some unknown creature. Fresh blood and much-disturbed earth scuffed the entrance.

"What in the nine hells could have done this?" Reeves muttered, glancing around the area for tracks or some indication of what creature or beast might call this lair its home.

"It's not big enough for a bear den or any larger beast I know that could so easily drag a man to his death like that," Weaver proclaimed nervously.

Callisto leaned down near the hole, inspecting it closer and running her hand across deep claw marks in the hardened dirt. No, she soon realized, they weren't animal claw marks, but marks left by desperate hands clawing into the earth of a terrified man.

"Captain, stay back," Reeves warned, expecting the creature to emerge at any moment to grab for her.

But Callisto had her flintlock pistol directed at the hole. It would taste iron for its efforts if anything were to come forth.

Shifting the dirt around, she pulled up a large purply green scale, much like that of a fish, but larger, near half the size of her palm. "Look at this."

Weaver took the scale. "Seems our beast likes the taste of man and fish."

"Too large for any fish I have ever seen," Reeves said,

looking down at it. "Strange colors too." He rubbed his fingers across the scale. "Almost feels more like skin than scale."

"Whatever it is, and whatever manner of creature this is, we know we are not entirely alone on this island now," Callisto confirmed.

"Want me to get some men and see if we can force the beast to emerge so we can kill it?" Weaver asked, an edge of excitement there.

"Aye," Callisto agreed. "Get ten men, rifles, pistols, and blades. Find a way to get it to come out, dig down, and force it to attack if you have to. I want it dead by day's end."

"You think Javier met the same fate?" Reeves asked, gripping his cutlass tightly.

Callisto looked around one last time, finding no indication the other man had been there. "I don't know. I hope not. But it might be likely, depending on how many of these things call this place home."

"Might be some fun sport for the men to break up the time here. Let them hunt the beasts. The group that brings in the biggest one gets an extra take when next we make port," Weaver offered.

"Let us find out exactly what we are dealing with before we send anyone out to hunt them. I'll not risk more lives for mere sport."

They returned to the beach and broke the news about Marcus and his untimely fate at the hands of some beast. Some men grew nervous, others wanted revenge and to hunt, giving Weaver more than enough volunteers to choose from.

Callisto dipped a mug in the water barrel, drank deeply, and was about to go for another when she saw a figure stumbling from the trees.

"Javier?" she called as the man fell to the sand and feverishly crawled his way to them.

Callisto was first to his side; he was naked and bloodied. Bite and claw marks riddled his flesh and oozed dark blood. "What in the nine hells happened to you?"

"Monsters in the dark!" he cried out weakly, his eyes radiating terror as she had never seen before. "Attacked us!"

"Calm yourself," Callisto told him as many others gathered around. "Get Toothless Jack, now!"

"Tell me what happened. Why did you go into the trees?" she questioned, wanting to be angry but was now more concerned.

"We were patrolling the beach when we heard something, like singing. It was soft and soothing, and we were sure it was female." He coughed, and gouts of blood came up. "We got closer to see who it was, see if maybe someone was afraid to come forward. Then there was more singing, coming from several places all at once. We were about to turn back and call for others, but—" his voice trailed off as he stared into nothingness.

"But what?" Callisto pressed.

Jarred back to reality, he focused again on her face. "But we couldn't. I mean, my mind was there, I knew something was wrong, but my body was like I couldn't control it anymore. We just started walking into the woods. Trying to find the singing, like it was calling directly to me, promising me things—pleasures beyond my wildest dreams. I knew Marcus could hear it too, but he wandered off in a different direction, but I didn't care what he was hearing. I could only care about what I was hearing. But then—" he swallowed hard, "but then—" the words were stuck there, and he trembled at the memory as he tried to force it from his lips.

"By the old god's Captain, the singing stopped, and I was alone in the trees, not knowing how far I'd gone or where exactly I was. But I saw something. A naked woman, yet she wasn't human—her skin was—it had a shine to it and was different colors. She wasn't of this world, and I wanted to run, truly, I did, but I couldn't. She was beautiful and monstrous, and I couldn't look away. Before I could do anything, she leaped at me, stronger than anything I had ever been hit by. Then—more came from the shadows—they—they—" his voice trailed off.

"Damn it, man, what happened?" Reeves shouted, his voice fearful of what was to come next. Everyone could see the wounds to know whatever it was hadn't been good.

"They clawed and bit me, drank my blood like some kind of lust had overtaken them as they took turns—having their way with me," he whispered. "By the time it was over, I thought for sure they would kill me. But they didn't. They grabbed me and tried to drag me to their cave. But my senses returned. I kicked and punched at them and was finally able to break free. I found my sword and fought them back. I cut down one, and the others fled, and so did I."

As much as those around wanted to discredit him and found his tale impossible to believe, his wounds could not be ignored. Something had attacked him, and that was enough with what had been discovered of Marcus. They were not alone. Something, creature or beast, was here with them and clearly was dangerous.

"Monsters rule this island," one man muttered and several agreed.

"Demons in the night, feasting on flesh," another said. "We aren't safe here."

"We need to flee this place, Captain, and quickly," Half Beard, the ship's quartermaster, said.

Callisto didn't like the direction these events were having on her crew, or herself for that matter, for fear did grip her tightly now.

"We can go nowhere, remember." Callisto patted Javier's shoulder and stood. "The ship is not ready to sail, our stores are far from full, and we have a long journey back. We are safer here than we would be out there for long. Least you fancy knowing the threat of thirst again."

There was truth in that. All the men knew it and could not argue that point.

"But until we know what is out there, you all are to remain on the beach. I want a barricade built around the beach this very day near as tall as a man. I want torches, scores of them, and fires set all along the front of the barricade. We will know anything that comes from those trees before it has a chance to strike," she ordered, and the men quickly went to work.

"Reeves, gather five men, armed and unafraid," Callisto ordered.

"Captain?" he asked.

"Javier said he struck one down. I would find it, or at least where it happened," she explained. "He said they were taking him to a cave. I would find that also if we can. It might give us insight into what we are truly dealing with here."

"I will come," Weaver said, though his tone proved he did not like the idea of going off into the woods again.

"No." Callisto stopped him. "I need you here, looking after the men, making sure that barricade gets set up and that our camp is defendable. Keep the men in check, do not let them twist up what has happened. Fear will break them faster than anything out there could."

"If that is your order, I will see it done."

"Plus, if something happens to me. They will need you to get them off this island."

"Aye, good luck, and return quickly," Weaver said. "If you are not back within a few hours, I will send the lot of them in to find you."

Callisto nodded grimly.

Hesitantly, Callisto and her group of five moved deeper into the trees, following the bloody trail Javier had left as he had fled his attackers. The man had lost much blood, and the deeper the trail went, they began to wonder just how likely it would be that he survived or how he had even made it back to them.

Sure enough, they began to find his clothing, much like they had in their search for Marcus. And soon, they found where the attack had taken place. The ground was torn up, and drying blood littered the area.

"I see no monster corpse," one of the men said, his eyes never staying in one spot for long.

"No, but this blood looks different," Reeves stated as he inspected the bluish ilk left behind. "Captain, look at this." He held up several more of the strange fleshy scales.

"His story was true then," Callisto whispered. As much as she had wanted to doubt Javier, she knew even before they had arrived here that he had not been lying.

"I don't like this, Captain," Slimy Fife stated nervously, his finger not far from the trigger of his rifle. "Feels like something is watching us."

"There are enough of us that nothing is likely to attack us, and we have enough firepower to stop anything that might think to try." Reeves tried to comfort the man, but he, too, felt the eyes upon them.

"Look, something was dragged off." Callisto held her pistol at the ready, following the disruption in the soil, where more of the bluish blood could be seen.

"Whatever they are, they returned and dragged off their

dead," Reeves said, examining the markings.

"And brought it down there." Barraka pointed into the crevasse in the rock face before them.

The cave opening was large enough for even the widest-shouldered man to move beyond with ease, and it angled downwards into the island's depths.

"The creature's lair, to be sure." Callisto pointed to where many more dried scales could be seen littering the ground, but there was also something else mixed among them.

"I don't much like this, Captain," Slimy Fife said again. "I think it best we be leaving. Get the ship repaired as fast as we can and sail away from this cursed place now and forever."

Callisto could agree with that, yet she had seen something just beyond the darkness of the opening, something that caught her eye. "Light a torch."

"You cannot be serious?" Reeves blustered out. "You mean to go in there?"

"Torch, now!"

With torch in front of her and pistol in her other hand, Callisto crept forward into the cave entrance, Reeves and Slimy Fife flanking her sides with rifles pointed into the darkness beyond. But they didn't have to go far before she had found what she was looking for.

Reaching down, she shifted the dirt and pulled up a small gold ingot.

"Whatcha find, Captain?" Fife asked.

"Gold," Callisto whispered, lifting the torch higher and seeing several more ingots and coins gleaming from the light.

"By the old gods and the new," Reeves gasped.

The others moved closer to see dozens of coins, gems, and ingots littering the pathway down into the darkness.

Grabbing several pieces each, they quickly exited the cave before going too far into its unknown depths. Each was wide-eyed, and the fear they felt moments ago was quickly replaced by the insatiable lust only treasure could bring out.

"Where do you think it came from?" Rusty Juan asked as he fingered the thick coin he held.

"The ships," Callisto said, suddenly understanding. "All the broken ships around the island. Whatever these creatures are, they have cleaned out whatever valuables were within them, it seems."

"There are two score ships around these islands," Fife added. "Maybe more long beneath the waves."

"Aye, that means there is bound to be a heap of gold and other goodies down that hole," Barraka replied, licking his lips in greedy anticipation.

"And likely a horde of whatever creatures inhabit this island guarding it," Callisto pointed out, though even she felt less fear all of a sudden.

That gave the men pause as they suddenly remembered why they were out there and what had happened to Javier and Marcus.

"What are we to do then?" Fife asked. "Sure as shit, we can't be leaving all that treasure down there."

"Aye," Callisto said, "but we'll not risk anything this day."

"What's the plan?" Reeves asked.

"We return to the beach and not a word of this to the others, at least not yet. I'll have all your words on that on pain of death." She held out her hands, took the pieces they had found, and stuffed them into her vest.

"Why keep it a secret, Captain?" one of the men asked.

"We are in enough danger as is. I'll not have anyone wander off on their own with the promise of riches only to end up dead, or we will never make it from this island. We need a plan, but first, we need to see what these creatures really are and how hard they are to kill."

By the time the sun began to set, the crew had erected as firm a barrier around their beach camp as they could with what they had to work with. Scores of torches were set all around, almost reaching the tree line, lighting up the area before them so nothing would slip by unnoticed.

Two dozen men manned the perimeter behind the barricade, bow, and rifles in hand, with orders to kill anything that showed itself. No chances were to be taken. It was now kill or be killed. And if pirates were good at one thing, it was killing.

As the final rays of the setting sun left the sky, strange, loud pitched calls began coming from the island's center. As they drew closer to the beach, the men felt their fear rising. Any who might have doubted that there were creatures on the island hunting them, that doubt was diminished now.

Hours slipped by, and the calls increased, forcing the uncomfortable truth that they were surrounded with their backs to the sea. An arrow let loose here, or a rifle shot thundered into the trees anytime someone thought they saw movement or a shadow lurking too close to the light.

Callisto paced around the water's edge, wondering if trying to hold the beach had been the right call. They should have returned to the ship and held the creatures there if they were foolish enough to swim out that far. But it was too late for those thoughts, at least for this night.

Another shot was fired to the left, and as much as she wanted to tell the men to stop firing until they could see the beasts, she wasn't sure that was really what she wanted. The random shots were likely keeping the creatures back and from making an attack against them.

"So much for a paradise island," Reeves muttered, holding

his cutlass tightly, his line of sight never staying in one place for long.

"We can hold them back like this. And during the day, we will just have to work harder while the sun is out," Callisto said.

"After a night like this, the men will be worn out," Reeves reminded her. "Not sure how much faster they will be able to work. They will need sleep."

"They will have to work in shifts and sleep in between."

"And up all night guarding the camp in fear of death."

Callisto couldn't argue with that. "Still better than the death we would have known by now had we not come here."

"Aye, but by how much?"

"Tomorrow night, we sleep on the ship. We should be safer there."

That was when they started hearing the methodical song from within the forest. One strange and wonderful voice at first, then another, until there seemed to be dozens with flawless harmony.

Callisto could see a strange calm come over Reeves then. As if somehow the melody was speaking directly to him, ensuring him that everything was okay.

"Reeves?" She touched his arm.

He shook his head as if trying to clear it. "What was that?"

A scream from down the beach pulled them from their conversation as they saw a man pulled back into the water, splashing wildly.

"They are attacking from the water!" Callisto cursed, and they rushed to help the poor man being dragged into the sea.

Callisto cleared half the distance when a scaled creature leaped from the shallow waters, pulling her legs out from under her. She crashed into the sand, knocking the wind from her.

Rolling over, trying to catch her breath, the creature climbed atop of her, and she stared face to face with a woman with tangled blonde hair, black eyes, and jagged teeth.

The creature was about to bite down at her but stopped. Confusion was plain on its face as it stared down at its prey.

"Yous—yous don't belong—" It croaked out in broken English.

Callisto had no time to register what it was saying, pulled her pistol, and fired into the creature's chest, throwing it off her in a bluish spray.

Before she could gather herself, a vice-like grip snatched her left ankle and began pulling her into deeper waters. She screamed and kicked, desperate to free herself, as another creature emerged to her right.

"With usss," the female creature hissed, grabbing a webbed fist full of Callisto's hair.

Throwing her spent pistol aside, she grabbed her other and fired up at the new threat, but the powder was wet, and no shot was fired after the dull click. Cursing, she threw it at the creature's face pulling her dagger, a dagger she had kept close since that fateful night a lifetime ago when she had been but a girl.

The blade bit deeply into her attacker's arm. It shrieked angrily, releasing her hair and pulling her head underwater. Callisto tried to get her face above the surface, but the beast pressed down, intent on drowning her as the other continued to pull her deeper into oblivion.

Knowing any moment, she would have to draw breath and would drown, her blade stabbed out and hit nothing. Again and again, she stabbed and slashed, feeling the blade score a hit here and a cut there. But still, the creature bore down on her, refusing to let her reach the surface to draw in a breath of life-saving air.

Finally, Callisto felt her blade sink into flesh, and instead of pulling out to stab again, she plunged the steel deeper still, twisting with every inch that impaled into her attacker's side. Even beneath the water, she could hear the ear-piercing wails. The creature released her and tried to pull away. But Callisto's dagger remained embedded, and she refused to let go.

Kicking again, she felt the other monster release her leg and quickly got them under her, found the bottom, and pushed up. Her head broke the surface, and she gasped for air only to be met by the snapping teeth of the creature stuck to her blade.

Callisto fought wildly, trying to keep the creature's maw at bay while still trying to keep her head above water. But here in the deeper waters where she could barely touch the bottom, she was at a disadvantage, and her head went under again, and so did the biting teeth of her enemy.

Callisto pushed her thumb deep into the creature's obsidian-colored eye, more to keep the dangerous mouth away from her face than any conscious effort to wound it. How it thrashed in agony, its teeth snapping all around her, mere inches from her face and neck.

Her dagger tore free of the beast's side, and she lunged it up, burying it into the monster's neck and pushing for all she was worth, feeling the blade slide into its brain. It thrashed in its death throes before going still and floating up.

Callisto pushed away, and her head broke the surface as a strong hand found her arm. She slashed at her new attacker only to stop short, seeing it was Reeves.

"Captain, are you alright?" Blood dripped from several minor wounds across his chest and arms.

"Behind you!" she screamed.

Reeves spun around, and his sword cleaved into the creature's neck, nearly taking its head off. "We need to get out of the water!"

Callisto didn't need to be told twice as the two half swam and half ran from the lapping deathly waters back to the mild safety of the beach's edge. They both fell to the sand and turned back to face the sea, almost expecting more of the creatures to be in pursuit. But it was done. The attack was over. A few more shots were fired while others climbed free of the waters that had almost been their graves.

Through it, all the eerie song had continued to play in the distant trees until now, when it simply stopped, and everything was deathly quiet as if nothing had just happened.

"What the hell were those things?" Reeves muttered, pulling himself to his feet.

Callisto grabbed the corpse that was washed up on the shore. The one she had shot. Soon torches were brought closer as men rallied around them, many with fresh wounds.

She flipped the naked woman over and gasped. The creature looked human, but nearly half her body was covered in the large fleshy scales they had found.

"What in the world are these things?" Kadir gasped, mirroring the words of several others.

"Some kind of half-human fish?" Weaver spat, tying part of his shirt around the bite mark on his arm.

"Mermaids are nothing more than myth," Three-Finger Pete said.

"Nay, not a mermaid. Those have tails like a fish," another added. "This thing still has legs." He moved closer. "But the feet and hands are webbed."

"I have no idea what they are," Callisto said. "But I know they can be killed, and that is all we need to know to stay alive."

"We need to leave this place, Captain," several of the men voiced.

"Repairs are far from done. We have barely begun work on

the new mast or patched the holes. We leave now, and we will die at sea within a week," Weaver stated.

"I'm willing to take that chance," another man cut in.

"Captain?" old Half Beard asked her. "What do we do?"

The time had come to tell them.

"If it is of everyone's mind, we will get the mast up and repairs what we must to be able to sail as safely as we can— but," she paused and fished out several of the gold and silver pieces they had found earlier and held them out for all to see, "there is more on this island than just the threat of death from these creatures."

Instantly everyone moved closer, eyeing the treasure with interest.

"Where'd ya find that?" one man asked.

"We followed Javier's trail to where he was attacked. We found their cave. Inside, we found this, and there was more further down," Callisto explained. "My guess is these things have emptied all the ships that have crashed here and hoarded everything of worth within their cave."

"By the old gods and the new," several muttered, their faces flashing with greed.

"There could be piles of the stuff as tall as a man," Kadir said.

"Aye, there could be," Callisto agreed. "Enough to fill the ship thick with treasure and see us all rich for a good long time."

"Not going to do us a lot of good if we are all dead before we can spend it," a man that had once been part of the Wind Spirit chimed in. "Three more were killed in the attack, and I saw half a dozen men wander off aimlessly into the trees once that singing started."

Callisto nodded. "There is truth in those words. But is this much more risk than what we face on the open sea each time we take a ship? Cannon fire could sink the lot of us each time. Arrows or bullets could snuff a man out before touching down on an enemy ship, or a blade could send us to the afterlife every time we find battle. And for what? We know not what will even be hidden in their hull. Could be riches or could be little of worth for the lives risked."

She let her words sink in, kicking the dead creature. "We know what we are up against now. We know they can be killed, and how they choose to fight now. We can prepare, and we can plan our attack. We have the advantage now." She handed the gold ingot to the man in front of her. "We know the rewards waiting for us to claim if we wish to take it."

"Aye, Captain," Half Beard replied. "But too many more losses, and we might not be getting off this rock in any shape to sail long."

"This is a risk I am willing to take," Callisto said firmly. "But I know many might not share that same thought. So, think about it. In the morning, if the majority wishes to finish repairs and sail away, we shall."

The men wandered back to their posts, guarding the beach, and now several had their attentions on the waterline, knowing that was just as big of a threat. The wounded were gathered, and once more, Toothless Jack put his limited skills to work. Sewing and washing out cuts and bites and applying wraps to the score of fresh wounds.

That night, no one slept. For tensions were high, and every noise set adrenaline running anew. But even more, the men talked amongst themselves about what course they believed was best. To flee or to risk death to get rich.

Morning came, and the crew was gathered around. They were exhausted, battered, and many showed wounds still bleeding through bandages. But there an eagerness behind all the doubt, worry, and fear.

"Out with it," Callisto called out.

Old Half Beard stepped forward, for he was the crew's spokesperson as quartermaster. "We'd follow you into the pits of hell and back to be sure, Captain. But we don't know how many creatures live here or how many hide within the caves. Treasure is a great motivator for us greedy lot, and if our numbers were more, and we didn't have so many wounded, we'd be more than willing to risk it. But dead is dead, and that is sure where we will find ourselves if we take such a bold step into their lair."

"You wish to set sail once we can?" Callisto asked, with more than a bit of disappointment in her tone.

"Aye, Captain," Half Beard replied. "To return to Glacia Island, hire a new crew, and better prepare. Then come back and take the fight to these fucking monsters and take every coin they be hiding under this cursed rock!"

The crew cheered in agreement.

Callisto wanted to argue. Wanted to belittle them. What kind of pirates would turn away from such a possibility? Yet, she didn't. For deep down, she knew they were right. They were in no shape for such an attack against numbers they didn't rightfully know they might face. A score of these creatures could be left, or a hundred—a thousand.

"It is decided then," she said. "We will get the mast up and repair what we can on the hull to see us out of here. Fill our barrels with water and food and set sail the first chance we can."

There was little excitement as they moved off to either get rested or to start the long list of work that still needed to be done.

"I fear with how things look, it will still be three to four days before we can leave this place," Weaver said once everyone was gone. "I suspect we will face these creatures several more times before this is done."

"If we remain on the ship at night, we should have an easier time, and hopefully, no one else will be lost to us."

"Aye, Captain," Weaver said. "We can pray for that."

By dusk, everyone was safely back aboard the Poseidon's Fury. Repairs had been slow, and work on the mast had taken priority. The tree they had fallen had been stripped and dragged out to the beach behind the barricade, where it had been measured and cut to the length and size it would fit. But that is as far as they had gotten that day.

The men were tired, many badly wounded, and even the threat of attack the longer they were on the island could only force them to work so quickly. If things went as planned, they would have the new mast moved to the ship tomorrow and set. The rigging and sails could be sorted out the day after.

The night was now upon them, and a score of men armed with bows and rifles patrolled the ship's deck, keeping their eyes firmly on the waters below. With ammo and powder in short supply, they were ordered only to shoot if they had a clear shot.

Callisto found herself at her desk, a glass of wine in hand to help steady her nerves. Though she suspected little would happen tonight, with them being on the ship, but doubt played in the back of her mind. If there were dozens of these creatures, and they coordinated a true attack, would they be able to survive even aboard the ship?

"Where are you, Ares?" she asked, with more than a bit of bitterness in her tone. The God of War had not shown himself since that night when he had shown her how to break the siege on Glacia's Island.

She was truly beginning to wonder if he had forsaken her since her run-in with Poseidon. But what was she to have done? To not give the god what he had asked would have doomed them all to a watery grave.

A hard knock at her door pulled her from her thoughts, and she was thankful for it, for her thoughts were growing darker.

"Enter."

Old Half Beard pushed his way in. "Sorry to bother you, Captain."

"Any sign of trouble out there?"

"Aye, the men claiming to be seeing things swimming in the depths, but nothing confirmed," he paused, "though none's doubting them at this point."

"We know they are part fish, or at least something like that," Callisto said. "I suspect they are just as comfortable in the waters as they are on land, maybe even more so."

He nodded. "Truth in that, to be sure."

"What do you need?"

"Not what I am needing, but Murphy wishes to speak with you." He shrugged. "Wasn't gonna bother you with the likes of him, but he seemed insistent about it. I asked him what for, but he wouldn't say, just told me it was for you to hear. I'll put him back in his cage if you wish, and I'll shut him up with a few knuckles for good measure."

Callisto held up her hand. "No, he has taken his punishment. I will hear what he has to say."

"Right, Captain. Want me to stay?"

Callisto smirked. "I would hardly think Murphy much of a threat, even less so now in his weakened state." She placed her flintlock pistol on the deck. "I think I will be safe."

"Aye, right you be, Captain."

Murphy was escorted into the cabin. He was dirty and haggard looking. His grey hair was matted and filthy, and a fortnight of growth had him with an unkempt beard that aged him a decade more than he really was. His wrists and ankles were red and swollen from the manacles he had been forced to wear far longer than necessary.

"Half Beard," Callisto called to the quartermaster before he departed.

"Captain?"

"Why is he still in iron?"

The man seemed at a loss for words. "He ain't no part of the crew, and this makes sure he doesn't try anything stupid, Captain."

"Remove them and do not return them unless he does something to warrant it. Murphy may no longer be part of the crew, but he isn't a prisoner aboard this ship."

"Aye, Captain," Half Beard said, unlocking the chains. "If that is your will."

Once they were finally alone, Callisto stared into the man's sunken-in, misty grey eyes. "I wish it didn't have to be this way. You were the only one I truly trusted at the start of all this."

"The fates are cruel, even to decent men." That was all he said in return.

All she could do was nod her agreement. "Once we are back at Glacia's, you will be released with a handful of coin to find whatever life you wish to start. That is all I can do for you. Now, what is it you wished to tell me?"

He limped forward to stand before her desk. "I believe I know what these creatures are."

"We killed a few last night. They seem to all be female, almost human, but with scales and gills of a fish."

"I inspected one of the corpses. I believe they are Sirens. A creature believed to be myth, except by those who have lived to tell the tales."

"And what do you know of these supposed Sirens?"

"Only what I heard rumors of decades ago when I first became captain of the Wind Spirit. I was in a tavern when a group of sailors entered. They looked worse for wear and unnerved to their core. They started on a tale of strange creatures that had lured them to an island with a faint song in the night. The crew was attacked or lured away in the dead of night, seemingly of their own will. They talked of how they were kept as captives, and the creatures stole their seed time and again, then feasted on their flesh as if they were no more than livestock. Those who escaped showed many of the same wounds I have seen on the crew."

Callisto listened intently, for the story fit well with what they had seen already. "And was this the only time you have heard such a tale? No others have brought it up?"

"Aye, it was."

"Hard to believe such a thing when only a handful of sea-lost sailors spoke of it."

"There is truth in that," Murphy agreed. "But I always remembered it. Their eyes spoke the words louder than their tale ever could. These were hardy men, true sailors who had survived storms, pirates, and beasts of the depths. But this had broken them, and not a one ever set foot on a ship again if rumors are to be believed." He shrugged.

Callisto poured herself a glass of wine and offered one to Murphy, who refused. "I cannot doubt the story, for given what we are facing here, it fits. Did they say how they escaped? What the creature's weaknesses were?"

"All I remember was they could be killed like a man could if you were fast enough, and they feared fire."

"Is that all?"

"Aye, that is all I can offer."

"I thank you for the information. That will be all. You may leave."

"Yes, Cap—Ms. SinClair," he replied and turned to take his leave.

"Murphy," she called to him as he reached for the door, and he paused but did not turn back. "I am sorry."

Murphy shrugged and left.

The night went by, and no attacks came, and in the morning, the crews rowed back ashore to find much of what they had left behind, tools, ropes, and gear, ruined or stolen. But still, they made do and went back to work with a new feverish need—a need to be away from this cursed place and the creatures that hunted them.

The following night, they were not so lucky.

The creatures were angry or hungry, who could rightfully tell? But they attacked the ship with a small force of nearly two dozen, climbing the outside of the hull and pulling themselves over the railing. But the men had been ready, and the beasts were repelled and sent back to the watery depths to flee.

Twice more that night, attacks came, each more dangerous than the last, as more of the creatures joined in, trying to overtake the ship and its exhausted crew. But each time, the Sirens were defeated, and by morning the Poseidon's Fury had only lost one man to wounds they could not help with.

"Tomorrow, we should be able to finish the repairs and set sail before nightfall," Weaver told her as they walked the beach, letting the men see them and offering their support where it might be needed. "We will be able to leave this wretched place behind us, at least until we return in force for the treasure."

"And how big of a force do you believe we will be able to muster with our coffers depleted?" Callisto asked in honesty.

JAMES FULLER

"Once we repair the ship and resupply, there won't even be wages for the men, let alone to hire on fresh crew."

"Our crew will understand, Captain," Weaver told her. "We have gone without many times before. Aye, coin is good when it is good, but not every trip is fruitful, even when we sailed under Blackmane."

"And the new crew? Do you truly believe they will sign on to sail with a ship that doesn't have two silvers to rub together?"

Weaver grinned. "Once word of your reputation spreads of your fight with Poseidon and seeing us through this fight on the island, there will be crew wanting to sail with the Queen of the Seas, just to say they did."

Callisto tried to take heart in that but couldn't.

"Chin up, Captain. We will find a way."

A sudden call broke the silence, and both were instantly drawn to the two naked figures emerging from the trees in a dead run. It was Marcus and another man they did not recognize.

Both men near threw themselves over the barrier into the waiting arms of the men on the other side. Their bodies looked much like Javier's had. They were bruised and bloodied.

"Marcus!" Callisto cried out, in both surprise and wonder at seeing the man they feared long dead.

"Captain!" Marcus gasped, trying to find his breath. "By the old gods and new, am I glad you haven't sailed off."

"We fear you and the others taken were long for dead."

"Aye," he huffed. "Some are, but many still draw breath, along with a score of others from ships stranded here from before."

Mutters and gasps echoed around as all the crew on the beach gathered at this unexpected event.

"They are alive?" Slimy Fife asked in surprise.

318

"Locked in cages they are. Being used for our—seed," Marcus explained. "They are using sailors to swell their bellies with child, to grow their numbers and eat..."

"How many are there?" Reeves asked. "Of these creatures?"

Marcus winced as Toothless Jack began cleaning his many wounds. "Tough to say for sure. The cave runs deep, and we only saw a small part of it. Three scores, four? Maybe a dozen more than that. No way to be knowing for sure. But there were fewer of them this morning, and many returned wounded. It was how me and Douglas here were able to escape. Most sleep during the day, leaving only a few to watch over us."

"So, they are weakened now?" Callisto asked, her mind racing.

"Aye, they number far less than when they first dragged me into their caves, to be sure."

"The others are still alive," Callisto muttered, stepping back, and all eyes were upon her.

"Captain," Marcus said, drawing her attention back. "There is treasure in those caves, more than any one ship could hope to sail away with."

That statement brought back unease among the men—a battle between greed and life.

Callisto's mind was already made up. "Our men are still alive; we have to go back for them."

"Captain," Half Beard intervened. "Not a man among us doesn't feel the pull to help our brethren, but the risk is too great."

"You would leave them to this fate?" Callisto snapped. "To be held as slaves only to be eaten alive by these—these things?"

"Nay, the thought sickens me to my core, but nor would I wish that upon any of the men standing here safe now. But we have less than thirty rounds of iron and powder. Two score of arrows, and half the men bear wounds that will hinder their ability to fight in any true capacity. What would you have of us?"

Callisto turned to her crew. "You pledged yourself to me a fortnight ago after I saved us from Poseidon, who would have seen us all dead. Then not, but days ago, you said if I willed it, you would follow me into the very depths of hell itself if I demanded it of you!"

Every man shuffled uncomfortably under her stern gaze, but none said a word.

"I'll demand nothing you aren't willing to give. But let me ask you this." Her eyes were hard and demanded their attention as she swept that gaze over each and every one of them. "If it were you in those caves, would you not hope help would come?"

She let the words hang in the air.

"I leave to save the crew in less than an hour." She turned and strolled away to prepare her gear and gather torches. If these creatures were afraid of fire, she would ensure she had plenty of it.

"Captain," Reeves called to her a short while later.

"Yes?" Callisto turned around to see twenty-nine men behind her, Reeves, Weaver, Slimy Fife, and Half Beard at the forefront. All of them were armed and ready for a fight.

"To hell and back." He grinned.

"And the others?"

"Wounded, Captain," Weaver stated. "They won't be much help to us in a fight. They will stay behind, get the ship ready to sail if we come running, and keep the ship safe while we are gone."

"Good enough." She spoke. "Let's go get our fucking crew back."

They marched into the trees, leaving behind the relative

safety they knew on the beach. The men gripped their rifles, pistols, and blades in firm but steady hands. They were a force. Many were battle-hardened by years of piracy, but all had taken a life before.

There was fear among them, for each man had their doubt, and each man pushed that doubt aside as they marched shoulder to shoulder with comrades who would fight beside them. Some had fought beside them a score of times.

They stopped at the entrance to the cave they had found before. Nearly every man was to carry two torches. For Sirens hated the light and feared the flame. Fire would be their biggest ally in this fight, or at least, they hoped.

"We free the captives first and foremost," Callisto told them firmly. "Treasure is second place in this fight. We will take what we can if we can, but only once we free those still alive."

Two men moved into the cave, torches held high, blades drawn. Behind them, four men were centered, bows at the ready. Reeves held a rifle, and Weaver had his two hatchets ready and flanking Callisto, who had one flintlock pistol in her left hand and her cutlass in the other. The rest moved in behind them, many barely containing themselves from grabbing at the coins and gold that rested atop the pathway down in the earth.

A hundred feet down and the putrid smell assaulted them. Rotting flesh, mildew, and feces. Each step intensified the smell, and many had to fight back, gagging. One many of them knew well. The tunnel was widening, and they knew they had to get close.

The group slowed to a stop as soft echoes bounced from the rock. Sounds of humming and soft screeches could now be heard. They were near the lair, and they all took a final moment to muster their courage, for the next bend and the light of their torches would announce their arrival. There would be no stealth attack here. The fight would be on in full the moment the light was noticed.

"We are pirates," Callisto told them. "We are the most feared thing on the seas and this fucking island. Or at least we will be when we are done here."

The men chuckled at that and found their wavering courage again.

"Strike fast and strike hard," Weaver told them. "The more of them we put down in the first moments, the less we have to deal with when we want to fill our pockets with gold."

That brought more grins and nods from the crew, for most of them were here more for that reason than any other.

Moving with haste now and trying not to slip on the slimy wet rock, the men knew these might be their last moments among the living. They steeled themselves to that realization, and within moments they roared a fierce battle cry as they entered the large cavern.

Torches were thrown far and wide. Some were extinguished when they hit shallow, murky pools where creatures slept, but most remained burning, bringing light to nearly the whole lair.

Sirens shrieked in surprise as they were disturbed from their deep slumber, turning their heads or shielding their eyes from the sudden light violation on their sensitive eyes.

Rifles were aimed, blasting the closest creatures dead. Bows snapped off their first round, and several Sirens went down dead or wounded before they knew what was happening. On came the pirates, their blades leading the way into the confused and startled creatures' nest.

Callisto charged ahead, ramming her cutlass deep into a Siren as it fought against the brightness of a torch that had landed beside it. Putting her boot to the creature, she pushed it off her blade as it withered in its death throes. Slashing left and right, she took the clawed hand from another that reached for her.

Within moments of the attack, a dozen Sirens lay dead, and twice that number were wounded and retreating. But now they understood that danger had come, and they fought back fiercely.

The sounds from their throats were deafening within the cave's confines, causing the pirates to stagger back against the piercing wails that assaulted their ears and minds.

Callisto felt as if her eardrums would burst and fired her pistol into the face of the Siren closest to her. The pain was nearly more than she could bear, and she felt as if her legs would give way, as several of her crews already had. Their heads were down to the ground with their hands over their ears, trying to dull the noise that cut to their souls.

But as fast as it started, it stopped, and the cave was silent once more as the Sirens escaped through the back tunnel, going deeper into their lair to warn the others. This had only been a small part of the nest, and the prisoners were nowhere to be seen.

"Get up!" Callisto bellowed out, though most of the men could hardly hear her as they looked up in confusion, their ears still ringing from the strange attack.

"What happened?" Reeves asked suddenly beside her. His sword slick with bluish blood.

"We have them on the run!" Callisto screamed, as much to hear her own voice as to inform the others. "Gather the torches and go before they can get coordinated!"

Many of the men were on their feet now, and without the fear of battle, their eyes widened at the realization that most of the ground they were standing upon was not earth but rather gold and silver coins, gems, and jewelry. Several grabbed handfuls and filled their pockets.

"There will be time for treasure once the fight is over and our brethren are freed!" Callisto spat, though she also felt the riches draw before them.

Half Beard slapped several men's hands. "You heard the fucking captain! Get after them fucking shrieking cunts and kill them all, and we can take our time filling the whole of the ship until she's ready to burst!"

That seemed to have the desired effect as the men grabbed their torches and pushed forward, reloading and notching arrows.

Callisto moved in behind them, Weaver and Reeves just in front of her. She was determined to find the others, and while the men fought, she would see to freeing whoever was still alive. But as they reached the next vast cavern, one near thrice the size of the last, the Sirens were prepared now. Over two score stood to meet them.

The Poseidon's crew entered with gunfire and arrows, taking a handful down in the first moments. But a physical fight wasn't what the Sirens had planned. They seemed to know they would be no match against the pirates' iron bullets and sharpened steel.

As several of their fellows were shot down, they began their song, raising their vocals to merge into one smooth unyielding voice that vibrated off the stone chamber around them—magnifying their enchanting song to heightened power.

The pirates faltered, not understanding what was happening. They shook their heads, trying to push the weariness they suddenly felt from their minds and bodies. Weapons began slipping from calloused hands as any thought of fighting these beautiful creatures or the promise of treasure was lost to them.

"What are you doing?" Callisto screamed, but if they heard her, they didn't show it. The Siren song muddled her thoughts, but her anger forced it back. This was how these creatures had so easily dominated sailors. Their song had some power over men.

Somebody screamed from the other side of the cave, but Callisto couldn't make it out. But she saw the cages against the rock and a score of naked men huddled within, several she knew to be her crew. They were pointing at their heads.

Callisto didn't have time to think about that as two creatures broke from singing, launching themselves at one of the dazed pirates. They bore him to the treasure-strewn ground, sinking their fangs into his throat and neck.

Rushing ahead, she slashed her cutlass across one of the creatures' backs, causing it to release its victim, howling in pain, its legs no longer working. She turned to see another diving at her and brought her pistol up in time to fire, tearing through the Siren's shoulder and spinning it away.

"EARS!" A cry cut through the cave.

Three more Sirens stopped their song, moving in on her. She was forced back, sweeping her blade side to side to keep the monsters at bay. She bumped into someone and turned to see it was Reeves, he too lost to the Sirens' beautiful and magical song.

"Reeves, you sonofabitch, I need you!" she cried, slapping his face hard before she lunged forward, burying her sword into one of the pursuing creature's chests.

The hit pulled him from the trance, and he instantly came forward, chopping his blade at another beast about to latch onto Callisto. "What the fuck happened?" he yelled as he kicked the dying Siren to the ground. But the song weakened his resolve. His arms grew heavy and dropped to his sides once more.

"Fuck!" Callisto pulled her blade free, not bothering to finish the wretched creature.

"Captain!" one of the trapped Poseidon's Crew screamed as loudly as possible against the loud harmonious singing.

Callisto looked up and saw the man grabbing the sides of his head. No, not his head, she realized. It was his ears. He was grabbing his ears! Of course!

"The damn song!" Callisto backstepped to give herself room from the two advancing creatures.

Reaching down, she scooped up a handful of slimy muck and slapped it across Reeves' ears, trying to push it in deep. Praying that it would block out the hypnotic magic of the Siren's song at least enough for him to fight it.

Reeves immediately found himself shaking his head to clear the confusion. Before realizing what had happened, a Siren leaped for him. With his weapons on the ground and no time to retrieve them, he fought with the only weapons he had, his fists.

He slammed a right cross into the creature's face, and the weight of the blow sent it back into another coming in close behind. Taking that free moment, he snatched his blade from the ground and caught sight of Callisto pushing mud into another crewman's ears.

Bringing his hand to his ear and feeling the blockage sealing his hearing, he understood. But he had no time to help the others, as more Sirens abandoned their controlling music and attacked. Taking down two other crewmen lost to the song with claws and teeth.

Reeves understood his role in this. He needed to buy Callisto time to free the others from the Siren's trance. With an angry bellow, he charged ahead, slashing, chopping, and stabbing any creatures within range of his devastating strikes. But more were finding their way to the cavern to join in the fight, and he knew he wouldn't hold them off for long, as he already bled from a dozen places.

Callisto scrambled as quickly as she could, scooping up mud and slime, covering ears as quickly as she could, breaking the spell that held the crew so they could continue the fight before all was lost.

She reached down again and was tackled to the cave floor, its razor teeth snapping for her throat as she struggled against its raw, violent strength. Her pistol came up, and she fired into the beast's side and quickly freed herself of its dead weight.

Two of the men she had helped were already fighting, with Reeves holding the gathering swarm back, while the other pirate realized the danger and began packing his brethren's ears with muck and shit. They could still win this; they just had to hold off a little longer until they had more fighters. But more and more Sirens were emerging from the deep waters of the cave and side tunnels.

Dread filled her.

They would be overwhelmed soon, for too many of her crew were still hypnotized and would likely be killed before they even had a chance to defend themselves.

Callisto ran ahead, driving her blade deep into a Siren about to attack one of her men from behind. She threw the creatures aside and kept forward, towards the cages. She needed more fighters, and they were all she had.

Ducking a wild charge of a Siren, she felt claws gouge her back as the beast went over her. She ignored the pain and kept forward. Stopping meant death. Her cutlass cleaving through clawed fingers, hands, and arms as she went. There was no time to kill; she needed to free those men.

"Captain, hurry!" a man cried from the cage, seeing a handful of creatures breaking off from the fight to give chase.

A Siren jumped in front of the cages and shrieked a challenge. Callisto wasn't about to stop. She knew others were right behind her. Dropping her shoulder, she barreled into the bitch, slamming it into the bars. Angry hands from within grabbed the beast, holding it in place. An arm came around its neck to squeeze the life from it.

Callisto chopped her sword down on the thick ropes locking the cage, but before she could strike again, a Siren grabbed her from behind and sunk its teeth into her shoulder.

"Take it! Get free!" Callisto cried, throwing her blade through the bars to the waiting men as she was pulled away.

Slipping in the muck, she fell, landing atop the beast, who relentlessly sunk its fangs deeper into her flesh. Punching back, she tried to dislodge it, but the creature refused to let go. She could feel her collarbone threatening to snap under the powerful jaws of the Siren.

Grabbing her dagger, she stabbed, burying the blade deep into the Siren's leg, but still, the beast held on. Again, she slammed the blade down, twisting and tearing the flesh of the creature's thigh, leaving it in bloody ruins. It screamed an ear-piercing wail as it released her. Callisto wasted not a moment rolling free and launching herself back at the creature. The dagger slammed into the Siren's neck, and Callisto tore it free, taking half its throat.

Falling back, she saw the cage door burst open, and nearly thirty men sprang forth. Their ears were packed with mud against the Siren song as they threw themselves violently into the fight, using whatever they could find, fists, rocks, or weapons littering the ground.

Callisto pushed herself up and saw they had quickly turned the tide of this fight. Nearly all her crew had been freed of the song's enticement, and those who weren't were coming to as the Sirens gave up singing to fight or flee into the murky pools and underwater tunnels.

Weaver ran to her side, his twin axes covered in gore. "Captain, you're hurt!"

She felt her shoulder and her hand came away thick with blood. "I'll live."

"I don't understand how such a spell could be cast," Weaver said. "I couldn't do anything. It was like my body was no longer my own."

"I don't know," Callisto admitted. "Somehow, there is magic in this song."

Within moments the cavern was theirs. Two score of dead Siren's littered the ground, and only ten men had fallen, six from her crew and four men from the various lost ships.

"Captain, the creatures have fled to a back chamber. We have them trapped in there. They don't seem to want to fight anymore," Reeves explained, a score of deep wounds marking his body.

Callisto grabbed a torch and moved to the opening, where a dozen men stood, ensuring the creatures could not escape. Holding up the torch, she saw nearly a score of Sirens fanned out protectively. Behind them, a group of nearly forty were huddled together, most with swollen bellies, thick with child. Others pushed their young behind them, trying to hide them from the enemy that had conquered their lair.

"It's a birthing chamber," Callisto whispered, and she saw the fear in the creatures' eyes. They knew they were beaten, and this would be the last stand for life or death.

"We can take them, Captain," Half Beard replied, priming his rifle with the last of his powder.

"Hold your shots," Callisto ordered. "There is nowhere for them to go."

"Captain?" several men asked in confusion.

Callisto made her way over to the side of the cavern where

several small barrels were scattered around, most showing a familiar symbol. "Help me, gather these up."

"Aye," Half Beard grinned maliciously. "I see it now."

The barrels of lamp oil were placed in front of the entrance. Several men began cracking them open and rolled them far into the midst of the cornered Sirens, spilling their contents as they went, soaking the ground all around the creatures.

The Sirens shrieked in confusion and huddled further against the back wall, unsure of what was happening and why the men weren't attacking them. But knowing the smell that came from the barrels surely wasn't good.

Callisto took a torch from Kadir and stood at the entrance, watching the strange creatures. She felt a pang of guilt for what she was about to do, but it had to be done as she looked at the men around her. Their wounds were many, and so many lives had been lost, not even regarding her men, as countless human bones littered the cave. Hundreds of sailors had met their end to these demons, maybe even thousands. She knew many of the creatures had escaped, and likely many more were hiding among the other islands, but they would do their part in weakening these demons.

The torch hit the ground, and flames sprung to life, following the oil-spilled pathways where they burst when they reached the half-empty barrels. Fire filled the cave within moments. The screams and shrieking from within were deafening, and even the hardest among the crew winced.

Several of the Sirens ran through the flames, making a final attempt to break free. They were met with gunfire and blades, stopping them cold in their tracks and only adding more fuel to the all-consuming flames.

"It is done," Callisto said bitterly, turning to what was left of her crew and those newly freed. She reached down, scooping up a handful of gold and silver coins. "Now we take what is owed."

The pirates were fast to work, filling their pockets and sacks and grabbing hold of chests and barrels they packed to bursting with all they could—moving as much of the treasure to the entrance above as they could before dark oily smoke filled the chamber and forced them to abandon the cave.

They made their way back to the ship, where they were greeted with cheers and mouths agape by the sheer volume of treasure they had recovered, and still more was coming. Men dumped off their loads and ran back to gather another.

"A mighty fine haul," Reeves said, running his hand over a pile of coins and ingots. "Five king's ransoms or more, and that is only what we could pull from the depths so far. The smoke will be cleared tomorrow, and we can go back in."

"I do not think we will get that chance," Callisto said, staring out across the waters to the other islands where the Sirens' calls could be heard. "They are gathering those that are left. Telling them what we did. We must leave this place before nightfall or be overwhelmed by every last one of them seeking revenge."

Several others had heard the calls and stopped what they were doing to stare out at the eerie sight of movement on the islands not far from them.

"But the rest of the gold?" Reeves asked, his greed over-playing reason.

"All the gold in the world will do us no good if we die here tonight," Callisto reminded him. "We have enough to see us all wealthy for a very long time."

Reeves looked back at the hoard they had already piled by the longboats and knew she was right. This was more wealth than he had ever seen in one place before. Hell, he was sure it was more wealth than he had ever seen combined in all his life.

"Start loading up the ship as quickly as we can. I want to be free of this place long before nightfall," she ordered the men.

Commodore Stephan Belfield stood at attention in the empty hallway in front of the double doors that led to the council chamber. The last time he stood before these doors, he had been given the rank of commodore, and now he wondered if he would lose it. General Jacob Knight, General Marcus Carpton, and Lieutenant General Ralph Wineton were within, hearing the tale from his lieutenant, James Featherstone.

There were benches in the hallway, and Stephan knew he could sit, as he had been standing for hours already. But he would not give himself that luxury. He would stand for as long as it took, with his chin up, back straight, and arms grasped above his lower back, at full attention. He had resolved himself to the discipline he had been trained for.

Already he had told his side of the story, for he had been the first to tell the horrific tale. But as was customary in such events, they would speak with each officer on board. And if that didn't satisfy them, they would interview the entire crew and hear each man's tale to fill in any gaps that might have been missed in another's.

Stephan suspected highly that the latter would occur. Losing three warships had not happened since the heat of the last war and never to pirates in a single battle. Such a defeat as they had suffered was not to be overlooked in any capacity.

Already he knew rumors would be thick in the city. It would fuel much discourse among the people and those who had investments in trade by sea. Often merchants would hire mercenaries or even other battleships to escort them across known pirate hunting grounds to help deter attacks. But only

QUEEN OF THE SEAS

the very wealthy merchants could afford such luxuries. What hope did mere merchant vessels have if pirates could sink three naval warships?

The Paradise had arrived in London late afternoon the day before, to the surprise of many, and at first, they had been greeted with cheers of admiration until it was realized they were three ships less. Then had come the crestfallen faces of the men who had marched from the ship.

Those men had been weary, their emotions stretched to their limits. None wanted to do anything more than to return to their families or to drink their fill to battle the demons they all felt haunting them. That hadn't been allowed to happen.

Soldiers had come to greet them with carriages and horses, and every man aboard the Paradise had been escorted back to the capital building. They had been housed overnight, awaiting a debriefing of the events, but soon, they would be given leave to return to their homes and families, at least for a while, before they were called to duty.

The door to the chamber opened, and James Featherstone stepped out; his face was stoic, and his demeanor distant as he looked upon Stephan. "They will see you now, Commodore."

"Thank you, Lieutenant." Stephan saluted and entered the room, where the three head powers of the naval military sat around a large table. All had firm and disgusted looks on their faces.

"Commodore, please take a seat." Jacob Knight, Stephan's old commander and mentor, motioned to the cushioned chair before them.

Stephan sat, straight backed, resting his hands on his lap.

"Would you like a drink?" Jacob asked, knowing the man had been waiting outside for hours.

"I am fine, thank you," he lied.

"Let us cut to the chase, Commodore," General Marcus

Carpton said. "These reports from yourself, Lieutenant Featherstone, Helmsman John Baker, and quartermaster William Stone are, shall we say, not cohesive in many key parts."

Stephan felt the back of his neck start to sweat. "How so, General?"

"Well, to be frank, they don't seem to match up," Marcus said flatly. "Aye, the beginning of your journey to this island you discovered, this, Glacia's Palace as it is known, seems to match up perfectly. Nothing to make us question it. But it is after your arrival there that the stories seem to falter."

"Which parts?" Stephan asked, confused.

Lieutenant General Ralph Wineton snorted. "How about the reason you didn't engage with the Poseidon's Fury when you first encountered her?"

Stephan cleared his throat, feeling his nerves creeping up on him. "I explained in my report. We were set to engage and cut the ship off from the island, but the new Captain, this Callisto SinClair, brought prisoners above and held them as human shields. I ordered a stand down not to risk the lives of innocents that might be spared."

"Only to discover they were slavers shortly after," Wineton growled.

"Information that was unknown to me at the time of my order, General."

"Be that as it may, a few lives would have been worth the risk in taking back our lost ship," Wineton countered. "As your officers reported, it was brought to your attention before it was too late."

"I thought it prudent not to risk the lives at the time."

"An order that was clearly a mistake," Wineton countered coldly. "In the face of a woman captain, no less. Hell, a woman pirate at that."

"Yes, General. The mistake is known to me now, and the

fault of it my own. But at the time, I had minimal knowledge of the events that came to my attention after the fact. I took an oath to risk no innocent lives if it could be avoided. This was avoidable."

"Do not talk to us about oaths," Wineton snapped back defensively. "More so when your own is in question."

Marcus Carpton leaned forward, ignoring Wineton's outburst. "The next morning is the part that bothers me, Commodore. You were greeted with the white flag of parley with the hostess of this rogue pirate island, correct?"

"Correct."

"And you thought it wise to risk yourself and a dozen men on said island, surrounded by those we deem traitors to the crown and enemies?" Carpton pressed.

"Yes, General," Stephan replied. "It was not a decision I made lightly. But I thought it judicious to go and see this island for ourselves. To gather what information about it we could in hopes to better understand it and its offensives and defenses in the event we needed to stage a large attack against it."

"What about the Poseidon's Fury?" Wineton cut in.

Stephan nodded. "It was also my hope to take stock of this new pirate captain. This woman who slew Blackmane and commandeered his ship—our ship. I had reason to believe she would see sense to return the ship with the promise of pardons and gold."

"Which you had no true authority to do, I might add, at least not in the capacity you presented it. The king would never agree to pardons to that crew," Carpton added with more than a hint of disappointment. "This woman, maybe, but the heartless killers aboard, never."

"What happened after? With this woman of the island?" Jacob said, remorse in his voice for his protégé.

Stephan stiffened a little. "She was most unusual and confident in her position as ruler on the island. She made that —clear. She also made it clear that she wanted no part in a war with the crown so long as we did not start one. But we were quickly dismissed after that. We sailed from the island. No harm came to any of us, as they had promised," Stephan explained. "We took to the waters around the island and began our hunt. You sent us out there to destroy pirates, which is what we did."

"Yes." Wineton ruffled through the papers in front of him. "You and your fleet sunk eleven pirate vessels, crippling a score more, that still found safe harbor around the island."

"Correct, General."

"A bold play to stay around a place so dangerously infested with that many pirates," Wineton said. "Almost like you were taunting them to band together and strike at you."

"With all due respect, General, they are pirates and not known for their loyalty among even themselves."

"Yet that is exactly what happened, is it not?" Carpton cut in. "Was it not the pirates banding together with this woman in command of the Poseidon's Fury that led to this disaster?"

"In the end, yes," Stephan admitted, with downcast eyes.

"Lieutenant Featherstone, John Baker, and William Stone tell us you knew well in advance that your supplies and arsenal were well past dwindled days before. Leaving you and the fleet vulnerable to attack, let alone any coordination. Even at the beckoning of your Lieutenant that you sail away days before to resupply, you pressed on," Wineton said.

Stephan stiffened again.

There it was, plain as day. James had betrayed him and altered the truth to place everything on him with the aid of the others, even though James's urgings had kept them there those days longer.

"Well?" Ralph Wineton asked. "What do you have to say for yourself, Commodore? Your report says a very different tale at this point and after. Like how you fled, leaving Sea Glory to the pirates when there was still hope to save her and her crew."

Stephan felt his anger flare, and he near jumped from his seat. "That is not what happened! I would never have left Sea Glory behind if there was even a shred of a chance we could have saved her!"

"You forget yourself, Commodore!" Marcus Carpton snapped, and Stephan tried to find his composure.

"Apologies," Stephan muttered bitterly. "That is not what happened."

"What's more, spending a week wallowing in self-pity, under the influence of drink while your men needed you?" Wineton jabbed further. "Maybe we were wrong about you, Stephan. Clearly, the pressure of such a station is not suited for those not bred for it."

Stephan gripped the sides of the chair in rage, and it took every ounce of control he could muster not to lash out at that statement.

"Gentlemen," Jacob Knight intervened quickly, knowing this would soon be said that could not be taken back. "It has been a long night and a longer day. I believe we have learned enough for today from Commodore Belfield. It is clear there is more here than what we have seen and heard and will require further investigation of the whole crew to paint better the picture of what truly transpired."

"Bleh," Wineton spat. "I think we know enough to deem Stephan Belfield responsible for this failure. All he is trying to do now is cover his hide and protect his title."

"Enough!" Jacob said forcefully. "We will follow protocol and investigate further on the morrow. When we are rested, and our heads have had time to cool." He turned a sharp eye to Wineton.

Carpton and Wineton stood and exited the chamber, and Stephan was about to do the same when a hand on his shoulder stopped him. It was Jacob, his mentor, and dear friend.

"By god, Stephan, what mess have you found yourself in?"

"James and the others are lying." Stephan sighed. "At least in part."

"About what?"

"It was James who convinced me we should stay and fight a few days longer, though I knew our supplies were low. I was ready to call us back and report our findings to the council. But foolishly, I listened to him, for we were defeating pirates easily."

"Why was that not in your report?"

Stephan sighed. "Because the part of me falling into despair and drink is not untrue."

"Yet, you left that out of your report. Even Helmsman John Baker did not add it, but your quartermaster certainly did, as did James, and his was in great detail. Worrisome detail, if I am, to be honest."

"James told me we would leave that part out, as with the part where we knew supplies were so low when we were attacked. We made a deal if I commended him in honor of the trip so that he might find himself as a Captain in the fleet."

Jacob leaned back against the table. "I see. That is a different tale to be told, one that does not see you free from guilt."

"I know," Stephan whispered. "I am sorry. I have failed you, the others, my crew, and the crown. I will accept whatever my punishment is. If I am to hang, I will not fight it."

"Mistakes were certainly made," Jacob agreed. "But I

QUEEN OF THE SEAS

wouldn't believe them to warrant your death. I do not believe that you are squarely at fault, even in light of what you've told me. You did do what we sent you to do. It is a dangerous job, and you were faced with a situation no one could have been truly prepared to face. Your knowledge of this island could be of great use to us. Not to mention the eleven pirates you defeated are no longer sailing the seas murdering and robbing innocent merchants."

"What will happen to me?"

"I do not know, my friend. I do not know." Jacob stood. "But for now, go home. Be with your wife and son. They will want to see you. We will get this straightened out, and I will do whatever I must to see right done by you. I promise. But first, tell me more about Callisto SinClair, this woman pirate. She intrigues me."

Stephan gently paced the large room with a slight bounce in his steps as he cooed down at Johnathan, his baby boy. He couldn't believe how big his son had gotten in the five months he had been gone, but already the child was twice the size.

"You will grow into a fine young man," Stephan whispered. "A fine young man with a bright future ahead of you. One in which you will be able to do anything you aim to do with your life. My son, you will not be held back by the blood that runs in your veins. I promise you that." He closed his eyes and fought back the tears that threatened to escape. "I will do whatever I must to ensure that for you, no matter the cost to myself. I swear it to the old gods and the new."

It had been three days since his meeting with the council, and still, he had heard nothing of note. However, the rumors were fast circulating throughout the city and countryside.

Some holding more truth than others. Most were beginning to paint him as the failure and James Featherstone as the savior to those few who had returned.

Stephan had no proof, but he suspected that James's words had fueled many of these rumors. He was making a power play, as all rich noble-born whelps did when they tasted opportunity from those they felt were their lesser.

He sighed.

He had liked James Featherstone. Yes, the man was brash, hot-headed, and not as conventional as he should have been, but he had seemed trustworthy and true. It had been a stab in Stephan's back what the man had done to him.

A deep part of Stephan wished to confront the young noble. To speak to him and ask why? They had discussed what would be said at length. Their stories would still have been confirmed, even if a few details had been omitted. But the blame would have fallen to the pirates, Stephan would have remained as he was, and James would have likely seen his rank jump to Captain of another ship. They both could have walked away from this disaster with honor, ready to seek revenge.

Not that Stephan had enjoyed altering the truth of what had happened. In fact, it weighed heavily on him, and he almost went against the plan and admitted everything in his report.

He stared down at his son, who snuggled into his chest, staring up with small sleepy eyes. He had only gone through with it for his son. To give the boy the best chance, he could at life, as was a father's job, as his father had done for him.

Now, it looked like it might all fall apart. That the Belfield name would be cut from its short reign as a notable bloodline, back to the squalor it had been born to.

"Breakfast is ready, my love," Mary said from the doorway, a bright smile on her face at the sight of her husband and son.

Stephan turned to face her, pushing down his negative thoughts. He didn't want her to see them, to know that he struggled as profoundly as he was.

In truth, he hadn't told her most of what was happening. Only they had suffered a significant loss, and things were being discussed what would happen because of it. He didn't want her to worry, though he knew the rumors would soon find her ears. But hopefully, by then, there would be answers to what their futures would look like.

"I have dreamed for months of having a homecooked meal." He smiled at her, his face portraying nothing of what his mind was thinking.

"Hopefully, you will be home long enough to enjoy many of them. That is until you realize I am not as good a cook as you remember," she teased, moving next to him. "Here, let me take him. I will bring him to Maranda, and she will watch over him while we eat."

Smiling, Stephan shook his head. "No, I will hold him. We will eat as a family, the three of us."

Mary beamed. "That sounds lovely. But we should get out there before it gets cold."

Stephan played with his son more than he ate as the three sat around the elegant table. It wasn't that the food didn't entice him; it wasn't that he wasn't hungry. But this moment was more important to him than food. These were the moments he wished to make and hold onto in the hard times that were sure to come.

"I was thinking since we have nothing planned for the day that we would go to the park down the street," Mary said as she cleared the dishes. "Some of the other wives are meeting up there with their children and husbands. Conny has organized a luncheon for the children with games and the like. It should be a grand time, and it would be nice if I could show you off to all those women who seem to forget you exist."

Stephan winced at the thought. "I am not sure I am up for that."

"Come now, Stephan. You were stuck on a ship for months at sea, and now you choose to be stuck in your house. It will be good for you to get out of the house. It will be good to walk around and see friends that you haven't seen in a while," she pressed. "I know several of your crew will be there with their families, so you won't be alone. Might do you good to be seen as a fellow family man and not just their commodore."

He wanted to argue, wanted to tell her seeing his crew was the last thing he wanted to do, but she wasn't entirely wrong. If he were seen among the others, with no fear, and no guilt, maybe it would help his cause.

"Aye, you are right, my dear."

She smiled warmly. "I always am."

The late morning sun was warm, and a slight breeze brought just a hint of the sea to mingle with the start of the fall air. The park was already bustling, with three dozen families participating in the activities.

Children chased each other this way and that, or kicked balls, climbed trees, and even a few kites graced the blue skies. Food and beverages were set up along several tables, each family bringing something to contribute to the festivities. It was peaceful, the picture of how civilization was meant to look.

Mary set the large platter of finger foods down on one of the tables, happy that she seemed to be one of the only people who brought them. "I am sure they will be a hit again. Last month I made them because I didn't know what else to make, and they were one of the first things gone."

"I am sure they will be again," Stephan told her.

"Mary, it is so good you were able to come with Johnathan and your—husband," a woman with a large and elegant up-styled hairdo said as she and a few others moved over to the table.

"Martha," Mary beamed. "We wouldn't have missed it for the world."

"I am just a little surprised to see your husband is all," Martha replied with a distant smile.

"Why would he not have come?" Mary asked, confused. "He is finally back from sea."

"Well, you know, with everything that is happening with —" she paused, "well, the investigation on what he did."

"What he did?" Mary was taken aback by the statement.

"Surely he has told you?"

"Told me what?" Mary looked at Stephan. "What is she talking about?"

Stephan did his best to remain calm. "It is nothing of concern. Just some formalities about the events need to be investigated and concluded."

"Yes, of course," Martha said with a bittersweet smile. "How silly of me to believe the rumors when nothing official has been said. I do hope you enjoy the day, Mary." With that, she and the other ladies walked away, laughing and glancing back over their shoulders.

"What was that about, Stephan?"

"There are always rumors that filter about after things of this nature happen. Do not worry about it. It will all be worked out soon."

She eyed him with a strange suspicion. "If you say so." She touched his arm. "You can talk to me; you know this. We have created this life from nothing, you and I. Do not feel you need to hide things from me to protect me."

Stephan did his best to smile warmly as he took his wife's

hand. "I would dream of no such thing. It is as I have said, you will see."

Mary seemed to accept that. "Let's go feed the ducks by the pond. Johnathan loves them so very much. You should see his face brighten up when they come close."

Stephan was about to agree when he saw James Featherstone and felt his anger rising. "I will meet you down there shortly, my love. There is someone I must speak with first."

Mary took Johnathan and made her way down to the large pond.

Stephan squared his shoulders, marching over to James, doing his best to stay composed. He needed to stay composed here. He could not let his emotions overwhelm him and catch him reacting foolishly. In truth, he should have gone with his wife and done all he could to avoid this man.

But he couldn't.

He had to know why.

"Ah, Stephan," James greeted him with a broad smile, "or Commodore for a little while longer, at least."

"Why?" was all Stephan could muster in response.

"Why what?" James asked in faint surprise.

"You know damn well what I mean." He tried to keep his voice down so no one would take note of them. "Why would you tell them all that you did? Why would you make me look like I failed at my duties and brought this ruin upon the fleet?"

"I merely told them the truth, Commodore."

"Liar!" Stephan spat. "You embellished far more of the 'truth' than what really happened. You purposely ran me through the mud."

"I don't know what you mean. I was asked to recount what I saw, and so I did. I am sorry if it painted you in a bad light, Commodore. But that was the light you stood under. You have only yourself to blame."

Stephan moved in closer. "We spoke of this. YOU spoke of this with me at length in how the story would go to ensure that blame fell on none other than the pirates. You wanted to be a captain, and I could have easily gotten you such a thing. We had a deal."

James grinned. "We did, and truly captain would have been a grand title to jump to so quickly. But the more I thought about it, the more I realized that Commodore would be a title better suited for my birthright. Don't you agree? You know, since I come from noble stock."

Stephan stepped back as if slapped. There it was. The truth. This man, whom he had considered a friend, had finally said the words aloud.

"It will not stand. The investigation will go through, the men will tell the truth, and I will come forth with the full truth of the events, all of them!"

"Do you really believe the men are on your side anymore? They had friends and family on those ships. Friends and family, your poor judgment got killed. A man of low birth got them killed because he reached higher than his station should have allowed him to," James sneered.

"You would try and ruin me for this? So you can jump rank faster? Why?" Stephan pleaded. "You could have had it all in time. I could have helped you. Three or four years, and you would have seen the title you so desired. Commodore of your own fleet. There is no need for any of this."

James shrugged. "Perhaps you are correct, and I could have, would have even. Or I can take what I want now and be the youngest noble to find such naval ranking. Oh, how that will grow the prestige of my family's name."

"You are a fool!" Stephan growled. "I will see this right, one way or another. If it strips me of everything, I have worked so hard for. I will risk it all to ensure you get nothing!"

James chuckled coldly. "It is already too late for that, Stephan. Even if you do decide to tell the truth now, it will only paint you in a worse light than the council already sees you. The men are already on my side, at least most of them. They would much rather follow a man of proper birth than a low-bred dock monger's son!"

Stephan wasn't even aware of the movement, wasn't even aware that his anger had reached that point, surging past all his reform of a base man. That was until he felt his fist connect with James's jaw.

James staggered back under the blow and looked like he would retaliate until he saw the growing crowd of watchful eyes. "Stephan, contain yourself, man!"

"Fuck you, you sonofabitch!" Stephan hissed, moving in to strike the man once more.

"This is no way for you to deal with your failures," James shot back, letting his voice be heard by all those around. "Not the way civil men act."

Stephan held himself, noting the wide grin on Featherstone's face. Suddenly he was very aware of the dozens of eyes upon them—nay, upon him. He composed himself quickly, seeing his wife making her way over to the scene with his son in arm.

"This isn't over," Stephan muttered loud enough for James to hear.

"Oh, but I believe this will be the final nail in your coffin, Commodore."

"What is going on here?" Mary burst out. Her eyes were wide with shock at what she had witnessed. "Stephan, what have you done?"

"Nothing," Stephan huffed. "A disagreement, and nothing more. Let's go home."

"By the gods, Stephan." Jacob Knight muttered. "What were you thinking? Striking a nobleman like that? In hot water, you already find yourself in."

"He is trying to destroy everything I have been able to create for myself, all because I was not born from the loins of a better man!" Stephan retorted as he paced his study.

"And you will make it easier for him to do with such actions. Hell, Stephan, you might have just handed it to him with this stunt."

"I did not mean to strike him." Stephan paused. "I lost control. I didn't realize I had hit him until it was too late. I was overcome with rage."

"You are already under investigation, Stephan. Deeply so. Every man aboard the Paradise and the few you were able to rescue from the Sea Lion are being drilled relentlessly for every detail from the moment you sailed from port." Jacob sighed. "Some still support what you say, at least in most. But many," he shrugged, "many share a similar tale as Featherstone. And now this transgression against a man of noble blood. A man whose claim against you is what started all this. It is not a good look, Stephan, and will only worsen your standing in the eyes of the council."

"He wishes to defame me!" Stephan shouted. "Wishes to take what I have built for myself as his own. Captain is not enough for him. He wants to see himself as Commodore and has conspired with many of the crew to just this end."

"Truly?"

"By his own words, only hours ago."

"Do you have proof of this?" Jacob questioned.

Stephan's shoulders slumped. "None as of yet, for I have only just learned of it."

"This might be a blessing in disguise."

"How?"

"If what you say is true, and James has talked to the crew about changing their tale to suit his need better, and those men were to come clean about it. It could see your name cleared of all this, or at least in part," Jacob explained.

Stephan dropped into his seat. "How many would you need to come forward?"

"As many as possible. The more that confirmed it, the better it would be for you. But even as few as half a dozen would be enough to build a creditable case on your behalf. Enough in the very least that the others on council wouldn't be able to deny the claim."

"I will see what I can do," Stephan said. "I will talk to them, find out what I can. See who will come forward."

"No, I don't think that wise," Jacob told him. "I want you to stay put, go out as little as possible. I will use my contacts to ask and speak with the crew. I want you involved as little as possible. If you are seen poking around too much, they might believe you bribed the men in some way."

"I am just to sit here, a prisoner in my own house?"

"Be thankful for that, for, after today's events, you were almost a prisoner in a cell. Only your good standing and my word have kept you from such a fate, and even that I cannot assure if James truly presses the issue."

Stephan hung his head in shame. "I understand."

"Know this, Stephan. That even with all this information, if we can prove it. The end result for you will likely not be great. You will avoid jail, but you will likely be stripped of your rank."

"How far?" he asked dourly.

"You might find yourself as far back as Lieutenant or quartermaster. If they even deem you acceptable to sail again."

"I understand," he said again.

"I will be in touch when I know more," Jacob said. "Until then, try to stay put and not find yourself in any more trouble."

Callisto opened her eyes and was standing in a grand temple and knew once more she was in the dream world of Ares. It had been long since he had summoned her, but she would never forget the feeling of what it was like and how different it was from her regular dreams.

"Ares?" she called out, and her voice echoed off the marble that made up the temple. "Where are you? Why have you not come when I have called for you?"

"You forget yourself and your place within this game we play," Ares said from behind her.

Callisto spun around. "But why have you been so silent?"

"I am not your pet to call upon," he chastised her. "You are mine, lest you forget who among us is the god, oh great Queen of the Seas."

She felt scorn behind that remark. He was indeed angry with her, and his eyes spoke volumes. "What was I to do? We were doomed. Caught in a violent storm of Poseidon's making. He called to me and demanded a sacrifice, or he would have destroyed the ship and all upon it."

"Yes, he certainly would have, so a sacrifice was required. I fault you not at all for the whims of my uncle," Ares responded coldly. "But who do you think was with you in that time of trial? Who do you think held the storm at bay and allowed you the strength to make it to the ship's bow?"

"It was you..." she whispered, finally understanding.

"It was I," he confirmed. *"I helped you defy my uncle, and you mocked me for it."*

"No! Never!"

"Who was that sacrifice?"

Callisto stiffened.

"Who?"

"I threw myself over the ship's rails into the waves."

"Why?" he demanded.

"Fortune favors the bold, does it not?"

Ares's laugh almost sounded as if it was one of mirth, yet it clearly was not. "Was there not a more perfectly suitable sacrifice among you? One that had already betrayed you and had scorn cast upon him?"

"Murphy..."

"The choice was obvious, and yet you chose yourself."

"I did not want to show my crew that I would so easily throw their lives aside," she argued.

"Mortal lives!"

"I gained the loyalty and respect of my crew! They are mine now! They follow me, and I no longer have to worry about a dagger in my back!"

"You will always have to worry about a dagger in the back! That is the cost of power! Fear demands loyalty and respect!" Ares's voice was full of violence.

Callisto stepped back from the sheer strength of his words.

"You are weak. I have chosen poorly."

"No!" she cried out. *"I am not weak! How can I prove myself to you? What can I do to make amends?"*

Ares paced around her, looking her up and down as if he was inspecting cattle for slaughter. "There is one thing you can do for me that would redeem this failure."

"What is it? Anything?" she pleaded.

"My spear was lost to me nearly a century ago. Retrieve and

return it to one of my statues, placing it in my hand, and I will forgive this foolish mishap."

"Where is it?"

Ares boomed with laughter as he began to fade. "You must find it."

The Poseidon's Fury's return to Glacia's Island was met with cheers by all those on the docks and countless others who had come down to witness the ship's return. Talk of what they had done to break the siege nearly three months prior was still the talk of the island.

The sight of the ship and its damages brought much curiosity to those around, wondering what tales of adventure and battle they had seen since they were last here. Their return was even blessed by the lady of the island standing at the end of the wharf.

"You have returned," Glacia announced with a wide smile. "Though it would appear just barely. Your ship will need much attention if it is to stand out as it once did and strike fear in the hearts of those who oppose you."

Callisto set a small chest down in front of her. "Breaking the siege here was the least exciting of our adventures."

"What is this?" Glacia looked down at the chest.

"Payment for docking, of course."

Glacia lifted the chest, her eyes widening at seeing several wonderful jewelry pieces. "Yet again, it is far more than what is required."

"We might need to remain here a few weeks for repairs. I just wanted to make sure that wouldn't be an issue. Plus, I owe a little for the flour and lamp oil I used, with interest, of course."

Glacia clapped her hands together and laughed. "You are ever a wonder, my dear Captain SinClair. Let us retire to my palace, where you can refresh and tell me about your adventures."

"My crew," Callisto glanced back as many of them were clasping's hands with friends or seeing to the ship.

"What about them?"

"They have been through a lot, as you will hear about shortly. I would ask for something extra for them this day. For we lost many, and hardship struck us bitterly, even if, in the end, we were rewarded. Payment is not an issue."

Glacia smirked. "I am sure we can work out something, yes. I will see to it the finest establishment is theirs to enjoy, with food, drink, women, men, and warm beds."

"You have my thanks."

"Now, come. Let us get you more comfortable, and you can tell me everything."

Callisto groaned as she submerged herself in the warm bath. A sensation she had not felt since the last time she had been here, months before. And one she greatly missed from her previous life. A life where the luxury of a bath was at her disposal nearly anytime she desired it.

She laughed at the thought of bringing a tub onto the ship in her cabin. It was absurd, and yet she wanted to do just that.

The scent of lavender wafted up with the steam filling her senses with something much more pleasant than the smell of the sea, fish, and sweat. She smiled; those were scents she had never expected she would have found comfort in the past, but now, she had grown used to it. As her crew titled her now, she was a pirate captain. Queen of the Sea

Callisto burst out laughing.

Who would have thought when all this started that she would find herself with such a title as that? She wondered how vocal her crew would be about it. Not such a bad way to be remembered in the history books.

"What is so funny?" a voice asked from the doorway softly.

Callisto opened her eyes to see Katrina standing there in a sheer, soft blue dress. "Oh, the fates do like to show themselves."

Katrina came in and sat near the tub. "How so?"

"You know it was you, not long ago, that first told me that I have the look of a pirate queen."

Katrina blushed. "I remember. You looked magnificent in your new attire."

"It would seem your words of flattery held weight with the fates."

"I am glad. A better woman to hold such a title, there is none."

"Why are you here?" Callisto asked. "Is Glacia that impatient that I cannot enjoy getting clean before telling her my tale?"

"On the contrary." Katrina smirked. "She informed me that you are to take all the time that was required and for me to help get you clean and—relaxed."

Callisto smirked. "That may take some time indeed."

Katrina let her dress slip from her slender shoulders, grabbed a cloth, dipped it into the water, and began washing Callisto's neck and shoulders. "You have returned with battle wounds," she said as she gently washed around the almost healed Siren bite in her shoulder.

"I wish I could say that was the only one." Callisto lifted herself a little to show the scar from the bullet on her side.

"Did they hurt?"

"Incredible."

"Such a dangerous and exciting life you live," Katrina said, an edge of wonder there.

"Since I was ten," Callisto admitted. "Though this new stage I find myself in certainly holds a higher level of danger."

"I can only imagine what it must be like—sailing the seas as a pirate—chasing down ships, fighting battles to board them, and plundering them when you win. It sounds so exciting. I have often dreamt about such a life."

Callisto turned to look at her. "You've dreamt of being a pirate?"

Katrina blushed again. "At times, yes. Others, just an adventure, discovering strange and beautiful places. Fighting off rogues and beasts. Talking with the gods."

Callisto laughed. "You sound like I did once upon a time."

"And now look at you. You are living such a life."

"Maybe I will take you sailing with me on one of my adventures, and you can see it firsthand."

Katrina's eyes lit up with excitement. "Truly? You would have me?"

"I see no reason why not. A pirate ship is not as fabulous as what you have here."

Her eyes quickly lost their luster. "The lady would never allow it, I am afraid. She needs me here and has done so much for me."

Callisto moved up and kissed the woman. "Adventure seldom starts with permission. I think I am clean enough, but I could use some help in the bedroom—getting dressed."

Callisto sipped her wine and ate more than she had at one time for months as she recounted her tale to Glacia. Starting from when they left the island and attacked the Sea Lion, setting the ship ablaze in a desperate attempt to help break the siege. To the great storm they were caught in, her throwing herself to Poseidon to save the ship and her crew, to the near death they faced afterward due to that same storm.

Finally, she finished her tale with the island of Sirens, which had nearly been the death of all of them and yet had rewarded them with riches worth a decade of successful raiding and plundering.

"Sirens?" Glacia gasped. "I did not believe them to be real —merely tales told by a handful of broken sailors. But what's more, you saw Poseidon? Nay, your whole crew witnessed the event. For already, while you were refreshing, rumors came to me of such a tale. By morning the whole of the island will know of it." She smirked. "Know of you as the Queen of the Seas, and your reputation has grown vast in such a short time. Well done, Queen of the Seas."

"Experiences I think I could have done without," Callisto admitted, showing her the two scars she had suffered for such newly found fame.

"Fame and power will always have their sacrifices," Glacia replied. "I know this firsthand. But you command your crew's loyalty, for they know you are god-touched. You truly are now and forever more the rightful Captain of the Poseidon's Fury. No man can claim that you are not any longer."

"I should inform you Murphy is no longer part of my crew."

"I suspected as much with what you told me of his performance. What will you do with him?"

"Nothing, he is your problem now." Callisto grinned.

Glacia cocked a brow. "My problem?"

"Only if you have use of him, of course. For he will not step foot on my ship again. Whether I forgive him or not, the crew will not. So, I will abandon him here to find his way. If he finds himself in your service, that won't disappoint me. But if he chooses to find a merchant ship to sail with or at least take him home, that will be his choice, for he is of no use to me any longer."

"Interesting. I saw in him a loyalty only seen in dogs when I looked at him when you first arrived. It surprises me that I was wrong about him."

"He is too honest. The pirate life was not meant for him. I cannot blame him for that."

Glacia nodded. "I will keep my eye on him to see what he wishes to do. Might be that I could use a more honest man around here for certain ventures."

"Enough of me. I feel that all I have done since stepping off my ship was talk of me. What about you? How do things fare here now that the siege was broken?" Callisto asked, finally pushing her plate away.

"It was slow for the first fortnight, but thankfully, pirates are pirates and need a place to sell their stolen goods and spend the money to drink and whore. It will still take time to replenish all that was lost, but it has not cut me too deeply."

"Repairs to my ship shouldn't be an issue?"

"They might cost a little more than usual, but it sounds like that will be well within your budget. You will have the island's full attention of carpenters, blacksmiths, and whatever else you need. I will see to it in the morning that repairs begin immediately. But did you not say you wish to stay awhile?"

"I do and will, depending on my next request and how fast you may be able to assist in it."

"Oh, this sounds serious."

Sidestepping to the left to avert the glare of the early morning sun, Callisto caught the glint of steel and barely managed to deflect the downward cut. She used her momentum and went into a full spin, dropping low against the reversing blade coming for her head. She slashed for her opponent's legs and caught only air as the man quickly stepped back.

"Almost." Callisto grinned as she launched herself forward, having Reeves giving ground now.

She slashed her cutlass in a figure eight as she pressed forwards. She wasn't trying to score a hit, only to off-balance him so that she could find an opening to strike. But his grin told her he knew well what she was trying. She pressed harder, determined to take that grin from his face.

Callisto reversed her blade and lunged forward, thinking she had him. Once more, she met only air, and only on reflex did she get her dagger down in time to turn aside his thrust for her ribs.

"Almost often still leaves you dead." He stepped back.

Callisto righted herself. "I will best you, sooner or later."

"I await the day, Captain."

"Let's go again. The morning is still early, and we have nothing of importance to get back to for a while," she said, enjoying the small clearing they had found to practice their swordplay—a change from aboard the ship.

"As the captain wishes." He came in, and the dance started anew.

"Seems the men are enjoying the respite these last weeks." She parried his blow.

Reeves stepped to the right and lunged again. "Nearly dying horribly a handful of times does that to men. They have enough wealth to enjoy Glacia's Island to the fullest."

"Aye," she parried again, reversed, and a ring of steel met her downward chop. "They deserve to feel like kings for a while. It hurts the ship's coffers now little."

Their blades rang out in song as they tested each other once again.

"Will you tell me your story now?" Reeves asked, nearly taking a cut to his exposed left arm.

"I was ten," she attacked again, "when my father took me to the house of Pablo Gasper, the nobleman we sold our fish to." She quickly worked her blade, countering his strikes as she told of that fateful day.

"He took your father's hand in front of you?" Reeves gasped, feinting an attack to her right, only to come in on her left, which she turned aside with her dagger, the same dagger she had killed Gasper with. "That is cruel indeed, and yet you were able to get your revenge."

"With the help of Ares," she admitted, for she held no illusions she would have even attempted such a thing without the god's support.

She ducked his swipe for her head and shouldered into his chest, forcing him back so she could find her footing again.

"When I returned home, I was met with anger and blame from my mother, who was distraught." She came in hard, and their blades rang loudly in the crisp morning air. "But men came looking for me, and so my brother woke me in the middle of the night and forced me to flee my home—my life—all I had ever known."

Reeves countered her wild charge, barely keeping ahead of each strike. "A hard life for a child to be forced out into with nothing. But he likely saved your life and possibly their own. Do you know if they survived?"

"They did, at least the last time I inquired, but that was many years ago." She sidestepped his attack and tried to slip her dagger between his guard, but it was slapped away with his short knife.

"How did you survive all those years on your own?" He rolled across the ground and was back on his feet, giving himself distance again. She was getting better, much better.

He knew he had to be careful, or she just might best him this day.

"The first few years, I was sure I would die more days than I expected to live." She came at him again, knowing he was becoming distracted by their conversation. "But it wasn't until I came into womanhood that I realized one of my greatest skills."

Reeves defected and parried her sword a half dozen times before he could move back on the offensive. "And what was that?"

Callisto grinned. "My womanly charm and the power of seduction. And just how weak the loins of men make them." She worked her cutlass perfectly, parrying each attack he sent at her.

"A curse most of us succumb to." He laughed as he forced her to give ground. "But how did that end you up on the Wind Spirit?"

"A lordling whose pride was wounded and couldn't accept that a woman had robbed him." She spun away from his lunge and slashed down on the top of his outreached blade, taking the weapon from his grasp.

She had him!

Callisto lunged in, but Reeves slipped to the side, his power hand clamping down on her wrist, locking her arm out to the side. She brought her dagger in for his belly, and he released his own and slapped it wide, knocking the blade from her grip.

He spun her around and crushed her with his arms, holding her tightly and squeezing until she dropped her sword to try and pry herself away.

"Almost," he whispered in her ear and released her.

Sighing, Callisto turned to face him. "I will best you—" her words were stolen from her as he pressed his lips to hers.

For a second, she kissed him back, lost in the sudden heat

of the moment. A moment she had thought about before. But quickly, she pushed him back, breaking the embrace.

"What are you doing?" she said, but there was no anger there.

"I think I love you," he whispered, surprised by the words slipping from his mouth as she was.

"Reeves, no," she pleaded.

"But I thought—we have a connection," he tried to reason. "Back at the island, you told me to come back to you. I felt it then as sure as I had felt anything."

"Reeves, no. This isn't something that can be."

"But why?"

"I am your captain. We are pirates. Certainly, there is something that this goes against in some code, or I don't know." She threw her hands up. "It wouldn't make sense."

"And how different would it be to anything else you have done?" he countered. "It doesn't make sense that you are a pirate, to begin with. A female pirate, a female pirate captain," he scoffed. "Hell, a female pirate captain blessed by the old gods. None of it makes sense, but why does it need to? Why does this need to make sense out of everything else that does not?"

Callisto knew she was about to hurt him, but she had to make things clear. "Love makes you weak. It gives you something that can be exploited. It makes you think differently, feel different, and react differently. It changes everything." She came forward and placed a hand on his cheek. "I cannot afford such a weakness."

The words stung, and Reeves flinched as he stepped back as if she had plunged her dagger into his chest. "Right," he muttered, collecting his things. "I understand, Captain. I overstepped. My apologies. It will not happen again."

Callisto felt her eyes moisten as she watched him walk

away but knew deep down it was better this way. Her only hope was that he would be able to move past it and that it would not affect his place on the ship. If it did, it would hurt her more to remove him from it.

The warm naked body shifted next to her with the light roll of the ship as light waves lapped at the side of the hull. Callisto took in the scent of Katrina's hair and moved her hand to find her other evening companion who had joined them. But Joshua was gone, the spot next to her was still warm, and she wondered if his leaving was what had woken her.

Glancing at the back window of the cabin, she knew it would be hours before dawn, and the man had likely gotten up to relieve himself and would join them again shortly.

It had been a fortnight since they had arrived back at Glacia's Palace and repairs to the Poseidon's Fury were nearly complete. A new mast had been properly fashioned, replacing the one the crude tree they had used to get off the Siren's Island. Nearly all the rigging and ropes had been replaced, and all but one sail had needed replacing.

The large crack in the hull where the Sea Lion had rammed them was gone, and if it weren't for the change in color of the wood, no one would ever know it had even happened. The only thing that would take more time was the blacksmiths repairing and casting the dozen new cannons to restore the ship to its former glory and strength.

The work had been considerable, and the cost for such speedy work had proven to be a lot. But it had barely put a dent in the hoard of treasure they had returned with. Even the extra wages she had given her men had done little to lessen their coffers. Half Beard had warned her that the men were spending foolishly, and she needed to tighten their rewards lest they find themselves broke before they set sail again.

Aye, it was true. She was paying them far more than required. But it was good for them to reap the benefits of such a thing. Plus, she knew the next adventure they took would be a personal one for her. She would need them, content for it. For it wouldn't be about treasure and gain for the ship alone. It would be about her finding good graces with Ares.

"Joshua, where did you go?" Callisto whispered, surprised the man hadn't returned.

Extracting herself carefully from her bed, she dressed and slipped out onto the ship's deck in search, wondering if the drink from the night before had caused him to get sick or pass out. But the deck was empty.

Wandering down to the dock, she caught sight of someone awkwardly stumbling towards the far end of the wharf and smirked. The foolish man had gotten lost on his way back to the ship.

Quickly she followed, calling out to him to get his attention, but he didn't hear her and wandered further into the lesser-used area of the dock, where very few ships resided.

"Joshua," she called to him again. "You are going the wrong way, you foolish boy."

She reached out, grabbed his shoulder, and turned him around, expecting to see the hazy eyes of a drunken stupor. But she was greeted with no such thing. Joshua's eyes were clear and alert, showing no intoxication signs.

"What are you doing out here?"

His eyes darted around nervously. "I—I am so sorry—but they made me an offer I couldn't refuse. I need off this island, and Glacia won't allow it."

"What are you talking about?" Callisto said when she heard the movement behind her.

Looking back, she was met with a fist to her jaw that staggered her into Joshua, who wrapped his arms around her tightly, holding her trapped.

"The feared Queen of the Pirates, aye?" the cloaked man who had struck her said. "Not so tough if you ask me. But I knew that already anyone with half a mind knew that on day one."

Seeing three others moving from the shadows, Callisto snapped her head back, crushing Joshua's nose flat to his face. He released her, and instinctively, she reached for her flintlock pistol and found nothing, for she had not thought to strap on her belt and weapons before leaving the ship.

The mistake cost her another punch to the midsection, which doubled her over, the air blasted from her lungs. She fell to her knees, gasping, trying to scream for help. But nothing but ragged gasps escaped her lips.

"Someone has missed you dearly, you stupid bitch," the man growled, lifting her chin.

Balling up her fist, Callisto punched up, following the trail up the man's inner thigh and connecting with all the strength she could into his groin. She sprung up as he came down, connecting her head to his nose with a loud crack. He hit the ground, holding his face and cock.

Before she could even think of what to do next, a boot found her side, and she toppled to the ground, where kicks and punches rained down on her. She tried desperately to fend them off, but she was no match for them. She found enough breath to cry out, but before the sound could come, a heavy boot connected with the side of her head, and all went dark.

Callisto came to, unsure of where she was or what had happened, but the pain that riddled her body let her know she wasn't dead, at least. It was dark, and she could see nothing, and it took several moments to realize that there was a hemp sack over her head.

She was in a chair, hands bound behind her back to something solid, and her feet were strapped tightly to the legs of the seat. It didn't take her long to know that whoever had tied her up had done so expertly, and there would be no chance that she could unravel herself anytime soon.

The sway alerted her to the fact that she was on a ship. She was no longer on Glacia's Island, nowhere near her crew and likely any help she might have hoped for.

She had been abducted.

Minutes or hours went by, and she couldn't be sure as she tried desperately to free her hands, but with each movement, she felt the course ropes biting into her wrists and could already feel the wetness of blood.

"Get the boss," a man from somewhere behind her ordered. "His guest has finally come to."

"Let me go and return me to the island, and I won't have you all killed," Callisto called out in vain.

She heard the man laugh and move in front of her.

"You are in no place to be thinking you hold any control of what is happening now, Captain." The words were said with venom, and she recognized the voice but couldn't place it.

"I know your voice. Who are you?"

The bag was yanked off, taking more than a little of her hair. Staring back was a man she did indeed recognize. A pirate who had once been part of the Poseidon's Crew. A man who had decided not to return to the ship to sail under her. His name she could not remember.

"Long time no see, bitch." He spat in her face.

"Looks like I missed one who was thinking of betraying me." Callisto glared. "You should have been on the ship with the others I executed."

He slapped her hard. "You killed my brother that day and a few of me friends, wench."

Callisto grimaced from the blow, her face already sore and swollen from the attack that had gotten her here. "Untie me, and I will send you on your way to meet them. I am sure they are waiting for you in whatever wretched afterlife awaits those of such cowardly stock."

The pirate lifted his hand to strike again when a commanding voice gave him pause.

"Enough, Astro. There will be plenty of time to teach this bitch all the things she has done wrong on our journey." The well-adorned man came down the stairs from the top deck.

Callisto felt the blood drain from her face as the newcomer entered the lamplight.

"Oh, so you do recognize me. Good, I was afraid I was just another faceless mark to your devilish trade."

"Antonio Dacordo."

She had not seen him in two years or more since she had seduced, drugged, and robbed him blind of a fair share of the wealth he had carried.

"Bet you didn't think you'd ever see me again." He pushed the pirate aside to stand before her.

"It would have been a dream, too, given I can still smell your breath upon me at times," she taunted and grinned at seeing his lips twist bitterly at the insult.

"Brave words for one in your position," he mused. "I would have thought you smarter than that. Where are your dripping charms now, whore? Your sweet words and seductive ways to convince me to let you go?"

Callisto snorted. "I hardly had to bat my eyes at you to get you to drop your trousers so starved for attention from a woman you were. And the little slug you call a cock was endured only because of the foolish amount of coin I knew I could take from you."

That did earn her a slap.

"Oh, but I prayed for the day I would see you again," Antonio hissed. "You stole much from me and made me look like a fucking fool!"

"If coin is what you are after, take me back to where you found me. I can double what I stole from you," Callisto said. "And the memory of our time shared you can keep as extra."

Again, he slapped her, slamming her head into the beam behind her.

"I will get my payment ten times over, wench."

Callisto licked the blood dripping from the side of her mouth. "Not out in the middle of the sea, you won't."

Antonio grinned maliciously. "There is quite the price on your head after your part in sinking those naval ships. A large sum of a thousand gold crowns, alive. Half that dead. Either will be more than payback for what you took from me."

"London?" Callisto said, fear flashing across her face.

"I am sure the king will want to meet the famous Pirate Queen, as they are calling you now," Antonio sneered. "Likely right before you drop from a rope in front of a crowd of cheering peasants like you used to be."

This was bad. Very bad.

"Antonio, please," Callisto begged. "You have my word. I can pay you that amount back at my ship. Twice that if it so pleases you. Thrice if I must."

Antonio burst out laughing. "There is the desperate begging I wanted to see. Oh, how the mighty have fallen. Do you truly believe this is about the coin? I am rich. Richer than anything you could have ever hoped to see in your wretched lifetime." He moved in closer. "This is about justice, not coin. I will see you hanged for your crimes against me. I will be there in the front row so that I can watch the light fade from your pretty little eyes."

"They don't care about the coin I took from you," Callisto growled. "They only care about what I did to their naval ships."

"But I will know," he countered. "I will know you hang because of me, and only because of what you did to me did I even care enough to capture you. So, you see. You will die because of what you did to ME!"

"Your ego knows no bounds."

He slapped her again. "And your mouth knows not when to keep shut!"

Antonio composed himself. "But you will learn before this trip is over." He grabbed her face hard and forced her to look at him. "But hopefully, I will put that mouth to use again before it all ends."

He stepped back. "Put the bag back on and guard her. She is a slippery one and has taken a ship once already. A mistake not about to happen a second time."

Before Callisto could protest, the bag was roughly put back over her head, and her world went dark.

Yawning, Reeves climbed the plank back aboard the ship. He had stayed out all night, drinking and gambling, and had even thought to find a woman to warm a bed beside him. But he had been in no mood for such a thing.

He had hoped to drink himself to the point of little self-regard, yet the rejection of Callisto had remained, no matter the liquor he had consumed.

He reached the deck to see the captain's cabin door open and Katrina, the captain's nighttime companion exit. He felt a pang of bitterness, knowing Callisto had enjoyed the woman and likely another, caring nothing for what she had done to him.

A worried look was clear on the woman's face.

"What is the matter?" Reeves asked anxiously.

"I do not know where Callisto or Joshua is. I awoke last night, and they were gone. I figured they would return, but they did not."

"Might be that they went for a stroll to find somewhere to work up a sweat without waking you," Reeves replied, trying to keep the hurt from his tone.

"It is not like either of them," Katrina said. "I am concerned."

"I wouldn't be." Reeves patted her on the shoulder lightly. "And do not take it as a slight either. Sometimes we all have a different appetite when the moment beckons." He tried to play it off.

"That is not what concerns me," Katrina snapped back defensively. "Joshua—he has been acting strange of late. Saying things about leaving the island."

Reeves shrugged. "Maybe the captain went to help broker him passage on another ship."

"In the middle of the night?"

He had to admit that would be a little odd.

"Nor would the lady allow one of her acolytes to leave. Not without her consent," Katrina was quick to add.

Reeves grimaced at that. For he had heard rumors of those Glacia kept around her. Beautiful men and women all. All in devoted service to her every whim and need, even the needs of those Glacia shared them with.

He shook the thought from his head, for that was none of

his concern, and in truth, such a life was still better than the average life most of them would find elsewhere.

"I am sure all is well, and both are about somewhere," he told her with little worry. "Only so many places on an island they can be."

"You are right. When you see her next, tell her I asked about her and for her to send word to me."

He watched the young woman leave and was about to find his hammock to sleep off the weariness and anger he felt, but something about the conversation nagged at him.

Pushing open the cabin door, Reeves saw the many empty wine bottles and discarded clothing. Callisto had had fun last night and was likely clearing her head and nothing more. He was about to close the door when he saw her weapon belt on the desk. Something that if she had meant to leave for a time, she would not have left behind, even here on the island.

"The captain up yet?" Alonso asked as he and Kadir climbed up on deck.

"You have not seen her?" Reeves asked the pair.

"Not since yesterday afternoon," Alonso replied. "But she has been spending much time at the palace with Glacia. Them two have become fast friends."

"Two women of beauty and power," Kadir said with a grin. "A man could only wish to be a fly in the room on what they get up to."

Reeves rolled his eyes, even though his mind had wandered there more than he cared to admit. "Keep your eyes open for her and ask around. If anyone finds her, tell her she is being looked for."

"There is a problem?" Alonso asked, concern in his tone now.

"I hope not," Reeves replied.

The morning and afternoon went by. The crew and laborers

worked on the ship's repairs as if nothing were amiss, for in truth, at the moment, none knew the truth of things. But by late afternoon, more than a few conversations began about their captain's whereabouts, and more than one crew member went into the town in search of anyone who might have seen her that day.

By that evening, no word had come of their wayward captain, and things began to get real. Callisto was the most talked about person on the island; the crew of the Poseidon's Fury had told their tales to any who would listen. They proudly boasted how their captain was blessed by Poseidon and saved them in the face of a storm that would have sunk any other ship. And how she led them to great riches and fought countless demons on an island full of Siren devils.

Yet none had seen her that day.

Finally, Weaver and Reeves' worry had grown enough that they ventured up to the palace, where they waited, pacing the large marble terrace to be seen.

"I don't like this," Reeves muttered. "Something is wrong. It is not like her to disappear. And where would she go? The damn island is only so big."

Weaver couldn't disagree with the statement, but he tried to keep a clearer mind about it. "I am sure she is here with Glacia and is simply busy. Who knows why or what has her attention."

"I just can't get this bad feeling to leave my guts," Reeves admitted, and he wondered if she were avoiding the ship and crew because she knew he would be there.

"No one would dare move against her here. Not now, and certainly not while we are on the island."

"You forget where we are, what we are, and who half these cutthroats are," Reeves reminded him.

"We will find her and put this all behind us," Weaver told

him, though the truth of Reeves' statement did not help his darkening thoughts.

"I am sorry for keeping you gentlemen," Glacia said as she stepped out to meet them in a gown better suited for a king's ball than that of an island full of pirates. "I heard word you are looking for your missing captain."

"She is here then?" Reeves cut in an edge of desperation in his voice.

Glacia held up her hands at a loss. "I wish I could put your mind at ease, but I have not seen her."

"Something happened," Weaver cut in. "She is missing, and I mean to find her!"

"Slow yourself," Glacia said, though she too felt a pang of fear creep into her now, for no one went missing on her island without her knowledge or encouragement. "I will get my people searching. We will find her."

Reeves' fists balled rightly. "I will kill anyone who has anything to do with her disappearance!"

Glacia's eyes darkened. "Do not forget yourself, Reeves, nor on whose island you are on. You will do no such thing. I will have my guard begin a search. By morning we will know where she is."

"And if she has been taken? Killed?" Reeves argued.

"If such a thing has come to pass, I will deal with it how I have always dealt with situations such as that," she stated firmly. "But let us not get ahead of ourselves. I suspect she is fine and merely enjoying herself or someone and lost track of time. Joshua has yet to return to my compound, and he was with her last night, and I suspect he still is." She smiled. "It has been known to happen here."

Weaver nodded, for he and the others had indeed seen Callisto with the young man and Katrina often enough. "We will be at the ship. Please send word to us the moment you have any news."

"You know that I will."

Callisto was startled awake as the bag was roughly removed, and before her sat Astro, his face bruised heavily from where she had rammed her head into his face when he had attacked her.

"Time to eat, bitch." He shoved a hot spoon full of greasy, flavorless stew between her lips.

It burned her mouth and throat, but she swallowed it, knowing if she were to have any chance at escaping, she would need every ounce of energy she could get.

"You know my crew will know I am missing by now and likely be on the hunt to find me."

Astro laughed, pushing another hot spoon full into her mouth. "Not likely. You think they care about you? Nay, they have likely already chosen a new captain and are glad for it."

Callisto grinned against the burning sensation. "You don't know MY crew and what we have been through together."

"I've heard the tales." Astro snorted. "And that be all they are, of that I have no doubt. Lies spread to make them feel more like men under the rule of a wench captain."

"If they hated me so much, why would they make up such lies?" She hit him with logic. "Or why wouldn't they have killed me by now?"

"So, they can continue to fuck you while at sea." He chuckled. "Only reason they are playing along is because you've no doubt spread your legs for each of them time and again. They play you for a fool and let you keep your little captain's hats so long as you let them fuck that wet hole of yours. Oh, and I am sure it is a fuck worthy of some praise from what our friend here has said." He grinned maliciously. "Might be that he lets the crew sample it before we get to London to watch you hang."

Callisto stared hatefully at the pirate. "Know this, Astro. I will see you dead before I am."

The heavy-set pirate's laugh rolled long and loud before he struck her. "Watch yourself, woman, lest I decide to care less about my payment for this job and decide to avenge my brother instead."

Before Callisto could say anything else, the bag was forced over her head, and she was left in its darkness again. But now she was left with darker thoughts. Things she truly had wished weren't going to play over and over in her mind.

Was she foolish enough to believe her crew would figure out what happened to her? How would they know which ship had taken her or where that ship was even headed? And on the off chance they did discover it, why would they think to come after her? They were pirates, after all. And a new captain among them would be a more straightforward solution than trying to catch up to them before they reached London.

And if they couldn't, it wasn't like they would invade the city in hopes of recusing her. How could they hope to? They weren't an army; they were pirates.

The realization was depressing and humbling.

They were pirates and would not risk themselves for such a bold move.

She was alone, and her survival would be up to her —somehow.

"I have survived worse," she whispered, with as much conviction as she could muster, but it was little more than desperate words she needed to tell herself.

Two days had come and gone. The island had been put on lockdown. No ships had been allowed to enter or leave until they had been thoroughly searched for the missing captain of the Poseidon's Fury.

Every inch of the island had been scoured, and a reward of fifty gold marks had been offered for any information, a price that would tempt even the tightest-lipped pirate. But nothing had been brought forth, and soon the island felt more like a prison than a haven.

On the third day, all hope for discovering what had happened was near an end. Nothing more could be done. Even Glacia and her guard could not hope to continue the lockdown with good conscience.

Reeves punched the mast, not for the first time. His knuckles were already cut and bruised from his previous assaults, but that pain was the only thing grounding him.

"Someone knows something!" he screamed, and the crew around them kept a wide berth. More than one had suffered a blow or verbal attack from him in the last few days.

Repairs to the ship were nearly completed, and they could set sail at their leisure at any time. Whispers of what would happen now were becoming less whispers and more open talk.

"We will have to make a decision soon," Weaver told him.

"What?" Reeves turned to face the first mate.

"You know what I speak of."

"You cannot be serious!" Reeves argued. "You cannot be thinking of giving up already!"

"I like it little more than you." Weaver's shoulders dipped in defeat as he ran a hand over his smooth, bald head. "But what choice do we have? We have nothing, have found nothing. Not even the full resources of Glacia and her network have found anything. Callisto is gone, dead, or sailed away of her own will or against we know not. Even Joshua has fled. Rumor is, he killed her and ran for his life."

"You cannot believe that worm could have overpowered her!"

"No more than a time ago I could have believed a woman could take the Poseidon's Fury from Blackmane..." he let the words hang in the air.

"There would be a body!"

"The sea is vast and hungry."

"No!" Reeves protested though he knew it to be the truth.

"We cannot sit here forever. We are pirates, and the crew has grown restless. They are just as angry as we are and need to vent that anger. They must hunt, kill, and accept—as we do."

Reeves was about to snap back that the men would wait as long as they demanded them to when he saw a horse riding hard towards the ship. "It is Gavin!" he gasped, pushed by the first mate, and nearly jumped from the ship to the dock.

"What news do you bring!" Reeves shouted, rushing up to the captain of the island guard.

"You two need to come with me," Gavin declared.

"What news, damn it!" Reeves growled, wanting to throw himself at the man but knowing better.

"Come now." That was all he said.

They rode up to the Palace and beyond, taking a back trail behind the vast home of the island's ruler, back to an underground bunker that Callisto had once visited on her first night on the island.

The horses were left to graze as Gavin led them to the hidden opening, where Glacia stood talking with Murphy.

"Murphy, you sonofabitch!" Reeves spat as he came

forward, ready to strike the man. "I should have known you were behind this!"

"Hold yourself!" Glacia commanded, and Gavin's sword was out in a flash and pressed into Reeves' chest, halting the man before he could move another step.

"You would protect him?" Reeves growled, the hate in his eyes never wavering.

"I would protect an innocent man who has, where we failed, uncovered what has happened to our dear friend and your captain," Glacia replied.

"What then?" Weaver asked, keeping himself more in check than his counterpart. "What do you know?"

"Follow," was all Glacia said as she pushed open the thick wooden door that led into the bowels of the ground.

Down the five went, deep into the rocky earth, where the sting of the torch smoke licked at their eyes and dried their throats.

Soon they were at the end of the stairs and down to the far end of the foreboding tunnel, entering a room where a man sat chained to a chair. A man Weaver and Reeves knew well.

"Gregor?" Weaver asked in confusion, for the man had sailed under the banner of Blackmane for nearly a decade but had left the ship and not returned when they had landed here many months before under new leadership.

"Long time, old friend," the pirate wheezed out through broken teeth and blood-caked lips.

"What did you do to her, you Scottish bastard!" Reeves hissed, and once again, Glacia's captain was there to remind him to keep composed.

"I did nothing."

Weaver turned to face Glacia in confusion.

"If what he says is true, then that statement is correct." She shrugged. "He didn't move against Callisto, but he knows who did."

"Who?" both Weaver and Reeves asked together.

"Tell them, Gregor, so that we may put this to an end."

"Not until you give me your words that I will not be killed for what I know," the man said, already having suffered greatly at the hands of a large torturer in the corner.

"You have my word. You will not be killed on my island," Glacia informed him. "Now speak."

"Nay, not good enough," Gregor muttered, spittle dripping from his mouth. "I know what happened to the others. I saw them executed on the ship before everyone. I'll not share that same fate. I am not to blame for this."

"Yet you weren't forthcoming with it either," Glacia reminded him.

"Why should I be? That bitch took everything from me and the others," he growled back.

"If you don't speak what you know soon, I will tear you apart with my bare fucking hands!" Reeves screamed.

Glacia smirked coldly. "And I'll let him."

"Your word is all I need."

"You have it damn it!" Weaver gave in.

"It was a man named Antonio Dacordo," Gregor finally said. "A merchant that was here. Someone who Callisto had wronged in her past life. Stolen from him a great amount, but worst yet wounded the small man's pride. He tried to hire me and a few others to help him capture her. I said no." He shrugged. "Astro and a few of the others did not. They had help from one of your very own, lady, one of your servants, who was spending time between the wench's legs."

"Joshua," Glacia gasped.

"Aye, that be the one. Fooled her good he did, led her into a trap where they took her at night and placed her on a ship."

"What ship?" Weaver demanded.

"The Golden Dahlia. She sailed out the same morning she was missing. Long gone now."

"Where were they heading? What was their plan?" Glacia pressed.

Gregor chuckled. "To London if what the sniveling lord said to be true. To collect the considerable bounty on her head from the king himself."

"How many are aboard his ship?" Weaver asked.

Gregor shrugged, for how would he know that? "Three of our old companions and that whelp of hers." He nodded to Glacia. "That lad wanted as far from here as he could get in a hurry. Without him, none of this could have happened."

"What more do you know?" Glacia asked coldly.

"Nothing. I told you everything." He pulled on his restraints. "Now, if you'd be so kind as to let me go on."

Glacia pulled the fine dagger she had concealed beneath her robes and ran it across Gregor's throat without a hint of hesitation. The sharp blade sliced through the fat of his neck like butter.

Weaver stepped back as they watched the betrayal register in the pirate's eyes as he struggled and gurgled, knowing his life was over. "Thought you gave him your word?"

"I couldn't have him reveal any of this to anyone else. His life was forfeit the moment my men had to gather him instead of him coming forward of his own accord," Glacia said calmly.

"London," Reeves whispered, not caring about what he had just seen, for he would have killed the man himself later anyway.

"Now you know what has happened and where she is heading. What is your plan?" she asked them once they were breathing fresh air once more.

"It is over," Weaver admitted.

"Over?" Reeves sputtered in surprise.

"You heard him. They are taking her to London. This bastard already has days on us in a faster and lighter ship. We couldn't hope to catch up to them even if we left now," Weaver reasoned.

Reeves growled at his friend. "We are just to give up and let them take her? After everything we have been through? We are to let her hang at the mercy of that fat, cocksucking king and those high-born pricks who will cheer when the rope goes taut?"

Weaver hung his head in defeat, not liking it any more than the others. "She is lost to us."

"We can save her still," Murphy said, stepping forward.

"Don't be daft," Weaver shot back. "What chance do we stand of catching the Golden Dahlia? Even if we did, the bastard would cut her throat before surrendering her back to us, knowing we wouldn't let him live."

"We will never catch the ship before it reaches London," Murphy admitted. "But that isn't where we can save her."

"How?" Reeves cut Weaver off. His eyes were wide with desperation.

"I have been to London many times," Murphy explained. "I know the city's lay and where they will keep her until they decide to execute her if that is indeed their course."

"We will never reach her in time," Weaver said. "She will hang before we even see the coast of England."

Murphy was shaking his head. "In most cases, you would be correct. But in this one, I suspect not. The first woman pirate captain? One who helped sink three of the greatest naval ships in their fleet? They will question her for weeks, if not months, before making a spectacle of her. Nay, they will keep her alive for a while. Of this, I am almost certain."

"There is a chance, then?" Reeves was near pleading.

"Yes," Murphy told him. "A slim one, but a chance none-theless."

"What are you fucking waiting for?" Reeves stammered, ready to set sail at that moment.

"We cannot make such a decision alone," Weaver reminded him. "We are captain-less. We will have to ask the crew. This is not something we can ask them to risk involvement in if they are not willing."

Reeves snarled at that, but he knew the truth of it. "Then let's go ask those sheep shaggers!"

Weaver turned to face Murphy. "And you? After what you did, the crew will not allow you back on the ship."

Glacia interrupted. "They might see reason knowing he was the one that discovered the whereabouts of your captain."

"How can we trust him?" Weaver said bitterly. "He has made it clear he doesn't wish to take part in the pirate's life."

Murphy shrugged, for it was true. "I still do not. Nor will I. But this is about rescuing a friend, not about piracy. This is a debt I owe her. Let me do this for her as my way to absolve myself of my failure to her and Alonso." His eyes were pleading.

"Good enough for me," Reeves said.

"Reeves," Weaver said as calmly as he could. "You forget yourself. I am in charge of the Poseidon's Fury as First Mate until—"

"Aye," Reeves turned back to him, his eyes a mixture of bitterness and fear, "you are. Are you willing to just let this go at this? That's it? You felt the same damn thing when you looked at her as I did. Can you really stand there and tell me you don't feel the call inside you? That this is far from over?"

Weaver sighed. "I cannot, no. I feel it too—still."

Reeves clapped his friend on the shoulder. "Then let's go get her back or die trying."

Weaver turned to Glacia. "You have our thanks, no matter what may come of this."

Glacia smiled warmly. "Think nothing of it. If you need a ship and a crew, all you need do is ask if yours are not up to the task."

"I would ask something else."

Glacia cocked a brow.

"If we leave for this, we cannot do so with a hull spilling with treasure. If sunk or caught, I'd not want those bastards to have it."

Glacia nodded. "I will send my men down to retrieve it and keep it safe for your return. But, if the word comes, you have failed, it will become mine."

"I would expect nothing else."

They moved off to the horses when Glacia touched Reeves' arm, halting him before he reached the others.

"Lady?"

"You love her."

Reeves was taken aback by the pure straightforwardness of the statement. It wasn't a question. But he couldn't begin to form a reply.

"Bring her back."

He nodded.

"And when you find her," Glacia slipped a piece of parchment to him, "give her this."

The crew of the Poseidon's Fury stood on the main deck, old and new alike. Men who had sailed upon the ship from its previous captain, those few remaining from the Wind Spirit, the Phantom Chaser, and others they had rescued from the Siren's Island.

Sixty-eight men in total. All eager to hear what was to be said about their wayward captain. Most feared the worst. They knew something big was in the air with how Weaver and Reeves had returned.

"We know who took the captain!" Weaver announced the moment the last man had climbed aboard. Time was not their friend, and the longer this took, the less likely they would succeed.

"Who?" Kadir called out, eager for a fight.

"A merchant bastard from the Golden Dahlia."

Mumbles and curses filtered through the men.

"Let's go get her back then!" Slimy Fife barked as if it was that simple. "Teach those fuckers what happens when they take something that doesn't belong to them!"

This was the energy Weaver and Reeves had wanted to see but would it last when they told them the rest.

"It is not as simple as that, for if it were, we'd already be setting sail," Weaver explained.

Alonso stepped forward, his wound healed now. "What is it, man? Spit it out!"

"They travel to London," Weaver told them. "They mean to collect the bounty on her head from the fat English king."

New murmurs and curses shifted through the men as those words sunk in.

"What are we waiting for?" Three Finger Pete called up. "We haven't a moment to spare. They have already got a start on us! I'll sail this ship right up Poseidon's arsehole if I have to!"

Many of the men supported that, yet others had worked out the truth.

"We won't catch them before they reach the safety of London," Weaver said with a heavy heart.

"We have to fucking try!" several of the crew yelled back.

"We won't. This we already know," Weaver stated. "But," he let the word hang in the air as everyone stared up at him, "that doesn't mean we have to give up hope of freeing her. We can sail to London and try and free her there, on land."

"Impossible."

"It would be suicide."

"How?"

Weaver waited until they were done.

"We have a plan or a start to one. But the risk to all of us is great, and there is no guarantee any of us will survive it." He motioned for Murphy to step forward. "You all know Murphy."

Many spat curses at the man.

"Aye, we all feel ill for what he did. But he has been to London. He knows the city and where they will keep her until they execute her. He has offered to help, to put his own life at the forefront of it all in hopes that we might save her. It is a small chance, but a chance all the same. But one I cannot force upon you as the first mate. This has to be something we are all willing to risk."

More murmurs rippled through the men.

Reeves stepped forward, grabbing the rail, his eyes fierce and full of fight. "You know damn well if it were anyone of us, she would come!" he yelled. "It was she who gave herself to Poseidon to save us when we were about to be swallowed by the storm! It was she who boldly marched into the lair of the Sirens to save those of you who had been captured! She spared you all a fate worse than death that day!"

He slammed his fist down, nearly breaking the railing before him. "No, it is not the pirate way to show such loyalty to anyone but oneself! Nay, we follow the coin, and those we believe will lead us to that coin. But you all know this is different! You all feel it within yourself! Know that she is something more than what we have always lived our lives around! This doesn't have to be the end! Not like this..." His final words were a plea. He knew it, and so did the crew.

Slimy Fife stepped forward. "Let's go get our fucking captain back! And show those cunts in London, the true terror of pirates!" he roared proudly, and all but three others added their voice to that statement.

"It is settled then!" Weaver announced proudly, likely more proudly than he had ever felt in his soul before. "We sail for London!"

Callisto found herself once more, deep in the dream world of Ares. Deep in her memory and back aboard the Poseidon's Fury, chained in Blackmane's cabin, naked. Everything about the memory was as it had been—the ship's sway, the smells of cheap wine, and the sea.

"Ares!" she cried out as she pulled on her restraints. "Help me!"

"How many times must I help you?" came the daunting reply as the god of war materialized in front of her.

"You would forsake me now?" she asked bitterly.

He shrugged. "You have not yet retrieved my spear and therefore have not gained my favor again. Yet you call to me as if I owe you anything."

"How can I do such a thing when an enemy has taken me prisoner?"

"You still draw breath."

"Not for much longer. Soon I will be in a place there will be no escaping."

Ares smiled coldly. "Only because you were too trusting and allowed yourself to be captured."

"I cannot serve you if I dangle from a rope!" she growled back bitterly, tiring of his games.

"Such a temper, my little pet." He shifted a piece of her long hair from her face. "Where was that fire when lesser men attacked you?"

"I was ambushed," she defended. "I had no weapons!"

"Whose fault was that?" he sneered. "Why would someone of your power and reputation dare to be without their defenses?"

"A mistake!"

"A costly one, it would seem. After I told you always to be aware of a dagger in the back."

She sighed. "Help me! Please! I cannot see a way from this."

"Did you not once believe that to be the case when you were in this very situation you dream of now?"

"Yes, but that was different."

"How?"

"I was..."

"Chains bound you on a pirate ship, surrounded by enemies you could not hope to overcome, yet you did."

"I had others who were also prisoners from the Wind Spirit. I do not have that now."

Ares shrugged. "Perhaps, perhaps not. Find a way to survive, for the end isn't certain until the rope goes taut."

He laughed as he began to fade.

"And do not call upon me again until you have my spear, or you breathe your last...."

Once more, the bag was removed, this time not as forcefully, and she was surprised to see it was Joshua who stood before her now. A meager ration of food in hand and shame-filled eyes.

"I am surprised to see you," Callisto croaked through dry lips.

He lifted a water jug to her mouth and let her drink for a

moment. "I was told to feed you, and so I will. Though my passage on this ship was assured for my part in—" he cut his words off and looked away.

"Say it."

"Why?" he muttered. "We both know what it is."

"But can you say it?" she pushed. "Can you say that dark truth that had put us both here?"

"I betrayed you for my freedom from that island and that horrible fucking woman!" Joshua snapped back.

"That wasn't so hard now, was it."

He looked at her, confused. "You jest at a time such as this? You know your life is over. You sail to certain death."

"Nothing is ever certain."

"That is where you are wrong," he whispered, putting the spoon to her mouth. "We are days away from the coast of London. Your time among the living is numbered."

"Because of you," she told him bitterly.

"Not out of desire! Nay, I hold no ill towards you. You were —pleasant to be with. Not like others."

That caught Callisto by surprise.

"What made you hate that island so much? Hate Glacia?" Callisto pressed. "From all I saw, she was good to all of you, kind, and gave you a life that most couldn't begin to dream of. Why betray her—betray me to leave that behind?"

"Not all of us wished to be there. To serve her and her goddess as acolytes."

"Didn't seem such a bad life to me. Have you been to the mainland? Seen what most people have to fight and do to merely survive?"

"At least they are given an option," Joshua countered. "On her island, we were little more than slaves, to do with as she demanded." He stared at her coldly. "Do you truly believe we came to your bed out of want?"

That was a slap to her pride she had not expected to feel.

"We were ordered to it. But you were kind, and I likely would remember our time fondly in another time and place."

"I—I didn't realize," Callisto said.

"Nor did you ever stop to consider it," he hissed back. "Why would you? You are a pirate captain. You are all-powerful and can just take what you want. Demand what you will, with no thought of who it affects so long as your desires are met. You steal and kill with ease and little remorse. Why would this be any different to you?" He sighed. "You are little better than she is at the end of everything."

"I would never have forced such a thing. Had you told me," Callisto tried to defend herself.

"What then? Glacia would have had me punished. Whipped, starved, and locked me away for a year. She has done that and worse to others who disobey her commands." He spat on the floor in disgust. "We are nothing more than slaves."

Callisto found she could hardly look at the man now. "I am sorry."

"So am I."

"If you help me, I swear I will do what I can to make this right," she pleaded, knowing the only person aboard this ship who she might be able to convince was him.

"To what end would that serve?" Joshua replied.

"To my survival and yours!"

"My survival is assured already," he told her flatly. "Why would I risk such a thing for you?"

"Because you do not hate me and do not wish to see me dead."

He shifted his eyes away from hers. "It is true. I do not wish to see you dead. But that is not for me to alter. The cards have been dealt for both of us."

"But they don't have to be that way. Free me and give me a fucking chance!" she urged him.

He was already shaking his head. "This is not like your grand escape from the clutches of Blackmane. You have no hope here, no allies that will help your cause. I am sorry."

With that, he stood, with sorrowful eyes, and placed the bag back upon her head.

She had been a prisoner upon the Golden Dahlia for weeks now. Days went by, and all that happened to her was she was fed and ignored. On other days she wasn't so lucky when a vicious hand of the Poseidon's old crew lashed out at her face and body—leaving her bruised and bloody, giving her no time to heal from the beating before.

On occasion, those vicious hands groped at her breasts or between her thighs, choked her neck, and she was sure they would rape her. Calloused hands and warm stale breath upon her skin were a stark reminder that she was at their mercy.

They had held off for a time, but soon a few came for her. They never took the bag from her head as they ravished her. But she knew it to be the three from the Poseidon's Fury as they held her down and took their turn.

She did her best to block it out and put herself somewhere else, far away in her mind. Reminding herself it was merely flesh they were hurting; her body would heal. But if she let them break her mentally and emotionally, she was done for.

Sometimes it was Antonio that came to her. He would belittle her, slap her, threaten to kill her, or worse. He mocked her, beat her, and detailed the death she would soon know over and over again.

He spewed threats that he would ravish her often, but

there was a fear in his voice and behind his eyes, and not once did he make an attempt though Callisto could tell the desire was there. But he was afraid of her. Afraid she would find a way to strike out at him and kill him the moment she was untied. But she knew he had watched the others, had smelled his perfume lingering in the air while they raped her.

She had even tried to play to those desires, desperation taking its course the closer they got to London. Joshua had made it clear he would be of no help to her. She had no one left except Antonio to convince her worth was more than his wounded pride.

Cooing to him that she would offer no resistance when he would listen. Would allow him all the pleasures he could want from her if he would just let her go. Would forgive her transgression against him. In truth, if she believed he would honor it, she would have. Each day she knew was one closer to the death that awaited her if they docked.

His bitterness and resolve always seemed to prove the stronger as he shunned her advances, ridiculed her attempts, and beat her some more at the end. She was left with the very real reality that she would reach London in chains.

Callisto had no idea what awaited her there. She knew the end game that would ultimately come. But how fast the process would be, she didn't know. Would they hang her the same day she arrived? Wait a day to gather a crowd? A week? Month?

She sagged in defeat.

No amount of thinking about it would help her. But she would fight. There were no certainties until she breathed her last breath. A chance could be found that she might still manage to escape. As small as it might be, she had worked with less.

She had no idea what she would do with herself if she did

escape. Finding the Poseidon's Fury seemed almost impossible unless she could find a way to get aboard a ship that would take her to Glacia's Island and wait until her ship and crew returned.

Ares had demanded that she find his lost spear. A trial that seemed daunting before when she had the resources to do so. Now it felt impossible.

She pushed such thoughts far back into her mind.

None of that would matter if she didn't find a way to escape certain death.

Weaver paced the ship's length, his watchful eyes criticizing anything he saw as not perfect in the rigging and sails. He demanded every detail, forcing the crew to adjust constantly so that they caught every breath of wind they could get in their sails to speed them to their destination.

Deep down, he knew it would make little difference, yet he couldn't help it. If they could reach London a half day faster, an hour—a minute. That might mean the difference between saving Callisto or not. He had chosen to fixate on it, for it was the only thing he had control of.

He glanced at Reeves near the helm. Three Finger Pete was steering the ship while Reeves trained endlessly with all crew members that weren't busy. The sound of his sword and dagger rang out like a death song against one opponent, two, three, sometimes four. It never seemed to be enough for him. And he defeated them all as if his very life depended on it.

Weaver grinned, for he knew why the usually relaxed man was training so fiercely. He saw how he looked at Callisto when he thought no one was looking, heard the difference in his voice when he spoke to or even about her, like a fool boy trying to impress a girl.

A foolish and dangerous thing, given who they were and what they did.

Weaver shrugged. It wasn't his concern. That would be between Callisto and Reeves.

The first mate stopped in front of the captain's cabin. A cabin which, by rights, was his for the short term until they either saved Callisto or elected another. Yet, for the two weeks they had been at sea already, he had not been able to bring himself to enter it. It didn't feel right.

He was about to walk away when a noise from within stopped him in his tracks, and he frowned. Someone was inside!

Barging in, he yelled as his eyes adjusted to the room's darkness. "Who is in here!"

He scanned the room. The bed was a mess, and several recently used plates and mugs were scattered across the table.

"Show yourself!" He moved further into the room, his hand near the hilt of his cutlass. "I swear if you show yourself now, your punishment will be far less than if I have to root you out like the dog you are!"

"It is only I," a soft, delicate woman's voice called out from behind the desk.

"Who's there?" he called back, confused as to why it was a woman's voice.

Katrina stood from her hiding place, looking scared, dirty, and ashamed.

"Katrina?"

She stepped out from behind the desk, showing her hands were empty and that she was no threat to the dangerous pirate.

"What the fuck are you doing in here?" he questioned. "Nay, what the fuck are you doing on the ship?"

"I hid so that I might come with you," she said meekly.

"Come with us?" he sputtered. "By the god's woman, why? We are sailing to what will likely be our deaths."

Katrina stood up proudly. "I don't care. I want to help rescue her."

"Help?" He nearly laughed. "And what help do you think you will be? Can you fight?"

"No."

"Know how to use a sword?"

She shook her head.

"Fire a gun?"

She said nothing.

"Then what help could you possibly be to us?"

She swallowed back her fear. "I have been to London before. I lived there as a child and grew up as an orphan on the streets. I know the city well."

"By the god's woman!" Weaver muttered in dismay. "We have Murphy for that. He knows the city well."

"No," she cried in desperation. "He knows the city as a man with purpose can know the city!" She moved closer to him. "I know the city as one who had to hide within it to stay alive. I know places and passages most do not."

Weaver pinched between his eyes in frustration. This was not what they needed now.

"Please! I swear I can help you."

"Does Glacia know you left with us?"

Katrina's eyes went to the floor. "No."

"For fuck's sake."

"She would never have allowed it otherwise. I snuck aboard while no one was looking while you and Reeves went with Gavin."

"What made you think this was a good idea?"

"I—I don't know."

"Because it's not, you stupid girl."

She bristled at that. "Callisto once told me: no good adventure starts with asking permission."

Weaver couldn't help himself and began laughing. "Oh, I believe that she said that rightly enough."

"What's going on in here?" Murphy stopped at the doorway and saw the two. "What is this then?"

Weaver merely shook his head. "Looks like we have another passenger and another set of hands to free the captain."

Callisto woke to the sound of movement, lots of movement. Shouting and calls that she knew were signs that they were docking. They had arrived. She felt dread fill her. Any hope she might have had of convincing Antonio to release her was forever gone.

Now it would become truly real. She would have to find a way out of this within the city's prison or try to escape before she arrived.

She winced as she tried to move. They had beaten her badly and often the last days at sea. Likely to ensure she would be too damaged to make any foolish attempts at just what she was thinking.

"It is only pain," she whispered to herself as she fought past it to force her stiff muscles to move what little they could.

"Pain is only weakness leaving the body," she growled through it. "Pain lets you know you are still alive."

"You will feel much more pain before stepping on the

JAMES FULLER

gallows." Antonio laughed, pulling the bag from his head. "We have reached your final stop."

Callisto glared at him, refusing to give him the satisfaction of seeing her afraid. Though she most certainly was afraid.

"What, no final pleas for your life?" he teased. "No, final begging to please me? To pay me back?"

Callisto smirked at him with violence behind her eyes. "It was better for you that you didn't fall for my charms again. I would have stolen more than coin this time."

Fear crossed Antonio's features before he shook it away, knowing he was safe from her. "I will cheer louder than anyone when they lead you up on the gallows. Watch for me."

"And you would do well to watch your back every moment from now until then. I will come for you if I find myself free again."

"You two put her in chains and get her on deck and out of my sight. The soldiers will be waiting for the dreaded pirate captain Callisto SinClair," he mocked.

No bag was put over her head as she was dragged up the stairs to the ship's main deck. The sudden brightness of the sun that she had not seen in nearly a month, and she flinched as it burned her eyes.

The sudden sounds of jeering and curses forced her to open them against the stinging, and she saw a crowd gathered along the shoreline. Hundreds had come out to see the captured pirate captain. The female captain led the attack that had sunk three prized warships and sent hundreds of their husbands, brothers, fathers, and sons to their deaths.

She could feel their hate in the air and knew if it weren't for the soldiers down below holding the crowd back, they would likely have swarmed over her and torn her apart with no remorse.

At first, she shrunk away from it and flinched each time a

394

rock or moldy fruit was thrown. But soon, she realized this was a form of power. Their hatred of her was based on their fear of her and what they knew she had done. And so, she glared back, stared them down, matching their hateful stares with her own.

Nothing was said to her by the armed soldiers that held her tightly as she was led through the dockyard to the awaiting carriage—an iron-bound cage on wheels.

She was thrown in with little remorse and crashed to the hard floor, and before she could right herself, the heavy door slammed, a thick lock was put in place, and then she was moving.

Stephan rolled from the bed, knowing it was well past morning. Likely closer to the afternoon. There was a time when he had prided himself on being up with the sun and getting a start to the day full of vigor and pride. Now he found little reason to get out of bed and only did so because he had heard his son crying and knew he should help Mary. He had also failed at being a husband and father of late, as he was failing at all parts of his life.

It had been six weeks since he had returned to London. Six weeks after giving his report and being caught in the deceptions and lies of James Featherstone and the crew that had sided with the Lieutenant. And he had heard little news about what was happening from Jacob or any other.

He was in limbo, and he hated it.

He hated that he still had no idea of what was happening.

What was going to happen?

Hated that rumors were being spread of bold lies and half-truths.

But mostly, he hated himself for allowing any of this to happen.

He had failed on so many levels.

Failed everything he stood for and that he had learned.

Failed those who had put their faith in him, their reputations, and had believed in him.

He was glad his father was dead for the first time in his life. He doubted he would have been able to stand the shame and disappointment that would have been in the old man's eyes.

Finally pulling himself from bed, he heard the knock at his front door. And for a moment, his heart nearly stopped. Could it finally be Jacob with news? Or could it be they had finally come to arrest him?

"Stephan!" Mary yelled as she ran up the stairs to the bedroom door. "Stephan, there is a man here to see you!"

"How many?" he asked, wondering if this was indeed it.

"Just the one, I think. I saw no one with him."

"What does he want?"

"I don't know. But he said it was important, and you'd want to hear it."

Stephan grabbed his pants. "Bring him to my study and tell him I will be there shortly."

Stephan stood outside his study door, thankful it was closed as he fought with his nerves at who might be inside and what information they might have that would be important to him.

He wondered if Jacob had sent the man instead of coming himself.

Taking a deep breath, he stepped in to see an averagely dressed man pacing fretfully in front of the fireplace.

"Ah, Mr. Belfield," the man said nervously.

"Yes, and you would be?" Stephan asked, suddenly unsure of what this might be about.

"Name's Conner, but that is of no importance."

"What is it I can do for you, Conner?"

"Nothing for me, sir," Conner replied, "but the news I have for you will surely brighten your day."

Stephan felt like rolling his eyes but managed to keep his composure. "You keep me in bated breath. Please explain."

"My apologies. Not used to talking with such high-statured figures and all."

"Out with it, man!" Stephan growled.

"Right, of course." Conner bobbed his head and licked his lips. "That pirate bitch that caused you so much harm. You know, the one that helped sink your ships and all? Well, some merchant just brought her into port in chains, he did."

"What?" Stephan gasped, his legs going weak, and he quickly grabbed the back of the chair in front of him.

"Aye, saw it meself. Guess she put up a good fight to be sure. They hauled her off the ship, all battered and bruised up good. Tossed her in the prison carriage, and off they went before the crowd decided to stop playing nice."

"She is here? In London?" He still could not believe what he was hearing.

"Aye, that's what I am saying, clear as day, sir."

Stephan could hardly draw breath.

"You gonna be alright, sir?" Conner asked, stepping closer. "Need me to call someone? To grab your missus?"

He shook his head to clear it. "No, no, I am fine. Thank you, Conner, for bringing this information to my attention." Quickly he fished in his pocket and pulled out a silver crown, handing it to the man. "For your time, I thank you."

Conner grinned widely and took the silver as he took his leave. "Much obliged, sir."

"She is here," Stephan whispered to himself. "Someone caught her."

"What was that all about?" Mary asked, coming into the room. "Is it good news? Is the investigation over? Are you cleared?"

Stephan pulled himself away from his thoughts. "No—well, at least not yet, but this may help." That realization hit him. "I have to go."

"Go where?" Mary asked as he pushed by her. "Stephan, what is this about? You are scaring me?"

"They caught her, Mary. They caught the pirate that did all of this," was all he said to her as he made for the door.

Stephan dismounted his horse and handed it to the man in front of the prison house as he made his way for the front doors. He knew he looked haggard, he had not dressed in his fine clothing that morning, and his face hadn't seen a razor in weeks. But he didn't care, couldn't care, so fixated on seeing Callisto SinClair behind bars in the flesh was all he cared about at that moment.

"May I help you?" a man behind the front desk asked, seeing the bedraggled man in front of him.

"Yes, I hear you brought in the pirate Callisto SinClair of the famed Poseidon's Fury."

The man eyed him with suspicion. "Yes, she was brought in just a few hours ago."

"I need to see her," Stephan pronounced boldly.

"That's nice. And I need a vacation and this rash on my foot to bugger off. Guess we will both be disappointed in how the day will play out."

Stephan straightened, and his features hardened. "Do you know who I am?"

"Not a clue and not a care," the man replied with just as much disdain.

"I am Commodore Stephan Belfield!"

If the man was impressed, he didn't show it. "Aye, you

mean the one everyone is talking about. Need to use that title as much as you can, eh? From the sounds of it, you won't be holding it for much longer."

The sheer disrespect portrayed had Stephan's anger flaring, and he nearly reached over to throttle the man. But he restrained himself only because of the man who entered from a side room.

"What is going on out here?" the guard captain asked as he took in the heated moment.

The officer behind the desk jumped to his feet. "Sorry, captain. Didn't mean to disturb you."

"What is this all about?" The captain came out to stand beside Stephan.

"Right, sir, Commodore Belfield wants to see the new prisoner. The pirate woman. I was telling him he wasn't allowed to."

The guard captain looked Belfield up and down with interest. "I see. You do realize, Kenneth, that that isn't a call you can make?"

"Captain?" The man went pale.

"Commodore Belfield outranks you, and though he has no official jurisdiction within the prison, his rank affords him privileges you aren't equipped to deny him."

"Captain, I was only going off your direct orders that no one was allowed to see her until the ministry came," Kenneth stuttered.

The captain waved him silent. "I, on the other hand, hold the power to grant such a request."

"I can see her then?" Stephan asked eagerly.

The captain motioned for him to follow down the hall aways before stopping. "What is the reason for this request? No official questioning has occurred yet, and it likely won't until tomorrow or the day after. You could request to be there for it. A man of your standing, no matter how wobbly it is now, should be given access."

"It is more personal than official."

"Personal business isn't our business here at the prison, you understand."

"I know this." Stephan sighed. "But I must see it with my own eyes. I must talk to her. I need this for me, but what's more, I owe this moment to the men I lost. To have this clarity."

"You know, my cousin was one of the soldiers aboard the Sea Lion. Tyler Conway."

"I knew him well. I sailed with him for several years aboard the Sea Lion. A good sailor, a good soldier, and a better man."

"Aye, he was, and he is missed." His eyes were hard, but only for a moment. "He talked highly of you. Said you were one of the best men he had come to know. How you gave him hope that even of low birth, there were acceptations that a man could work his way to the top." The guard captain ground his teeth. "That is the only reason I will allow this. Rumors be damned. I trust my cousin's words over the garbage that spills from the flapping lips of idiots."

"You have my thanks, Captain."

"I can only give you a few minutes, likely a little more. So, you best make it count, Commodore."

Stephan nodded as he was led down the hallway to a large, locked door and into the dungeon, where the worst criminals were housed.

"Straight down the stairs, to the left, the cell with the lantern burning in front of it, that'll be your woman. Keep away from the bars, she hasn't tried anything foolish yet, but I suspect, seeing you, she might feel inclined to try."

Stephan took the lamp and began down into the damp darkness of the prison. The smell of feces and urine assaulted his senses and almost made his eyes water. He took out a handkerchief and put it across his nose, drowning out the stench only a little.

Each step set his nerves rattling anew.

He stopped at the end of the stairwell to collect himself, seeing the lantern down the hall that marked his destination. He had no idea why he was so nervous. No, not nervous, he reasoned, but scared. Truly scared. For this woman, nay, this pirate, had very well destroyed the foundation of everything he had done in his life, had built, had achieved, had proven!

A cold sweat began down his back, even though the temperature within the underground cell room was cool.

He thought of turning back, not facing this woman for a moment. But then flashes of the Sea Lion, The Highlander, and the Sea Glory entered his mind. The flames and screams of his men dying hardened him, and he forced his feet toward the light.

Stopping in front of the cell, he set his lantern down on the small table and glared at the woman who lay upon the dirty cot.

"Get up," he ordered, with as much authority as he could find in himself.

A condescending chuckle came from within.

"I said get up!"

"Why should I?" she replied. "What are you going to do? Put me in a cell? Hang me?"

Stephan gripped the bars tightly, wishing he had the strength to tear them open. "We have unfinished business, you and I!"

"Commodore Stephan Belfield. Can't say I expected to see you, at least not as my first visitor." Callisto lifted her head to regard him. "Though I would have suspected a man of your nature would have put a little more effort into your appearance," she scolded him. "Clearly, you haven't been doing too well since last we cast eyes upon one another. You certainly don't look as happy to see me as I expected. I would have thought seeing me behind bars would have given you much enjoyment."

"It does."

"Your eyes tell a different story." She walked over to the bars, showing her battered and bruised face. "Have you come for a little fun too? Need to feel like a man and take a few swings and bloody your knuckles?" She stared him straight in the eyes. "Will it help? Or maybe you are here for something else, hmm? Hold me down and wet your stick?"

"I don't strike women, nor do I—"

She laughed bitterly. "Oh, the sweet lies men tell."

Callisto grabbed the bars and pressed her face closer. "But you would have killed me. Shot me in the chest or plunged your sabre through me had we crossed blades. I am a pirate, after all. Isn't that your job?"

"I—I would have tried to disarm you and take you prisoner to stand trial," he said with as much conviction as he could.

"Locked in chains aboard your ship, surrounded by your men." Callisto pressed closer to the bars. "Do you know what happens to female prisoners aboard ships?"

Stephan averted his eyes shamefully.

"I bet you do, and so do I," she hissed. "Do you want to know how many times they raped me before they got me here? How many different men took part in it?"

"That—that would not have happened aboard my ship."

"No?" She laughed bitterly at him. "Why? Do you believe your men to hold that much more honor? Or is it because you would have kept me for yourself?"

"No, never!" he stammered.

"Are you so sure? Who would know? Who would even care what you did to a pirate?"

"I would care," he stated firmly. "You would have been safe and not harmed."

"Such honor, even after that same honor seen me sail right by you to the island's safety," she taunted, pushing herself away from the bars. "You might have done what you claim. That is until what happened afterward." She grinned wickedly. "You remember that, don't you? When I grew tired of you and your fleet outside the island. When I sailed your beloved Poseidon's Fury out to meet you?"

"Shut up!" He slammed his hands on the bars.

"That's why you are here, isn't it? Some form of closure for all those men lost. For yourself and leading them to their deaths?"

"I just wanted to see it for myself. To see that it was truly you behind these bars."

"But something is bothering you about it." She searched his eyes "You wanted to be the one. You wanted to be the one to face me and win. But that is gone now. Your chance at absolution was taken from you by a slimy lordling who played his hand well against me."

Stephan grimaced, for those words held more truth than he cared to admit.

She smirked. "Open the cell, let me escape, and you can chase me across the world until one of us finally kills the other."

"You are caught and will pay for your crimes. That is all that truly matters to me."

She laughed wildly. "Oh, the lies men do tell themselves."

"You know nothing of me, you wretched woman!"

"I know you feel broken inside. Twisted with guilt, and your pride has been forever altered. You feel anger, hate, and a deep rolling wave of rage building inside you, only to be trumped by despair at failure. And I know the only way you feel you could have conquered those feelings was revenge against me. And now," she shrugged, "that chance has been taken away."

Enraged, Stephan grabbed the bars. "Yes! You're right! Is that what you want to hear? Yes, I wanted to be the one to bring you down! I wanted to bring you back in chains with your head hung in defeat! I needed it! I—needed it." His tone slipped into anguish as he stepped back and fell into the dusty chair against the wall.

"You have no idea what you've taken from me," he whispered. "What you have done to everything I have built. I will likely lose everything because of you."

"Good. I can die happy knowing I at least achieved that much, even if I won't be able to fulfill my other promise to you." Callisto's laugh was full of contempt.

"Promise?"

"I told you if you came for me, I would kill you before our time together ended." She smirked. "I still draw breath. I suppose there may still be time."

Stephan stood, no longer able to look at her, and picked up his lantern. "You will hang Callisto SinClair, and I will know peace once more."

With that, he walked away.

Callisto paced her cell like a caged wolf against every protest of her body. The time aboard the Golden Dahlia had not been good. The beatings had come often and had taken their toll. The guards in London had been just as kind and had come down with hatred in their eyes and taken their turns beating her.

She had fought back and had tried for the door, but in her current state, she could not hope to overpower them. And so, she had inflicted what damage she could before being beaten unconscious or left withering on the floor, whimpering in defeat.

The desire to give up haunted her, at the back of her mind, like a piece of glass rooted into her brain, forever cutting a little at a time. She could see no way out of this. These men despised her, and no amount of seduction would hope to trump that hate. They were too careful, too ready to ensure there was no escape. And she had no one to help.

There had to be a way out of this. That was the hope she held onto. Sooner or later, before she was walked to the gallows, a chance would come, no matter how small. She had to be ready, so she paced like a caged animal. Rolling her shoulders, stretching muscles that screamed at her to stop, begged her to let them rest, but she refused.

She used that pain to fuel her hate. To fuel her drive and numb her hopelessness.

She was so lost in her thoughts that she hadn't heard the newcomer's approach. And he was already before her cell when she saw the new light.

"You are awake, good," the finely dressed man said, taking a seat in the chair in front of her cell.

"And who are you?" she asked coldly.

"I am General Jacob Knight."

Callisto scoffed at the title. "Have you come to watch the guards beat me? Or maybe dirty your own hands with the chore?"

"I must apologize for that. Nasty business running a prison, and sometimes the guards forget themselves. Other times examples must be made, and wills broken," he replied. "It would seem your will is far from broken. That only adds to the testament of how a woman found herself in control of one of the most feared pirate ships and crews the seas have known."

"If you mean to flatter me, this is hardly the place."

"No flattery intended, my dear woman. Nay, just a factual observation."

"What do you want?"

"To have a conversation. A real conversation. One where we can look past our differences, our hates, and our baser nature."

"Why not," Callisto muttered. "Not like I have other plans at the moment."

"Good. Do you want to die here?"

"I thought we were having a real conversation."

"We are. And it is a simple and direct question with great importance of how the rest of this talk could go. So, I ask again, Ms. SinClair. Do you want to die here?"

Callisto stared at the man, trying to figure out what this was. What game was he playing? "I hardly believe I have a choice in the matter."

"Yes or no, Ms. SinClair."

"No," she growled. "No, I do not want to die here."

Jacob leaned forward, resting his hands on his legs. "Good, now we are getting somewhere. There is a good chance you don't have to die here, dangling from a rope in front of thousands."

"I hardly doubt you have the power to spare me such a thing unless General Jacob Knight is the name you use for fun when you are not being King William the Third," she said sarcastically.

Jacob smiled. "It is true. The final decision is, of course, up to his majesty. But his mind can be swayed in such matters as this if he believes more good is to be gained from such a prospect."

"And what prospect would absolve me of such crimes as I have partaken?"

"Absolve you? No, nothing will absolve you of what you have done. I doubt even the Lord above would forgive you for your sins. I did not state you would find freedom. Just that you wouldn't have to die," he was quick to add.

"So, instead, I remain down here a prisoner. Beaten daily, fed food not fit for rats, and to rot away?" Callisto laughed. "I think I'd prefer the rope and crowd."

"A prisoner, yes. But this," he motioned, "doesn't have to remain. We have better accommodations for prisoners of war that are, how shall I say, helpful. Far more comfortable than this. More like an inn, with better food, better view, time allowed outside, and of course locks and armed guards."

"And pray tell, what it is you would want from me for this fine offer?"

"A simple one, really. One that a pirate with little loyalty to others should easily be able to comply with. We would want detailed information on this pirate island you make port in, Glacia's Palace."

"What?"

"Information on its weaknesses. How many soldiers does this Glacia command? What weapons do they have? How many ships does she command? What pirates are often there, and their numbers. What would cripple them from the outside, and so an invasion could be executed with minimal losses."

"You can't be serious."

"I am as serious as the rope that awaits you if you refuse," Jacob replied.

"You want me to betray my own to save myself?"

"What else could you offer us in our war against the scourge of your kind, except ways to help us rid ourselves of your kind?"

"I know of an island with more gold and treasure hidden within it than likely the king himself has in his castle."

"I am not interested in fairy tales, Ms. SinClair," he scoffed. "The only thing that might save your neck is this. Betray those upon the island with information we can use to defeat or hang them. But know this. The island's time will come with or without your help, for we cannot let such a place survive any longer than we already have."

"If you don't even need me, why make the offer?"

"As I said. Your information will help us minimalize our losses, that is all. Which might make up for the men who found their deaths under your attack."

"You ask a lot," Callisto growled.

"And offer you a chance to live out your days alive and treated fairly in your imprisonment," he replied. "Though I find it odd that a pirate such as yourself holds such moral objections to betraying your fellow cutthroats. A trait I have never seen before from your ilk. You know anyone in your shoes would have no problem doing such a thing to save their worthless hides."

Callisto suppressed a snarl as she stared hard at the man. The man offered her the only way to continue to draw a breath that she could see. And with that, sooner or later, she might find a way to escape whatever place they put her.

"I have wasted enough of my time in this foul-smelling place, and it is apparent you do not wish to partake in my offer." He stood and brushed himself off. "I will pray for you, Ms. SinClair, though I doubt god will show mercy."

Before he had taken two steps, Callisto grabbed at the bars. "Fine—"

He turned to regard her. "Fine, what? I must hear the words, Ms. SinClair.

"I'll do it."

"Very well. I will see what can be done."

"My apologizes that I haven't come by sooner," Jacob Knight said to Stephan, accepting the cup of tea from Mary as the woman quickly left the room. "The investigation has been— difficult as we knew it would be."

"Am I cleared?" Stephan asked eagerly.

Jacob sipped his tea before setting it down. "Not entirely, but the rest of the council has come to realize that it isn't as open and shut as they once believed. On questioning two of the crew, they hinted that James may have persuaded them to change their story slightly better to implicate you as the guilty party in this mess."

"That is good news." Stephan sighed in relief.

"It is, but not good enough yet, I am afraid. There is still too much evidence against you. Too many higher officers are still taking James's side in this. But it has been enough to stay the council's hand in a ruling. Though for how much longer I cannot know."

"I see. Who would be enough to sway them?"

"The biggest two would be John Baker or the quarter-master Tomas Lavington."

The two names stung Stephan, for he had known both men a long time and sailed beside them near half his career. Having saved both their lives in battle before and in kind had his own saved.

"If I could just talk to them in private. I am sure I could make them see reason and come forward with the truth."

Jacob was already shaking his head. "I understand your frustrations in this; truly, I do, Stephan. But it would be seen as meddling in the investigation if it were discovered. Likely to cause more harm to your case than good, even if you were to convince them to speak the truth. Others would think you bribed them or threatened them."

"Then what am I to do?" Stephan asked, defeated once more.

"I will see if I can arrange something. A meeting with them, for myself and you. Something safe and from prying eyes."

Stephan nodded. "Again, you have my thanks."

"You should know something else."

Stephan looked up from the fireplace in wonder.

"The pirate who started all this has been caught and is here in London, as I am sure you might have heard."

Stephan held back the emotions about his meeting with her, hoping he didn't portray anything. "I had recently heard. That is good news, and hopefully, when she hangs, it will send clear messages to others."

"About that." Jacob cleared his throat. "I spoke with her yesterday, at length. And a deal may have been reached."

"A deal? What kind of deal?"

"One that would see her life not end at the gallows."

"What!" Stephan nearly jumped from his seat. "Why?"

"Calm yourself, Stephan, and hear me out. She knows things about that island. Information that could prove very valuable in its demise. Helping us clear at least one more haven for pirates close to our seas."

"After all she has done. All the lives that were lost because of her. You would offer her life?"

"Yes," Jacob said flatly. "What she may know could well save countless others in our attack on the island. And if we are

410

successful, countless others with fewer places for the pirates to find safe ports."

"You cannot do this, Jacob!"

"My request has already been sent to the king. Along with the other council members who as much as they would like to see Ms. SinClair hang for her crimes, understand the advantage her information might hold for us."

"I can't believe this," Stephan said bitterly, running a hand through his hair.

"I understand your anger. But I felt it should be me who told you. It is not a guarantee that the king will approve, and she may still hang. But given that the whole council felt it worthwhile, I suspect the king will find merit in it. This doesn't buy her freedom, merely her life. She will remain a prisoner of the crown for the rest of her days. She will cause no more harm to anyone."

Stephan rubbed his hands trying to contain himself. "I do not like it, but I understand your position in making this decision."

"I know it is hard, but it is for the good of the country. Have faith, Stephan." Jacob rose from his seat. "I will bid you a good night and will be in touch when I know more."

The straw-filled wagon waited in the gloomy alleyway as dusk was fast setting in on the city of London. Most of its inhabitants were already in the comforts of their homes, leaving only a few remaining wandering the streets. Many of them were city guards patrolling the streets or those finding their way to taverns and whore houses in hopes of drinking and fucking away the stresses of a hard day's work.

Weaver pulled the hood of his cloak tighter around his face, ensuring his features were obscured. Though Glacia had given them clothes that would help them blend into the city's crowds, his face and the others belied the truth of who they were.

"He is taking too long," Reeves grumbled from the back of the wagon, hidden under the straw with Kadir, Alonso, and Javier.

"It is fine. It hasn't been that long," Weaver muttered, glancing at Katrina, who sat next to him. In truth, he was beginning to worry, for it had been over an hour since Murphy had gone into the tavern to find out if they were already too late.

Katrina had gotten them into the city safely with the ruse of the wagon they had purchased from a farmer at twice the price it should have been. But they needed it and stealing it would have caused problems they couldn't afford. They were in the heart of enemy territory, and to be found out would see them all dead long before they knew where Callisto was.

The Poseidon's Fury had dropped anchor a dozen miles away from the city and its active port. The small group had rowed the longboat ashore and stashed it for a quick escape. If it came to that, they all expected it would. They could not afford the ship to be recognized by watchful eyes.

"Easy for you to say. You're not the one with straw up your arse," Reeves grumbled back.

"Maybe I should go in and check on him," Weaver whispered to Katrina.

"No, they would see through your disguise quickly in there. It is a naval tavern," she reminded him. "Might even be some of the men from the Paradise in there. I will go."

She was about to climb down when Weaver stayed her with his hand.

"He comes."

Murphy idly made his way to the alley, checking over his shoulder often to ensure no one was paying him any attention before slipping into the darkness and down to the waiting wagon.

"What news?" Weaver helped the man up beside him and Katrina.

"She lives," Murphy replied, thankful. "They have not hung her. She remains under guard at the prison."

"Let's go get her," Weaver stated boldly.

"That will be no easy task," Murphy reminded him. "It is a prison, after all. There will be a dozen guards or more and only six of us."

"We will fight our way in if we have to!" Reeves said from the straw.

"And invite the whole of the city's soldiers down upon us in short order," Murphy interjected. "We need a plan."

"We can move on foot to the prison. We will be less noticeable if we stay in the alleyways and shadows," Katrina told them, climbing down.

"Aye, best see what we are up against," Murphy agreed as he helped the other three out from beneath the straw they had used to hide.

Slowly the group made their way through the city's darkness, often having to wait for many minutes for a section of road to be clear before they sprinted across open ground to the safety of the shadows on the other side.

The city was large, but the prison was not so far, yet it still took the group nearly two hours to get within sight of the place, for caution and secrecy were paramount.

Three guards lingered outside the stone building, armed but paying little heed to the few people wandering about at this late hour. That was a good sign; they had been on duty long enough this night to get complacent.

"Three outside, and the gods know how many within."
Reeves grazed his fingers over the flintlock pistol he had in his
belt.

"We cannot try and storm the place," Murphy reminded
him. "We wouldn't get far, and the noise would alert the whole
city. We would never see tomorrow's dawn if we tried brute
force."

"Then what?" growled Reeves. "We can't just wait around.
We will be seen sooner or later or waste the night. The longer
the Poseidon is near the coastline, the sooner someone will
spot it, and they will be forced to flee, leaving us trapped
here."

Murphy knew that to be true. They were indeed on a time-
sensitive mission, and they all knew it. This had to be done
tonight.

"There may be a way inside without being detected,"
Katrina said. "But you aren't going to like it."

"What is it, lass?" Murphy asked.

"The sewers all connect underground. Many of us used
them when I was an orphan to get around the city and into
places we couldn't reach above ground," she explained. "But,"
she looked to Reeves, Weaver, and Javier, "they won't be able
to fit through the hole that drains from the prison. Alonso,
Kadir, and I should be able to."

"Aye, but she will be locked tight. We will need the keys."
Murphy rubbed his head as he tried to formulate a plan.

"How long will it take you to move through the sewers and
get inside the prison?" he asked as something came to him.
Something risky and would likely see them all killed, but it was
all they had with time running short.

"We can enter just around the corner over there. Twenty
minutes at most," she told him.

"You get in and find her." He slapped Weaver and Reeves

on the shoulders, looking at Javier. "We will go through the front doors and get the keys."

"Come on, you fucking thieving drunk!" Murphy barked as he pushed Weaver forward, his hands falsely bound in front of him.

"What's this now?" one of the three guards called out as the two men approached.

"Fucking drunkard was trying to steal my damn horse while I was taking a piss," Murphy said, reaching where the three men were standing. "A good night or two in a cell would do him good, me thinking."

"You arrested him yourself?" one of the guards said, looking the big man up and down and back to Murphy, who was nearly half the man's size.

"Aye, got lucky he is so drunk, or else he likely would have beaten the spit out of me." Murphy laughed. "Still had to hit him a dozen times with my club to get him down, though."

The three guards shared a chuckle.

"Where were the guards patrolling?" the first guard asked. "You should have called for someone. No point risking yourself when that's what we are paid for."

"I would have had it not been for that big brawl down at the Sinkhole tavern. The place got busted up, and I saw two dozen guards rushing in to help break up the fighting."

The guards looked to each other with concern, for they had heard nothing of it.

"Aye, let's get him inside and somewhere miserable for the night. John, help me get him inside, grab three or four others, get down to that tavern, and help our boys out. Take the back door and some horses. It'll get you there quicker."

"You got it, Captain." John grabbed Weaver's arm while the other guard took the other, leading him up the stairs and inside as the pirate kept up the ruse of being intoxicated and struggling only a little against the two smaller men.

Murphy licked his lips nervously. There was no going back now.

"You have done good," the lone guard said once the other two were gone. "We will keep him for a few days, make sure he sobers up and pays a fine for his foolishness."

"Aye, good to know. I love that horse," Murphy replied, doing his best to keep the guards' eyes on him as another figure came up from behind.

"Well, you be all done here," the guard said. "Best you get on home before you find yourself in the path of some other unruly sort."

"Like the one behind you," Reeves said, grabbing hold of the guard's head, twisting viciously, and breaking his neck.

"You were supposed to knock him out, not bloody well kill him!" Murphy gasped, making sure no one had seen anything as Reeves and Javier drug the man behind the stairs.

"Dead men don't come back to fight later," Reeves muttered. "Now, let's get inside. The others should be in place, and those extra guards should be gone by now."

Murphy glared at the pirate but knew it was too late to change anything. They had a job to do, and they were all in for better or worse.

Murphy opened the door slowly, and a muffled gunshot could be heard from the back and below. He cursed and pushed his way in.

"Something is happening below. You three, go check it out!" the guard ordered the men milling around the desk as he struggled to hold onto Weaver with another guard.

As soon as the three men were out of sight, Weaver broke

into action, tearing his hands free of the fake bindings and thundering a punch into one guard's jaw, dropping him coldly to the floor.

"I need help in here!" the other guard cried out, backing away and pulling his club.

Four more guards were moving out of the side room, having heard the gunshot but turned their attention to what was happening with a prisoner.

"Fucking pirates," Murphy muttered, knowing it would be a full-on fight and flight now.

"Quick, man, help us get this brute under control!" the lead guard from outside cried back, seeing Murphy and who he thought was his man from outside.

Reeves shouldered by Murphy and drew his cutlass, and before the other guards knew what had hit them, two more were cut down by the pirate's sudden attack.

"What the fuck?" a guard cried out, seeing Reeves pulling his sword from one of the men's backs. "Call for help!" the guard screamed as he took a jarring right hook from Weaver that sent him stumbling into the wall, where Javier quickly slashed his blade across the man's throat.

A guard broke away, running for the back hallway, hoping to find reinforcements.

"Catch!" Javier tossed Weaver his prized hatchets.

Weaver caught the axes and sent one spinning end over end, which embedded into the running man's back, dropping him to the floor, his spine severed.

"I—I surrender!" the last guard stuttered, discarding his club and dagger.

"We have to get down below," Murphy ordered them. "The others will need our help!"

Weaver grabbed the whimpering man. "Keys to our captain's cell. Where are they?"

"I—I can't," the guard sputtered.

Reeves was there, pressing a dagger into the man's ribs. "I think you can if you want to live."

"He—he has them." The man pointed to the guard, whose throat Javier had cut out.

"Thank you." Reeves drove the dagger through his ribs and into his heart.

Weaver snatched the keys and started down the hallway. He stopped long enough to pry his axe from the crippled man's spine.

The door leading down was wide open, and fighting could be heard below. All three rushed down into the darkness, cutting off any retreat the guards may have hoped for.

The fight was over in moments.

"Why did you shoot your pistol!" Murphy growled at Kadir.

"There was a padlock across the grate," Kadir reasoned. "It was the only way to get through. I knew we were running out of time."

"Callisto!" Reeves screamed, ignoring the others, and not caring for being quiet any longer.

"I am here!" came a reply, not far away.

Callisto woke to the loud sound of a gunshot coming from somewhere inside the dungeon. Rolling from her cot, she slowly moved to the bars, wondering if she would catch a glimpse of what was happening.

Was someone trying to break out? Would they free her, too, if she offered to help?

She could faintly make out voices, voices she was sure she recognized before the door above banged open and the sound of guards yelling and soon the sound of clashing blades.

Then she heard the sweetest sound in all her life. A voice she never thought she would hear again.

"Callisto!"

It was Reeves.

For the briefest moment, she forgot all else as she realized they had come for her. Her crew had come for her.

"I am here!" she cried out.

"Captain!" Weaver laughed, coming up to the cell door with the others in tow. His hatchets and clothes were marred with fresh blood.

"You came for me," Callisto whispered, hardly believing her eyes.

"Of course we did, Captain." Reeves fumbled with the keys, trying to find the correct one.

"We need to hurry." Murphy looked over his shoulder, knowing others would soon show up. There had been too much noise.

By now, the others within the dungeon were up and at the bars of their cells, calling for help and begging to be freed, claiming their innocence or loyalty. Anything that might buy them a chance to escape the noose that surely awaited them for the crimes that had landed them here.

"Murphy? Katrina? What are you two doing here?" she asked in surprise at seeing the others.

"Hopefully, we will have time for all that later," Murphy said. "Right now, we need to go!"

The lock clicked.

She was free!

"Here, Captain, thought you might want these for this next part." Reeves handed her the weapon belt with twin flintlock pistols, cutlass, and dagger.

"Javier, take the keys and release as many prisoners as possible," Callisto ordered, strapping on her weapons.

"What are you doing? They are not our concern!" Murphy reminded them.

"We don't need all of them," Callisto said. "Just enough to create more confusion."

Half a dozen prisoners were already freed and standing outside their cells, confused about what to do next.

"Listen up, you fucking cunts!" Callisto barked at them. "You are free men because of me, and all I ask is one thing in return."

"What's that?" one man dared to ask.

Callisto's eyes burned with violence. "Wreak havoc tonight in this cursed city. Start fires, break windows, and hurt people. Become devils of the night."

Several prisoners grinned and nodded, running for the stairs. A few stayed behind, unlocking more of the cell doors to their criminal brethren.

"Now it's time to go," Callisto said.

They made their way down the hallway to where Weaver and the others had left carnage in their wake. Already a dozen prisoners had picked up the dead guards' fallen weapons and made for the exit.

They were met almost instantly by resistance from outside, and gunfire and the clashing of steel could be heard just beyond the door. But it didn't deter the prisoners as they knew this was their one chance at freedom.

"We will never make it out that way," Murphy said, seeing several soldiers moving through the entranceway.

"We got trouble!" Weaver yelled, seeing rifles rising to greet them.

"Halt, or we will open fire!" one soldier screamed.

Without a thought, Reeves grabbed a burning lantern and

threw it toward the soldiers. It burst into flames as it hit the floor.

Several rifles went off.

Reeves was clipped in the shoulder and ducked to avoid another that might find him.

"We will have to find the way out the back!" Weaver yelled over the sudden turmoil.

They all turned to flee out the back when they saw Murphy standing wide-eyed as blood pooled from his midsection. His legs gave way, and he crumpled to the floor.

"Murphy!" Callisto crawled to him.

Weaver cursed, knowing that each second wasted was another they came closer to being overrun. "We have to go!"

"We can't leave him!" Callisto stared down at the man and his mortal wound.

"You must," Murphy said weakly. "I will only slow you down."

"No! I will not leave you like this. Not after you came for me."

Murphy lifted his hand from his wound, saw the thick blood, and smiled weakly. "I am already done for."

"Fuck, Murphy!" Callisto screamed at him. "Why did you come back for me?"

"We are even now."

"What?"

He winced. "You saved me on the Poseidon's Fury, and now—"

Kadir grabbed her arm and pulled her up. "Captain, we are running out of time."

"Go," Murphy whispered.

"Fuck!" Callisto screamed and was about to follow the others when she saw the guard on the floor moving, a terrible axe wound in his back.

Growling, she moved quickly and grabbed a fist full of his hair. "Where does Commodore Stephan Belfield live?"

"What?" the man groaned.

"Where does he fucking live!" She shook him, and he cried out in agony.

"Captain, we have to go!" Kadir fired his pistol through the growing flames at the soldiers beyond, trying to keep them at bay.

Callisto grabbed a nearby lantern and threw it against the wall near the guard. It burst into flames, mere feet from the wounded man.

"Tell me where he lives, or I'll let you fucking burn to death, you worthless swine!" she hissed. "It's a horrible way to die, feeling your flesh blister and blacken. Your flesh melting from your bones while you feel every fucking moment."

"Alright! Alright!" the terrified man wailed, watching the fire spread closer. "He lives on Folgate Street, number sixteen! Now pull me free!" the man cried as the flames began to nip at him.

Callisto ignored him and his growing screams of agony and quickly followed the others to the back of the prison, guilt and shouting following her every footstep.

Now knew where he lived.

She would get her revenge before she left this fucking hell-hole of a city.

The back entrance was still clear of soldiers, but they all knew that an army would be coming at any moment, and they needed to move quickly. The fire inside the prison was already taking hold, and flames could be seen breaking through the windows as black smoke rolled into the night sky.

"Horses!" Alonso pointed to the paddocks, where a score of the beasts stood saddled and ready for the mounted patrol groups.

"Where are we moored?" Callisto asked.

"A dozen miles west of the city," Weaver informed her, pulling himself up on his mount.

"Where is Folgate Street?" she said with bitter determination.

"Not far from here," Katrina admitted. "I know the way."

"Good, we go there before we leave," Callisto said determinedly.

The others exchanged nervous glances.

"Captain, we have worn our welcome out. We need to leave," Weaver told her as he and the others slapped the rumps of the other horses, causing them to run free of the stable and into the street.

"I made a promise to kill someone. I mean to keep my word."

They kicked their mounts and took off, thundering down the street behind the prison, barely avoiding a dozen soldiers trying to stop the horses from scattering into the city.

A loud knock came from the front door as Stephan paced his study deep in thought. Everything Jacob had told him the day before had continued to play in his mind. If what he had told him came to pass, that wretched pirate woman would live out her days in comfortable captivity. The notion did not sit well with him. Not at all.

The knock grew louder and pulled him from his thoughts.

Who would be knocking this late? It was already near midnight.

"I will get it," Stephan called out, hearing Ms. Pots, their maid, making her way downstairs to answer it.

"As you wish, Mr. Belfield," she called back. "I will be up for a bit if you have need of me."

"Thank you, Ms. Pots."

Stephan opened the door to see Conner, the man that had come with information before.

"Sorry to bother you so late, Mr. Belfield," Conner said nervously.

"Do you bring news from Jacob?" Stephan asked eagerly.

"Aye, from Jacob. A meeting has been set with some of your pals from your ship. You've been requested to meet with them." The man licked his dry lips as he kept searching the streets.

"This late of an hour?" Stephan asked.

"Aye, this late, Commodore," Conner replied. "Fewer eyes about since it is a sensitive meeting and all."

Stephan thought back to his conversation with Jacob, and he had said he would try to set up a safe meeting. In the dead of night like a vagabond was likely the best he could do for this kind of meeting.

"Where?"

"Down at the old bakery, the one that burned down months back. Few blocks away from here. Said they'd meet ya in the back."

"Right, I will get my things and follow you there."

"Beggin', your pardon, Commodore," Conner said, his eyes edgy. "My job was to deliver the message, not to bring ya. Too much is on the line for me to get caught up in this further. If you know my meaning."

Stephan wanted to argue but didn't. The man was right. Stephan had no right to risk this innocent man further than they already had. "Fine, I shall find it on my own. Thank you for informing me."

Conner nodded as he started back down the stairs. "I wish you luck, Commodore."

"What is going on down there?" Mary asked, seeing Stephan gathering his sword belt and night coat.

"I must go for a short while."

"What?" Mary gasped. "It is the dead of night."

"Aye, I know. But Jacob has set up a meeting with those I need to convince to tell the truth of Featherstone's treachery. This might be my only chance to clear my name and keep all we have been able to build, Mary."

"So late?" Mary pressed. "Surely Jacob could set up a meeting at a more appropriate hour."

"I wish it were so. But this is a sensitive thing. We cannot have prying eyes upon us. The risk would be too great during the day," he reasoned.

"When will you return?"

"As soon as I can, my love. And hopefully, with good news that will set this all beyond us." He kissed her cheek. "I must go, for they are already waiting for me."

Stephan kept his hood covering his face as he moved down the dark, empty streets. Whenever he heard or saw someone, he quickly found a dark shadow to hide within, like a thief in the night, until the way was clear. It made him feel dirty. Like he was indeed one of the very people he fought his whole life to stop.

But this was different.

He was not hiding because he was committing a crime. He was hiding to help uncover one. One that, if wasn't resolved, would leave him and his family in ruins.

This was a mission of the utmost importance that required this stain on his conscience.

It was not long before he found himself in front of the old bakery. Its blackened frame barely stood from the fire that had gutted it months before. The smell of charred wood still lingered in the calm night air.

"Stephan! Over here," a voice called from the darkness of the alley.

Stephan knew that voice. It was John Baker, his helmsman of the Paradise. A man he trusted and had known for nearly a decade. A man who he hoped would do the right thing this night and help clear his name.

Moving to the alley's darkness, a dirty lantern burned barely provided enough light to see more than a few feet. "A strange place for a meeting."

"Aye, there is truth in that," John replied, his tone slurred by drink.

Stephan looked around. "Are we the only two here so far? Where is Jacob?"

"Jacob won't be coming to this meeting, I am afraid," an all too familiar voice said from behind him.

Stephan turned to see James Featherstone, Conner, and another man he didn't know blocking the way he had come.

"What is the meaning of this?" he asked, suddenly very aware of his dire situation.

"I think you know what this is," James replied, his hand dangerously close to the hilt of his sabre. "You and Jacob have been prying too deeply. Asking too many questions and turning my plan against me. You know I can't let that stand. I will not let a low-born bastard ruin this opportunity for me."

"You lured me here to what? Force me into submission? To beat me until I give up and allow you to destroy everything I have built?"

James chuckled menacingly. "If only I believed that would actually work." He pulled his blade, and the others did likewise, and a drawn weapon could even be heard behind him where John stood. "But we both know that would not stop you, and a more drastic step is required to silence you for good."

Stephan pulled his sword and shifted his stance so he could

see John behind him. "Murder is a deed most foul. I knew you were a rat when you first joined my crew." He turned to regard John. "But you were an honest man, a good man, and a man from nothing well on his way to breaking those chains as I was able to do. This is beneath you."

John's eyes showed his shame. "Aye, I am from nothing. But this is my way to becoming something more, and you stand in that way, Stephan. I wish it weren't so, but it is."

Stephan needed no more convincing of the trouble he was in and lunged at John with his blade; the drunken man barely parried the attack. But it had been a feint, and Stephan shouldered into him, slamming John into the brick wall behind him, knocking the wind from his lungs.

Turning, he met the swing of Conner's blade and parried it out wide, kicking the man in the knee and forcing him into a quick retreat. On came the other brute, lunging in for Stephan's exposed side. But with reflexes honed from a hundred battles, he found his pistol in hand and fired. The sound tore through the silent night as the iron ball took the man square in the chest, throwing him back and down into the dirt.

"Just fucking die!" James screamed as he came in feverishly.

Stephan worked entirely on the defensive as James came in violently. The man's sword work some of the finest Stephan had ever seen. And worst, some of the hardest he had ever had to defend against. In the dim alleyway, he could barely keep the hungry blade from finding him, and already he had felt the sting of the sword tip a handful of times across his arms and legs.

Conner had finally gathered himself and came in from the side, and Stephan was forced to give ground and knew the wall behind him was looming closer. He was running out of space to go and was cornered. He could not win this fight like his.

Conner launched forward, swinging wildly but with little true sword-fighting talent. Stephan ducked the blow, slammed into him, and bulled him forward, crashing him into James in a tangle of arms and legs.

Pushing with all his might, Stephan disengaged as both men hit the side wall and lost their footing. He lunged down, driving his blade deeply into Conner's back, thinking he had finally gained the upper hand when his side suddenly flared in pain, and he spun away.

John lunged again with his bloodied dagger, but he was drunk and still dazed and missed his mark. Stephan hit him with the pommel of his sword, staggering the helmsman back. He needed to find help. Killing these men would bring him little pleasure but exposing the attack upon himself would clear his name faster than anything else.

Seeing an opening to the street, he took it. Forgetting the fight and running for all he was worth.

Weaver held the group back as he peered around the building, watching a group of soldiers rush down the street. There were many of them about now, all calling for arms and buckets to put out the many fires that had mysteriously started throughout the city.

He grinned at that.

They had started fires with the help of the dozen other prisoners they had released. Nearly a score of them by now had flared up throughout the city. The desperate confusion was what they needed now more than anything. As people were awoken from their homes, peering from their windows, or coming out to stop, a guard or soldier rushed by to question.

It was this confusion that would keep them distracted. Likely most of the soldiers and guards had no idea the most dangerous prisoner they had locked up was now at large. All they knew were some fires needed to be put out quickly before they could spread.

Only once had they come across guards that had called them to halt, seeing them riding city mounts, yet were not of the city guard. And those two men had not been prepared to face what fury of pirate blades that had come next.

"Let's move!" Weaver called back as they moved their mounts into the open street and down. A handful of people were standing near their doors, but none seemed to pay them any heed as they looked at the smoke filling the sky above.

"Here," Katrina said. "This is Folgate Street."

They turned down the broad street and sped their horses along until they found their destination, number sixteen. It was a large three-story home, modest compared to many houses within the city but grander by far than most of the houses the citizens called home.

"What's the plan, Captain?" Reeves asked eagerly, though his shoulder screamed at him. What he had thought was a grazing hit back at the prison had not been, and the iron bullet was buried deep.

"We break in and kill the bastard!" Callisto growled, drawing her pistols and motioning for Reeves and Weaver to break down the door.

Both large pirates nodded and charged, putting their shoulders and full weight into it, and the door tore from its hinges and crashed to the polished oak floor within. They moved in quickly and heard the startled cry of a baby upstairs.

"Alonso, Kadir, Javier, search the main floor and make sure

there is no one down here, and keep your eyes on the door, do not let anyone in!" Callisto ordered. "Katrina, stay hidden. Weaver, Reeves, with me."

Even though she was hurting, her muscles and bruised body screaming at her to slow down, Callisto took the stairs two at a time.

"What is going on out here?" an older woman called out in fear, lifting a lantern as she came out from her room to see what the noise was all about. Seeing the intruders, she cried out and tried to run back to the safety of her room, but Weaver was there, grabbing a fist full of her hair and slamming her against the floor.

"If you value your life, you will not move or say another word!" he told her, one of his hatchets resting across her neck, with no doubt that he would kill her if she disobeyed.

Callisto pointed her pistols at the other door, where a light could be seen shining through the cracks, and a baby's cry emanated.

"Come out right now, Commodore, and face me!" Callisto yelled. "Or I'll cut the throat of your maidservant!"

"Please, he is not here!" came a woman's voice from within the room.

The words were a blow to Callisto. She had come all this way, risked her life and crew for this moment, and he wasn't even here!

"Come out now!" she hissed. "And if you try anything foolish, you'll die here this night."

Slowly the door opened, and a young woman stepped out in her nightgown with a baby held tightly to her breast. "Please, he isn't here. Please don't hurt us. Your fight is not with us." Her eyes widened as she saw the group before her, but more so the woman before her. "It's—it's you!" she stammered. "The pirate woman!"

Callisto grinned. "Aye, it's me. Now, where is your coward of a husband!"

"I—I don't know. He left not too long ago for a meeting. Just leave us alone. We have done nothing to you. You have found your freedom, take it, and run before it is too late for you," Mary pleaded.

"We can't stay here much longer," Weaver reminded her.

Callisto was about to abandon this ridiculous plot when she looked over to the mirror in the hallway and wished she saw Ares's reflection to guide her. But he had told her he would not help her again, not until she had retrieved his spear.

What would he want her to do now? Run and find her revenge later? Or—she looked at the woman and baby.

If she took Stephan's family as hostages, he would come for them. And that would lead him to her.

"We bring the woman and child with us," Callisto ordered.

"Captain?" Weaver asked, confused.

"He will follow, for they will be all he has left to try and save or his miserable life," she sneered.

Reeves grabbed the screaming woman and child and hauled them downstairs towards the door, needing no more motivation than that.

"And you," Callisto said to the maid. "You will tell him what I have done. Tell him he better come before I grow bored of his family's company and give them to the sea."

Callisto grabbed the lantern the maid had dropped and threw it into the bedroom, where it quickly burst into flames.

"Let's go!"

They mounted their horses. Reeves held Mary and the child in front of him as they thundered down the streets. They turned and weaved through the city to the western road that would take them out of the city, along the coastline, and back to their waiting ship and crew.

Scores of guards and soldiers were frantically running about, working with fire crews to gain control of the growing fires that mysteriously assaulted their city. Few knew of the escaped prisoner, and fewer would be concerned as more pressing matters were before them.

Only a small handful of guards were manning the western road out of the city, and most had already heard the fire bells and seen the dozens of plumes of smoke rising around the city. They called for the halt of the group that rode towards them with all haste, knowing something was wrong.

But they didn't get their rifles up as Callisto led the charge, her two flintlock pistols firing, taking one man in the shoulder and another in the leg. The remaining guards threw themselves out of the way as more shots were fired from the group on horseback as they rode clear of the city.

Stephan had to slow his run, for the wound in his side was bleeding badly; he pulled his hand away and saw the dark blood. He needed to tend to this before he bled out. But he was almost home; he would go there and get Mary and Jonathan and take them to Jacob's house. They would be safe there until they could get this straightened out.

The smell of smoke was thick in the air now, and he just noticed it and the growing amount of people who were out of their homes and in the streets—pointing and shouting up at the sky, where thick plumes of smoke could be seen.

What was happening?

He rounded the corner to his street, and his heart sank. Flames burst forth from his house as a handful of men and women tried vainly to douse the fire with buckets of water from several loaded wagons.

"No!" Stephan cried out, forgetting his wound, and ran to the scene around his home.

"My family?" he cried but knew he couldn't enter, for the front of the house was engulfed in flames.

"Mr. Belfield!" Ms. Pots cried from the far side of the street.

Stephan ran to the distraught woman. "Where are they? Where is my family?" He looked back to the flame, tears streaking his face already.

"No, Mr. Belfield, they aren't in the house."

"Where then?" He searched the crowd but could not see his wife anywhere.

"She came with men—with pirates," Ms. Pots cried out. "They took your family."

"What? Who?" Stephan grabbed the woman. "Who took them?"

"That horrible pirate woman, Sir, the one that was brought in not long ago. It was her. She came for you, meant to kill you in the night, but you weren't here, so she took Mary and Jonathan."

"No..." Stephan whispered, feeling the weight of everything crashing around him. "Sweet heavens, no..."

"She told me to tell you that you best come looking for them. She wants you to come to her."

"Where are they?" Stephan yelled, shaking the poor older woman. "Where did they go?"

"I don't know!" Ms. Pots cried out, trying to break his iron grip.

Stephan stepped back, his legs giving out, and he crashed to the ground. The chaos going on around him, he hardly registered any of it. For none of it mattered. Callisto had taken his family. Had crossed that final boundary after taking everything else from him.

"Commodore!" a soldier called to him as he slowed his

horse. "What has happened here?"

Stephan pulled himself from his thoughts and stared up at the man. "They're gone. My family—taken..."

The soldier climbed down from his mount. "Sir, get ahold of yourself. The pirate captain Callisto SinClair has escaped. Her crew infiltrated the prison and broke her free."

"I know that!" Stephan raged, wanting to strike at the man, but held himself back.

"I was sent to gather you, sir. You are needed at the Paradise at once!"

"What?" Stephan could hardly understand the man. Why would he be needed at his ship? What good was his ship to him now?

"The Poseidon's Fury has been spotted several miles down the city's west coast. They are fleeing on horseback down the coast to reach the ship. Soldiers are being rounded up to give chase, but the Paradise is needed to cut them off and stop the ship from escaping the coast."

"The west coast?" Stephan muttered.

"Aye, sir."

Realization hit him then, and he scrambled to his feet, shoving the soldier out of his way, and mounted his horse.

"Sir, what are you doing?"

"Get out of my fucking way!" Stephan screamed, kicking the horse's flanks.

He thundered down the cobblestone streets towards the western city exit.

He could catch them still.

He could stop this from going any further.

He could save his family.

434

Callisto's heart leaped with joy as they rode around the bend, and she caught sight of the Poseidon's Fury sheltered off the coast. Her ship—her crew. They had come for her. They had risked everything, put aside their pirate code to replace her as captain and move on, and instead sailed across the sea thick into enemy territory to rescue her.

They pulled up their horses on the beach, where the long-boats were hidden. A dozen men armed with rifles, pistols, and blades stepped from the concealment to greet them with cheers at the success.

"Fucking hell." Slimy Fife laughed as he helped Callisto from her horse. "They fucking did it!"

She hugged the burly pirate. "Aye, they did. Thanks to all of you."

If the man could blush, he indeed was. "Couldn't let these cocksuckers think they could take what wasn't theirs to take. No one steals the Queen of the Seas from her crew without a fight."

"A fight it was," Weaver said, clapping the man on the back.

"Seems you lost one and gained two others," Fife replied. "What happened to Murphy?"

"He is gone," Callisto said. "Fallen to save us."

Fife grunted his understanding. "Good man, even if he stumbled when you needed him."

"He earned my forgiveness this night," Callisto replied.

"What of the woman and child?" he asked.

"Prisoners. The wife and child of our friend Commodore Belfield," Callisto said coldly.

"You mean for him to come after us, don't you?"

"I have a score to settle."

Fife nodded and said no more.

"Time to get moving. It won't be long before they realize

what happened, and an army will be behind us if one isn't already," Weaver explained.

"What's that there?" Reeves asked, pointing in the direction they had just ridden. "A lone rider, coming in fast."

"I'll take care of him," Fife muttered, lifting a rifle as the man approached.

"Hold," Callisto said, her eyes burning with hatred.

He had come already.

"It is him, coming for his family." Callisto laughed, grabbing the woman who was still cradling the crying child. "And this is my fight, do not intervene."

"Please don't hurt us," Mary whimpered.

"Be still, woman, and let the final act of this play be finished," she growled, pushing the woman forward.

Stephan fell from his horse long before it had stopped, and he hit the ground hard but forced himself quickly to his feet. He had lost so much blood, he was weak, but he was desperate.

"You found us," Callisto called to him.

"Please, let them go." He stumbled, barely keeping his feet under him. "This doesn't concern them. It is me you want, so here I am. Just let them go, I beg you."

"I made you a promise."

"You have already taken everything from me. My career, men, honor, home, and all I have built in this life." He stared into her bright green eyes, pleading as a man with nothing left could plead. "I beg of you. Don't take my family."

"And why should I spare them or you?"

"I have nothing left. I am no longer a threat to you, your way of life, or any other pirates who sail the seas. I am defeated." He crumpled to his knees. "I am done. Let them go, and I will never set foot on a ship again."

"Nay, this isn't over. I promised to take everything from you before I killed you."

"My life for theirs. Let this end with me. You will still have taken everything with my life."

"No, Stephan!" Mary cried out, trying to pull away, but Callisto's grip was unrelenting.

"Shut up and stop moving!"

"Captain," Reeves said behind her. "Torches coming, dozens of them. The soldiers are approaching. We haven't gotten long before they are here."

"You want your family?" Callisto asked coldly, pushing the woman and babe to Stephan. "You may have them..."

Mary dropped down, embracing her husband in terror.

"Oh, Stephan!" Mary wailed. "I knew you would save us!"

The silver flintlock pistol fired into Mary's back, launching her forward in a spray of blood.

"No!" Stephan cried out, his wife and babe slipping from his arms to the sand.

"No! God damn it!" he wailed with trembling hands as his son shifted, revealing the bullet had killed both mother and child.

Stephan pulled his eyes from his family. "Why?" he whimpered. "Why—you had already won—there was no need to—to do this...."

"Now, I have truly taken everything from you." Callisto glared down at him.

A rage-filled scream tore from Stephan's throat as he launched himself at her, his sword suddenly in hand.

Callisto parried the frenzied attack, kicking out his legs as he stumbled and crashed into the sand.

"You are nothing!" Callisto laughed. "You have nothing! I have taken your entire world and destroyed you!"

Stephan pushed himself off the sand, turned to her, and fired his pistol, but the only sound that happened was the snap of the firing pin hitting an empty chamber. A flash from the fight he had already found himself in that night went through his mind.

Throwing the empty gun at her, he slashed his sabre, hoping to catch her off guard. But she quickly sidestepped the discarded weapon and attack, and he felt the bite of steel across his leg as she counterstruck.

Stephan kept his footing and squared off as she came forward, slashing left and right. He parried each attack with ease, his anger forcing his attention. His pain fueling his every move. He cared about nothing else anymore, only that he wanted to see her dead before his own life ended, which he knew if he bled, much more would be ensured.

He could beat her.

He could already tell he was a better swordsman.

He just had to fight a little longer.

He just had to deny God his soul for a few more moments.

Callisto knew he was tiring, could see his steps falter more. Blood was pouring freely from his side from a wound he had had when he arrived. But she had to be quicker. Soldiers were approaching the beach, and they wouldn't be able to win that fight, not with most of her crew still aboard the ship. But she would still have her victory over this man.

The moment came, he lunged, and Callisto parried the feeble attempt. But before she could counter with a slash that would have left his guts on the ground, his free hand snapped out, grabbing the wrist of her sword hand. She tried to pull back, but he came forward and snapped his head into her face, causing her to fall back and release her blade.

Stephan let her weight pull him with her so that he was bearing down on her. And he had to act fast, for he could already see from the corner of his eye pirates moving in to stop him. This was his moment.

He pulled his dagger from his belt. "This is for my family!"

"Pirates don't fight fair." Her second pistol pressed into his stomach and fired.

Stephan's eyes went wide, and he felt his strength fail him, and the knife slipped from his grasp. "No..." he whispered. "It can't—end—like this."

Callisto pushed the dying man off her with no remorse, yet now that she had defeated him, she felt little pride in it as he stared at her with those broken eyes. Knowing he had lost everything, even the last chance he had had to avenge all she had stolen.

Pulling her eyes away from him, she felt a wave of guilt. This was a man truly shattered in every sense of the word. This was the power she held over her enemies. It was empowering and terrifying.

"We are out of time!" Reeves said, grabbing her arm and pulling her towards the waiting longboats.

Callisto ran, hearing galloping horses coming down the bank to the beach. She glanced back to see Stephan crawling to his wife and son's bodies so he could be with them in his death. But even in that, he had failed, as his body went still mere inches from them.

Climbing into the boat, they pushed off and put their backs into it, rowing as hard as they could, putting distance between the beach and the dismounting soldiers who were readying their rifles, though their range was too far.

Callisto pulled herself over the railing of the Poseidon's Fury to see dozens of her crew's eyes light up at seeing her. But there was no time for that now.

"Fire the cannons!" she screamed. "Kill them all!"

No questions were asked, and flame was set to wicks. The ship rocked as all twelve cannons on the port side fired, ripping through the night. Iron balls whistled through the air, striking the beach where the soldier lingered—spraying sand, adding confusion and terror to the deadly attack. The sweet music of men and horses screaming in death could be heard all the way to the ship's deck.

"Again!" she ordered once the long guns were slid back into place, primed and ready to fire.

Once more, the cannons rocked the ship, and the men on the beach died.

"Pull anchor," Callisto ordered, beginning to feel her strength waning. "We have left our mark here; they will not soon forget who we are or what we are!"

All around her, the crew cheered.

"Where to, Captain?" Three Finger Pete asked from the helm.

"Captain," Reeves said, pulling a parchment from his pocket. "Glacia gave this to me before we left. Told me if we found you that you would need it."

Callisto broke the wax seal and read the note, a grin spreading across her face.

"Three Fingers, set our heading south for Portugal."

"Aye, aye, Captain!" Pete called back.

"What's in Portugal?" Reeves asked.

"The next piece of my destiny," she whispered back.

Glacia sat nervously upon the throne of her audience chamber. A new guest had come to the island, one that she had hoped never to see again. Possibly the only person in all the world she had ever met who truly terrified her. She drank deep from a wine bottle, caring too little to pour it into the crystal goblet next to her, for she needed to calm her nerves quickly.

"My lady," Gavin said, entering the chamber quickly and nervously.

"Yes?" she asked, trying to compose herself, knowing what he was about to say.

"The captain of the Crimson Tears has arrived."

"Are the men in place?" she asked.

"Yes, my lady."

"Good."

"Do you believe there will be a fight?" Gavin asked, his fingers grazing the polished oak of his flintlock pistol.

"I pray with all that I am that there is not," she freely admitted. "But one can never be so sure with him."

Without another word, a large boorish man with a mane of reddish-white hair and a thick, oiled beard strolled in as if he owned the place. A dozen pirates followed in behind him, their eyes radiating violence.

Glacia sat straight on her throne as they moved closer, eyeing everything in the room like hungry hounds.

"Sharktooth, it has been too long since you last visited," she said, keeping her voice calm and even. She was the ruler here; she was in control.

"I am not here for pleasantries," Sharktooth said, his tone dark and menacing.

Glacia dipped her head. "Then pray tell what it is you are doing here? So that I might help speed your departure."

"What happened to my brother?" His tone was level but dangerous.

"Your brother is dead."

Sharktooth's eyes darkened. "How?"

"Killed on his ship by a prisoner."

"Who?"

"Captain Callisto SinClair, of the Poseidon's Fury." There was no point lying; he already knew the truth. He wouldn't have been there otherwise.

"Where is she?" He growled.

ABOUT THE AUTHOR

 James Fuller was born and raised in the heart of the Canadian Rocky Mountains. Spending most of his childhood in the small town of Revelstoke BC, then moving to the small town of Golden BC at 10, until leaving at 19 to live in Kelowna BC, where he still resides at 35 with his beautiful wife of 16 years and son.

James gathered a passion for reading at a very young age. Diving into the works of Tolkien, David Gemmell, R.A. Salvatore, Terry Goodkind and many other great authors. It was not long before the larva of reading blossomed into the butterfly of writing.

It did not take long to win the surprise of his English teachers in high school when short story assignments came up. Soon short stories weren't enough, and the need to create a full-length fantasy world was born. A few years later he published his first book The False Prince, to his series The Fall of a King.

Now years later, he has broken into several genres from fantasy, dark fiction, horror, dystopian, paranormal erotica, thrill and drama.

To learn more about James Fuller and discover more Next Chapter authors, visit our website at www.nextchapter.pub.